G000136910

Tom McNab's career spans both sport and the arts. Seven times Scottish triple jump champion, he played football for Scottish Youths and rugby for Bermuda, and has coached at world-level in athletics, rugby union and bobsleigh.

In 1963, he became a National Athletics Coach, created the Five Star Award Scheme, the world's most successful children's athletics programme, and the National Decathlon initiative which produced Daley Thompson. In 1973, he was coach to Chelsea FC when they won the FA Cup, and he helped take the English rugby union team to a silver medal in the 1991 World Cup.

It was in 1978 that he started work with Colin Welland as script advisor on the Oscar-winning film *Chariots of Fire*, later becoming its technical director. It was in the same period that, having written definitive technical works such as *Modern Schools Athletics*, he wrote his first novel, *Flanagan's Run*. This went to the top of the best-seller lists in its first week, into 25 languages, and is now in film development. His next major novel, the sports-western *The Fast Men*, was declared the best book ever written on track and field athletics.

A member of our London Olympic bid team, Tom presented a play on the Berlin Olympics, 1936, which showed successfully at Sadler's Wells in 2012. His play on the German film director Riefenstahl, *Leni. Leni.*, featured as a short film at Cannes in 2016, and *Whisper in the Heart*, featuring Riefenstahl and Orson Welles, will show at the Camden Arts Festival in August, 2018. He has recently written *Orwell on Jura*, and now has in preparation *My Name is Joseph Knight*, based on the famous Scottish slavery trial of 1778.

Still coaching back in 2003, he transformed a 16-year-old football player into a world-class long jumper. His name was Greg Rutherford.

Dedication

To Hammie Smith—a great coach and a great friend.

Tom McNab

READY

AUSTIN MACAULEY PUBLISHERS™
LONDON • CAMBRIDGE • NEW YORK • SHARJAH

Copyright © Tom McNab (2018)

The right of Tom McNab to be identified as author of this work has been asserted by him in accordance with section 77 and 78 of the Copyright, Designs and Patents Act 1988.

All rights reserved. No part of this publication may be reproduced, stored in a retrieval system, or transmitted in any form or by any means, electronic, mechanical, photocopying, recording, or otherwise, without the prior permission of the publishers.

Any person who commits any unauthorised act in relation to this publication may be liable to criminal prosecution and civil claims for damages.

A CIP catalogue record for this title is available from the British Library.

ISBN 9781787108172 (Paperback)
ISBN 9781787108188 (E-Book)

www.austinmacauley.com

First Published (2018)
Austin Macauley Publishers Ltd.
25 Canada Square
Canary Wharf
London
E14 5LQ

Chapter 1
The Old Man

9 a.m., Friday, July 7th, 1995

Marty had liked his face best when it had been three yards in diameter. Now, expanded to over five times that size, it had somehow morphed into a cheesy, Uncle Tom look. It would have to go, and quickly. He took a final glance, grimaced, shook his head, closed the left-hand rear window of the stretch, and settled back into its soft leather womb. The Cadillac glided silently on Sunset and Vine in the light early morning traffic, dwarfed on each side by massive 'Wheaties' billboards featuring a smiling Martin Luther Jones.

He was dressed for business. Marty lay back, cocooned in the black softness, in his immaculate grey Nike tracksuit and white polo neck shirt. Only his favoured, worn shoes, cracked and thin-soled, hinted at the reality of athletic life.

Marty did, indeed, look better than the billboard, his light coffee-coloured skin almost translucent, his smooth, boyish face dominated by blue eyes always hovering on a twinkle, surprisingly consistent with his Spartan, polished head. Only his mouth detracted from the picture. For, although generous and full-lipped, a pouting arrogance hovered at its edges.

Marty lay back and half-closed his eyes. No question, he decided, Wheaties would have to ditch it. Somehow, the larger billboards brought out something in him to which he could not put words but which he did not like.

He leant forward and called to the front seat. "Bo, buzz that guy at Wheaties," he said.

Bo Robertson, his manager, fat, avuncular, sat beside their chauffeur, his eyes glued to a television screen before him. Bo flicked it off and turned to face Marty. "What you saying, champ?"

"Buzz Wheaties," repeated Marty. "Those boards, they gotta be history by tomorrow."

"What the Jack you trying to tell me, man?"

"Those big Wheaties boards. I want them out. Gone. They make me look bad."

They had stopped at lights. Bo opened his window. On his left, was a smaller Wheaties billboard, featuring Marty in an identical pose. Bo scrutinised it for a moment and shook his head. "Look real cool to me," he said.

"That's the small one," said Marty. "Sunset and Vine is five times as big. Makes me look Jack Shit."

Bo shook his head again, closed the window and checked his gold Rolex. "Can't do nuthin' now, man," he said. "Only a quarter of eight. But I'll be right on to those Wheaties boys at nine, MLJ. You can count on it."

"You just do that," said Marty flicking on the television in front of him.

"We got Bill Easton," observed Bo. Now facing them was NBC's Bill Easton, deeply tanned, immaculate in sky-blue blazer and razor-edged slacks, his lean, leathery face betraying only a hint of $50,000 worth of modification.

"*And today, as MLJ travels towards the pre-even press conference at the TAC World Championships trials in Los Angeles Olympic Stadium, the world is asking if the Californian all-rounder can be the first decathlete on earth to break the magic 9000 point barrier.*"

"No problem," whispered Marty to the screen.

"*But, whatever happens tomorrow at the stadium today, there is always the same nagging question asked by every sports fan – is the decathlete merely a Jack of all Trades and Master of None?*"

"You don't know shit," snarled Bo at the screen.

Marty switched off and again settled back in the darkness, closing his eyes.

"Jack of all Trades, yes," he said, "but sure as hell master of decathlon."

The black Cadillac stopped in the road in the thin early morning sun, directly outside the main entrance to the stadium. Marty opened his right side window and peered out. Even from here, he could see the upper sections, empty tracts of the stadium. And they would remain empty, echoing throughout the first day of decathlon only to the shouts of parents, coaches and partners. Marty sighed and shook his head. Here he was, poised to make the greatest decathlon score in track history but, within a stadium capable of accommodating 80,000 souls, there would be not much more than three men and a dog. He was on the Wheaties box, on Pepsi commercials. Hell, he would soon have his own late night television slot, and yet with the exception of Olympics and World Championships, only a handful of people had ever come to watch him at work. Marty could already see most of the next day's audience, crowding around the glass-fronted entrance to the stadium offices, restrained by security guards. There they were, the usual bunch, a cluster of kids, track nuts, coaches, aspiring decathletes and the inevitable smooth, lean, leggy women who respected the vertical man but served only the horizontal one.

Marty opened the door and made his way towards the entrance, his driver gasping behind him, sagging under the weight of two bulging Nike bags. Bo, surprisingly light on his feet for a fat man, stepped in front of him, easing a path through the children who had rushed to the car from the entrance on its arrival.

"Nine thou," someone in the crowd at the doors started to chant, and it was taken up along the corridor through which he now travelled towards the stadium entrance.

Marty stopped, wet his right index finger and tested the warm breeze. He smiled. Tomorrow, the wind would almost certainly be behind him in the 100 metres and next day in the hurdles, but inside the legal limit, so not too strong to cause him problems in the 400 metres. That breeze was worth fifty extra points for sure. Perhaps more.

Nine thousand points. The magic nine. No one had ever done it, not Hingsen nor Thompson, not even the great Dan O'Brien. Grinning in PR reflex, he stopped and looked around him at the smiling, chanting crowd, cocooned in his thoughts. All the decathletes in the '80s had competed for nine events, every goddamn one of them, but they had flunked out at the fifteen hundred metres. If the Big Nine was even remotely within reach going into the final event, the fifteen hundred metres, then he would have to go for it, deep into that oxygen desert.

He had rehearsed it, in his imagination, time after time. First day, 10.4 seconds 100 metres; 8 metres long jump; 15 metres shot put; 2.10 metres high jump; 46.4 seconds 400 metres. Second day, 14.0 seconds 110 metres hurdles; 48 metres discus; 5.20 metres pole vault; 65 metre javelin and a 4 minute 25 1500 metres. That would do it by a clear hundred points and, if by chance a few points did happen to melt away prior to the final event, then it would be eyeballs out and digging deep to where he had never been before, close to 4 minute 10 seconds in the 1500 metres. It was all there. He could almost taste it.

Still deep in thought, Marty reflexly signed autographs for the crowd, now a noisy blur around him. Decathlon was like walking a tightrope ten times; a hurdle touched, a toe a fraction over the broad jump board, a discus a mere centimetre out of the sector, a shower of rain, the slightest error in pace in the 400 metres and you were gone, history. And decathlon was not like sprinting or shot putting, where an athlete could shrug off failure, come back and try again, next week. No, for the decathlete there were probably only three good shots at it per season and only one where he would be in perfect shape, the weather mild and Lady Luck smiling down sweetly upon him.

"Nine thou; nine thou," the chant was lamely taken up by some of the older members of the crowd as the glass automatic doors of the stadium slid open for Marty and his entourage. He turned and, smiling, looked into the crowd which now pressed around him. A lean, copper-skinned young woman, essentially a pair of legs with a head on top and tits from here to San Diego, thrust a leather-covered autograph book into his hands. Briefly, their fingers touched and Marty's blue eyes took on their reflex twinkle. He scrawled his autograph and put his telephone number directly below it.

Marty raised both arms to the crowd, his eyes fixed on hers. "See you," he shouted, and her eyes told him that he would. He turned and the glass doors closed behind him.

9 a.m.

Marty, sitting on stage at a long table, surveyed the journalists milling below him and blinked as the television arc lights shunted on, bathing the improvised platform in white light. On Marty's immediate right, sat his grey-haired, crepuscular track coach, Vince Harris, alongside his psychologist, Lena Millar, and his weights coach, Fritz Hall. On his left, sat his nutritionist, Brenda Klemm, with his agent, Bo Robertson.

None of the other decathletes competing in the Trial were with him on the dais, not even the blond Penn State man, Dutch Janner, a mere two hundred points behind him on the world rankings. No, out in the semi-darkness Marty could just pick them out, glowering away at the back of the room, Janner, Simmons, Dubose and half a dozen others. They were not at top table, for they were not MLJ. For, though Marty was a decathlete, he had never truly been one of them. MLJ was a loner, polite and diplomatic, a man with many admirers but few friends. When they had first met six years ago, Bo had asked him what he had thought the colour of success would be. Marty had been nonplussed, unable to reply. Green, Bo had replied that it was green, pure green, the colour of envy. Marty knew that Bo had been right. Track was, certainly, not a sport for the generous of spirit.

Bo, now sweating, the buttons of his sky blue Armani suit stretched to bursting, stood with both arms raised and looked around the room. He reflected that only one decathlete on earth could attract such attention from the world's press. Bo tapped the microphone in front of him. It was live. He withdrew a white handkerchief from his top pocket, wiped his brow and cleared his throat.

"Ladies and gentlemen." The microphone let out a screeching, nasal whine, and Bo raised a sweating finger to the sound engineer standing at a console at the back of the seething conference room. The technician nodded and adjusted the levels.

"Ladies and gentlemen," Bo said again. He smiled in relief; the sound was good. "We got…" he checked his Rolex "an hour befo' MLJ has to go back for his rub-down. So could I please have some questions from de floor?" Bo always affected a street patois, despite a middle-class upbringing and a Master's degree in Business Studies at Harvard. His eyes ranged around the room.

The first voice was that of a woman; it was Clare Fox, of the London Times, sitting in the front row. "Your Mr Easton said this morning that the decathlete is a Jack of all Trades and Master of None. How would you define the decathlete?"

Marty smiled. It was a feed. Somehow, Bo had got to Fox. "A decathlete, Miss Fox, is a series of injuries held together by ligaments and a desire for points," he replied.

There was laughter all round and Bo smiled.

"Did you say points or pints, Mr Jones?" responded Clare, grinning.

"Points for decathletes, Miss Fox," he replied, "pints for football players."

There was, again, laughter. This kind of banter had made Martin Luther Jones the darling of the press. Decathlon itself was like watching paint dry, but MLJ, always good for a quote, was money in the bank.

"Bill Martin, Chicago Evening Post." The voice came from the front row again. "Nine thousand points, is it possible, MLJ?"

Marty groaned inwardly. Journalists were such lazy assholes. They had been asking him the same fool question since he had taken the world title back in 1991. His face assumed the billboard, watermelon smile. "Just a figure, Mr Martin," he said. "Like your four-minute mile. Couple of years back, some Ethiopian – don't know the fella's name, ran two miles in close to eight minutes. So that was two four-minute miles."

"So, is it possible?"

"I've done it lots of times," Marty replied. He tapped his forehead with his index finger. "In here. In here I scored the Big Nine many a time. In here, it's always two metres okay wind behind in the dash and hurdles, and I even got me a following wind in the four hundred metres."

There was laughter once again. Bo glanced uneasily along the table at Marty. He hoped that all this mind games bug-a-boo would go no further. Marty's visits to Roswell and his membership of the Aetherian Society were not good medicine. He stood and grinned. "It's like sex dreams, boys. You allus meets a better class of folks. Same with track. In yo' dreams, you allus pick up all them points that you need."

Marcus Allenby of the New York Times stood up, clipboard in hand. "You talked about dreams, MLJ. I've heard tell that you use psychic techniques to improve your performance."

Bo's eyes started to roll. This was the Twilight Zone.

"If you mean I use visualisation techniques, then yes, that's right, I do." Marty replied.

"So how exactly does that work?" Allenby sat down as he spoke.

Marty paused. "I just sit at home and meditate, get my mind empty, loosened out. Then I think my way into the stadium and into each event."

"You actually SEE yourself there?"

Marty shook his head. "No, Mr Allenby, I AM there."

There was scattered, uneasy laughter. Bo looked along the table at Marty's psychologist Lena Miller, cueing her in. Lena, a slim, handsome white woman in her mid-thirties, leant forward to the microphone, her thick lips pursed. "Mr Allenby," she said, "it's a basic element of modern psychological training. Standard practice."

"Psychological, but not psychic?" Allenby pursued his point.

"Yes," said Lena smiling, "the only board in decathlon is in the broad jump take-off. There is no ouija board."

There was immediate laughter. Bo smiled in relief.

Marty shook his head. It was the same every time with the press. To them, decathlon was like some strange, mystic planet. All that they sought was some angle, some quotation which would prompt a distant sub-editor to print a catchy headline. After that, it was off to the bar in the hospitality suite. His eyes ranged around the crowded room searching for someone who might come up with an intelligent question. As he did so, through the glare of the arc lights, he caught sight of an old man standing alone at the back of the room, in semi-darkness. The man looked to be in his early sixties, with a brown, lined, almost Asiatic, face. He was dressed in an ill-fitting, rumpled, grey tweed suit, his shirt collar open. Marty saw the old man's lips move, but heard nothing. The old man smiled, revealing broad white teeth. Then, out came his voice, booming, as if amplified by a microphone. To Marty, the deep, sonorous voice seemed to fill the room.

"Are you ready?" asked the man.

Marty peered out into the audience. For a moment, the sound and depth of the old man's voice disarmed him. There he stood, at the back of the room, his lank black hair shining in the reflection of the arc lights from a mirror on his right, his face half-shadowed. Marty looked to each side, to the other members of his entourage on the dais beside him. But they looked directly ahead, as if unaware of the question, as did the journalists in front of him.

"Ready," he replied. "Of course I'm ready."

Bo's eyes darted at him in surprise, then to Lena Miller.

"Ready?" he hissed, out of the side of his mouth. "Ready for what?"

Marty pointed to the back of the audience, to the old man. "That guy back there – he asked me if I was ready."

Bo peered out into the audience, scanning it. He shook his head, scrambled to his feet and put his hand on Marty's shoulder. "That's it, boys," he said. "It's rub-down time. We gotta be off." Brow furrowed, he looked questioningly at Marty, who was still staring out into the crowd, shaking his head. Clearly, Bo had seen and heard nothing. Marty continued to peer into the audience, then the lights went on.

The old man had vanished.

The first day went like a dream. The following wind in the first event, the 100 metres, had locked in at the allowable limit, two metres per second. He poured, he flowed. It was like a training run. Only the time of 10.38 seconds told him otherwise. It gave him 1004 points and Dutch Janner was already 50 points adrift.

In broad jump, Marty's first leap was almost invariably crabby and cautious. This time, in contrast, it was a fluid, balanced 8.0 metres – a decathlon best, giving him 1061 points. Free of restraint, Marty attacked the board in his next two jumps. Both were massive, well beyond the eight metres, but both were marginal fouls. It did not matter, for he was now well ahead of schedule.

In his first attempt in shot put, the implement had felt a kilo light. It flew out to 15m 2 cm, another decathlon best. His next two attempts, eyeballs out, were as if he were putting for accuracy at 14m. 39cm and 14m. 38cm. It was always the same. The good ones felt easy; add more effort and technique invariably crumbled. But Marty was now deep in the Zone, ahead of a 9000 points schedule, with Janner, though going well, trailing 91 points behind him.

This had always been a good high jump venue for him. The crossbar, framed against the high stands, had always looked low and today, warm and windless, it looked no different. Marty played safe, coming in at 1m 90cm and he sailed over easy, in Coach Harris' words, 'Like a goddam sack of potatoes'.

Between jumps, he lay on his stomach on his camp bed on the infield, his head covered in a blanket. It was a necessary part of his ritual; Marty never liked to see the crossbar until his attempt was called. He did not experience a failure till 2m 10cm. It was one of these days when he seemed to flow up from his approach run. In flight, there seemed to be aeons of time to flip his heels clear. He ended with a third – time clearance at 2m 10cm and withdrew to save himself for the final event of the day, the 400 metres.

Dutch Janner peeled off his track bottoms and looked across at Marty. Only twenty odd points per event separated them in the world rankings, yet MLJ's income this year would be well in excess of $5 million, whilst his would barely cover his mortgage. At first, MLJ had seemed to be one of the boys, good for half a dozen Buds and a pizza with the guys after a decathlon. But now he was MLJ, a star, partying with Jack Nicholson, Geena Davis and Ted Turner, his world as distant from theirs as a dancer in the New York Ballet.

Dutch was unable to separate his dislike of Marty from sheer envy and, being a fair man, that made him angry with himself. He knew that if things took their likely path, Marty, now 175 points clear, was out of reach, all set for 9000 points and into decathlon history. But Dutch wanted this one, the

400m., and he knew that decathlons could vanish in a moment, like a mirage.

A week before, he had run a 300 metre time trial in an easy 33.6 secs. That meant that he was surely good for a sub 46 second 400 metre run, a full half second ahead of MLJ's best. Whatever the result at the end of ten events, he would surely take him here and edge closer to him.

Dutch had drawn the perfect lane, lane four, inside two mid 47 second runners, Dellinger and White, with Marty on lane seven. He would have his rival in his sights all the way.

From the crack of the gun, he knew for certain that he had his man. He poured round the first bend, first eating up the stagger on Dellinger, then taking in White half way up the back straight. Dutch's eyes now fixed on Marty, outside him, in lane six. He was taking him apart. He would gobble him up on the final curve and spit him out in the home stretch.

Dutch burnt through the back straight, hitting the 200 metre mark in 21.8 secs, but feeling full of gas, as if he had only just started. He knew that he had taken two metres out of Marty in the first half of the race. All he had to do now was to stay loose and he would take at least the same distance out of him in the final furlong, sucked in to the finish by the following breeze. He took the last curve like greased ice, his eyes glued to Marty's rippling, sweating back.

But it did not happen. Dutch held form, stayed tall and loose, but it simply did not happen. For the stagger did not close as they entered the home straight almost level, the other competitors wallowing ten metres or more behind them. Outside him, Marty's rhythm was remorseless. His leg speed did not drop and, coming off the bend, he slowly started to draw away. Dutch felt loose, felt fluid, knew he had never run better, but it was irrelevant, for Marty simply poured away from him. As he hit the tape three metres down, he looked up to the scoreboard to see that Marty's winning time was 45.75 seconds, his own 46.02 seconds.

"Fastest any man ever run at ground-level in decathlon," grunted Bo, handing Marty his sweat suit. "Bill Toomey ran

45.6 in Mexico at altitude in 1968, some English guy Gabbett ran 46.07 at ground-level in Munich."

"Gabbett, Toomey, those guys are cold potatoes," said Marty, pulling on his track bottoms. He looked up to the scoreboard to check the first day scores. The board was blank. Then the first print appeared, in capital letters, massive upon its black surface. It said, 'Are you ready?'

It was nine o'clock. Marty stood in the gathering dusk, high in the stands looking down upon the track. The energy had now drained from the Coliseum. Only hours before there had been a power, an energy in its bright red synthetic surface. The decathletes had poured the product of thousands of hours of training into its circles, its lanes, its runways. Now empty, it was merely grass and red rubber, real estate, devoid of meaning.

He watched an empty plastic cup, captured by the light breeze, bobble along the track, its passage audible even from the distance at which he now stood. It jumped and spun unevenly under the ten flights of high hurdles already assembled for the first event of the second day. Marty had stood many times in such athletic deserts at the end of a first day, already seeing himself in the sixth event, feeling himself flow sweetly over the barriers, then spinning a discus into infinity, looking down on vault crossbars far below him, rifling javelins that hung forever in flight. Only the final event, the 1500 metres invariably resisted such positive imagery, no matter how hard he tried. Somehow, Marty's eyes were glued to that plastic cup. It had begun its erratic journey at the first hurdle and, picked up by a zephyr of a breeze, had taken an uncertain path under the hurdles towards the finish. Now it had been blown infield, and rested at the base of the pole-vault landing bed.

Marty suddenly became aware of a pair of trousered legs and black boots and his eyes travelled upwards to see someone sitting on the edge of the vault bed, legs dangling. It was the old man from the Press Conference, dressed in the same coarse, ill-fitting grey tweed jacket and trousers and open-necked white shirt. Even at this distance, Marty could see that the man was old, probably in his sixties. He looked up towards Marty, raised a hand in recognition and moved his lips. Marty somehow did not have to hear the words, for he knew exactly what they said. They filled the stadium, causing seagulls to flutter up into the sky above the Coliseum. He rushed down the stadium steps, through the empty stadium's echoing corridors, and out onto the track, the word "Ready?" still ringing in his ears. When he reached the vault-bed, the plastic cup was there. The old man was not.

The decathletes called them 'spaldings', the yellow tranquillisers shaped like footballs which guaranteed a good night's sleep between the first and second days of competition. Marty had found that one 'spalding' represented oblivion. As he washed it down with a gulp of sparkling Perrier, and lay back on his bed and closed his eyes, he fixed in his mind the first event of the morning, the 110 metre hurdles.

There they were in front of him, ten three foot six barriers, glistening with morning dew. But no, these were not standard hurdles, rather they were strange, wooden T-shaped obstacles, the same height as hurdles, but thick, implacable, solid, closer in nature to steeplechase barriers.

The gun exploded and, strangely, he could hear himself run, an alien, crunching sound. But the track upon which he ran was not springy and resilient and he could feel it soft beneath his feet, see it black ahead of him. Marty ran on blackness, with only the hurdles and more blackness before him. He cleared the first barrier, but he was too far away and much too high. He landed, sagged in softness and struggled on through the blackness to the next hurdle, and the next and the next. Then, suddenly, it was over, and he tumbled on to black mud. Gasping, he sat up, looked down on his legs and saw that the ankle of his trailing knee now streamed dark blood.

Then it was the old man, but no, rather a fresher, leaner, younger version. He was in long shorts and vest, smiling, pointing to high jump uprights on which rested a thick, wooden crossbar, standing next to what appeared to be a broad jump pit. He then ran towards it and cleared it with a strange little hop-type jump, landing in the sand pit on one foot. Returning to his feet, he beckoned Marty to follow him. But as Marty ran towards the bar, it appeared to steadily rise until it was far above him. He went under it, falling into the harsh grit of the sand pit.

Then he was back again on the black track, this time on a pole vault runway, but the pole felt heavy as he ran sluggishly towards the vault-box. Jesus God, there was no vault-box or landing-bed, only a hole and a flat pit filled with sand. Then he was into the pole-plant and take-off. The plant was hard and Marty felt as if he had been ripped from the ground. For the pole did not bend, he had therefore no time to lay back and line himself up for its recoil. Marty turned and wriggled over the heavy wooden bar, taking it with his chest and chin as he did so. He landed on his butt in the unyielding sand as above him what looked like a tree branch hit the crossbar taking it down towards him. Both the branch and the bar landed upon him.

Then, then there was only steam. He was in now what seemed to be a vast kitchen. It was a hell of steam, great bubbling vats of soup, mountainous piles of greasy dishes, a stone floor slimy with detritus. Suddenly, there was a hellish, strident ringing. Marty awoke, groped for the alarm clock. It stopped, and he flicked on his bedside lamp. His sweating hand came to rest upon the message pad beside the telephone which stood beside the alarm. Gasping, for no reason that he could understand, he picked it up and looked at it. In pencil, in crude, clumsy writing, were written the words ‘Are you ready?’

The first three events of the second day poured out of him like molasses. First, there was a 14.02 second 110 metre hurdles win which had seemed to Marty like a training run, leaving behind Dutch him Janner and ten untouched barriers. Then there had been a loose, big-arm first round throw in discus which had landed sweetly straight up the middle of the sector at exactly forty-eight metres. Finally, there was the pole vault, where he did not experience a single failure till his final height of 5.10 metres. Thus, if he could make even par performances in the final two events, the Big Nine was definitely his.

The dream continued with his first javelin throw. He gave the spear a loose, massive pull, and it flew away from his hand. It seemed to linger forever in the soft summer air and flew, way out, far beyond the sixty-metre line. But the javelin landed flat and the throw did not count. In his second attempt, he panicked, tightened up, and tried too hard. He rushed his strike, short-arming the javelin and hooked it wildly around his left foot. It went long but flew well outside the throwing sector, leaving him only one throw to achieve a score. From hero to zero in two throws. He was now in deep shit.

Marty sat on the competitors' bench alongside the javelin runway, feeling sweat bead upon his flushed face, sensing the almost palpable smiles and stares of Janner and the rest of the pack, as he restlessly awaited his final throw. He tried to breathe slowly, deeply, as Lena Miller had taught him. There was no question about what had to be done in the final throw. It would have to be safe, right back to basics. A short, cautious, seven-stride approach run, the javelin held well back in the withdrawn position, novice-style. Then a long high pull and a prayer that the javelin would land somewhere around sixty metres, point -first

Everything went as planned, at least in terms of the technical quality of the throw. The throwing arm was long, loose, the approach run slow and controlled, the pull on the javelin rangy and direct. But, Jesus, it was all too soft, too cautious. There was no bite, no urgency, lacking sharp, flailing viciousness in the delivery. It was flabby, gutless and, though it landed safely, point-first, it was well short of his target, at a miserable fifty-one metres fifty six, garbage. Vital points lost, he was now in deep trouble.

"You got eight thousand one hundred and twenty-seven points," intoned Vince. "Four minutes ten seconds. That should do the trick. Yes, that should do it, with a few points to spare. The big nine."

Just like that. Vince had omitted to say that this time was fully four seconds faster than Marty had ever run in decathlon.

Marty sat in his tracksuit high in the stands, surrounded by his now silent entourage. Only a few yards away, the press huddled, modems poised, awaiting his next words. Marty looked across at them. Only half an hour ago, he had been free and clear, perhaps, ten million bucks clear. Only a weeny sixty metre javelin throw and he could have cruised easily round the fifteen hundred metres, singing Dixie, to take the Big Nine and put himself into the history books.

"Pin yourself on Janner," growled Coach Vince, closing his points tables booklet. "He's got silver for sure and he can run four eight. He can take you there."

Marty looked across at Lena Miller. She quietly beckoned him to sit beside her. He observed her. Lean and ascetic, he had always thought of Lena as some dropout from an Amish sect. She looked at him solemnly with her deep, sad spinster eyes. "Dream it," she intoned. "Then do it."

Bo put it quite differently. "Them that never gives up is never beat," he said.

Dutch Janner did exactly as Marty had anticipated, taking a stretched field through the first lap in a steady sixty-seven seconds, perfect pace. Marty locked himself in directly behind him on his right shoulder, acutely aware of the stilted artificiality of his 1500m stride. But he felt loose, easy, oblivious to the scattered shouts for a faster pace echoing from the stands.

It felt far too slow, but as he heard the official shout 'sixty-eight' as he passed he knew that Janner had judged it well. Marty resisted an irrational impulse to go ahead of Dutch, his eyes pinned on his broad, freckled back as he cruised through the eight hundred metres in two minutes eighteen seconds, still perfect pace. He became aware of the redness of Janner's neck, of a thin trickle of sweat beginning to track its erratic way between the freckles, leaking down on to the surface of his white vest. Marty flowed easily down the back straight into the third lap. He now began to feel his breathing, but it was still coming easy. He suddenly became aware of a runner on his right shoulder. It did not matter, because this was not a race, rather a struggle against a confection, an abstraction, the decathlon tables. Marty involuntarily quickened his pace, almost stumbling over Janner's heels as he did so. The passing runner was Dubose and he passed suddenly and was on Janner's right shoulder, penning Marty in. Janner, galvanised, took off and the two men surged away from Marty into the curve at the end of the back straight, into the final six hundred metres. Marty was suddenly adrift, in limbo. He ventured a glance behind him. The tracking group, flat-footed, was well over twenty metres back, running at too slow a pace to be of any help.

Marty quickened his leg-cadence and went after Janner and Dubose, feeling, as he did so, his breathing begin to deepen. By the curve, he was directly behind Dutch, who was now only five metres behind Dubose. Now, feeling his diaphragm tighten, it was starting to hurt, too early. Five hundred metres to go. Suddenly, in a few metres, Marty had passed beyond that measured comfort zone where fatigue and oxygen intake maintain a fragile, precarious balance, and he was hurting as he tracked Janner and Dubose down the home straight into the final lap. Gasping, he desperately tried to focus in to hear the final lap time, as the bell clanged. Three minutes six seconds. A final lap of sixty-three seconds, that, or something close, was all that he needed.

In the stands, his coach Vince Harris anxiously checked his flickering stopwatch. A shade over sixty-four seconds would just do it, squeeze MLJ beyond the nine thousand point total, but he could see that Marty was losing leg-speed, dropping back on to his heels, with Janner moving steadily away from him. Dubose, paying for his earlier exuberance, began to crumble, legs bowing, in the middle of the back straight, and Janner began to pull him in. Vince Harris stood and, cupping his hands, bellowed at Marty, though knowing full well, that his man was now far beyond hearing. So were all the runners, yet the spectators stood, bellowing, united in imperative vocal impotence.

Marty could feel himself fading but, lungs stretched and screaming, he passed a sagging, broken Dubose and, eyes focused on the circle of sweat that now engulfed Janner's vest, struggled to regain the shape of his running. Even now, in his deep fatigue, he knew that when form and shape crumbled, you were dead. Marty could hear his breath rasp from deep inside, tearing his lungs, feel himself settling back on to his heels. Oblivious to the chasing pack now closing in on him from behind, he struggled round the final curve, Janner now fixed at ten metres ahead of him. As he hit the home straight, Marty gathered himself and produced a desperate, bow-legged, pathetic parody of a sprint. As he did so, the pack closed in from behind, engulfing him. All co-ordination now gone, he flailed his way up the home straight. Somehow, he stayed with the pack, finishing twenty metres behind Janner, and flopped across the line. His legs gave and he wobbled left on to the infield, landing flat on his face on the grass. Through his pain, he knew that he had blown it.

Marty felt strong arms around his trunk, pulling him on to hands and knees, then gently turning him on to his back on the dry grass. He lay back, eyes closed, feeling only the deep rasp of his breathing. Marty was suddenly aware of the strong, sickly smell of tobacco. He opened his eyes and looked up to see, only inches from him, the brown, lined face of the old man. His lips moved. Though Marty could hear nothing, he knew exactly what he was saying.

Chapter 2
Factor 2000

Marty just loved the way those English dudes talked. Every Saturday night, it had been his custom to sit with a couple of Buds in his Santa Monica condo, pinned to a regular source of English programmes, *BBC World*. When there looked to be any shortage of such entertainment, then he would hire himself a pile of English videos – *Dad's Army*, *Fawlty Towers*, *Monty Python* – he knew many of them by heart. His particular favourite was *Yes Minister* and Marty could perform a passable imitation of its leading character, Sir Humphrey, albeit one which thankfully never left the confines of his condo.

It was now approaching eleven o'clock and time for shut-eye. Marty sat watching *BBC World*, the final episode of Blackadder in the Great War. It was the third occasion on which he had seen this particular episode. He never tired of it, but when Blackadder and his regiment finally scrambled over the top into a hail of fire, Marty's eyes invariably filled with tears. He wiped his eyes with the back of his hand and went back to the kitchen to locate some tissues. As he did so, he inadvertently touched the television remote control lying on the chair beside him, and an ESPN programme appeared on the screen. It was the urbane, ubiquitous Bill Easton, speaking directly to camera.

"*And as the 1995 track and field season draws to a close, with MLJ so desperately close to the world's first 9000 points decathlon, tonight we take you briefly over the history of that ultimate test of the all-round athlete.*"

Marty withdrew a tissue, wiped his eyes again and blew his nose. He picked up the controls. Track history, even the history of decathlon, was of little interest to him. The past. Boring.

But then, suddenly there it was on the screen, staring out at him. It was the face of the old man. Marty sat down and pushed up the sound, but the programme had now moved on to some hazy, flickering film of the 1912 Stockholm Olympics. Then it was on to Antwerp 1920 and, for some reason, an American high jumper called Osborne, lying side on over the crossbar in a strange, twisted position.

Marty rushed to the telephone and dialled NBC. But no, no one was now available at Sports Desk. And no, Mr Easton's home telephone number could not be disclosed. Yes, they would take his message and Mr Easton would be in touch with him on Monday.

"Jim Thorpe, Marty. That guy you saw on my programme on Sunday night was Jim Thorpe. Come on, you don't mean to tell me that you never in your life heard tell of the great Jim Thorpe?"

Marty sat in a worn brown leather armchair in front of Bill Easton's desk in the journalist's cramped, book-lined NBC office. He smiled and shook his head in mock disbelief. Easton rose, went to a book-filled shelf on his left and withdrew a large, leather-covered volume. He laid it on his desk, first checked the contents page and then, licking his index finger, he slowly flicked through the bulky tome. He stopped and nodded. "Here we are, Marty," he said. "Page 21. Stockholm Olympics 1912. Jim Thorpe, U S A." He rose and with both hands passed the volume across to him across the table. There was Jim Thorpe, standing, hands on hips, looking out at him from the page, in the knee-length shorts of the period. He was just as Marty had seen him in his dream, a younger, leaner version of the old man. Thorpe looked to be about six feet tall, and about a hundred and ninety pounds. He was copper-coloured, lean and chunky, with a flat, almost Asiatic nose.

"As I recollect, Jim was a Navajo," said Easton. "No I'm wrong, a Sac + Fox Indian. Went to Carlisle Indian College, ran track and played football for Pop Warner."

"Pop Warner? That name rings a bell."

"One of the top college coaches of the period. Coached track, football and baseball. Full of crazy ideas. You've heard of the Pope Warner Baseball Programme?"

Marty nodded. "That's it. When was this photograph taken?"

"Just before the First World War," replied Easton.

"And when was that?"

Easton smiled. "I see you didn't major in history, Marty. About 1914. Yes, but for Uncle Sam the War must have been just after then, around 1917. Jim won Decathlon and Pentathlon in Stockholm in 1912."

"Decathlon AND Pentathlon. So, what was Pentathlon?"

Easton shook his head. "Five events, but which ones? You got me there, Marty. No idea." He paused. "Anyhow, Jim won both events, but the Suits took away both his Olympic medals."

Marty looked down again at the book, then back at Easton. "Why was that?"

"As I remember it, Jim had played some semi-pro baseball a year or so before, just beer money, you know how it goes. All the college boys did it back in those days. But some eagle-eye newshawk picked it up and an AAU asshole called Sullivan declared that Jim was a pro and took away all his Olympic medals."

Marty looked down again at the book, shaking his head. Easton smiled. This was the longest conversation that he had ever pursued with Martin Luther Jones. Somehow, he sensed a story in the offing. "So why all this sudden interest in ole Jim Thorpe?" he asked.

Marty, his eyes fixed on the photograph of Jim Thorpe, did not reply for a moment. Then he spoke. "No reason, Bill," he said. "No reason at all."

"Marty tells me that he keeps seeing an old man," said Lena Miller, removing her spectacles and rubbing the grooved red bridge on her thin, ascetic nose. They sat around a polished oak conference table in Bo Robertson's office, Vince Harris, Fritz Hall, Brenda Klemm, Dr Paterson and a sweating Bo Robertson.

"So what?" said Robertson. "I keep seeing my old woman."

"He keeps saying *are you ready?*" pursued Lena.

Bo grinned. "So does my old woman," he said.

"Come on, Bo," said Vince. "This is a serious matter."

"You're right, coach," said Bo. "Ten million bucks serious. It could've lost him the Big Nine."

Lena rose and walked over to the coffee percolator behind her and poured herself a cup of black coffee. She turned to face them. "An old man," she said. "Marty's father disappeared, didn't he?"

"No, not disappeared. Marcus has been on a round-the-world trip for the past few months," volunteered Dr Paterson. "Marcus Jones, he's my patient. OK, so he's a little odd, taking his wife's name, all that psychic stuff, but he's in great shape." Paterson nodded as Lena proffered the coffee jug to him, and pushed forward his cup, which she duly filled. He spooned sugar into it and stirred. "Marcus Booker Jones, Doctor of Engineering, UCLA," he said. "One of the smartest guys I ever met, or ever likely to meet." He lifted his cup and sipped his coffee. "But the clock keeps striking thirteen with Marcus." Paterson paused and shook his head. "He's into all this psychic hoo-ha," he said. "Roswell, ESP, astral sex…"

"Astral sex?" said Lena.

"Don't even go there, Lena," growled Paterson. He paused again, and then went on. "Still, it might explain ectoplasm." Paterson saw that his well-practised joke had no meaning to anyone in the group except Lena, who responded with a disapproving frown.

"You don't think this old man stuff might have something to do with his father?" asked Brenda Klemm.

Lena shook her head. "Could be…who knows?" she said.

"But do you think it bugged him in the decathlon?" asked Bo.

"No, Bo, I don't think so," replied Lena, firmly. "Marty was well-focussed. I've checked back and all my pre-competition evaluations confirm that. I don't think this old man stuff affected him in any way."

Dr Paterson spoke. "How was he eating, Brenda, before the decathlon?"

"Normally," replied the nutritionist. "Marty always has been very particular about what he eats. It's a sort of family trait. Everything has to be pure, organic. He won't even take aspirin. You must know that."

Vince Harris stood and moved to the window, then turned to face them. "You know the difference between a javelin landing flat and one hitting the ground point first close to seventy metres?" he asked.

"Ten million bucks?" volunteered Bo.

The coach smiled and shook his head. He lifted his thumb and index finger so that only millimetres separated them. "This much," he said. "And that's what did it for Marty. Not some old man."

He shook his head.

"I've seen the best javelin men on earth foul out in big meets," he said. "Guys who can rifle it out to ninety metres in their sleep. The decathlete, he's different, he's a man of half-skills. So fouling out, it's always on the cards, even for great athletes like Marty. It happens all the time. And that's all it was, you just have to take my word for it."

Lena laid her cup down on the table. "Marty seems to have abandoned all confidentiality on this business of the old man. That's why I've brought you all here. I've said it before and I'll say it again. This could be a very serious matter."

"So what does he say this old guy looks like?" asked Bo.

Lena picked up a folder on the table in front of her and withdrew some sheets of white paper. She slid a sheet to each of those assembled round the table. "Marty's something of an artist. He drew this impression for me."

There was silence as each of the group surveyed the sheet.

"Looks like Marlon Brando in the Godfather to me," growled Bo.

"Sort of Chinese," ventured Vince.

"You're right, Vince," said Lena.

"Asiatic," agreed Dr Paterson, nodding.

Bo stood, surveying the sheet. "Jesus," he said, "It don't matter to me if it's Chairman Mao. What do we do about it? What do we know?"

"I've got a strange feeling that Marty knows who this is, "said Lena.

"Then why doesn't he tell us?" asked Vince.

"I don't know."

"Marty's always been a loner," said Vince.

"Does he have lady friends?" asked Anna Klemm.

"They're always friendly but they ain't no ladies," answered Bo.

"Marty's not your normal profile of a decathlete," said Lena. "They're usually gregarious men by nature, always helping each other out all the time."

"Not him," said Vince. "Marty never helps anyone. Give him steel wool and he'll knit you a stove." He shook his head. "It's some of these people Marty and his father hang out with," he went on, laying the sheet down in front of him. "They could be the problem."

"You mean the Aetherian Society?" asked Fritz.

"They're harmless," said Lena. "Fruitcakes."

"You think so?" Bo exploded. "I met one of 'em once at a party up at his father's house. This guy, he showed me some pictures he'd taken of the sun. I said 'great, keep up the good work'. You know what he came back with?

Lena shook her head.

"He said, 'What I want to know is, what is the sun trying to TELL us'?"

Vince lifted both hands, palms up. "What could it *tell* us?"

"Beats me," said Bo.

"No," said Lena. "Marty's like his dad, he's always been into this psychic thing, though, not to the same degree. So this old man thing, it's *real* to him."

"*How* real?" said Vince.

"*This* real," said Lena, returning to her folder and passing out another half a dozen sheets of paper. "These are photocopies of a message Marty says he found beside his bed."

"What is it?" asked Paterson.

"I just told you," replied Lena, tartly. "It's a message."

"Are you ready?'" read Bo. "Ready for *what*, for Chrissakes?"

"Couldn't he have written this himself?" volunteered Paterson. "In his sleep?"

Lena shook her head. "No," she said slowly. "I've had this analysed by a handwriting expert."

"And?" pursued Bo.

"This was written by an uneducated man," she said.

Marty had often wanted them to stay on for a cuddle and a chat, but somehow few of his lovers never seemed to do so. Perhaps Carol Ross might be different, because she did not possess the same anonymity as the others. She had, up till a fortnight ago, been the assistant to Dr Voderman, the specialist recommended by Dr Paterson to administer his monthly vitamin injections at his nearby Santa Monica clinic.

Carol Ross stood at the kitchen doorway, naked except for her black panties, a quiff of pubic fluff showing tantalisingly above the elastic. She held a steaming jug of coffee. "Decaf," she said, wrinkling her nose.

"But strong decaf," he growled from the bed.

“Man,” she said, “I’ve seen all those herbs you got in there. You sneeze you’re gonna cure somebody.”

Marty smiled and propped himself up in bed.

“I’m thinking of leaving my body to science,” he said.

“Science fiction, honey,” she replied, pouring him a cup of coffee and handing it to him. She poured a cup for herself and laid it on the glass-topped bedside table, sitting beside him on the bed. “You know what us girls down at the clinic used to call you?”

He sipped his coffee and shook his head.

“The Ice Man. That’s what the girls used to call you. No heart.”

He continued to sip his coffee. Somehow, he began to wish that Carol Ross had gone, like all the others.

“My heart’s in track,” he said.

“Not that heart. The other one,” responded Carol.

He laid down his cup. “Carol, I try not to take life too serious,” he said. “I know I’m not going to get out of it alive.”

“Always the wisecrack,” she responded, shaking her head. She pointed to the kitchen. “When I go, you’ll find something in there I’ve left for you. From one of the lab girls. Someone you ditched last year. Not a friend.”

“What is it?” he asked.

She placed a slim brown finger on his lips, pulled over the duvet and lay down beside him. He nibbled her finger as he felt her toes slide up inside his thighs and nestle beneath his crotch. She leant over him and gave him a deep, thick kiss, sliding her hand under the duvet.

“Are you ready?” she asked.

Carol Ross had left behind her more than pleasant memories. In the kitchen, she had left a phial of clear-coloured liquid, marked ‘Vitamin B12 MLJ’. It was identical to the phials from which his vitamin B12 shots were given to him each month by her former employer, Dr Voderman. Beneath the phial had been a note '*Suggest you take this for analysis. Carol'*. Marty had dispatched the phial that morning by Federal Express to the pharmacy laboratories at UCLA. A week later, he had been asked to come to UCLA to meet an old college friend, Carl Schneider. Marty had been surprised that it had been Carl that he had been asked to meet, for Schneider was not a member of the faculty's pharmaceutical department. Marty had not seen Carl for six years. On that occasion, Carl, foaming at the mouth, had staggered over the finish line in a decathlon 1500 metres to record a bare one-point beyond his lifetime goal of 7000 points. Carl Schneider was one of nature's plodders, gangling, uncoordinated. Already balding at 26, he had gone on to take Honours in Sports Medicine, and was now looked upon as a coming man in his profession.

"Seven thousand and one," said Marty, pointing his index finger at Carl as, almost tripping over a file on the floor, he stumbled into Schneider's tiny, cluttered office. He was barely able to close the door behind him. Marty shook Carl Schneider's hand warmly.

"That was my big day, Marty," said Carl. He placed his hand on the telephone. "Is it still strong decaf?"

Marty nodded and Carl picked up the phone to order coffee for two. "You're looking good," he said. "Sorry about the Big Nine." Carl sighed and lay back in his chair for a moment, surveying Marty. He then leant forward, reached into his desk drawer and withdrew a half-empty phial of liquid. It was the one that Marty had sent to UCLA for analysis. "Just exactly how'd you happen to come by this?" Carl's voice had become a tad sharper.

"It was left with me," replied Marty. "And I was told to send it in here to UCLA."

"Okay, Marty, I'll buy that," said Carl, leaning back in his chair as the coffee arrived, brought in by a young female student. The student immediately recognised the identity of Carl's guest and asked him to autograph her wrist and T-shirt. Carl smiled wryly as Marty did so, and the girl made an ecstatic, flustered exit.

"Okay," he said again. "Let's get back to business. Let me tell you what this is, Marty. No, let me re-phrase that – let me tell you what's in it and then I'll tell you what I *think* it is." He laid the phial down on his desk. "Let's be frank here, Marty. You could fit the number of men who've broken 8500 points without drugs into a Volkswagen boot and still have room for President Bush." He stood up. "Except you. When I first met you, you were like a god to me. Hell, you ran ten five and high jumped two metres at High School. And you hadn't just got talent. You were a worker. You had the talent for having a talent. So when you got close to nine thousand, I thought, heh, this is real. You didn't take anything. Hell, you never even smoked grass."

"So what is it?"

"It's a kind of cocktail," said Carl. "No, not your Manhattan or your Harvey Wallbanger." He paused. "We've been getting noises on the grapevine about this stuff up here at UCLA for the last couple of years. It's a mixture of drugs. And listen, this is Bam Bam Alakazam. It passes out of the system in less than twelve hours."

Marty felt the sweat hot on his neck. "So what exactly does it do?"

"What do you think? Pretty much the same as the good ole anabolics, only more so. Strength, power, work-rate. Take it from me, Marty, this stuff is dynamite."

"And does it have a name?"

"They call it Factor 2000," replied Carl. "A perfect way to celebrate the Millennium."

"And it isn't detectable?"

Carl shook his head. "Apart from that twelve hour window, no," he said. "And you take at six of an evening and the chances of random testing picking it up are close to zero."

Marty shook his head. "So how many points do you reckon it would it be worth?"

"How on earth would I know?" answered Carl. "Who knows where a man ends and drugs begin? But I'll tell you this much. I'll tell you what it's worth per shot – about two thousand bucks. So a man's got to be in a profitable line of business to afford much of this stuff."

Marty felt himself involuntarily sag. Carl noted it immediately, and raised both hands.

"Hold on Marty," he said. "We're only at chapter one. Your Factor 2000 is, as the rules presently stand, completely legal."

"Legal? How?"

Because it's a compote, a sort of pot-pourri of substances, some of them drugs, but all of them completely legal in the amounts that you are taking. As far as the authorities are concerned, even if they picked it up in some new test, you're in the clear."

Marty shook his head.

"Only with them, Carl. Only with them. Help me, Carl, what was it that Arthur Miller once said, in one of his plays?" I took it in drama at high school-View…view…

"View from the Bridge," said Carl. "And Miller, I think that he said something like this "all the law is not in the books."

"Miller was dead right," said Marty. "OK, what I'm taking, so it's not strictly illegal, but what my people are doing is dancing on a razor's edge. The guys who are a few hundred points down on me, they sure as hell won't be getting any Factor 2000, just three square meals a day."

"You all right?" asked Carl, noting the change in Marty's expression.

Marty stood, breathing deeply. "Thanks, Carl. I've got to get back," he said.

Not many folks ever came now to Carlisle's Jim Thorpe Room, Marty could see that. It was, perhaps, not surprising. After all, it was not exactly your modern Hall of Fame with interactive television, computers and holograms. No, this was your regular, old-style museum, a dim collection of faded photographs and rusting medallions, dusty objects in misty glass cases, ill-lit by the light of stained-glass windows. The

Jim Thorpe Room lay in the basement of the Carlisle City Library, a solid brownstone relic of the early twentieth century.

When Marty entered, it was empty and there was no one at the desk to collect his dollar entry fee. As he passed the desk, he laid a ten dollar bill on it and moved on into the small, single-room museum, feeling the creak of springy, polished wooden floorboards beneath his feet. The wall on the immediate right featured a full sized, blow-up photograph of Jim, standing hands on hips. It was the same one that he had seen in Bill Easton's book. Underneath the photograph had been printed '*Jim Thorpe, American Athlete of the Half Century, United States Association of Sports Writers, 1950'*.

"*His* half century," muttered Marty. "Not mine."

The next exhibit was a glass case containing Thorpe's vest, shorts and running shoes from the 1912 Stockholm Olympics. The material for the vest and shorts looked to be coarse and heavy. The black leather spiked shoes, with their blunt, stubby spikes, looked clumsy and ponderous.

"Chariots of Fire," said Marty to himself, shaking his head.

Thorpe's medals and trophies occupied two entire cases along the right hand wall, and contained row upon row of medals, plaques and cups for track, football, baseball and basketball. Hell, Thorpe had even place-kicked a football sixty-one yards, only one yard short of the present record. The next photographic blow-up, on the wall directly facing the entrance door, was of the Swede, Hugo Wieslander, who had finished second to Thorpe in the 1912 Olympic Decathlon. Wieslander, an angular, clean-cut, handsome man with a middle parting in his hair, stood fully clothed in a coarse rumpled suit of the period. Below the photograph lay the caption, '*Hugo Wieslander (Sweden) who refused to accept Jim Thorpe's Olympic gold medal when Thorpe was disqualified in 1913. Wieslander returned the medals to the International Olympic Committee, but they disappeared from view. Wieslander, in a visit to the United States in 1925, unsuccessfully attempted to contact Thorpe.'*

"Loser," grunted Marty. He moved on to the next case in the corner on the far left, containing yellowing letters and photocopies of newspaper reports. Jim Thorpe, the Principal of Carlisle Indian College, Dean Mackay – in the dim yellow light afforded by the stained glass windows, the names were now almost impossible to read. Marty walked back to the light switch at the entrance and pressed it, to no avail. He returned to the case of letters and peered into it, but it was difficult to distinguish much more than the bold headlines of the newspaper articles. Shaking his head, Marty moved on to the left hand wall, where two large, man-size glass cases were devoted to Thorpe's career in baseball and football.

Suddenly, the lights went on behind him. Marty looked round to the door to see a petite, dapper old lady in an impeccable white linen blouse and long black dress which almost touched the floor. Her face was small and wrinkled, her iron-grey hair pinned back in a tight bun. Marty noted that she wore thick black woollen stockings. The woman stood, hands clasped in front of her, smiling. "Can I be of any help to you?" she asked.

Marty walked to the desk, retrieved his ten dollar bill and handed it to the old lady. "There was nobody here," he explained. "So I just came on in."

She went behind the desk, placed the ten dollar bill in a black tin box, locked it and put it back in the drawer. "No," she said. "Not many people come here now. They have a whole town in his name now, Jim Thorpe town, I think they call it." She opened another drawer and withdrew a pair of spectacles which she placed on the end of her nose, peering closely at him. "I thought so," she said. "You're MLJ, aren't you?"

Marty smiled and nodded.

She offered her tiny, wrinkled, liver-spotted hand to him. "I follow everything you do," she said. "But I didn't know you had an interest in track history."

Marty considered saying that he had not and never would have, but held back.

"I'm Helen Mapstone," said the old lady. "I've been here since 1953, my grandad Hiram Mapstone put this room together, after the movie."

"The movie?"

"Man of Bronze," she said. "Jim Thorpe's life story." She pointed to the left of the entrance desk, to a full-size blow-up photograph, which was not of Thorpe. "Burt Lancaster played the part," she said, her brows furrowing. "He came up here once. Lovely man, but thirty-seven. Far too old for Jim. Far too old." Helen Mapstone looked around the little room, and spread her arms. "So how can I be of help to you?" she asked again.

Marty turned and pointed to the case containing the letters and press cuttings, over in the left corner of the room. "Before you came," he said, "I was trying to read those."

"Then let's see what we can do," she said moving with him towards the case of letters and clippings. She opened the case and withdrew a framed photocopy. "Yes, here's a letter from Pop Warner. He was the coach at Carlisle. And this one here, this is from Jim."

Marty looked at the letter and his heart missed a beat. The handwriting looked to be identical to that on the slip which he now carried in his inside pocket. He grunted. Miss Mapstone noted the grunt, but chose to ignore it. "And here's a letter from the Dean of Carlisle, Mr Mackay."

Marty breathed deeply. "What are those drawings?" He pointed to a link of tiny sequence drawings of a long jumper in the bottom left hand corner of the case. There was a text below.

"Now these, Mr Jones, these are very strange," Helen Mapstone said. "Very strange indeed. They're sequences of a long jump performed by Jim back in 1912."

"What's strange about them, ma'am?" asked Marty.

"Because they show a hitch-kick action," the curator explained.

"So what's wrong with that, Miss Mapstone?"

"Well, the hitch-kick didn't arrive till around 1925," she replied.

Marty felt himself flush. "He might have done it by accident, I suppose," he volunteered.

Miss Mapstone smiled. "Most successful track techniques are done by accident, young man," she said. "Then the sports scientists go back to the laboratories to see if they also work in theory." She shook her head. "No, it's the time – much too early. That's the problem. No one has ever explained it, at least not to my satisfaction."

Miss Mapstone turned from the case and moved along the left hand wall, past the glass case dedicated to Thorpe's career in baseball and football, and stopped at a massive, hazy, sepia photograph. It was a posed photograph of the Carlisle 1911 track and field team. There were three lines of eight men, in white vests bearing the letter 'C' on the front. They were surprisingly small men, with creased, nut-brown skins, staring unsmilingly out at him from the past. In the front row, arms folded, sat Jim Thorpe and Pop Warner, side by side with Dean Mackay. Suddenly, Marty felt a bead of sweat form on his forehead. For on Jim's left sat a chunky, muscular black man, his face set in a cheesy, Uncle Tom grin.

"Shit," said Marty, involuntarily.

Miss Mapstone removed her spectacles and surveyed him. "*Mr Jones*," she said.

"It's clear enough to *me*, Marty. He wants you to come back. Jim Thorpe wants you to come back."

Only the photographs around Bob Goldstein's living room betrayed their owner's background, but they were a strange mixture. Above the desk was a lean, cadaverous Goldstein dunking a basket for UCLA in 1963, next to a photograph of Professor Goldstein some twenty years later standing beside Uri Geller, whilst in the corner was a grotesque cartoon of a smiling Goldstein shaking hands with the Great Randi, the scourge of all psychics.

Goldstein, six foot six tall, but now slightly bowed and with the merest hint of a small but perfectly rounded pot belly, stood and refreshed Marty's mug of coffee. He had been a founding member of the Aetherian Society and its President for six years.

"Back where?" Marty asked.

"To 1911"

Marty shook his head. "Get real, Bob."

"Then you tell me just what the hell this is all about," said Goldstein in his dry, cracked voice. "You see an old man. You *hear* an old man. Goddammit, the same old guy even writes to you. He keeps asking 'are you ready'. Then you find out it's someone you've never, may God forgive you, never heard of, Jim Thorpe. This is exactly what the Society's been waiting for since it got started."

"But the Society," said Marty. "It's not like the X-Files. It's always been about the scientific analysis of the paranormal."

"You ever read that English guy, Hawkings?" asked Goldstein jabbing an index finger at Marty. "He says that time, it's not like we thought it was."

Marty shook his head wearily and reached into an inside pocket. He withdrew an envelope within which was a photocopy of a section of the 1911 Carlisle photograph. He handed it to Goldstein who studied it for a moment before getting up to go over to his desk. He withdrew a magnifying glass and peered at the photograph for several moments. "Jesus H Christ!" he said. "Where on earth did you find this?"

"At the Thorpe Museum," replied Marty. "In Carlisle."

"Then you *made* it, Marty. You're there! Holy shit!"

Marty shook his head. "That could be anybody."

"There's one way of proving it," said Goldstein. "Let me see if I can bring this photograph up on the Net." He put his hands on Marty's shoulders. "Marty, play it cool. You just sit there and think about it. Finish your coffee and I'll call you when I've got it up on my screen."

It took only three minutes before Goldstein called Marty down into his office in the cellar below. Marty could feel the pulse of Goldstein's energy as he entered the room. It was almost palpable. The older man, sitting in front of his computer screen, beckoned him to sit down at his side. "Got it," he said in excitement, the sweat dripping down his lined features. "Jeez, they've got a whole site here on ole Jim."

Before them on the screen appeared the 1911 team photograph which Marty had first seen at Carlisle.

"June 1911," said Goldstein. "There they are – Jim, Pop Warner, Louis Tewanima – he was a distance runner – and, god help me – *you*!" He looked to his right to Marty, who was now transfixed. He withdrew a white handkerchief from a trouser pocket and mopped his face. "You bust your left wrist, didn't you, at karate back in '92?"

Marty nodded and lifted his left wrist. There was still a visible white stitch mark, about four inches long.

"So let's go find it," said Goldstein. He pressed a button to secure focus on the Negro's arm. "Got the arm," he said peering at the screen. He shook his head. "Can't see anything, can you?" The older man looked closely at Marty again.

"I must be la-la," he said. "Marty, go, go look at yourself in the mirror. Have a look at your face!"

Marty stood and walked across the room to the mirror which hung on the wall beside the office door.

"So?" he said.

"That tiny mole you got, just above your lip on the left."

Marty nodded and turned. "Let us have another look, Bob," he said joining Goldstein at the computer. Goldstein focused in on the Negro's head.

"Let's us just close in," he said, focusing on the mouth.

"Jesus wept!" yelped Marty.

"There it is," said Goldstein turning to Marty. "There it is!"

For there it indisputably was, that tiny mole on the lip of that long-dead man, staring out from a faded, long-forgotten photograph.

"Let's us just print this out," said Goldstein. He pressed the 'print' button and in moments a copy of the computer picture was in their hands. Goldstein handed it to Marty. "So you made it," said Goldstein. "Like father, like son."

"My *father*?" exploded Marty. "What's Dad got to do with it?"

Goldstein sat back in his chair, put his hands to his lips and sighed. "Your father and I. We've studied time travel for years – since the Sixties. Never put anything on paper. We knew that astral bodies could move. Hell, the CIA and the KGB knew that. So back in 1988, we started by moving objects like pencils."

"And did it work?"

Goldstein shook his head. "Sometimes it did, sometimes it didn't. Like most psychic phenomena, it wasn't easy to repeat. Then finally we managed to do it consistently."

"But this is the PAST, Bob. This is *people*. It's not just moving pencils from one room to another."

Goldstein nodded. "We went to friends' homes, selected rooms and objects and tried to put them back into the past."

"So how did that work?"

"We would put the object, say an ashtray, in a room on a Thursday. Our aim was to bring back that object to two days before, to the Tuesday."

"So, let me get my head round this. You put something in a room on a Thursday and you already had it there on the Tuesday?"

"Yes. We had photographed the room on the Tuesday. No ashtray. Then we sat together on the Thursday and thought it back, re-checked the photograph, and allah shazam, it was there."

He paused.

"I know what you're gonna ask me, Marty," said Goldstein. "But don't ask, cos it hurts my head. And you can see what would happen if I ever tried to publish."

"I'll tell you what I can see, Bob," said Marty. "I see a one-way ticket to the Funny Farm." He stood up and examined the photograph. "So what you're saying, what you're telling me, Bob, is that people can go back into the past."

Goldstein nodded. "We've *done* it, Marty," he said.

"With who?"

"With *whom,*" Goldstein corrected. He paused. "With a lady, then your father," he said.

Marty returned to his seat and his shoulders sagged. "What are you trying to tell me?"

"Your father and I talked about it for years," said Goldstein. "He wanted to go back to 1900."

"1900. Why?"

"To work with Edison," replied Goldstein.

"But I got postcards from him all this year, since he left. And he left messages on my tape."

"We fixed these before he went," replied Goldstein. "The first year."

"Come on. Dad said he was going on a world tour. How do you know he isn't just sitting in some bar in Paris?"

"Your father doesn't drink," replied Goldstein. "I'm telling you, Marty. He made it back last year."

"So why didn't he tell anybody he was going?"

"Jeez, Marty, Marcus got enough stick back in 1972 when he married a black woman – and changed his name to hers a year before she died. Think of it. The Time Machine Professor. He would have been a laughing stock. So would I." Goldstein replied.

"I still can't get my head around this, Bob," said Marty.

"How do you *know* he made it?"

"He gave us a name, Marcus Klumberg, that he would use," replied Goldstein. "Now, up till a year ago, there was never any mention of a Klumberg in any of the biographies of Edison. Then in a new biography it suddenly appeared, around 1900, a few days after he left."

"OK," said Marty. "So why didn't my dad come back?"

'Because he didn't want to," replied Goldstein. "At least, not yet."

"So how do you know that?"

"Marcus and I, we decided on a method of keeping in touch, telepathy again, by having him trying to transmit a code word," said the older man." It was picked up here by one of our telepaths, and the rest of the team all combined to try to piece together what he was trying to say. It wasn't easy, because it was a sort of spaghetti of words, but they, eventually, worked it out and we were in business."

"And you were able to reply?"

Goldstein paused.

"That hasn't always been so easy. Your dad only got a six on his telepathy tests, but we occasionally get through, though only in fits and starts."

"So where is he now?"

"We don't know, at least not exactly."

He paused.

"Houston, we have a problem. We sent him back to 1900, but one night he went to sleep in New York, and woke up next morning in Rhode Island in 1906."

"This…this is one helluva lot to take in," said Marty.

Goldstein reached forward and placed his hands on Marty's shoulders. "I know you don't drink," he said. He walked over to a cupboard high in the left hand corner of the room, opened it and withdrew a bottle of Scotch and two crystal tumblers. "Glenmorangie," he said. "Scotch malt whisky. You know your father liked a shot every now and then." He poured out shots in the two tumblers, replaced the bottle and sat beside Marty. He handed him a tumbler. "Get this into you," he said. "Edison was an asshole," he said. "Stole everything your dad ever invented. So Marcus took it all back off him at poker."

Marty surveyed his whisky. "Yes," he said. "He could always count the cards. They wouldn't let him play in Vegas."

Goldstein raised his glass to Marty and sipped his malt, nodding. "Like you. Almost total recall," he said. "So he took Edison for a ride and put his money in movies and vaudeville." He sipped his whisky and coughed. "Your father said he would die fit," said Goldstein, smiling. "He took good care of himself, no smoking, an occasional malt. Worked out with the weights. Vitamins like you can't imagine."

"Vitamins," repeated Marty dully.

"I remember, I said to him – before you go check out your health – no Medicare in those good old days. And your teeth – get yourself a dental audit."

"Jesus H. Christ," said Marty, continuing to sip his drink.

"Fillings," continued Goldstein. "No fun in 1900, or 1906, for that matter. Extractions, agony."

Bob Goldstein had expressed neither surprise nor shock when Marty had told him of the UCLA analysis of the "Vitamin B12" phial's contents. It was now one o'clock in the morning and they sat together in the dim light of Goldstein's tiny, book-lined office, sipping the older man's powerful decaffeinated coffee. Marty had, since a child, always thought of Goldstein's voice as dry sand. It rasped, it crackled, but behind it there was always the sharpness, the certainty of thoughts that had passed many times through the filter of intellect and experience.

"It's been a dung heap since Mexico 1968," growled Goldstein, laying down his mug on the stained brown roll-top desk in front of him. "Marty, when I was a boy, I used to keep all the track and field rankings. The names, they probably wouldn't that mean much to you now. Bob Hayes, Ralph Boston, Wilma Rudolph. Great athletes." He paused, to replenish his empty mug from a percolator bubbling black on a bookshelf above on his right. "Then one day – it was August 1st 1971 – I stopped keeping them. Just like that." He poured cream into his mug, failing to find a spoon, absent-mindedly stirred it with a pencil. He lifted the mug and sipped his coffee. "Men like monsters and women like men," he said. "That's what Marcus used to call them." He paused. "But like some chicken running around with its head cut off, I still went to track meets, still watched the Olympics on television. God knows why." He shook his head, and continued, as if speaking to himself. "You know, a buddy of mine asked me a couple of weeks ago – he said – Bob, you're the expert, tell me which women's world records you can be certain of, hand on heart – no steroids, no growth hormone, no nothing." Goldstein held up three fingers to Marty. "Three, that was the best I could do," he growled. "Even then, I wasn't too sure."

Marty sat silent, aware that this was something that Bob Goldstein had wanted to say to him for a long time. "And what about me?"

"You, you were always Marcus' boy. Like Caesar's wife, above suspicion. Hell, you were like shit off a shovel back at High School, so I thought…" He paused.

"But you weren't completely sure."

Goldstein shrugged. "Who is, these days?" he answered. "If any man has scored eight thousand five hundred points clean, then I tip my hat to him."

"Do you think I knew?"

"Look, when you took up with Bo and Vince back in 1991, you put on over five hundred points in a year, twelve hundred over three years. Didn't you ever stop to ask yourself why you were running out of suits and shirts that fitted?"

Marty did not reply. He felt a sickness at the pit of his stomach.

"It's not sport anymore," continued Goldstein. "It's become a contest between pharmacists. Hell, they should have Laroche and Glaxo up there on the podium with them, taking medals." He paused. "You conned yourself, Marty. You didn't *want* to know. If it makes you feel any better, in your place I would probably have done the same. But no man wants to believe he isn't real."

"Real?"

Goldstein's voice was beginning to tire. "Sport is what you are by nature and what you put in by hard work. Brain and train. Me, I've got no problems with psychologists, physiotherapists, all that stuff. That's part of the brain and train. But drugs, that's a whole different ball game. That's not real." Goldstein stood, took Marty's empty cup from him and re-charged it. He handed it back to the younger man.

"You've probably heard all of this before, Marty. The ramblings of an old man. You guys don't think that way anymore." He shook his head. "Reality. Truth. The big 'Who am I' question. You know, Marty, I still jog. I can just about knock out twenty-four minutes for three miles, downhill with the wind behind me. Sometimes, twenty-four-ten, sometimes twenty-four-twelve. But twenty-four minutes, that's my limit." He paused. "Now if you gave me some of your Factor 2000 to shoot up with, I might suddenly run twenty-three minutes. So, Hallelujah, I've run a minute faster. But where is the 'me' in that sixty seconds?" He rose, took an almost empty bottle of Glenmorangie from the shelf above, removed the cork and poured a shot into his coffee. "No, there's no 'me' in that minute, Marty, just some stuff from a hypo. That's all there is and I'm conning myself if I think any different."

Marty sat silent for several minutes, as Goldstein finished his Glenmorangie. Goldstein's words bit into him. He had lived as a stranger to himself. There was no knowing what he had achieved, for there was no knowing who he had been. It was all nothing. And now here was old Jim, calling out to him from a sepia past, giving him a chance to make it all good. He became increasingly aware of the empty, sick feeling at the pit of his stomach. He knew what he had to do.

"So when do I go?" he said.

"Jeez," said Goldstein. "You didn't take long to make up your mind, did you? Why?"

"I want to be real."

Goldstein nodded.

"I can see what you mean, Marty."

"Just one other thing," said Marty. "Can you think a man back here?"

"Yes."

"So you've got someone back. It's not a one way ticket."

Goldstein pursed his lips.

"Marty, do you remember Miss Boggis?"

Marty nodded.

"Who could forget Miss Boggis?"

"Because she was our top psychic, ten out of ten in all disciplines. She was the first to go back-and she was the first to GET back. We had been moving people for almost a year, usually only a few days back at a time, and getting them back here, but she wanted to go back to 1924, to Paris, to meet Picasso. "Picasso", that was her code word, and we got her there, then back here safe and sound. And that was when your dad saw that it could work, and he decided to go. "

"So how did it work?"

"She placed herself at the exact spot in Paris where she had arrived, and sent out the code words "Picasso return". It came out to us loud and clear. Fifty-one of our best and bravest got to work, and next morning she was back. We will use the same mechanism with your dad, and with you."

"One question I've got to ask you, Bob. Miss Boggis, she could have been back there for life. How did you know all of this was going to work?"

Goldstein re-charged his drink.

"I didn't. We didn't. Sometimes Marty, you simply have to jump out of the plane and build your wings on the way down."

"You've jumped a fair way," said Marty. "But how do you time it so I can get back for next year's Olympics?"

"I don't," said Goldstein. As I just said, it's not an exact science, hell it's not a science at all. Marcus went back to 1900, but in a couple of weeks he was sending back messages from 1906. He had lived six years in about fourteen days. So the time power-weight ratio seems to be pretty good."

"So say I go back to March 1911, and compete in the 1912 Olympics and beat Thorpe you're telling me that I get back here in a few days."

Goldstein nodded.

"We set you a date back in 1912 for getting back, you go to exactly where you started, and we think you back here. Your father has got a word for it-psychokinetics."

Marty sipped his coffee.

"Bob," he said, "I've got a feeling that he knows."

"Who knows?"

“Jim Thorpe. He knows that I’m a fake. That we’re all fakes.”

“Then, perhaps, you’re Jim’s last chance of the century, Marty.”

“And he’s mine,” replied Marty. “So I have to get back there and kick ass. Then come back here and kick more ass. But clean…” He paused. “So what do I have to do?” he asked.

Goldstein stood and withdrew a calendar from a hook on the wall. He surveyed it. “You go to Carlisle, you book in at a hotel, close to where the old track used to be. You wear some track gear of the period. You take a couple of spaldings and you go to sleep, thinking your code word. That’s when the Society will get to work, all fifty-one of us, led by the redoubtable Miss Boggis. We will THINK you back to Carslisle, 1911.”

Marty shook his head.

“I don’t believe this,” he said.

“You have to,” said Goldstein. “Because we need to have everything going our way.”

“When?”

“August 20th,” replied Goldstein. “A week from now. And have you got any idea of your code-word?”

“Yes,” said Marty immediately. “Nike.”

Miss Mapstone looked somewhat incongruous in Taco King, but she had insisted on eating there, rather than in the French restaurant which Marty had offered her. Engulfed by her taco, she nibbled at it for a moment, then laid it down. She reached below the table, into a cracked brown leather briefcase, withdrew a file of papers and handed them across the table to Marty.

“The Carlisle College records of that period were destroyed in a fire, about twenty years ago,” she said. “This was all that was left – I had them photocopied.” Miss Mapstone returned to the unequal assault upon her taco.

Marty opened the file and leafed through the photocopies. “So have we got anything here about that black guy?”

“Roother,” said Miss Mapstone, sipping her root beer. “I think he might have been the groundsman – but then he might have been a rubber.”

“A rubber?

“A masseur. Massage, it was all the rage for track athletes back in those days,” she replied.

“So that’s all you know?”

“There weren’t many blacks in Carlisle in those days, though, there was a black sector in the town.”

Marty nodded. “Did you manage to get a blow-up of that section of the team photograph?”

“Yes,” said Miss Mapstone. She, again, reached down into her brief case and withdrew a foolscap-size photocopy. “Here it is,” she said, handing it to him.

Marty took the photocopy and scrutinised it. He looked at “Roother,” and was surprised that Miss Mapstone had not noticed the resemblance. But there was no question of it. There was the tiny mole, above the left lip. Marty felt himself redden.

“Any photos beyond 1912?”

“All burnt in the fire,” she replied.

“And where exactly was the Carlisle track back in those days?”

“Somewhere up there,” she said, pointing above her to the twinkling lights of the Holiday Inn.

“Just below that hotel. The Majestic, it was called, back then.” She returned to her taco.

It was an hour to midnight when Marty registered at the Holiday Inn. The receptionist had, oddly, showed no surprise when he had pre-paid for two months and had insisted on Room 1911. His last words as he drifted into sleep were “Nike.”

Chapter 3
Carlisle

When Marty awoke, he was lying on a shelf. He lay there, in hot, inky darkness, curled in a foetal position. It was fortunate for him that the shelf was both broad and thick, for he had plenty of room and it could take his weight. He was breathing hard, through mouth and nose, and became aware of a sweet, sickly smell which was difficult to identify. Marty felt the sweat bead on his forehead, and trickle hot down his neck.

He opened his eyes and raised his head, cracking his forehead hard on the thick plank of the shelf above him. Marty shouted in reflex and tumbled from the shelf, spinning as he did so and pulling down over him a pile of soft, fluffy materials. He turned and landed backwards on his butt, in a bamboo basket directly below him, his arms and lower legs dangling over its edges. Gasping, he pulled his legs and arms down into the basket and drew himself up onto his knees. He put his index finger to his forehead and felt a salty trickle of blood run down his right nostril into his mouth. Marty fumbled beneath him and felt what seemed to be a bath towel on the side of the basket. He pulled it up and dabbed gingerly at his bleeding nose.

Marty stood up in the basket and ranged blindly around him with both hands in the still, warm darkness. Nothing. He then reached down with both hands and made contact with the thick, woven thatch of the sides of the basket. He gingerly scissored over the edge of the basket, to stand in the darkness on a hard stone floor, and again reached out blindly with both hands and took hesitant, uncertain steps forward. This time, his right arm made contact with a shelf and with what felt to be a pile of thick bath towels, which dropped down on to the floor over his feet.

Marty slowly groped his way around the room in a clockwise direction, stumbling over towels and the wheels of the laundry basket as he did so. He felt what seemed to be more towels, sheets, pillowslips and bathrobes, resting in piles on shelves which rose above him.

Suddenly, he made contact with something hard, a series of large, heavy tin cans, standing on a shelf just below shoulder-level. Then, in a corner, there was what felt like a row of brooms or mops, all standing vertically. Finally, he stumbled into some buckets at ground-level in the same area.

Marty stopped and leant back against the shelves, breathing heavily. He now knew that he was in some sort of laundry room. That much was for sure. He turned and put his hands beyond the shelves, to touch a rough brick wall and continued to fumble his way clockwise around the room, seeking the light-switch. Finally, he felt the smooth painted surface of a wooden door. He passed his hands slowly down the door until he reached the doorknob, and he twisted it. It was locked. Marty groaned, turned and slid helplessly down the door, sitting on his backside on the cold stone floor in the darkness, his back against the door, hearing only the sound of his own breathing.

He tried to gather his thoughts. Perhaps the whole thing had been some elaborate plot, a hoax. They had all been in on the scam – Bo, Vince, Bob, Miss Mapstone. He had seen it all before, in an old movie starring Michael Douglas, *The Game*, a few months back. Douglas had been assaulted, almost drowned, had all his money stolen and ended up falling a couple of hundred feet through a skylight, to land on an airbag. In the end, it had all been nothing more than an elaborate hoax, all set up by his brother. So, perhaps, Carl and Bob Goldstein's budget couldn't run to a cast of actors or special effects and he had simply landed up in a laundry basket, but it all fitted perfectly.

Marty slowly got to his feet, turned to face the door and again tried the knob, pulling on it in rage. It was firmly locked. He banged on the door. Nothing. He slid his hand up the left-hand side of the wall, seeking a light switch. There was nothing. He tried the right-hand side of the door, and there it was, a thick, bulbous switch. He flicked it on, and suddenly the little room was bathed in light.

He was, indeed, in a laundry room. It was one which was now in chaos, as in his confusion he had pulled whole shelves of towels, sheets, pillowslips and bathrobes down on to its stone floor. Marty lifted a bathrobe in order to replace it, and began to fold it. He noticed letters ornately worked in blue onto the left pocket of the white, fluffy robe. They were not printed letters, but were fluid and stylish. The letters were 'M H'. Marty examined the pillowslips, sheets and towels on the floor around him. On all of them, the letters 'M H' were monogrammed in blue. He was in the long-forgotten Majestic Hotel.

The tiny laundry room was like a sauna. Sweating, congealed blood mixing with his sweat, Marty looked down to the bottom shelf, where the hand towels were stacked. Below the shelf, on the floor, was a line of what appeared to be thick, white china bottles with cork stoppers. He lifted one and, holding it to his ear, he shook it. It was empty. Marty put it back, bent down and knelt on one knee, scrutinising the objects on the floor below the bottom shelf. Behind the bottles was a row of big, white enamel bowls. Marty withdrew one and lifted it. Suddenly, he knew exactly what it was.

It was a chamber pot. He had seen one once in an old English movie. He put it down as he felt the blood, again, trickle down his chin. He picked up a towel to staunch the flow, and heard a key turn in the lock behind him, and the door open.

"Where you bin?"

The voice came from the open door behind him. Marty turned to see a slim young black woman dressed in a long, black maid's uniform and a full-length V-shaped white apron. She held in front of her a thick pile of newspapers.

The young woman did not wait for a reply. "We bin a-waitin' for you this half hour," she said. "Plumb forgot yo' name."

"Marty Luther…"

She did not allow him to finish. "Marty Roother, that's it. Me, I go by the name of Mary Lou Barrow. Well, I gotta say is, you done made a great start, Marty." She stepped forward and checked his bleeding nose. "You bin in some kinda fight?"

She turned, closed the door behind her and laid down the newspapers on a shelf behind her. She looked at him again. "And what you all dressed up like dat for – Mardi Gras?" She bent down and picked up a newspaper, which she thrust into his hand. "You read this – if'n you can read," she said. "Me, I'll go down and rustle up some kinda uniform for you. Maybe we can make this work."

She turned, picked up the remaining newspapers and opened the door. Then she faced him. "Marty Roother, don't you go answer to no one till I gets back," she said. She closed the door and he heard the key turn in the lock.

Marty, stunned, stared at the door. "Marty Roother," he said to himself, lifting the newspaper in front of him. It was headed "Carlisle Clarion." The date was March 11th, 1911.

It was just as it had been in his dream. The kitchen of the Majestic was like some vast Turkish bath, with clattering stereophonic sound. Marty stood, sweating, at Mary Lou's side in the great throbbing, echoing kitchen, a hissing hell of noise and steam. The smooth, red-tiled floor of the kitchen was wet, its hot air thick with the odour of long-forgotten meals. Through the steam, Marty began to pick out indistinct figures moving about in white overalls and high, bulbous chef's hats, waving their arms and shouting at each other.

He moved gingerly forwards with Mary Lou deeper into the cavernous kitchen and now saw Negroes standing on wooden platforms, staring ahead, silently stirring bubbling, glutinous vats with long wooden ladles. Marty was now dressed in coarse, ill-fitting white overalls and the same flat-topped peak-less white caps as the men who now stirred the vats. He felt Mary Lou's hands behind him, on his shoulders, gently pressing him forward, deeper into the kitchen.

From out of the hot mist loomed a giant. He was a white man, at least six foot four in height, dressed in chef's hat and black and white striped jacket and white trousers, his ample belly straining at the broad leather belt encircling his waist. The man's face was round, hairless, his neck a terrace of fat rolls down which sweat cascaded.

"This Chef Bassett," said Mary Lou, pulling Marty forward.

Chef Bassett did not respond, but reached forward, grabbed Marty's right bicep and squeezed it hard. "Who this fella?" he grunted. "Who this heah boy?" He continued to press Marty's upper arm. "He Mistah Sandow hisself?" He released Marty's arm, and he shook his head, sweat spraying on to Marty and Mary Lou. He pointed at Marty. "This heah's an eighteen inch arm. Never seen no nigra with no arm like this. Not never. What's his name?"

"Marty Roother," said Mary Lou, nervously. "He come here to work."

"Where you hail from?" boomed Bassett, his great tombstone teeth flashing.

Mary Lou pursed her lips to speak.

"Let the boy speak for hisself, Mary Lou," said Boss Bassett. "He got a tongue in his head."

For the first time in his life, Marty was lost for words. His mouth was dry. He gulped. "Alabama," he said.

"Alabammy?" roared Bassett. He leant forward and poked Marty in the abdomen with his index finger. It was rock hard. Boss Bassett's eyes narrowed. "Must feed you nigra boys real good down Alabammy way," he said.

Bassett turned towards piles of dirty dishes behind him on a heavy wooden kitchen table. He lifted the first pile, raised it in front of him to shoulder level and, grinning, dropped it on the floor. The plates shattered, scattering all over the red tile floor. Bassett did the same with each of the four piles until the floor was now a wilderness of splintered plates. Marty and Mary Lou stood, transfixed. Finally, Bassett easily picked up a steel urn containing cold vegetable soup, tipped it up, turned it, and slowly poured it into the shattered plates.

"I keeps me a right clean kitchen heah, Marty," he said. He pointed towards a mop behind Marty in the corner of the kitchen. "Fetch me that mop, boy," he said.

Marty dutifully fetched the mop.

"Don't want to see nothing laying on this heah floor, not never," he said. "And when you done, you gets them biceps of yourn set to the kindling out there in the yard, with ole Abner Pyle." Bassett turned and crunched his way across the broken plates, shaking his head. "Alabammy," he growled. "Don't that beat all."

Marty looked helplessly behind him, but the girl, Mary Lou, had now left him to pursue her duties upstairs. He surveyed the desolation in front of him and tentatively pushed the wet mop up the kitchen floor. Securing a small iron shovel, he scooped up the first of the wreckage and placed it in a bucket. As he did so, he became aware of the stares of the other kitchen staff, stirring vats or frying up on black griddles in the hot steam and din of Boss Bassett's kitchen. Around them, waiters bellowing orders swept in and out of swing doors bearing trays of plates or swept out into the dining room with steaming food.

Marty finally filled two buckets with the chaotic jumble of plates and soup, then looked around him helplessly, for the exit.

"*Out*, boy, out!"

It was the booming voice of Boss Bassett, from somewhere behind him in the mist. He felt two heavy hands on his shoulders pressing him to his left, beyond the kitchen sinks where rows of Negroes stood, hands in hot water, dwarfed by high piles of greasy plates, towards an outside door.

Marty found himself stumbling into a cobbled yard, in bright sunlight. There stood row upon row of coloured maids industriously beating carpets which hung suspended on washing lines, the dust from the carpets rising slowly in the warm spring air. On seeing him, as if on command, the maids stopped their rhythmic beating. Marty stood with the buckets, suspended in both arms, aware of their gaze. He looked at them. Jesus, they were like something out of 'Gone with the Wind', wide-eyed, thick-lipped young mammies.

He stumbled across the bumpy, cobbled yard, a bucket suspended in each hand, towards a row of corrugated bins set against the red brickyard wall. He lowered the bucket in his left hand to the ground, opened the bin, and swung the other bucket up, pouring its contents clattering into it, then did the same with the second bucket. He turned to face the maids. They had not resumed their beating but now stood, hands on hips, observing him. In the row directly in front of him, a slim, lean coffee-coloured girl, essentially a pair of legs with a head on top, nudged Mary Lou, smiling. "Looks like you got yousself some kinda man there, missy," she said.

Mary Lou frowned and shook her head. She laid down her beater on the cobbles and walked towards Marty, as the other maids resumed their work. "How you doin', Marty?" she asked.

Marty wiped his sweating face with his right hand. "Cool. It's cool," he said.

"Cool?" she replied. "You'se sweating like a pig."

"*Boy!*"

Behind him, Marty heard the boom of Boss Bassett's voice through the kitchen door. Marty retrieved the empty buckets and made his way back to the kitchen. As he passed through the kitchen door, he received a solid thump on the back of his head which sent him reeling forward onto the tiled kitchen floor, dislodging the pails. He lay on his front, gasping for breath, as above him Boss Bassett placed a heavy foot on his back.

"Jest you keep yo' eyes offen them gals," growled Boss. "They'se good gals. They'se ladies. Not for the likes of Alabammy boys like you."

Marty turned, got to his feet and looked for his pails. Boss Bassett shook his head and handed him two other pails almost twice the size of those he had carried into the yard. "Next time, use one of these heah," he said. "Ergonomics." Boss Bassett had sought the occasion to use that word ever since he had first encountered it in McFaddens Magazine the year before. He smiled to himself in satisfaction, turned, and was, again, lost in the steam of the kitchen.

It took Marty an hour and a half to clear the kitchen of debris. Then he got on to his hands and knees to retrieve the sharp fragments of plate still lodged in crevices and corners. During the whole period, no one spoke to him. The Negroes wordlessly stirred their vats or stood, hands deep in the greasy water of the sinks, cleaning dishes. Around them whirled the white chefs and waiters, shouting, berating, denouncing.

Then, after a barely edible meal consisting of grey pulp in which lodged fragments of meat which he could not identify and washed down with lukewarm milk, Marty was dispatched to the yard at the rear of the hotel to chop kindling wood. There, he found himself in the company of Abner Pyle, an iron-haired, sinewy black man in his mid-fifties. Pyle, stripped to the waist, appeared to possess little in the way of muscles, his sweating body apparently consisting of a series of veins held together by ligaments. But the old man was like a metronome. A log was placed on the block and dispatched in one loose, easy swing, to be replaced by another, to be, again, sliced easily in half with a movement that appeared to contain nothing in the way of effort. Behind him lay a mountain of kindling, a veritable Everest of activity.

Abner Pyle acknowledged Marty with a shrug as he continued to churn his way remorselessly through the logs in the thin March sunshine. He pointed Marty to another oak block in which an axe was sunk, withdrew a red handkerchief from his jeans pocket and wiped his forehead and face. Marty looked for a moment at the pile of logs towering over Abner Pyle.

"Shit," he said, withdrawing the axe and placing a log on the oak block.

The first logs went easy, split in one clean swing, and for the first half hour Marty relished the work as, out of the corner of his eye, he observed Abner swinging steadily. After a few moments, he began to pick up and match Abner's rhythm, and his little pile of logs slowly began to rise. Then it suddenly started to hurt. The pain started, slowly, slyly, in his neck and upper back, spreading gradually to his shoulders and then down into his forearms. His rhythm started to flag and he stopped for a moment, gasping, his sweat blinding him. But a few metres away, Abner's relentless destruction of the forests of Pennsylvania continued remorselessly. Marty resumed, but the pain returned early and he stopped again, feeling his arms and hands now tremble with fatigue. He looked at his hands. Already blisters were rising in both of them. Just a few swings later, the blisters burst and both hands began to bleed. Marty grunted and stopped.

Abner Pyle stopped, looked over and walked across to Marty. "Lemme take a look at them hands, boy," he commanded in a dry, hard voice. Abner turned over and inspected Marty's palms, and shook his head. "Yo's a big strong buck, but yo' ain't chopped much in the way of logs in yo' young life, has yo'?" he rasped. "Nuthin' there that can't be mended," he said. "Just yo' wait right here." He left the yard, rounded a corner and was out of view. Marty sat on the block and observed his hands.

"Fuck me!" he groaned.

A few moments later, Abner returned, carrying a basin of water. "Salt water," he explained. "Like that there John L Sullivan used for fist fightin' in de ole days." He took Marty's hands and placed them in the basin. Marty resisted the temptation to shout as the salt bit into the cuts. "We soon get them hands of yourn hard, boy," said Abner. He looked up to the darkening sky. "'Bout stoppin' time, anyways," he said.

The stench of Main Street cut deep into his nostrils. Marty and Mary Lou stood on the boardwalk of the 'Majestic', looking down on the teeming dirt surface of the main road through Carlisle, bisected by the lines of a trolley car. Marty noted that it was yellow with excrement, and below them a young Negro in blue overalls was busy scooping steaming horse-dung into buckets. The boardwalks thronged with white men and women. The men, almost invariably moustachioed, were dressed in bowlers and suits which buttoned to the neck and sealskin trousers, the women in long dresses which reached to the surface of the boardwalk.

Directly across the street was Mulligans' Hardware Emporium, only its entrance visible, with its shop-front a chaos of suspended pots and pans, while beneath on the boardwalk were sack upon sack of nails, nuts and bolts. Directly to the right of the Emporium stood Bells Temperance Hotel, and to its left was the Electrical Picture Palace.

On Marty's right, Main Street seemed to stretch for about a quarter of a mile, intersected by at least four streets on each side at right angles to it. On his left, the street took a sharp right turn, descending as it did so. Directly in front of him, a horse and buggy stopped and the horse defecated, its yellow turds steaming on the dirt surface of the road. In moments, they had been removed by the Negro child and dispatched to his bucket. Marty's nose wrinkled, but again, Mary Lou did not seem to notice the smell.

"You got kin hereabouts, Marty?" she asked.

Marty, bewildered by the scene and stunned by the smell, did not immediately answer.

"You got kin here, Marty?" repeated Mary Lou, impatiently.

"No," replied Marty, distractedly. "No kin. No nothing. No one."

Another horse, directly in front of him, excreted as it moved forward, and Marty winced as the acridity of the odour stung his nostrils. Again, Mary Lou did not appear to notice.

She stepped off the boardwalk down on to the street, avoiding the boy, who had run forward to remove the excrement. She pointed down the hill to the left. "We lives down thereaways," she said. "Bracken Flats." He followed her down into the street, narrowly avoiding a horse and rider. "My brother Jake, he got a room to let."

Marty did not reply. He felt as if he were deep in some dark dream, and continued to look around him in bewilderment. Jesus, it was like something out of Dodge City. For these were dirt roads, with rarely a car in sight. They walked together down the hill as it curved down to the right. As they did so, Marty looked down to his left, through a space in the passing horses. And there, a couple of hundred feet below him, he saw it. The track. Its contours were clear. A black, unlined cinder track, encompassing a green sward whose winter football markings were still visible.

"Is that it?" he said, pointing down to this left.

"What?"

"The track."

She nodded. "Where them Indian boys runs and plays football."

They continued to walk down the winding dirt road in the gathering gloom.

"You ever heard tell of an Injun, a fellow name of Jim Thorpe?" he asked.

Mary Lou nodded. "Everyone hereabouts knows Jim Thorpe," she replied. "He can run like a hare and jump like a deer."

It was a hovel. Marty would not have classed it as a house, rather as a hut, composed entirely of slats of cheap wood and strips of corrugated iron. Its main room contained merely a wooden table, four chairs and a black stove with a funnel reaching through the ceiling, and its curtains seemed to consist of frayed sacking. But the room was scrupulously clean. Indeed, the gnarled, uneven surface of the wooden floor seemed to shine.

Before him stood Beth, Mary Lou Barrows' sister-in-law, a woman in her early thirties, but already plump and greying, looking at least ten years older. Around her, on each side, clinging to her apron, were two boys of four and six, and two girls of eight and ten, wide-eyed, thumbs in mouths. Beside her stood her husband, Jake, Mary Lou's brother, a big, wide-mouthed, smiling man in check shirt and jeans, his hand proffered to Marty.

"This here's my brother, Jake," said Mary Lou. "This his wife, Beth."

Marty shook their hands and Jake beckoned him to sit at the table.

"Marty Roother," explained Mary Lou. "He workin' with us now down at the Majestic."

"With Boss Bassett?" asked Jake.

Mary Lou nodded. Jake sat down and beckoned Beth to the stove to the black coffee pot, while Mary Lou took four iron mugs from a shelf to the right of the table and placed them on it. "Then Marty here will need a cup of Arbuckles," he said. "That Boss Bassett, I hears that he don't take easy to no nigra boys."

Beth poured four cups of steaming coffee. "Where you say you come from?"

"Alabama. He come from Alabama," said Mary Lou.

Jake nodded and beckoned to Marty to drink his coffee. Marty sipped it tentatively. It was strong, aromatic, unlike anything he had ever tasted. He smiled.

"One thing to which my brother is devoted is his coffee," said Mary Lou. "Always Arbuckles."

Beth nodded. "Do without his grits; do without his chicken; but jest you forget his Arbuckles and Jake's a real unhappy man, sho' enough."

The children had now become accustomed to the stranger and had abandoned the security of their mother's apron. They clustered around Marty as he sipped his coffee. He noted that, though cleanly and sparsely dressed, they were all bare-footed.

"Jake here works at the Indian school," Beth said.

Jake sipped his coffee and nodded. "The Dean, he allus calls it his College," he said. Couldn't work with a better class of man," he said. "And that Coach Warner, he's sure somethin' special."

"Pop Warner," said Marty.

Beside him, Mary Lou's brows rose in surprise.

"The very same. That man, he know more 'bout sporting matters than any man alive," replied Jake, beckoning his empty mug to be replenished.

"Marty here was askin' 'bout Jim Thorpe," said Mary Lou.

"That Jim Thorpe, he ain't no man," interrupted Beth. "He somethin' else entirely."

"Why do you say that?" asked Marty.

"Jim Thorpe, he can wrassle an alligator and jump a house," said Beth.

"At the same time," added her husband.

Chapter 4
Jim

When, on June 5 1904, Jim Thorpe arrived at Carlisle it had been almost a quarter of a century since Lieutenant Richard Henry Pratt had brought one hundred and forty-seven Indian children to the Carlisle Barracks at the north end of the town.

When Pratt had first travelled out to the Dakota Territory, it had not been easy to convince the Indian chiefs to deliver their children to him and make the long journey east in the 'moving house' to Pennsylvania. The pivotal figure in his negotiations had been Spotted Tail, the veteran lawmaker of the Brulé Sioux. Spotted Tail had argued that the white man had invariably reneged on his treaties, and that he had no wish for Sioux children to be corrupted by his ways. But Pratt countered, making the telling point that had the Sioux and the other tribes possessed an adequate command of English, then the lies of the White Eyes would have been transparent to them. This conveniently ignored the fact that Pratt himself did not possess a single syllable of Sioux.

Spotted Tail had paused and reflected on the Lieutenant's arguments for some time, puffing slowly on his long, white clay pipe. Around him, his braves sat in anticipatory silence, while Pratt had sipped a Sioux brew of coffee strong enough to float a horseshoe. Then, Spotted Tail had nodded and a day later had offered Pratt five of his children. By November, Pratt, accompanied by a teacher, Miss Mather, had gathered a hundred and forty-two other children, mostly Crow and Chippewa, and they had made their winter way by rail to Carlisle.

The 'School' had then been little more than a desolate, abandoned barracks, going back to the War of Independence, and only the humane intervention of the local Society of Friends had made its chill halls remotely habitable. Even then, the incompetence of the Indian Agency had meant that on the first night the children had slept upon cold stone floors on straw mattresses.

The original, if unstated, aim of the Indian Schools, immediately subsequent to the Little Big Horn in 1876, had been to deploy Indian children as hostages. Pratt would have none of that. His aim was to control the Indian, not by fear, but by making him into a white man. 'I believe in immersing the Indians in our civilisation and, when we get them under, holding them there, until they are thoroughly soaked'. Carlisle's curriculum was that of an industrial school, based mainly on manual skills, from basket weaving to typing and engineering. Boys and girls were strictly segregated and, dressed in cast-off army uniforms, they drilled each morning with muskets in the yard. And when, in 1895, the German strong man Eugene Sandow had visited the College with his manager, Flo Ziegfeld, he had donated his exercise programmes and a hundred light dumbbells and wands.

The Indian children had, surprisingly, taken well to Pratt's military drills, but they showed markedly less enthusiasm for Sandow's barren callisthenics with wands and dumbbells. It was a year later, in 1896, that the Carlisle boys, supported by the school orator, had come to Pratt to ask his approval for the formation of a college football team. Pratt, now a brigadier, had been cool in his initial response. Football, derived directly from English rugby union, was both a brutal and a brutalising game. Indeed, Pratt had argued, had not over ninety blue-blooded Limeys been killed on the Rugby Union field in the previous five years? The students had patiently listened to the Dean's arguments, but had persisted with their request. Finally, Pratt had nodded his assent, and presented his conditions.

"First, that you never, under any circumstances, slug. That you will play fair and, if the other fellows slug you, you will in no case return it. If you slug, people who are looking on will say 'There's your Indian for you. Just look at them. They are savages and you can't get it out of them'. White boys do a lot of slugging and no one says a word, but you boys, you have to represent your race. So if those white boys slug and you do not return it, very soon you will become the most famous team in the United States. If you can set such an example, you will do a work in the highest interests of your people."

There had been a silence for a moment; then the students said with one voice, "Sir, we agree to that."

"My other condition is this. That in the next three or four years you develop your strength and skill to such a degree that you whip the biggest and best football teams in the country. What do you say to that, gentlemen?"

There was a longer silence, as each player looked to the man beside him. Then again, as one, they replied "Yes, sir. We agree to that."

When the boys had left, Pratt had sat silent at his desk, tears running down his face, his eyes set on a framed photograph in front of him. It was a faded portrait of Spotted Tail.

The early years of football at Carlisle Indian Industrial School, whilst not disastrous, had not been quite as auspicious as Pratt had hoped. The average weight of the Indian boys was only around 150 pounds, a full thirty pounds less than well-fed Eastern college teams, and although, the Carlisle boys were brave, fast and agile, slugging by opposing sides ensured that they rarely finished a game with a full team. For the Indians were slugged mercilessly and long before the final whistle, usually required the services of a dentist or a doctor more than those of a coach. But never once did they fight back.

But they did need a coach. And in 1904, Pop Warner had arrived, from Cornell University, at the princely salary of $1200 a year. Pop would never know exactly why he had made the decision to come to Carlisle. It was, certainly, not the salary, only a few bucks more than he had made at Cornell. For the boys were scrawny creatures, more suited to distance running than a power sport like football. Yet, somehow, there was a strange inevitability about his decision, one that Pop would never have occasion to regret. For under his rigorous tutelage, Carlisle soon became a team to reckon with. Pop drilled his Indians mercilessly, adding both system and guile to their natural courage and athleticism. By 1906, Carlisle had secured a 6 – 0 record and were becoming one of the most feared teams on the Eastern Seaboard. Pop was already recognised as one of the most creative coaches in the game, to be mentioned in the same breath as Walter Camp, its creator.

Pop used every ploy in the book, and when a tactic had been sussed out and countered, Pop threw away the book and wrote his own. Using salt and pepper pots, he used the table of the College refectory as a training field to devise new moves. In 1906, he had even devised the 'hidden ball' ruse, by encouraging players to stuff the ball under their jerseys. And when he had been temporarily banned from touchline coaching because of the ripeness of his language, he had devised a complex code of birdsongs in order to communicate with his players.

When the Crow Jim Thorpe had first arrived at the College in 1904, at the age of sixteen, he had been 5' $5^1/_2$" tall and weighed in at a willowy 115 pounds, soaking wet. In Pop's words, 'Jim had to stand on a penny to see over tuppence'. Jim had, nevertheless, revealed early athletic ability as a high jumper and had cleared within an inch of his own height in his first track season, using a primitive 'scissors' technique. But for all his early success in track, Jim Thorpe's true passion was the pigskin. But, though Jim never missed viewing a team practice or an inter-collegiate game, Pop stubbornly refused to let him play football. Jim, he reasoned, was a good high jumper, and beginning to develop a fair turn of speed in the dash and over the slats, but he was far too slight, too fragile for the rigours of the gridiron.

Football apart, Pop Warner's passion was the internal combustion engine; ultimately, no man in the area would be able to strip down a Model 'T' Ford like Pop. But in 1906, he did not yet own a Ford and was in possession of an ailing 'Stanley Steamer', a steam-based car. Jim, by now a strapping 155 pounds, had offered to help repair Pop's Stanley, on condition that if he successfully mended the vehicle, Pop would let him try out for the football team. Warner had grudgingly agreed, for the sickly 'Steamer' was his pride and joy, and Jim had spent the entire weekend slaving over the ailing Stanley. On Monday morning, he had driven it to Pop's door, its engine hissing with pleasure.

Pop was now between a rock and a hard place and agreed to try out Jim that very afternoon, placing him at halfback in the reserve squad, a skeletal melange of Chippewa, Cheyenne and Lakota Sioux. His pre-match advice to the members of the opposing first team had been simple. When Jim was hit, he was to be hit hard. Pop's aim was that by the end of the practice, Thorpe would be glad, indeed grateful, to return to the safe, non-contact world of hurdling and high jumping.

Jim had taken the punt from the kick-off at the twenty-five, catching it cleanly. He ran, supported by his tiny blockers, but had no need of them. For Jim seemed to find space where none existed, gliding effortlessly through the first team defence, leaving tacklers grasping at air. And, when body contact was made, Jim simply ran through and over the tackler, or handed him off. He ran a full seventy-one yards for that first touchdown. Within half an hour, he had run in three more, and Pop Warner knew that for the first time he had seen the future for Carlisle. For now, in Jim Thorpe, he had lightning in a jug.

The rent was a buck a week, all found, though Marty had no understanding of what exactly that involved. In any case, he had no idea how much he was earning at the 'Majestic' and had been afraid to ask Mary Lou before she had left.

That night, they had eaten a stew which, though delicious, was composed of a gamey flesh which he could not identify and about which he did not care to enquire. To follow, there was a generous wedge of pumpkin pie, washed down by steaming mugs of strong, dark Arbuckles. He rightly sensed that any request for decaf would meet with incomprehension. The meal was eaten by the light of two smelly, flickering oil lamps in the damp, dark little cabin. Marty was glad that they had lit the log fire just before dinner, for he could feel the chill begin to creep into his bones. He wondered if it was always so cold, so dark.

He had been unable to respond immediately when Jake had asked him to say grace. He had, however, once heard grace at a dinner held in his honour. 'For what we are about to receive, may the Lord make us truly thankful', he had mumbled, and that seemed to serve well enough.

He was thankful that neither Jake nor Bess had been too inquisitive about his life in Alabama, though he sensed that they were eager for him to volunteer them some information about his background. For though Marty had created a past life for himself via his studies on the Internet, he was uncertain if it would stand up to close scrutiny.

That first meal had given reality to the moment. Up till then, Marty had felt strange in his own skin, not yet in the year 1911, and once during the meal he had gently prodded a fork into the top of his thigh. As the fork pierced his trousers, he knew that this was real. It was 1911 and he was in Carlisle. And soon he would meet Jim Thorpe.

"Are you ready?"

It was Beth. She stood above him, holding to her bosom a black and white striped pillow and pile of rough grey blankets. Beside her stood Jake, bearing a torn, lumpy khaki-coloured mattress from which wisps of straw were spilling on to the dirt floor of the cabin.

"Out back," said Jake, pointing behind him. "Beth – she got it done it out, real nice."

They walked out of the back of the cabin into the darkness, the light of the oil lamp held by Jake spilling ahead of them. Beth pushed open a broken, slatted wooden door, held crazily on a single hinge. Jake moved ahead of her and the light of the lamp revealed that they were in a shed, about six yards long by four yards wide. The floor appeared to be composed of soft dirt. In the left corner, stood a pile of kindling in the middle a table and on the right a bare, wooden-slatted bed. There was nothing else. Jake laid the mattress on the bed, while Beth carefully arranged the pillow and blankets.

"Sorry, we don't run to no sheets," she apologised.

"If'n you wants to go…" said Jake.

"To the John?" volunteered Marty.

"John who?" said Jake. "To the privy. It's out back"' He pointed to the right into the darkness.

Marty nodded and laid down his sack of clothing on a wooden table beside the bed. "Cool," he said, "Cool." He did not notice their surprised response, or the looks that they exchanged as they left him in the guttering light of the smelly kerosene lamp.

Marty decided to sleep fully clothed, for it was too cold and he did not relish the rough blankets against his skin. He removed his shoes, retaining his socks, placed the kerosene lamp on the bedside table and put it out, eased himself uncertainly on to the lumpy mattress and pulled the rough blankets over him, feeling as he did so his stockinged feet press against the hard base of the wooden bed frame. He sniffed. There was an odd, dank smell in the shed which he could not identify. He felt a lump in the mattress at the base of his spine.

"Jesus wept," he groaned, turning on to his left side.

There was a sudden crack and the mattress sagged, causing him to bend in the middle. He turned on to his back and felt, through the lumpy mattress, his butt touching the floor below. Marty levered himself up on his elbows, turned, and sat on the pillow, both legs over the side of the bed. He reached behind him and passed his hands slowly to the centre of the bed, under the mattress. There was now a gaping hole. Marty groaned, pulled off the mattress and placed it on the dirt floor, and fumbled around for the blankets and the pillow. He placed the pillow at the end of the mattress, put his head on it and lay down on the floor, dragging the rough, holed blankets over him.

It was an hour before he finally slipped into sleep. Then he awoke, suddenly, with a shout. Something was walking slowly across his face.

He didn't talk like no boy from Alabama, decided Mary Lou. Marty Roother didn't talk like no feller from nowhere. No, more like some fancy Dan college boy, like one of them fellers from Harvard when they had first come up to try to whup the Carlisle boys at football, five years ago, just a couple of years after Pop Warner had arrived. Them young Harvard boys, they spoke and moved real slow, like they all had plenty of time, like their lives had no troubles. And when they spoke, there was no 'them things' or 'we was'; no, nothing like that. And them young fellers, they looked right through you when they passed by you in the hotel, like you was nothing much, nothing much at all. But this boy Marty Roother, he weren't like that, no, not him. For, though he talked proper, just as if'n he were white, he looked at you real straight, like you was zactly the same as him. Like you was someone. Like you was somebody.

But he didn't seem to know nothing, his hands were soft as your pocket and they cut up real easy, like he had never done no work, not never. Indeed, only good ole Abner Pyle had saved his skin that first week, for Abner had set Marty to collect and stack the kindling 'stead of chopping it, so's his hands would get time to heal up. It had meant that ole Abner had been forced to chop near twice his normal batch, but Abner, he hadn't said nothing. Luckily, Boss Bassett, he had been fixed heavy in the kitchen making vittles for some rich folks up for Easter from New York, so he hadn't seen nothin' of Marty, or that the boy from Alabama hadn't done nothing in the way of chopping.

And when Marty had been brought into the kitchen to clean dishes, it was sure as Satan to Mary Lou Barrow that he had never touched no dish in his mortal life. Thus he took the whack of Boss Bassett's tongue and hand. So Mary Lou, she tried to figure out just what Marty had ever done in the way of work, but noted that when he had come into the yard to the kindling, all the maids had come round in twos, just to check him out.

That Alabama boy, he sure was something to behold. Her friend Ellie, she reckoned that Marty was built like one of them fellers in them big history books in the Carnegie library that both of them enjoyed so much Yes, like one of them there Greeks, like that there Ulysses or Hercules, only black.

Pop Warner had long since decided that track and field was not a sport. No, it was a bunch of separate sports which merely happened to take place within the same arena. Hell, discus was as different from high hurdles as football was from baseball. Yet he had to coach them all, always he had to be the all-knowing God-coach, the expert who could respond to every fool question on every event.

Pop squinted into the weak, afternoon, spring sunshine and adjusted his worn, peaked cap. He sat high on the cracked wooden bleachers above the black, cinder Carlisle track, waiting for the members of his track team to arrive. Pop, stocky and avuncular, was now in his mid-thirties, but he had always been "Pop," even in his sophomore year at Cornell. From the outset, he had been the old head, even when pubescent pimples still lingered on his open, sunny face. For he had been from the outset a natural coach, even when he had known next to nothing, always feeling the need to pass on to those around him whatever knowledge and half-knowledge he possessed. It was what he called "the power of positive ignorance." Thus, he had gone direct from college football into coaching, first at Cornell and now here at Carlisle, with these cockamamy Indians.

Even in such a diverse sport as track and field, the Indians were rarely the right type; too small to propel shot or discus much beyond their left feet; rarely tall enough for high jump; lacking in the speed and thickness of thigh required for sprints and hurdles. Their main forte had been distance running, and there Pop possessed a pack of runners led by Louis Tewanima, a Fox who could run till hell froze over and who had made the 1908 London Olympic team in marathon. In a club meet, Tewanima would take on every distance from half mile to three miles, and pick up points, and never so much as break sweat.

Track and field had been a desert at Carlisle until Jim Thorpe had begun to show them his paces. Though Jim had kicked off as a high jumper, he had soon revealed more than a fair turn of speed and this had led to success in hurdles, long jump, even pole vault. In the latter, Jim's technique was simply to sling the bamboo pole into the box, shut his eyes and grin that toothy grin when he cleared the bar and hit the sand, usually on his ass. And when he had matured and football had fleshed him out, Jim had proved that he could also throw, launching shot, discus and javelin out to distances which picked up precious points even against those Irish whales from Cornell and Notre Dame.

No, Pop had never in his coaching career met anyone or anything to remotely compare with Jim Thorpe. For there was nothing that the Crow Indian could not do. At the diamond, he could pitch like Leon Ames; he could hit like Sam Crawford and there was no ball which he could not somehow lure into his mitt. And when the Carlisle basketball team, short on height, had asked Jim to play, once the umpire had informed him that this was not a full contact sport, he had dominated every match.

Pop reached into an inside jacket pocket, withdrew a stick of chewing baccy and took a long slow chaw. He reflected that Jim had never shown much taste for training. No, that was unfair. For Jim was, quite literally, a playboy in the true sense of the word. He did not like formal training, but he sure loved play. Thus, when Pop had offered Jim a milkshake if he could launch the sixteen pound shot beyond forty-two feet, the big man had smiled his slow, lazy smile, and had propelled the implement a foot beyond the target-peg. That week, Pop and Jim had been regular visitors to the Kretschmer's drug store, with Jim consuming six milk shakes as he had proceeded to rip the Carlisle record book to shreds in every event from discus to broad jump.

"Lap it!" roared Pop, as Jim appeared with members of the squad on the track below, dressed in shorts, black sneakers and a holed woollen Carlisle team jacket. Pop shook his head. The big mutt would not limber up unless he ordered him to do so. No, Jim would amble straight to a high jump or a dash without so much as a stretch or a jog.

Pop shook his head in mock anger as Jim looked at him, his open brown face cracking into a wide grin. He stepped forward and moved slowly into a straight-legged handstand position, and held it. Then he bent his arms and rhythmically pushed himself up ten times without a quiver. He dropped his feet to the ground and looked up at his coach. Pop grunted and smiled, shaking his head. He could never get mad at Jim, for the boy could always do the business. When the time came, Jim would always deliver. He stood, raising both arms and cupped his hands to his mouth. "Get your Injun asses around that track!" he roared. "*All* of you!"

Jim nodded and, joined by the others, he ambled lazily around the inside of the black, cinder track, followed by the other athletes. Pop watched them go, and scowled. The track, untended since the 1910 season, was soft as pudding, and the jumping pits undug, and the vault boxes and take-off boards were rotten. This was his fault and he knew it. Their last groundsman, tired of Pop's cussing, had left in the middle of the football season to pick up bigger bucks over in the deep anthracite mines at Scranton, and had not been replaced. Aided by team members, Pop had been able to keep the football field in some sort of shape, but the track required more time and more specific knowledge than he possessed. Something would have to be done or his track team would soon be laid low with Charley Horses, and all manner of other injuries.

Marty had recognised Pop Warner immediately. The coach, dressed in blue suit and waistcoat, was younger than he had expected, but then the museum photographs had been indistinct and the blurred picture on the Internet had been of a much older Pop, only a couple of years before his death in 1954. Marty wondered what Warner would say if he told him that his face would one day adorn a US mail stamp half a century later, or that Little Leagues would be named after him.

Marty took time to scrutinise Jim Thorpe as he ambled down the home straight towards him on that first lap, leading a score of Carlisle athletes. Jim looked to be around five foot ten, with thick, well-defined thighs and calves, and a bulky upper body accentuated by his holed, chunky Carlisle jersey. His brown face was dominated by a broad flat nose and an open toothy smile, and he looked older than his twenty-one years. Marty knew that Thorpe weighed around 175 lbs, but even as he trotted away from him to complete a second warm-up lap, he could sense in Jim a raw animal power that went far beyond his size.

Marty sat high, about six rows behind Pop Warner on the worn, unpainted bleachers and reflected that it all looked so rough, so casual, so amateurish. The unlined track was stodgy, its black cinder surface as soft as the broad jump and high jump pits, themselves overgrown and choked with moss and grass. And apart from Thorpe, all the Carlisle athletes looked tiny, like nut-brown children. He noted that none of them had their legs covered and tried to recall when sweat suits had first been invented. 1940? 1950? No, he had seen them in that old English movie, "Chariots of Fire," and that was surely based some time back in the 1920s. Perhaps, he thought, he could turn an honest buck by inventing them. At fifty cents a day at the Majestic, he could sure do with the money.

The Carlisle team had undertaken nothing remotely resembling a warm-up, only a couple of laps of desultory jogging and a few casual arm-circles; then they had split into event groups. Jim Thorpe had peeled off to the high jump, with Pop departing the bleachers to join him at the high jump fan. Marty made his way down the bowed, creaking bleacher steps and walked slowly up the home straight, around the outside of the track to get a closer look at the high jump area. He examined the high jump sandpit and shook his head. The undug sand was close on half a metre below ground level, full of moss and rabbit-droppings, with God knows what else lurking below its undug surface. Marty reflected that more sand had dropped out of his shoes after a day at Santa Monica than was contained in the Carlisle landing area.

But neither Pop nor Jim appeared to be much troubled about its lack of sand, its hygienic shortcomings or its potential dangers. Pop picked up a broken garden rake lying beside the pit and scraped for a few minutes at its shallow surface, then nodded to Jim that all was well. Thorpe walked to the pit and lifted to the vertical two thick ponderous wooden high-jump stands. He struggled for a moment with a rusty screw on one stand before releasing it, pushing upwards an inside spine of wood and fixing the screw tightly to secure it. He did the same with the other stand and placed a thick wooden lathe on top of the vertical spines, before walking back on to the soft cinder runway.

The height of the lathe looked to Marty to be about 1m75 but it was difficult to judge for, unlike modern stands, the crossbar had been placed on top of the uprights. Thorpe did not appear to measure a formal approach run. Instead, he simply scratched a line in the soft cinders on the left of the stands about twelve yards out, faced the cross bar and ran in with a soft, springy motion. For a moment, Marty did not know from which foot Jim would take off. Then he leapt from his left, his inside foot and cleared the crossbar, lying flat on his left side and landing on his take-off foot, a sort of modified hop. It was an easy clearance.

Marty heard Pop shout out "six feet," and saw him, cussing, struggle for a few moments to adjust the rusty stands and then place the wooden crossbar on top. It now looked high, much higher than six feet.

Again, Jim sauntered up and rolled over with a light, lissom action, landing on the hard sand on his take-off foot. At the next height, six foot three, it was the same, an easy clearance, by a clear couple of inches. Marty grimaced as Jim rolled over on the thin blanket of sand. This was a something close to full contact sport. Then Pop shouted something that Marty could not understand, and the crossbar was taken down. The high jump session was apparently over.

Jim, led by Pop, moved over to the holed, rutted running track to the start of the home straight. He picked up from the grass verge what looked like a small steeplechase hurdle, heavy, ponderous, unpainted and T-shaped. Now joined by two other athletes, Jim located in the long grass what looked to be three sets of four 3'6" hurdles. Marty could not see how the Carlisle athletes could possibly know where to place them, for there appeared to be no lane or track markings, but, when they finally set them up, the distances between the hurdles looked to be close to the standard ten yards.

Pop sat, chawing on his stick of baccy on the bleachers at the side, as Thorpe and his two diminutive colleagues, using trowels, proceeded to dig holes in the cinder track fifteen yards from the hurdles. Marty knew immediately what they were doing. They were digging starting holes; he remembered it from that same old English movie. Marty circled around the track to the back of the bleachers to find a place on them directly behind Pop and above the hurdlers.

As he did so, Jim recognised Marty's presence for the first time, and looked across questioningly at Pop. The coach glanced round at Marty, back at Jim and shrugged his shoulders in a "how-the-hell-do-I-know" response. Jim shook his head and settled down into his holes. Marty had not noticed the exchange of looks between them, and climbed up the cracked, splintered wooden bleachers to sit further back, on the top row, directly behind the Carlisle coach.

Pop bent down and reached into the black canvas bag on his left side. He withdrew from it what appeared to be a white piece of hinged wood, about two feet long, and flexed it into a V-shape on its hinges. He stood, holding the wood in the same V-shape in front of him. "Get to your marks," he bellowed.

Thorpe and his two colleagues settled into their holes.

"Get set!"

Their hips slowly rose. Pop paused for just a moment, then drew the pieces of wood sharply together with a crack.

Jim was a yard ahead in the first couple of strides. He reached the first barrier about three yards up and soared over it in a lithe, easy action. Behind him, the two Carlisle runners stuttered uncertainly and leapt wildly over the first hurdle. Jim poured over the first three barriers. True, his action was gauche, clumsy by Marty's standards, but it possessed a liquid, animal grace. He had touched down at the third hurdle before his colleagues had even cleared the first two.

Pop stood up, shaking his head, and strode over to the two tiny Carlisle men now walking back towards him. "You boys gotta *run* over the goddam' hurdles!" he roared. "*Run!*"

The two Indians nodded. Pop looked at Jim. "Flatter, Jim," he said. "Get low over the hurdle."

Marty watched the session for a further twenty minutes before Pop moved away to join the distance runners at the end of the track, while Jim moved on to the broad jump pit. By that time, it was clear to him that Pop was, certainly, no hurdles coach, for nothing that he had said had been of much practical value either to Jim or his two teammates. True, Pop clearly understood that hurdling was not jumping, but that appeared to be the full extent of his knowledge. His exasperated exhortations had, not surprisingly, made little impact upon Jim's two training mates. Lacking either a consistent approach to the first hurdle or the most rudimentary of clearance techniques, the two Carlisle athletes oscillated wildly between grotesque leaps, smashing through the barriers, or complete refusals. A quarter of an hour into the session, their ankles and knees dripped blood.

In contrast, Jim Thorpe had simply proceeded to smooth out his raw technique, ignoring both Pop's ministrations and the soft, rutted surface upon which he ran. After a dozen repetitions, he had achieved a surprising fluency.

Marty watched Jim amble slowly towards the broad jump approach run, a single strip of overgrown black cinder running parallel to the track but outside of it, at the end of the home straight. He followed behind him, as on the infield Pop bellowed orders to the distance runners circling the track through a battered tin megaphone. There were no bleachers above the broad jump pit, and Marty stood in the reedy, unkempt, long grass a dozen yards away, as Jim looked distractedly around for a rake. The broad jump pit was little different to the high jump area, being more suitable for mining than for jumping. True, there was sufficient sand, but most of it was heaped at either end, leaving a deep hollow in the centre, filled with rabbit-turds. Marty walked forward on the grass parallel to the runway and tripped, almost falling forwards. He looked down at his feet. It was the rake. Marty lifted it. It was rusty, its wood grey and cracked, green with slime. He picked it up and walked over to Jim, who smiled a broad, toothy smile. His voice was deep, husky, just as Marty had remembered it.

"Knew that rake was somewheres around. Musta been lying here since last track season," he said, reaching out his right hand for the rake.

Marty shook his head, stepped into the pit and began to push sand with the back of the rake into the centre of the pit. Jim smiled and walked away up the soft, pitted cinder runway. Marty stopped raking and scrutinised the pit. It could not, he estimated, be more than twenty-five feet long, a distance he had exceeded many times. He looked at the take-off board. It was cracked, unpainted and barely visible, its width well short of the eight inches required by the rules. He looked back up the runway. Jim now stood about thirty yards away, his hand raised, ready to jump.

Then he started his run. Jim ran as if there was to be no jump at the run's conclusion, churning up the soft cinders as if he were in a dash. Marty knew that with such an uncontrolled run, there was little hope of an effective jump. Then Jim hit the board and took off. He soared. He flew. Jim did not hitch-kick, rather he simply strode through the air in a giant stepping motion, as if shot from a cannon, landing lightly only a couple of feet from the end of the pit.

Marty looked at him, slack-jawed, for Thorpe had just jumped nearly twenty-three feet from an improvised approach, on a chicken-shit runway. He looked at Jim, unable to speak. Marty knew now that he had just seen something special.

Chapter 5
Settling In

From the outset, Marty had been shocked by the smell. Or rather the smells, for they assailed him from every direction. Pretty much everything in Carlisle smelt real bad. Every minute of the day, its streets were yellow with dung, and the cobbled surface of the Majestic's stable yard was covered with a permanent skin of dung slime, which Boss Bassett required him to remove. The earth closet at his lodgings unquestionably harboured the product of many centuries of dedicated defecation. Marty had never before speculated where all the ordure of the world, eventually, ended up: where he had come from, there had never been any need to enquire. He now knew that here, at the beginning of the 20th century, most of it simply stayed put and even when some of it had been lodged in the depths of the earth, it returned to haunt you, with hellish odours.

But no one seemed to care. Indeed, no one even appeared to notice. The smells were part of the established order, something to be taken for granted. It came to Marty, after the first week, that the pristine, odourless, flush toilets of the Majestic might well prove to be his salvation, the saving of his sanity, in this world of ghastly smells. The only alternative was to dedicate himself to constipation as a full-time, albeit unpaid, profession.

The earth-closet at his lodgings suffered from a second, if less important, handicap, not olfactory in nature. For the john was dark, stygian. Marty had always deployed the john as a sort of Alternative University, reading novels, track manuals and men's magazines. That was now impossible. Fortunately, the Majestic's high-ceilinged john, deep in the catacombs of the servants' cellar, offered him a certain level of security. Alas, he did not have the time to indulge in either his excretions or his reading in the casual manner that he had enjoyed in his Santa Monica condo, for always there was Boss Bassett to look out for. However, his daily dump in the Majestic's john meant that he was at least spared the horrors of the earth-closet at 25 Lime Street.

Marty had also been unprepared for the impact of the endless grind of daily work, ten hours of unrelenting labour, punctuated by a snatched lunch and ten minute breaks morning and afternoon, mostly spent in the john. For all his fitness, he was drained at the close of each day's work, and he wondered how Old Abner, essentially a collection of bones held together by ligaments, managed to get through such a prodigious volume of logs and continue to enjoy any sort of life. For Marty, ten hours of manual labour was proving infinitely harder than a three-session day in the world of 20th century track and field.

The food did not help. For during the day at the Majestic, Marty fed on scraps, leftovers from the previous evening. At 25 Lime Street, he ingested coarse, repetitive meals, often containing ingredients about which he did not care to speculate. Marty could almost feel his body shrinking and, after the first fortnight, he decided to check, using a tape purchased for five cents at Mulligan's Hardware Store. But no, there had been no shrinkage; the work on the kindling had probably seen to that. Chest 45"; waist 32"; thigh 25"; calf 16" and upper arm still a healthy 18".

It was probably just as well that he was so tired, for there was so little to do after work. Life after the Majestic consisted of a quick wash at the rain barrel, dinner, then a seat with Beth, Jake and Mary Lou on the porch, observing the passing life of Lime Street. Then it was back to that dank, rodent-ridden room, to bed down on a straw mattress. Luckily, Beth had bought a cat for a dime and the mice had soon departed to pastures new or to Mouse Heaven.

If the smell of ordure was constant, so also was the smell of people. Marty had never really smelt other people before. Deodorants, yes sir; perfumes, thank you ma'am; but people, never. After a few days, he had begun to smell his own body and he had not enjoyed the experience. For it was a strange, sweet-sour musty odour and he wondered if the others smelt it, too. Thus, each night before retiring, he stripped naked in the dark at the rain-butt and washed down with Pears Coal Tar soap.

And, though he had been surprised at the sheer volume of horses in Carlisle, the big surprise to him had been the trolley car. Every day, it pursued its noisy, clanging course from Clay Street, up Main Street, past the Majestic and down the hill, stopping short of the Negro Quarter before returning on its route back uptown. But already there were open Model T Fords chugging through town at a steady ten miles an hour, causing the horses to fret and rear. Only whites appeared to own them and never once did Marty witness a black travel as a passenger. And, when he had paid his five cents on the trolley and had sat down in the empty lower deck, he had been told by the conductor in no uncertain terms to strap-hang at the rear.

For the blacks of Carlisle were like some X-Files aliens, lying parallel to whites but several layers below them, performing the anonymous, menial tasks of the town: shovelling horse-dung, labouring in the fields, working the hotels as maids and bellboys. There was little obvious racism, but every Carlisle Negro knew exactly where he was placed, what he was expected to do, where he would live. This would be his black life till Hell froze over.

Jim had been surprised to see the black boy again, as had Pop Warner. He had turned up a week later, the next Wednesday, at exactly the same time, the beginning of practice.

True, some of the Negro community had come to watch Carlisle in the football season, though in Pop's view the game was no sport for blacks and never would be. No, it was Pop's firm opinion that your Negro, he had no taste for physical contact, no joy in the sting of battle, and never would have. For it was not in their nature. True, many of them were well-set young fellows, but they were not contact athletes; he had seen a peck of them in his time, and it was clear as crystal to him that your nigra boy had no taste for the big hits.

When Jim had once countered with Jack Johnson, who had taken the biggest hits the whites had to offer, and converted vertical white dreams into horizontal nightmares, Pop had chawed for a moment, his plump face contorted. When he finally answered, it was to say that Johnson was merely the exception that proved the rule. Jim had thought of answering that surely it was the exceptions that disproved the rule, but he did not pursue the argument. For Pop was no mean judge of a sportsman, even if it had taken a coon's age and Jim's skill with the Stanley Steamer to give him a chance to express himself in football.

Still, no question that this Roother feller could sure rake up a soft, flat, broad jump pit. He had even topped up the broad and high jump pits with material from a pile of builders' sand that had arrived that week from Mulligan's. Indeed, he had gone further and trimmed off the grass at the sides of both pits and their runways, so now they looked real tidy. And, though the Negro was fully clothed, Jim could see that he would strip big. Big arms, close on eighteen inches, and below the stretched, patched jeans, Jim could sense thick, chunky thighs. Yes, this boy Roother was surely a big-set fellow.

On the third Wednesday, Pop had pulled the Roother boy across, and had offered him a quarter to rake and roll the track. Jim was surprised that Pop had come up with so much, as the coach was well known to be stingy with a buck. He was not surprised that Marty had immediately taken him up on the offer. It had taken Roother till late that evening to finish the track. Jim had brought him down a bottle of milk and a sandwich at nine o'clock as Marty was slowly dragging the heavy roller round the outside lane. He had done his job well. Next day, the track was sharp, yards faster, though its basic composition was still too loose, too dry. Pop had flipped Jim a quarter to hand on to Roother at the weekend, when the Indians of the Industrial School were allowed into town.

Marty had been surprised to see Jim at the Majestic that bright Saturday morning. Jim had come to the stable yard with little Louis Tewanima, and had stood for few minutes watching Marty, stripped to the waist, working through the kindling with Abner Pyle. Marty, his hands now hard, worked remorselessly, with rhythm and energy, at the same speed as his older colleague. Jim and Louis had said nothing, but stood observing at the corner of the yard, in the bright sunshine, eying up the maids.

Finally, Jim spoke, nodding smiling recognition to Abner, who stopped and raised his right hand. "You sure sweat real good," he said. "Ain't never seen no man sweat like you." He reached into the front pocket of his patched, worn jeans and withdrew a silver dollar. He handed it to Marty. "From Coach. From Pop."

Jim did not add that the other seventy-five cents had come from the members of the Carlisle track squad.

"What's this for?"

"The track," said Jim. "You got it two yards faster. Ran ten-five yesterday for the hundred."

Marty nodded placing it in his back pocket. "Yards or metres?" he asked.

Jim looked at him in surprise. "Don't get your drift, Marty," he replied.

"A hundred yards or a hundred metres?" responded Marty, picking up a rag from the cobbled yard to wipe his forehead.

"Never run nothing but yards here, Marty. Not at Carlisle," said Jim.

“Not in the United States,” interrupted little Louis. “Them French, them Germans. They run metres over there. Not us.”

Marty realised that he had now moved into No Man’s Land. “Thanks for the buck,” he said, picking up his axe.

“Pop,” said Jim,” He’d like to have a word with you. Down at the track. When you’re all clear here.”

Marty nodded. “Just you tell Pop, I’ll be down there right after work.”

Jim raised his right hand, palm to Marty and he and Tewanima strolled out of the yard. Abner Pyle stopped his work and leant on his axe.

“What the Sam Hill was *that* all about? he asked. “Yards or metres? You gone crazy or sump’n?”

Marty did not reply. There was no point.

Marty arrived early at the track, limbered up and pursued a session of six by sixty metres dashes in his sneakers on its black, cinder surface. His diligent work with rake and roller had vastly improved the quality of the track, but he doubted if he could run better than ten-seven for a hundred metres on its dry, powdery surface. Whatever happened, his first priority would be to purchase a pair of running spikes.

He had earlier discovered that there was nothing remotely resembling a sports shop in Carlisle, and had resorted to Mulligan’s, where he had secured a Sears Roebuck catalogue. Alongside the Sears catalogues had been piles of other catalogues, mostly for patent medicines and Marty, his curiosity aroused, had selected a batch. His concern for the purchase of a pair of track shoes had momentarily evaporated as he studied them.

The first extolled the virtues of Peruna. Its inventor, Dr Samuel Baker Hartman, appeared to believe that catarrh was the modern equivalent of the Bubonic Plague, and that Peruna was the only answer. Marty had always imagined that catarrh was essentially an ailment of lungs and throat. But no, for in Dr

Samuel Baker Hartman's opinion, catarrh was to be found everywhere, in the bowels, the bladder and even deep in the pelvis. Marty wondered how it had resisted the temptation to stop there and failed to make its insidious way down to the hamstrings.

It was therefore, perhaps, not surprising that most of the American population seemed to suffer from catarrh in one form or another. From the Peruna catalogue, it seemed that United States Senators were particularly prone to its rigours. Senator Ogden of Louisiana, Senator Sparkman of Florida, Senator Wilber of New York, and dozens of others. Even the military did not escape, in the form of the wife of Admiral Winfield Scott Schley, 'The Hero of the Battle of Santiago Bay."

Marty smiled, laid down the Peruna catalogue with the others, as yet unread. They would all make good reading in the john at the Majestic. But he must set about his task then hightail it back home, and that task was to whup Thorpe and take gold at the 1912 Olympics. He picked up the Sears catalogue and leafed through it till he came to the sports pages.

The track and field section was nothing if not comprehensive. Bamboo vault poles, high jump and pole vault stands, discus, shot and javelin, hurdles, but, he noted, no starting blocks. He finally reached the clothing section and the track shoes.

Like all of the other equipment, the running spikes were sketched rather than photographed. They appeared to be not much more than black outdoor shoes, with six spikes protruding from each sole, and looked heavy and ponderous. These were the 'dash' shoes, 'as worn by the 1908 Olympic champion, Reginald Walker'. They were priced at three bucks, more than a whole week's wages. Other shoes had a cross strap and two spikes in the heel. These were 'for high jump, long jump, pole vault and hurdles, as worn by the inventor of the Western Roll, George Horine'. These shoes, also made of black leather, looked even more cumbersome than their running counterparts and were priced at $3.50.

"You thinking of taking up track, boy?"

It was Pop Warner, standing behind him on the bleachers, dressed in dark blue suit and waistcoat. Marty looked up at him. Every button on the coach's waistcoat was doing its job, for though Pop was only now in early middle age, his age had already reached his middle.

"Could be, coach."

"No big bucks there, Marty. You might pick up a few clams indoors, if'n you're fast. New York. Boston. Phillie. Amateur. Brown paper envelopes. No real living in it, though." He took the Sears catalogue from Marty and scrutinised it. "But there are still some big pro races up Connecticut way," he said. "Scranton, at New Year. Crooked as a corkscrew. And at those crazy Scotch Games, where they toss logs."

"Cabers," volunteered Marty.

Pop's bushy eyebrows rose. "Yes, however, did you know that?"

Marty did not reply.

Pop handed the Sears catalogue back to him. "No, you best keep your money and stay well away from track, Marty. Never seen a nigra boy in track worth a bucket of warm spit. Best leave track and field to the white boys." He paused. "But I got a little business proposition for you, Marty," he said. "You did a real good job here last week. Real good." He loosened the top buttons of his waistcoat. "By the way, did you get that quarter I gave Jim to give you?"

Marty nodded.

"Worth every cent, Marty. Every dam' cent. He placed his hands on Marty's right shoulder. "How much do they pay you up at that the Majestic, Marty? Four bucks? Five?"

"Three bucks. All found," replied Marty.

Pop paused. "Three," he said. "I think we might just stretch to that."

"For what?"

"College groundsman," said Pop. "Take care of the track, cut the grass, repair the equipment, the whole shebang."

"What about vittles?" asked Marty. "They feed me like a prince up at the Majestic."

“Vittles? Jim or Louis’ll bring you down a bag at lunch and at track practice. Hell, so perhaps, it won’t be your grits and your watermelon, but sure as Hell you won’t go short.

Marty nodded. “One thing, coach,” he said.

“Yes?”

“Do you have a john – in the pavilion?”

Pop found it difficult to conceal his surprise. “Yes, boy, I think we can safely promise you a john.”

“A proper one? Flush toilet?

Pop was surprised, but nodded. Marty put out his right hand. “Then I think you have yourself a deal, coach,” he said.

Pop paused for a moment and then shook Marty’s hand. He later reflected that it was the first time in his life that he had shaken the hand of a Negro.

Angus Mackay, Dean of Carlisle Industrial College, looked down on to the schoolyard from the high window of his office, withdrew his half spectacles and rubbed the bridge of his bony, bird-like nose. He had known for years that the Indian boys and girls called him “The Eagle”. Hell, so did most of his staff. Truth to tell, Mackay quite liked it. As a boy in Scotland, he had watched golden eagles circle lazily above the sour mosses and deserted crofts of his native Sutherland. There was a lot to be said for eagles. Those birds did as they pleased, and took what they wanted. And they had the big view.

Yes, that was all he had in common with the eagle. The big view. For Carlisle had always, since its early days, been underfunded, invariably struggling to make ends meet. The barracks which housed the school had always been just that, a military base built by Hessians two hundred years ago, bearing as much resemblance to a school as to a railroad siding. True, improvements had been made since Lt. Pratt had made his winter journey with 147 shivering Indian children back in 1879 to Carlisle’s bleak corridors, but the school was still closer in nature to Sing Sing than to Harvard. And every year since his appointment in 1904, there had been a desperate battle to balance the books, the nit-picking economies. "Raisin cutting" his mother had called it when he was a child.

And behind all of their funding problems with the government and the Indian Agency had been the baleful presence of the editor of the Carlisle Chronicle, Cyrus P Gilbert, whose elder brothers, Joseph and Matthew, had died at George Custer's side at Little Big Horn. Mackay's protestations that the Indian wars were long past, that the Hostiles were no longer exactly hostile, had cut little ice with Cyrus P. Gilbert.

Mackay turned from the window, went back to his desk and picked up a sheaf of papers, the 1910-11 accounts. Yet again, despite rising receipts from Pop Warner's team, he would have to draw upon shrinking reserves. Alas, though Pop's boys drew big crowds wherever they played away, there simply wasn't enough money to pay for a covered stand or to develop bigger bleachers for home matches.

Carlisle possessed only shallow rows of open-air bleachers, no place for the faint-hearted in chill Pennsylvania winters. The school therefore played most of its games away, against colleges like Notre Dame and Yale, in front of tens of thousands of partisan fans, to be slugged mercilessly by both fist and voice. This being so, their split from away matches helped keep his college afloat.

No, reflected Mackay, it was surely Jim Thorpe who kept Carlisle afloat. For even those with no interest in sport would travel long winter miles merely to see Jim, just as they had in his Scottish youth to see the great Highland Games athlete, Donald Dinnie. Thorpe and Dinnie, he mused, had a lot in common. Both were great all-rounders; both were tough and uncompromising. He sometimes reflected that it was a pity that time could not be compressed and that the two men could not somehow be brought together in competition.

He was aware of a knock at the door behind him. Mackay bellowed, "Come in," to see that it was Pop.

"I think we've got ourselves a new groundsman, Dean," said Pop, as Mackay beckoned him to sit in front of his desk. "A nigra boy, name of Marty Roother," Pop continued. "Alabama boy."

Mackay pointed his right index finger at the coach. "Only two questions, Pop," he said. "First, what's your fancy for the 2.30 at Belmont?"

Pop's response was immediate. "Scotch Mist, Dean," he said, smiling. "Might be worth a buck or two."

Mackay nodded. "And second, what fraction of my precious bawbees are you proposing to squander on this Roother boy?"

"Three bucks a week, Dean."

Mackay nodded. "He's hired," he said.

"Plus vittles," added Pop.

Mackay shook his head. "He's fired," he said, but smiling.

Marty had tried to lip-synch the hymns, always a fraction behind the other worshippers but it had been, for the most part, impossible. There were a few occasional, if fragmentary successes, like 'Come we will gather by the river.' He had once heard it in an old John Ford western, though he could only remember the first line, and the same was true of 'Mine eyes have seen the glory of the coming of the Lord.' He felt himself blush as hymn after hymn came up, all totally unknown to him, as around him swelled a torrent of sound.

He hoped that Mary Lou on his right, and Beth and Jake on his left, could not see his lips or hear clearly the sounds which issued from them as he mumbled through each hymn. Here, the volume of sound, the passion of the tiny congregation, proved to be to his advantage. He hoped too that they did not note his lack of response as from the congregation came the reflex and voluble reactions of an audience transfixed by the passionate preaching of the Reverend Obadiah Meek, rotund, white-haired, standing above them in the pulpit in the Spartan little Baptist church.

The Church was packed to the rafters, the passion of its congregation almost palpable. Marty tried to look within himself, to draw on something in order to relate to his new environment. He could not. Instead, he groped his way through the ceremony, hoping that his embarrassment, his uncertainty, would pass unnoticed.

Marty with Mary Lou, Beth, Joan and their children walked out into the bright spring sunshine to be greeted by the Reverend Meek who proffered a plump hand to him in greeting. “Alabama boy, I hears,” he said, his sharp blue eyes glinting behind half -spectacles.

Marty nodded.

Meek looked at Marty’s companions. “Let’s us see this here Alabammy boy at the Barn dance, next Saturday night, Jake. Put the boy through his paces.”

Marty put in his notice at the Majestic first thing that Monday morning, said his goodbyes to Abner Pyle, presenting the old man with a bottle of Peruna, in case he might fall prey to the dread catarrh. It had cost him 50 cents but it was worth every cent, for old Abner had surely saved his hide that first terrible week at the Majestic.

He arrived at the Carlisle track on the following morning with not the slightest notion of how he might embark upon his new employment. He first checked the track equipment. The roller, though rusty, was in good shape, there were plenty of rakes and spades but there was only a manual, garden-size grass mower for what was a pampas-like infield area.

He did as Coach had always done each pre-season, listing his work-priorities on a blackboard used by Pop in the football season to chart team tactics.

1) Grass cutting

2) Track lining
3) Throws distance marking
4) Track equipment overhaul

Marty shook his head. No, he decided, throws markings could take lower priority; they probably didn't have them in 1911 anyway. He wiped them out at (3) and pushed them to (4). He also wiped out 'grass cutting' and put it in 3rd place. Hell, discus and javelin were the only long throws and the risk of losing the implements in the long grass would have to be accepted.

He possessed little in the way of working clothes. Fortunately, the previous groundsman, now working in the deep mines in Scranton, had left behind him a pair of patched, greasy dungarees on a peg. The man, Marty decided, must have been more a place than a person, for the dungarees engulfed him. He also unearthed a pair of massive, cracked leather boots. They were covered in fungus and mud and it took him fully half an hour to clean them up.

His feet sliding around within the boots, Marty then lumbered out on to the college track. He had no intention of re-measuring its lanes. In any case, he had no idea of how that might be done. Instead, he crouched on both knees on the track's black cinder surface, attempting, like an archaeologist, to locate the dim, half-visible track markings of 1910. Finally, he began to distinguish them, as through a glass, darkly. They were there, like the long-buried ruins of Olympia, albeit marked in lime. It took him all of that morning to re-mark the home straight in white lime and by lunch he was almost exhausted. He looked up the home straight, as down the hill towards him came Jim Thorpe, bearing his lunch in a brown cardboard box. Marty turned and grimaced as he looked down the jagged, wayward lines. Hell, some of them started at four foot wide and had narrowed to a foot less by the finish. Others, jagged and irregular, looked as if they had been drawn by some booze-blind drunk. His work was shit.

Jim stood, hands on hips, surveying Marty's work. "Like I said before, this marking don't zactly suit your pistol, do it, Marty?"

Marty sighed and walked with Jim to sit with him on the bleachers. Jim opened the box and handed it to Marty. "Chicken sandwich, piece of apple pie and a bottle of milk," said Jim. "Same as what we get."

Marty opened the box, bit into the sandwich, chewed and shook his head. Jim pointed to the track. 'But I seen worse in my time, Marty. Weren't no markings to speak of when first I got here."

Marty took a gulp of milk.

"The last groundsman, ole Jack Duckworth," continued Jim, "he allus used spikes and string to mark them lanes. Laid the strings on the track and poured lime over 'em. I seen ole Jack do it every spring. Eat up your vittles. I'll try to show you how."

Jim had used the remainder of his lunch break to show Marty how to deploy strings and spikes to line up the track, working in the back straight. Then, he had made his way back up the hill to college, leaving Marty to complete his work. By six o'clock that evening, he had re-lined the remainder of the track with a precision which had amazed him.

Looking up the home straight, he could not now bear the clumsiness, the sheer incompetence, of his earlier work. Marty ignored his hunger, his fatigue, laboriously brushed out his wretched morning markings and re-lined the home straight. At nine o'clock that night, standing in the twilight, he stood on the hundred yards starting line, looking up the home straight, at its now straight, pristine lanes. He reflected that he would remember 6th April 1911 as the first time that he had ever undertaken manual labour. He could not exactly say that he had enjoyed it, but it had somehow given him a strange, unexpected satisfaction.

Then Marty looked at the now pristine long jump pit. On its level sand, was the letter "N", clearly etched on its surface.

Psychokinetics. The Aetherians had got through. Marty struggled to keep back the tears.

"I bin a-watchin' you. You, you works like Booker T."

It was Mary Lou. She stood on the slope behind him, on his right side, wearing a simple blue calico dress. He looked at her. The short dress sure made her bare, slim legs look real good. Marty wiped his eyes with his handkerchief.

"Booker T who?"

"You sure are some Alabama boy," she said, shaking her head. "Booker T. Washington, that's who."

They walked slowly up the home straight, back towards the equipment shed. Marty deposited the strings and spikes, pulled the shed's heavy brass lock together and closed it. They continued up the road, away from the track.

"Booker T, he always tells the story when he was a little boy, when he was told to clean the floor of this here room. So he goes around cleaning it with this cloth. Then he stops, looks, and he thinks, good 'nuff. Then Booker, he sees a peck of dust, then another, so he goes around again. Booker, he done go round that there room ten times, does Booker, till he can see his face in that floor."

"And this fellow Booker T. Washington, is he still around?"

She turned to face him, her face mock-stern. "Where you bin? You should read yo' Chronicle. He here next week at the NAACP."

Marty did not dare ask her to explain the nature of NAACP. Mary Lou sensed his uncertainty and spoke. "The National Association for the Advancement of Coloured People," she said. "I'se a member, but not Jake nor Beth."

Everyone and everything in the Big Barn seemed to be moving. Marty stood with Mary Lou, Beth and Jake at its entrance, in a thin pool of light spilling out into the dusk. As they moved in, there appeared to be hundreds of dancers spinning wildly on the Barn's brown dirt floor.

At the far end of the Barn, on a platform a few feet from the floor sat a group of fiddlers, ancient grizzled men from whose instruments sprang a jaunty, compulsive melody which Marty could not identify. Below the fiddlers throbbed a rage, a passion of dancers performing what he assumed was a jig. The dancers held each other, sometimes at the waists, more often by hand and waist, but there was no intimate body contact, nothing overtly sexual in the dancing. As they moved round to sit on vacant bales of straw, Marty noted that all of the dancers were without shoes, and that as they danced, sweat spurted and dripped from their arms and faces on to the dirt floor. It was a strangely pure Bacchanalia, exuding enough energy to meet the combined power needs of Los Angeles and New York.

Marty felt the pressure of Beth's hand on his shoulder. "Get yo'self out there and show us what you can do," she said.

Marty rose and found himself at the edge of the floor, facing Mary Lou. She raised both hands and Marty placed both hands in hers. He did not move. Mary Lou pulled on his right hand and gave him a light kick in his right shin with her foot.

"Let's us get going," she ordered.

For the first time in his life, Marty could not move. Mary Lou, again, jiggled impatiently with both arms and Marty twitched for a moment, without moving forward. Mary Lou released her hands, reached down and removed both shoes, throwing them to her brother. She beckoned Marty to do the same. He did so, and again, took her hands. He stumbled forward into Mary Lou's feet but, miraculously, she somehow avoided him. She pulled him forward and the nightmare began. For Marty had no idea of the rhythm, no feeling for the movements of the dance. They stumbled round the floor, surviving only because of Mary Lou's surprising ability to avoid his feet and by the nimbleness of the other dancers. Fortunately, the dance ended in a few moments, and Marty, sweat pouring from his face, plodded, head down, from the floor to where Beth and Jake sat.

"Don't think the St Louis Rag has made it down Alabama way yet," said Mary Lou, ruefully. "What kind of dancing you boys do down there?"

Marty did not reply. Jake sensed Marty's embarrassment. He reached below him to the floor and lifted a grey earthen keg to his knee. He uncorked it, lifted it to shoulder height and took three deep gulps. Jake wiped his mouth with the back of his hand and proffered the keg to Marty.

"Jungle Juice," he said. "Put some lead in yo' pencil. Help you in them there dances, for sure."

Marty looked uncertainly at Jake. He was lost. He lifted the jug to shoulder level, rotated it, spilling some of its contents on to his shirt front. Finally, he got it to his lips and took a tentative swig. It was sweet, like a sort of cider, only slightly thicker. He took a more substantial gulp, then another.

"Easy, boy, easy," said Jake. "That's pow'ful medicine you got there."

Mary Lou rose. "Yo' want to have another try?" she invited, as the music started up again. "The Pennsylvania Polka."

"Is it…Is it fast?"

She placed both her hands on her waist, elbows out. "Waltzes is slow, Marty. Polkas is fast. See how it works now?" she said, her soft red lips pursed, schoolmarm fashion.

"Give me time. Let me loosen out for a moment, Mary Lou," he said. "Just to get the beat."

"Just to get the beat," she mimicked, mocking him and winking over his shoulder at Beth and Jake as they rose to take the floor.

Marty stood and shut his eyes, absorbing the music. It was fast, but he could pick up the rhythm. *Dee-dum-tee-dum-tee-dum-dum – Dee-dum-tee-dum-tee-dum*. Jesus, he had conquered every dance step from the Twist to the Lombardi, he had even competed in ballroom dancing at Blake High. He would be damned if he could not master these hick stompings. Finally, he opened his eyes. "Got it," he said. They stepped up to the outer fringe of the seething, spinning dancers. "Here goes nothing."

Marty took Mary Lou's hands, launched himself forward and suddenly he was on the move, his actions clumsy, jerky and primitive, but embodying the raw rhythm of the dance. Marty kept Mary Lou to the edge of the floor to give himself freedom of movement, realising that a single contact with another dancer would destroy his precarious, fragile rhythm. He grinned. It was now almost there, more fluid, less jerky, and he gambled and essayed the perky lateral up and down movements, mimicking the other dancers. He looked out over his right shoulder at the dancers in the heart of the Barn.

"Let's us go for it," he said, spinning Mary Lou towards the main body of dancers. His head felt light. Suddenly, Marty was deep in the Zone and they were spinning in perfect balance through and round, the social centrifuge of the dancers in the Big Barn. Now he was locked into it. It was easy, like a series of effortless discus-turns. He looked at Mary Lou. Her face was now radiant.

Suddenly, before he would have wished, it was over. She stopped and, smiling, looked at him. "Wow!" she said, dropping his hands, the sweat dripping from her face. They walked back to Beth and Jake.

"Thought, you told me you couldn't dance," said Beth.

"Must be Jake's Jungle Juice," replied Marty.

"Looks like we got us a break," said Beth, observing that the musicians' platform was now emptying.

"If'n you two want to go out back…to cool off," said Jake.

Together, they walked out of the Big Barn, into the cool darkness. The Barn was surrounded by woods on all sides and already couples, hand in hand, were wending their way along woodland paths into its blackness. Marty now felt slightly giddy, the result of both the Jungle Juice and the vertigo of the Pennsylvania Polka. Impulsively, he reached down for Mary Lou's hand and felt no resistance, and they entered the woods. Marty shook his head to try to clear it. All around him, he could hear rustlings and the unmistakable sounds of sexual pleasure.

Embarrassed, Mary Lou turned and looked up at him. "You like it workin' down at the track with all dem Injun boys?"

He nodded. "They haven't scalped me yet."

"That Pop Warner, ain't nuthin' in God's earth he can't get them Injun boys to do. Pop's some kinda man, and no mistake."

Marty turned impulsively, took Mary Lou by both shoulders and kissed her. Immediately, he felt that this was right. It was comfortable. They fitted perfectly. There was no resistance, and without thinking, he slipped his tongue into her mouth and let his hand slip down to her left breast. Her response was immediate. He reeled back as Mary Lou smashed him on the left cheek with the flat palm of her right hand.

"You got some nerve," she spat out the words. She strode quickly away from him along the path, back towards the light from the Big Barn.

"Ouch," he said, seconds after the blow. He shook his head, for he still felt woozy. Then he ran back up the path, stumbling over the roots of trees, to be greeted at the entrance by Jake, his face sombre. Jake stopped him and placed his hands on Marty's shoulders, looking him straight in the eye.

"I gotta tell you, Marty, that there Jungle Juice, it ain't no lemonade." He drew Marty round to the back of the Barn to a horse trough, at the side of which stood a metal pump. Jake cranked the pump for a few moments until the water began to gush fitfully from it. "You git yo' head down there," he ordered, pulling Marty forward. Marty obediently bent forward and felt the cold water flow over his head and neck. After a few moments, Jake pulled him up. "How you feel now?" he asked. "You all ready to go back in there?"

Marty spluttered for a moment and wiped the water from his eyes and face with his right hand. "Sure, that's cool," he said.

"Cool." Jake shook his head. "Now I don't know what'n you said out there and I don't know what you done."

Marty spat out some water. "Nothing much," he said. "Didn't get much of a chance."

"My sister, she's some feisty young lady," said Jake, smiling as they walked back through the darkness. "No man round these parts ever got far with her. No ways."

As they re-entered the Barn, they were greeted by the insistent thud of a drum. The Barn's central floor was still empty, except for what looked like a huge, bulbous black barbell at its centre. Marty sat with Jake, his eyes avoiding those of Mary Lou.

The Reverend Obadiah Meek, plump and sweating, waddled up to the centre of the Barn, stood in front of the barbell and raised both hands for silence. "My friends," he said. "The Good Book is fair bustin' with athletes. You jest take Jacob. What a dingbat rassler he was. Enoch, why he was a whiz-bang distance runner. And what about David? Wasn't young David a Jim-dandy pinch-hitter?"

The audience howled their agreement. Meek, again, raised his hands for silence. "And, ladies and gentlemen, why I haven't mentioned yet ole Samson, God's strong man. Samson, poor feller, betrayed unto those dag-blasted Philistines by that agent of the Devil, that there wanton woman, Delilah."

There were mumbles of agreement.

"Samson, that boy, he teaches us God's lesson, my friends. A man's gotta keep hisself to hisself, keep his seed, retain his God-given strength, least till the time come to join with a young lady in matrimonial union." Meek pointed to the barbell resting on the barn floor. "So that's what this here is, my friends. The barbell. That there strong man, Mr Sandow, he's shown us the way, like Mr Roosevelt. The barbell, it's a symbol of a man's strength, the work of the Lord. That's why we allus have you young bucks try out with it. So, who's a-gonna be first up?"

Marty leant forward and scrutinised the barbell. It had no sleeve and looked to be a solid, roughly-cast piece of black metal, bulbous at both ends, perhaps, 200 pounds or so in weight. But no problem.

Two young men dressed in blue dungarees walked slowly and uncertainly from the opposite sides of the Barn to cheers and applause. Marty reflected that they were both big men, around 190 pounds, thick in arm and thigh. The first man, in his early twenties, had clearly no idea of how to address the weight, placing his feet too far from it and too wide apart. Marty felt the impulse to shout out, to help him, but resisted the temptation. There was no need. The young man hoisted the barbell to knee level, shook his head, lowered it and walked back into the crowd, head down, to applause and laughter.

The second youth, who looked to be in his late teens, addressed the weight with a more efficient technique, placing his feet under it, gripping it firmly, hands shoulder-width apart. He pulled the bar to chest height, the audience roaring their approval. But the bar would not budge from his chest. Eyes bulging, sweat pouring down his face, he strained to push it to the vertical, but it would not shift. Defeated, he dropped the weight to the floor with a thud, to groans from the crowd.

Reverend Meek placed both hands on the young man's shoulders. "Well done, son," he said. "You done good. Real good."

The boy walked back into the crowd, to scattered whoops and cheers. Reverend Meek, once again, raised his hands for silence. "There but one feller here," he said. "But one who can lift this here weight. Elmer Dobbs."

The chant went up from the crowd. "Elmer…Elmer…Elmer."

Marty looked at Jake. "Who's this guy Elmer?"

"Elmer Dobbs, just 'bout the strongest feller round these parts, that's who," replied Jake.

From the audience emerged a giant, around 6'4" in height and about the same in circumference. Marty reckoned him to weigh in at more than three hundred pounds. Elmer lumbered forward into the centre of the Barn, shook hands with the Reverend Meek and pulled his black leather belt more tightly around his bulging belly. Elmer Dobbs clearly knew what he was about. Addressing the bar in perfect form, he cleaned it quickly to his chest. Then, to the ecstatic cheers of the crowd, he bent his knees and slowly pushed the barbell to arm's length. He lowered it easily to the ground and, smiling, shook hands with the Reverend Meek. The crown now took up another chant, one which Marty could not understand.

"The Big One…the Big One…the Big One," they chanted.

"The Big One? What's that?" he asked.

Jake pointed into the centre of the Barn. "That's the Big One," he said.

Four burly youths, struggling with the weight, lugged into the centre what looked like the axle and wheels of a railway wagon.

"The Big One," said Mary Lou. "No man round here ever lifted the Big One."

Meek raised his arms for silence and spoke again. "Now, no man on God's earth has ever lifted the Big One," he said.

"I done told you," whispered Mary Lou.

Meek reached into an inside pocket and raised a piece of paper above his head. "Now I got me in my hand a twenty dollar bill for the first man here who lifts this here weight."

"Reverend, you had that there twenty dollars since Moses got them Israelites out of Egypt," shouted someone from the crowd. There were roars of laughter and Meek smiled. "You want to take another shot at it, Elmer?"

The big man grinned and nodded, and there were renewed cheers. There was silence as he moved to address the weight. Marty scrutinised it. It was tough to call, but this looked closer to three hundred pounds, and again, with no rotational sleeve to facilitate the clean to the chest. The Big One was one pig of a weight and no mistake. Elmer settled himself on the weight, head up, back flat. The bar started to move, slowly, painfully. It reached Elmer's waist, but it was not moving with sufficient speed and he could not clean it to his chest. With a grunt he dropped it to the floor. Elmer re-set himself and tried again. This time, it did not get above his waist and the giant dropped the weight, shaking his head. He shook Meek's hand and walked off to consoling cheers and applause.

Meek looked around him. "Anyone else here like to try, fore'n we gets back to the dancin'?" he shouted.

Marty stood up. "I'd sure like to give it a try, Reverend," he shouted.

Mary Lou pulled restrainingly on his sleeve, shaking her head, but Marty was on his way to the centre of the barn before she could stop him. There were derisory boos and whistles as Meek shook Marty's hand. He grabbed Marty's biceps and nodded his approval.

He held up his hands for silence. "I read somewheres," he said, "about some Baron in Europe somewheres, who said the big thing was to take part, not a-winnin' but a man a-doin' the best that he could do. And I reckon that there Baron, he was saying what the greatest athlete of them all, the dear Lord Jesus hisself, what he woulda said. So lets us give this Alabama boy here a sportin' chance."

There was now a respectful silence.

"You stone cold sober, boy?" Meek hissed out of the side of his mouth.

Marty nodded. "Yes, Reverend," he answered.

He looked down at the weight. Close up, it looked even bigger. The clean would have to be real quick, because of the absence of a rotating sleeve on the bar. There would be no possible room for error. Marty addressed the bar, placing both feet well under it, hip-width apart. He put his hands on it, pressed his knees out into his elbows and lifted his head. Marty drove up with his legs, arms straight. The bar went just above hip height, but that was enough. In a flash, he was under it, in a squat position, with a quick roll of the elbows. He slowly rose to an upright position, and the crowd was now silent. He knew that he dared not hold the weight long on his chest. Marty bent his knees and drove up straight, splitting his legs fore and aft and straightening them as he did so. His arms locked out, he brought his feet together, and for a moment stood frozen in the centre of the Barn, with arms straight, the weight directly above him. There was no sound. Marty slowly lowered the bar to his chest. Then he bent his knees and drove it up again, to straight arms and stood with the Big One again directly above him, still and fixed.

The Barn erupted.

For the first and last time in his life, the Reverend Obadiah Meek blasphemed. “Jesus Christ,” he said.

Chapter 6
The Dash

By April 1908, Mary Lou had read Mark Twain's *Huckleberry Finn* fifty-one times, and everything on Buffalo Bill Cody that Ned Buntline had ever penned. In the spring of 1909, she had set out with similar vigour upon the plays of George Bernard Shaw. When she had exhausted the Carnegie Library of Shaw's plays, she had moved on to his critical essays, which she had found harder going, since they usually reviewed music which she had never heard, and never would. At first, Shakespeare had been tough, too many *thee's* and *thou's* for her taste, but she had then deployed *Lamb's Tales from Shakespeare*, before returning with enjoyment to the Bard.

Mary Lou was voracious, profligate, taking six books home each week, the maximum allowed under the Carnegie Library rules, straining her eyes in winter months as she remorselessly pursued her reading in the guttering light of a kerosene lamp. Now, in spring, she was coming into her Reading Season, the time when she could pursue her wild, random studies without effort, deep into the summer evenings. Like most people lacking the discipline of a formal education, Mary Lou was promiscuous, indiscriminate, reading everything from classics to potboilers. And each week she committed herself to learning at least one hundred new words from Mr Webster's Dictionary. True, she had no idea where or when she might use them, but she was confident that she would be able to do so when the occasion arose.

The intensity of her studies and her dedication to the NAACP separated Mary Lou from her friends, but this did not unduly concern her. Neither did it trouble her that she could find no immediate practical use for her studies. Somehow, she felt instinctively that the muscle of her mind was thickening and developing, responding to training, just like Pop Warner's athletes and footballers. Mary Lou did not feel superior to her work-mates at the Majestic, merely different. She was popular with her colleagues, sharing with vigour in their practical jokes and horseplay, but the moment she crossed the Majestic's threshold each evening, she became someone else, even with her family. Somehow, she did not know how, there was a way out, and her books would take her there.

Marty had proved a disappointment to her. He talked in a strangely educated manner, more like a white than a black, but his conduct at the Big Barn had been no different from any other randy buck. But she had felt a pull, there was no question of that. It had been the touch, that first physical contact, in the disastrous St Louis Rag that had done it, when they had first held hands. There had been something good about it, something comfortable, something right, something inevitable. And when they had touched lips, that had been comfortable too, as if Marty had come all the way from Alabama for her alone. If only he had simply stopped there, that would have been just dandy.

But earlier, when Marty had lifted the Big One, her feelings had changed to something more animal, and that had troubled her. It was the way in which he handled the colossal barbell, the grace, the assurance, the manner in which he had focussed upon it with a massive, hidden energy. It was unnerving, and Mary Lou had felt herself shiver. She wondered if John and Beth had noticed.

If only Marty had just been nice and friendly, that would have been enough for the moment. Mary Lou had often wondered if young men and women could ever be just friends. In this sense, the NAACP was a haven, as most of the members were grizzled veterans like Abner Pyle, well beyond their springier days.

But the comfort, the rightness of that first moment lingered with her. So did the exhilaration of the Polka and the memory of Marty standing upright with that weight. She decided to give him another chance.

The parcel arrived by first post on the morning of Saturday, 6 May 1911. Marty went back to his quarters to unwrap them, feeling like a child at Christmas. He sat in the flickering light of the kerosene lamp and scrutinised the spiked shoes. They were black, with a pristine yellow leather sole, and they were stiff and heavy. Marty reckoned they must have weighed more than two pounds. But they fitted snugly enough. That night, he laced them up and pranced about on the spot on the dirt floor of the shed.

But something strange had come with the spiked shoes, an extra item from Sears Roebuck. It was two corks, slightly bigger than those used for wine bottles. Each cork was sewn into a loop of elastic. Alas, the package from Sears Roebuck contained no indication as to their purpose.

It would have to be a handicap race, Pop decided, for Half Moon, a sprinter only a couple of yards slower than Jim, had sustained a Charley Horse in training and would not be able to put weight on his injured leg for at least another week. Jim simply had to have a hard, realistic dash for he would soon be up against Heffelfinger, a Yale boy who was said to have run a yard outside even time for a hundred yards.

Pop groaned inside. It was the same old story, coming out of a football season, track athletes picking up shin splints and Charley Horses, and now the changed speed of the Carlisle track, though surely welcome, had not helped. For Roother had surely made the Carlisle track the fastest outside of Penn State University itself. It was sharp and crisp, even if still a mite too dry.

From high up in the bleachers, Marty could hear Pop call Louis Tewanima through his tin megaphone to run against Jim, off a ten yard start. Tewanima was clearly unhappy about running in a dash, but Pop was adamant. Marty could hear him bellowing imprecations at the little Indian from the top of the bleachers. He rose, walked down the wooden steps on to the track, stepping across it on to the infield to join Pop, Jim and Tewanima. He placed a hand on Pop's right shoulder and, realising what he had done, withdrew it. Pop, absorbed in delivering orders to Louis Tewanima, was not immediately aware of Marty's intimacy. Then he turned, his face red with shouting.

"So, Marty, what can I do for you?" he asked, abruptly.

"Can I help you out, coach?"

Pop was for a moment disoriented. "Help me out? How?"

"By me running against Jim, instead of Louis." Marty held up his Sears Roebuck shoes. "I got me these here new running shoes. Sears Roebuck."

Pop took them from him and scrutinised them for a moment. "Jesus Christ," he said. "These shoes must be more'n three bucks, Marty. How you gonna eat?"

Marty did not reply. Pop's tongue rolled below his lip as he pondered. Finally, he nodded. "Okay," he said. "Louis, you're off the hook. Off you go and give me two miles in ten minutes. Rest for five, then another two miles in ten. No more, no less, or I'll whup your ass good. You got it?"

Louis, relieved, nodded and jogged off. Pop turned to Jim and Marty. "You ever raced track, boy?" he asked, pointing at Marty.

"A bit," Marty replied. "Picnics and things. You know how it goes."

"This ain't no picnic, Marty," said Pop. "Jim here can run ten flat. Even time. You have any idea what that means?"

"It's fast," replied Marty.

"You're goddam right it's fast. Jim here can put out the light and get into bed before it's dark."

"Give Marty a chance, coach," pleaded Jim. "I hear tell he lifted the Big One."

"Those goddam railway wheels? No man born of woman can lift that. Even Eugene Sandow hisself couldn't get it overhead."

"Marty did it. Twice," said Jim.

Pop shook his head. "Anyhow, Jim, this ain't lifting no dumbbells. This is fast country, not muscle mountain."

"Let me try, coach," said Marty.

"Okay, okay. So how many yards you want?"

"You mean a start, in other words?"

"Not in other words, Marty, those are the exact words," replied Pop.

Marty shook his head. "I don't want any start, coach," he said. "I want to run level with Jim."

Pop tried to control his impatience. "You're not with me, Marty. You're just not with me. You see, this is what we in track call a time trial." He pointed up to the bleachers at the finish, where Dean Mackay now sat. "The College Principal is up there, Dean Mackay. Now, he's Scotch. He knows running. He knows runners. He's putting fifty bucks on Jim's back against this Heffelfinger guy. Like I said, he's Scotch. He likes to stay close to his money."

"Bawbees, Pop. The Dean calls it bawbees," volunteered Jim.

"Just like I said, Jim, he's Scotch. Whatever he calls it, he wants to keep it," growled Pop.

"I'd still like to run level," insisted Marty.

Pop frowned and turned to Jim.

"So what do you say, Jim?"

"I say we run level," said Jim, smiling his big toothy grin.

Dean Mackay squinted down the track into the bright sun. The Carlisle track was looking much better, though he noted that the infield grass still needed a good cut. For three bucks a week and vittles, he would expect no less. Still, the black boy Roother looked to be doing a fine job, and at that sort of money each week, any black could live like a prince.

Mackay knew Fast Men from soup to nuts. In his springier days, at Edinburgh University, he had followed the "Peds," the fastest professional sprinters that Britain could produce, running at Edinburgh's Powderhall in the New Year Sprint Handicap. Hell, he had seen the fastest sprinter of the nineteenth century, Harry Hutchens of Putney, running thirty seconds flat for 300 yards. Even time, running around four men in the cold, midwinter gloom, finishing at a trot, crivvens, that was running. He had wept, with others in the crowd, even before the time had been displayed, for he had known, as Hutchens had cut through the field like butter, that he had just witnessed something special. Mackay had no need of a stopwatch to tell him that.

Jim Thorpe, well, he was not quite in the Hutchens class, though with Scottish training Mackay felt that Jim could go as low as two yards inside even time. It was a pity that Jim was not a "pro," for big money could have been made on him at professional meets like Scranton, at least before the bookies and handicappers got wise to him. Enough to pay Mackay's bookmaker, Goldberg, to whom he was in hock for a thousand bawbees.

Pop arrived, sweating. "Got this Roother boy to run against Jim," he said.

"In the trial?" said Mackay, looking up the stadium to the start through his field glasses. "The black boy?"

"Yes," replied Pop.

"How much of a start?"

Pop paused. "I thought it best that we have them start level."

Mackay lowered his glasses and looked at Pop, scowling. "Pop, this is supposed to be a time trial. I've got fifty wheels on Jim at 3 – 1 against this Hefflebanger."

"Heffelfinger."

"Finger, banger. I dinna give a docken, Pop."

Pop noted that Mackay always became more Scottish as he got angry.

"A trial is a trial. I've seen top peds in training, Pop. This groundsman, this Roother, should be given a day's start, or your trial's a waste of time."

"Let's just see how it goes, Dean," said Pop, defensively.

Mackay took another look down the track through his glasses. "I've got this Negro boy in my sights now," he said. "He's doing a lot of dam fool stretching, like some hoor at the Follies. Now, I ask you, Pop, why would he be doing something like that?"

"I don't know, Dean."

Mackay continued to look through his glasses at Marty. "And, Jesus wept, look at him now! The boy doesn't seem to know how to dig his starting holes. Jim's having to show him how."

Pop looked down the straight, through his own field glasses. "Roother, he's a well set-up young feller," he said, defensively.

"So are some of the bucks down the Scranton mines. But I wouldn't try to run 'em against Jim. It's common knowledge that black boys don't make fast men, Pop. You know that as well as I do."

"What about that Negro Mackenzie, up in Canada?" said Pop.

"He was a Canadian, a half-breed," said Mackay. "Anyhow, I heard tell he'd got some Scottish blood in his veins."

"Let's just see how it goes," repeated Pop, removing his stopwatch from his fob pocket.

"Don't keep saying that, Pop," said Mackay, tetchily. "Who's starting?"

"I've got Half Moon on the gun," answered Pop.

"Least we've got **someone** who knows what he's about," growled Mackay.

Marty felt it all beginning to come back to him, the feelings of fear and uncertainty vital for athletic performance. Certainty was death. Necessary was that nagging scintilla of doubt, squirming deep in your gut. That and only that produced the adrenalin rush that triggered peak performance.

He had re-checked his starting holes. Hell, he had even forgotten the shallower angle in the front hole, automatically set in modern starting blocks, but Jim had pointed it out to him. But Jim had now retreated into his shell as he prepared to compete and was no longer the gentle giant of only a few moments before. Marty settled into his holes for a practice start. He felt his feet press on their rough cinder walls. He raised his hips, then ran out, feeling his Sears shoes bite into the hard, dry cinders. Half Moon, standing on their left, blew a whistle and raised his arm to Pop and the Dean at the finish. Pop stood and raised his hand in response. The Carlisle athletes clustered behind Mackay and Pop, up in the bleachers.

Marty felt his mouth suddenly go dry.

"Get to your marks."

Marty looked sideways at Jim. He suddenly looked much bigger. His thick thighs looked well-defined, balanced by his burly footballer's shoulders. Marty settled into his holes, Jim on his left side.

"Get set."

Both men lifted their hips, Marty's higher than those of Jim. The gun exploded, unleashing both runners.

"Jesus Christ, Pop, he's taken Jim," said Mackay.

For Marty had taken almost a yard out of Jim in the first twenty, accelerating out of his holes as if shot from a gun. Jim, rugged and ungainly, struggled to hold the gap as they approached halfway.

"Come on, Jim," growled Pop. "Pick him up."

But Marty slowly started to slip away and Jim started to tighten up. When they hit the tape, there were three clear yards of daylight between them.

Pop did not bother to look at his watch. "Forget about Heffelfinger," he growled. "Jim's had it."

"Wheesht, man," said Mackay. "You haven't looked at your watch yet."

Pop looked at his stopwatch and gasped. "Nine and four fifths," said Pop. "Nine point eight." He shook his watch close to his ear. "Must have dust in it," he said.

"Then we share the same dust, Pop," said Mackay. "My watch is in hundredths. I got him at 9.69."

"That means Jim ran close to ten seconds dead," said Pop.

"Jim ran well," said Mackay. "Right up to form. Only this man Roother took a full three yards out of him, singing Dixie."

"No man on earth can run that fast, that easy," said Pop, disbelievingly.

"This man Roother can," said the Dean. "So just you keep him under wraps, Pop. I got plans for him. Big plans. Our boy Roother, he's money in the bank."

"Strip off," ordered Pop.

Pop and Marty stood in the dusty locker room of the now-deserted pavilion.

"You mean…" said Marty.

"To the buff," growled Pop, arms folded. "You bashful?" He delved into a rusty locker, fumbled within it for a moment and returned with an ancient shredded jockstrap. He threw it to Marty who deftly caught it. "Here, put this on, if you've got problems."

Marty scrutinised the jockstrap. It was tattered, yellowish, but odour-free and clean. It would be all right. Aids was seventy years away. He peeled off his shirt, vest and shorts, pulled on the jockstrap and stood before Pop. Pop put his right hand, supported by his left, under his chin and scrutinised Marty for a few moments. "How much you weigh, boy?"

"One eight six, one ninety," replied Marty.

"At least. And no fat either."

"I eat good, but it burns up fast," volunteered Marty.

Pop stepped forward, bent down and, alarmingly, grabbed his thigh. "This must be close on twenty-six inches," he said. "Where the Sam Hill did you get legs like these? The railways?"

Marty resisted replying that he always travelled by plane. "Weights," he said. "I work out with weights."

Pop shook his head and continued to examine him, peering at his deep, powerful chest. He grabbed Marty's upper arm and squeezed it. "Saw Hackenschmidt himself a coupla years back, in Scranton." he said. "Rasslin' at the Garden. You got bigger arms than Hack, you know that?"

"Hackenschmidt? Who's he?"

"Jesus Christ," groaned Pop involuntarily. The man had never heard of Hackenschmidt, the greatest wrestler on earth, a household name. Still, he was from Alabama, so it was only to be expected. But he possessed a magnificent physique, more like Sandow than a track athlete. Pop had never seen anything quite like him. True, Jim was big, but at least twenty pounds short of the Negro, and with nowhere near the same levels of muscular definition. This boy had muscles in his hair.

"Put your clothes back on," he ordered.

The two men walked out of the pavilion into the bright spring sunshine. On the track below, the Carlisle squad were now finishing their workouts.

"Now Marty, I'm going to give you a piece of good advice," said Pop. "I don't reckon to know that much, but one thing I do know for sure. Weights are no good. Give 'em up. Weights make you slow."

To Angus Mackay, it was all blindingly obvious. It was payday, Eldorado and Sutter's Creek, all rolled into one. He would clear his debts to Goldberg, with enough left for a month's holiday in Cape Cod, and a Model T Ford. The Scranton New Year Handicaps were only eight months away, the biggest professional footrace in the United States. OK, so it was all as crooked as a dog's hind leg, but Marty was money in the bank, an ace in the hole. The Scranton prize money was $1000, enough to clear him with the Jew, but the real money would lie in the bets. He would deploy the Carlisle syndicate, bringing in Gilbert and a few of the city's leading businessmen and cream off 20% of their winnings. Mackay could already see the greenbacks. He would eat them with a knife and fork, and there would be money for the College too. The Negro boy Roother, he would pick up a few bucks. Twenty a week in training and all the meat he could eat, $100 of the $1000 prize money, perhaps, a lick of cream from the betting too, if he kept his nose clean.

Central to everything was the fact that Roother was an unknown, with no form. Thus, the handicapper would be forced to give him a novice's handicap, perhaps, five or six yards. If Roother played it canny, took it easy and won by a short yard, they might drop him to three yards for the next big handicap. There, even on that mark, he would still win and even cut down to one yard he might still be worth a few bucks. After that, it would be scratch championship races against the fast men of the Eastern seaboard, perhaps, even against visiting Aussies or Sassenachs. If only Roother could be trained to play it smart, and run strictly to orders, win by a vest. If so, they would cream the Eastern Seaboard before it became clear that they had in Roother a man who could run four yards inside even time, perhaps, even better. Came the moment, came the man. Roother was a money-machine and Angus Mackay was just the man to set that machinery into profitable motion.

When he had put it to Pop, Mackay had been surprised at Pop's immediate response, for his coach was not a gambling man.

"Count me in," said Pop.

"We have to keep your man Roother under wraps, Pop. So no more of these trials against Jim. Nothing public, at least. And can you keep all our Indians quiet?"

"Does a fish shit in the sea?"

Mackay chuckled. "You've a quaint turn of phrase, Pop."

"I saw this Roother stripped off," said Pop. "Forget about your Hackenschmidt, forget about Sandow. Roother's got muscles in places where I don't even have the places."

"But how d'you think he'll run – with money on his back?"

"No telling," replied Pop. "You must know that."

"You know," said Mackay, "I once met Wyatt Earp – it was over in New York, at Barnum's Museum. Earp said that the average shooting gallery shot is fast, but he's no damn good in a gunfight. Not used to having that split second before his living and his dying. Same with a fast man."

"Football fields the same," growled Pop. "Life and death. You know, we had near a hundred deaths in five years, before Teddy Roosevelt stepped in a few years back."

"Forget football, Pop. Give me your honest opinion about this boy Roother. You know what we're up against. Those boys up in Scranton at the New Year Handicap will take the hairs from your arse and sell them for a brush. Can this fellow Roother do the business?"

"Like I said, there's no telling," replied Pop.

Mackay scowled. "D'you know, Pop, you have a nasty habit of repeating yourself."

"It's the coach in me," said Pop. "You know, Angus, this boy Roother isn't your ordinary run of the mill Negro."

"Run of the *cotton* mill Negro," said Mackay.

Pop chuckled. "No there's something about him – I can't quite put my finger on it."

"Try," said Mackay."

"I wanted him to run off ten yards," said Pop. "But no, Roother, he said no, I'll run level. Right to my face. Wouldn't budge."

"And he was right," said Mackay.

"But down there on the track, Angus, what I say goes," said Pop.

"Just as well it didn't this time," responded Mackay. "You might just have cost us ten thousand bawbees."

"That much?"

"Maybe a lot more, if we can just teach him to run a wee bit slower and still win by a vest. That's what pro running in handicaps is all about."

"That won't be easy," said Pop.

"Football's your game, Pop. Running, that's mine. Roother runs to orders, always wins by a thin vest. Keeps the odds up, till the bookies finally get wise. By that time, we're all in Paris, France."

Pop shook his head. "What about fair play?"

"Fair play, Pop, is a jewel," replied Mackay. "But me, I don't give a docken for jewellery." He paused. "The big question is – can Roother run with bucks on his back?"

"You said that before," said Pop.

"But that's what it's all about. I saw them every year in Edinburgh, at the Powderhall Handicap, Pop. Ran fast in their trials, but died the death when you put big money on their back. It's called stripping big."

"I know what you mean," said Pop. "Jim has it in spades. Intestinal fortitude."

"Come again?"

"Guts."

Mackay nodded. "You've got to get to him, Pop. You could talk a dog off a meat wagon. Get him in shape."

"Roother **is** in shape."

"Then keep him in shape, but under wraps. And feed him well. Peds always feed well. I'll put up for meat."

Pop nodded. "Roother's a big boy. He'll need a horse between two mattresses."

"Anything it takes, Pop. We have to plan it neat. So get that boy to my office on Monday, ten o'clock sharp."

"He said no," said Mackay, his hands flat in front of him on the black leather surface of his desk. "The Negro said no."

"Did you tell him how much it would be worth to him?" asked Pop.

"Aye," said Mackay. "A hundred dollars training expenses, another hundred in prize money, two hundred from the syndicate. That's four hundred dollars, well over three year's earnings for a buck like him."

Pop nodded. "It's a lot of dough," he said.

"So what did he say?"

"First, he asked me why he wasn't getting **all** of the prize money. Me, I said we were keeping it for training expenses."

"And what did Roother say?"

"He asked me to list the training expenses. Then he said he could win it without us, simply get on a train to Scranton and pick himself up a thousand dollars."

"Well, that's true," said Pop.

"You're right, but I don't expect some buck from Alabama to tell me so," said Mackay. "Anyhow, that's not the point. We're the brains of the whole clanjamfry. We put up the mind and the money."

"But now he tells you he thinks that he could do it himself," said Pop.

"He's not a pro," said Mackay. "He doesn't know what I know. He's a nigra. If brains were leather, he wouldn't have enough to saddle a bug. Roother needs managing, Pop."

"He doesn't seem to think so," said Pop.

"But that's no' the end of it, Pop," said Mackay. "It wasn't just about the split, Pop. No, I upped it to a grand and he was still thrawn."

"Thrawn?"

"Thrawn, Pop," said Mackay testily. "Stubborn." He shook his head. "No, he let me talk just to get ma dander up. He said he didn't want tae run for any money."

"Why not? He's only getting three bucks a week."

"And vittles," said Mackay.

"And vittles," said Pop. He was, in some strange way, enjoying Mackay's discomfiture. It was not often that the Dean was thwarted.

"He could pick up enough to buy a house and set up a business," he said.

"Just exactly what I said to him, Pop," growled Mackay. "Ma very words." He stopped. "Pop, I've never in my life asked you the meaning of a word, have I?"

"No," agreed Pop. "Your Scottish education."

"Decathlon," said Mackay. "What in the name of Rabbie Burns is a decathlon?"

"Not pentathlon?" said Pop. "They had something called pentathlon at the 1906 Olympics in Athens." He stroked his chin. "Met up once with a Harvard boy who took part. Four track and field events, ending up with rassling. Our fellers were well up till the rassling, then those goddam Greeks and Krauts took over. They were the only ones who knew the goddam rules."

"Let's use our heads here, Pop," said Mackay. "Pen equals five, dec equals ten."

"Got it," said Pop, abruptly. "Got it Decathlon. Ten events. An all-rounder. I remember they had it at the St Louis Olympics in '04. Some Mick called Keily won it."

"What was in it?"

Pop shook his head. "Just about everything except marathon," he said. "Hell, they had a 56lb weight for distance and a one mile walk. All on one day. Like Hell on stilts."

"Well, that's what Roother told me he wants to do," said Mackay. "Decathlon."

Pop raised both hands in mock despair. "Now, however, would an Alabama boy like Roother get to know about decathlon? Down there, they only started walking erect a coupla months ago."

"Well, that's what he wants to do, Pop. Decathlon in the Stockholm Olympics."

"I didn't know anything about a decathlon in Stockholm," said Pop. "I was thinking of Jim competing in high jump and long jump and Louis Tewanima in the long track runs."

"Well, this boy Roother seems to know more about these Olympics than you do, Pop, and that's put paid to Scranton."

Mackay breathed deeply, rose and turned to face the bay window behind him, his back to Pop. He was silent for a moment, then turned. "Unless…" he said. "Unless we call his bluff…" He pointed a thin, bony finger at Pop. "If he decides to go it alone to Scranton, we'll threaten to blow the gaffe on him and he'll get low odds."

"And if he still won't go to Scranton for us?"

"Then he can look for a new job," said Mackay.

"You're a devil, Angus," said Pop.

"Pop, life would be hell without the Devil," said Mackay.

Chapter 7
Together

It was like a cell. Jim lay on his back in his lumpy bunk, head cupped in his hands. He reflected that, had he been incarcerated in Oklahoma's Bellemont Prison, he would probably have lived in quarters such as this. A bunk, a chest of drawers, a chair and a desk, that was all there was. Even the john was a communal one, evil-smelling, contingent upon row upon row of washbasins further down the corridor. Jim's earthly possessions constituted one change of shoes and clothing, a football uniform and boots, and a pair of running spikes and jumping shoes. And three jock straps.

No. There was the most important possession of all and it hung on the wall directly above him. It was an oil painting of his great-grandfather, Chief Black Hawk. It was a fanciful portrait by Pop Warner, an accomplished amateur artist. It featured Black Hawk charging into battle against the Osage, astride a palomino, in his most famous victory. Black Hawk, a feared warrior, had battled against both Indians and whites, but he had been wise enough to know when to give up and had retired to the Indian Reservation at Des Moines. Many years later, an Irishman by the name of Thorpe had come to live near the Reservation, and had taken as his wife Black Hawk's granddaughter. From this union had come Hiram Thorpe. Though only half Indian, Hiram was completely Indian in looks and was a big man, '6′ 2″ tall and 230 pounds, and no one in the locality could match him in running, jumping and of feats of strength. When the laws of the Reservation had proved to be too restrictive, Hiram had moved to Indian territory in

Oklahoma. Some years after the death of his first wife, he had married Charlotte View, one quarter French and three-quarters Sac & Fox. Seven years after the birth of their first boy, George, Charlotte had given birth to twins, Charles and James.

Jim raised the thick earthen jug to his lips again, his gaze still fixed on Black Hawk. The brown liquid splashed around his mouth and on to his neck. He sighed. How he and his brother Charlie had played. All day long, they had run, jumped and wrestled, winter and summer. And with the other boys, there was always the 'follow' game. This was played by over twenty boys and involved following the leader wherever he took them, up trees, over barns, even underneath horses. And if you chickened out, your punishment was to crawl under twenty boys standing with legs spread, and that was tougher than any of the rigours of 'follow'. Then suddenly, at the age of eight, Charlie had died of pneumonia. Jim, now lost, had grown ever closer to George and his father. Hiram Thorpe was like a god to Jim. His father was inexhaustible, could run, wrestle and jump and would vanish for weeks on hunting trips. And when there was no room on his horse for a deer that he had killed, Hiram Thorpe would simply sling it over his back and walk home for twenty miles with it across his shoulders.

Jim's drowsy eyes stayed fixed on Black Hawk's grotesquely painted face. Sometimes, he thought that it would have been better had he been born in the time of Black Hawk, to have ridden into battle with his great grandfather and his warriors. Now the war against the whites was fought with a pigskin, hitting the secondaries against thugs, sons of the Good and the Great of the East Coast. For the players from Harvard and Princeton were no more principled than their forebears, who had broken every Indian treaty to which they had committed themselves.

Jim had always remembered the day that the Carlisle quarterback, Running Deer, had been slugged on the ground by a Harvard man. He had risen slowly to his feet, wiped the blood from his mouth, spat out his broken teeth and looked his assailant in the eye. "Who's the savage now?" he had asked, through bloody, broken lips.

Who was the savage now? Jim took another swig. Jesus, in this Land of the Free he was not even by right an American citizen. None of them were. All winter he hit the line for Pop and all summer he ran track or played ball for him, just for board and lodging, but he was not even allowed to vote.

But he loved it so. To Jim, competing for Pop was simply the play of his childhood with his brother Charlie transferred to gridiron, diamond or track. It was a joy simply to test himself there, a delight of childhood which he would stretch for every possible moment into the future, till he could compete no more, just as Hiram and Black Hawk had done. Hiram. Jim had been at school in far off Kansas when news came that his father had been hurt in a hunting accident. He had walked for two solid weeks to get back to Oklahoma. His father had recovered, but a few weeks later his mother had died of blood poisoning. From that day, their relationship had deteriorated and at the age of twelve Jim had run off to Texas. There, he had learned to tame wild horses and had returned with a string to Oklahoma, to an approving father. Three years later, a Carlisle representative had arrived at the North Canadian River Territory and offered Jim an education at the school.

Jim reached down again, lifted the keg above him and felt the last drops dribble slowly into his mouth. He could now paint, was a fair carpenter and no mean car mechanic. Not that there would be much call for mechanics back in the dust of the barren Oklahoma Territory. Back there, he had seen them at the Reservation, shiftless drunks hovering outside agency offices, waiting for handouts, sad shadows of past warriors. Whatever the limitations of his college education, Carlisle would surely lead to something better than that. So he was not leading warriors against the White-eyes, even Black Hawk had seen the futility of that. But every winter week he was cutting through their defensive lines like butter and he was tearing their track and field record books to shreds.

Jim reached under his bunk and withdrew a half-empty bottle of beer. He uncorked it with his teeth and poured it down his throat. He grimaced, for it was now warm and flat.

At least, he reflected, he was not a black, for they were truly at the bottom of the heap, invisible. They did not play football against the whites, or run them into the ground. That was why Roother had been such a surprise to him. For that week, Pop had gone off to the Midwest, scouting for players for the football season, and the Negro had offered to help him in his track training.

They had started with shot-put. Here, Roother was quite different from Pop, whose advice had always been simply to hit the sixteen-pound ball harder. Alternatively, Pop would advise him to throw his heart out to the required distance and the shot would surely follow. Jim could get Pop's general drift, but it didn't explain how he was going to improve his performance. Roother was quite different. First he had got him to settle deeper at the back of the circle, at the start of his shift, and to keep his throwing elbow higher. This had produced immediate improvement. Then, Marty had tried to get him to land in the circle-centre with his weight back over his right foot, facing backwards. In no time, he was launching the shot out to near forty-five feet, time and time again, as if he were putting for accuracy. But then, the strangest thing had occurred. Marty had demonstrated a put from the standing position, and the shot had flown out to over forty-six feet. It had rocketed from Roother's hand as if shot from a cannon. Jim had asked him to repeat the put, and the sixteen-pound shot had gone even further. Jim had thrown against the best men on the Eastern Seaboard, but few of the beer-bellied Irish whales of Chicago and New York could match such distances.

And it had been exactly the same when Marty had worked out with him on the high hurdles. In demonstration, the Negro had skimmed the barriers, running between them like a sprinter. Jim reckoned him to be a fourteen and a half second man, and that was world record time. Then, Marty had broken down Jim's technique, working first over low hurdles, isolating each aspect of lead leg and rear leg movement. In no time at all, Jim had been flowing rhythmically over the 3'6" barriers.

Finally, aware of Jim's coming match with the Yale man, Heffelfinger, Marty had broken down his sprint technique, stressing relaxation in arms and shoulders. Soon, he was pouring down the crisp cinder track, Marty at his side, talking him on. All that week, the two men had worked out together.

It had been the same story when the other members of the track team had come to Marty for advice. Marty had changed Half Moon's javelin grip, got him to position the spear flatter, parallel to his shoulders. The little Chippewa was soon throwing 150 feet, more than twenty feet beyond his previous best. In the week before Pop's return, Marty Roother had transformed the performance of at least a dozen of the Carlisle track team. In return, they had helped him out with ground-maintenance and, as a result, the infield was now cropped and flat, with clear, well-defined throwing arcs, and the long jump and vault boxes had been replaced.

Jim laid down the now empty beer bottle at his side. No question of it, this Roother boy surely knew his track and field, and was no mean athlete himself. His coaching method was, however, quite different from that of Pop. When Louis Tewanima had discussed Pop's coaching methods with Marty, the Negro had responded by saying that Pop didn't know jack-shit. Louis had asked him later about Jack Shit, and Jim had replied that he was probably some ole black boy from Alabama.

Aloysius P Gilbert stood, his back to Angus Mackay, looking out of his office window onto the main street below, his hands clasped behind him. It was a strange relationship. For years, they had been fast friends, despite Gilbert's steadfast opposition to the *raison d'être* of Mackay's life, Carlisle Industrial School and the education of Indians. Still, Gilbert's attitude to Mackay's predecessor, Brigadier Pratt, had been no different and Pratt had been an Indian fighter.

Out of snow you cannot make cheesecake. That had been the view of another of Gilbert's *confrères*, Aaron Wildstein, on blacks and Indians. You could make a man out of the Indian, but you couldn't take the Indian out of the man. The friendship of Gilbert and Mackay had gone back to the New York Highland Games, when Gilbert had been a cub reporter on the *New York Times*. Mackay had been a competitor, and Gilbert had picked up fifty bucks on him in a mile handicap. They had become firm friends, that friendship extending beyond Gilbert's move to the *Carlisle Chronicle* as assistant editor in 1900. In 1907, the two men had met up again when Mackay had become Dean of Carlisle.

Mackay and Gilbert were both gambling men, meeting each Friday night with Wildstein and other Carlisle cronies to play Five Card Stud in the editorial offices of the *Chronicle*, losses limited to twenty bucks. Their activities at Belmont racetrack were more adventurous, but the syndicate usually broke even. However, Mackay's Achilles' Heel had been the Scranton Pedestrian Handicap. For the past three years, the Scot had come up with certain winners of the $1,000 Handicap, but his valediction was the kiss of death. Thus, the Carlisle syndicate had since 1907 lost close on $10,000 on Mackay's "certainties".

Gilbert turned to face his friend. "Now let me get this clear, Angus. You're telling me this year that your *groundsman*, this nigra boy, can win at Scranton? A stone cold certainty?"

"Aye."

"You've clocked him?"

"Took Jim by three yards, a week past."

"How fast?"

"Nine point seven for a hundred yards," replied Mackay.

"Jesus," said Gilbert, sitting down at his desk. "Are you sure? No man alive can run nine seven."

Mackay stood in front of Gilbert, both hands on the desk. “I’m telling you, Aloysius. I saw it with my own eyes. This nigra Roother, he’s money in the bank.”

“So was that Italian waiter with the birthmark last year, the guy you told me to put my shirt on.”

“The stop-watch doesn’t lie, Aloysius.”

“Okay, so tell me, where’s he been all this time? Mars?”

“You’re close, Aloysius. Alabama.”

Gilbert sighed and shook his head. This was too good to be true. “So you want the syndicate again? To put up the money?”

“That’s right. I need two hundred up front, just for training expenses. We’ll take him up to the boondocks, out of sight; feed him like a king…”

“Then we enter him and lay early money around.”

“Big odds, Aloysius. Roother’s an unknown.”

“How much?”

“Two, three thousand. We’ll get 6-1, 8-1.”

“What time won it last year?”

“Twelve point six for one hundred and thirty yards, off a handicap of five yards. That’s the equivalent of about ten point two for the hundred yards, off scratch.”

“And your boy ran better than that off scratch, against Jim?”

“Easing off,” said Mackay. “Singing Dixie.”

“That means, if he plays it smart, he can take it easy and win it in, say, twelve-point-four,” said Gilbert, stroking his chin. “Don’t show too much right away.”

“Then we’re off to Chicago for another handicap in November.”

“Pick up another twenty grand in the Windy City.”

“He could score three big wins before the handicapper gets wise and brings him down to size.”

“We’re looking at real big money here, Angus. I’m in, and I’ll lay bets on Wildstein too.”

“And all the other Steins,” said Mackay.

Gilbert nodded.

"But one thing, Pop-we can make two hits here-we save your man Roother for 1913, because we already have a guy in preparation for this year, a Canadian, by name of Rae. We've had him under wraps for two years. So we get two bites of the cherry."

The Dean shook his head.

"Roother wants to compete at the Stockholm Olympics," he said. "In the decathlon."

"Decathlon? What the Sam Hill is that?"

"Ten events," said the Dean.

"Whatever it is, he'll be exposed, and there will be nothing in it for us at Scranton in 1913. You will have to convince him otherwise, Angus."

Professor Hunter's Electric Picture Palace was clearly the social event of 1911 for the Negros of Carlisle. Hunter had taken over the Palace for the night and had begun, not with a movie, but with Mack's Minstrels, a group of ancient banjo-playing Negros dressed in frayed, striped blazers. They were led by Professor Hunter himself, a blacked-up white man who conducted a puerile patter act with a gormless member of the band. To Marty, it was excruciating stuff, but the audience appeared to love it, whooping and hollering at every piece of dim badinage. So did Mary Lou and her vast family.

Then there was Marko, featured as the Man of a Thousand Voices, who imitated Teddy Roosevelt, Eddie Foy and George M. Cohan. Marko had changed his headgear on every voice, so whatever else he was, he was, certainly, a Man of a Thousand Hats. He ended by playing 'Yankee Doodle Dandy' on a multi-instrument strapped to his chest, consisting of mouth organ, cymbals, trumpet and drum. Then, to end the vaudeville section, there was a half-hearted sparring exhibition between a couple of bloated, flat-nosed pugs, followed by an interval.

At last, came the movies. The first was a ponderous farce, *The French Maid*, featuring a man wearing an ill-fitting wig and a wobbling moustache, his wife and a French maid. Marty reckoned the movie could not have cost more than fifty bucks to make, but the Carlisle audience responded as if it were witnessing classic comedy by quite literally rolling in the aisles. The following movie was a maudlin affair, starring a little girl who had lost her dog. Marty looked to each side of him. Every one of Mary Lou's family was now in tears, and even old Grandpa Lincoln was blubbering.

Finally, there was a Western about a bank robbery, featuring a crowd of errant, middle-aged buckaroos, dressed in strange, woolly leggings. It ended with a head-on shot of a train coming towards the audience, which caused most of them to duck, screaming, to avoid it.

The best thing about Professor Hunter's entertainment was the audience itself. They amused Marty more than anything that appeared on the rumpled white sheet which served as a screen. But the true star of the show was the local church organist, Miss Louella Bright, acting a pianist. From her honky-tonk piano flowed a stream of melodies far superior to any of the clod-hopping melodramatics on the screen above her.

The audience, still bubbling, poured out into the dying spring sunshine of Cameron Street.

"So what you think, Marty?" asked Mary Lou. "Somethin' special, eh?"

"Never seen anything like it in my life," replied Marty. He put his hand on his heart. "Truly."

Then they had made their way to Mary Lou Barrow's home, only a couple of hundred yards short of his Lime Street lodgings. The Barrow house was constructed of wooden slats and was twice the size of his lodgings, a single floored bungalow consisting of living room kitchen and three bedrooms. As they took their places at table for dinner, Marty took a closer look at Mary Lou's mother, Alice Barrow. Alice was still lean and trim, her lined, handsome face fringed by grey-flecked hair set in a bun. This, he reflected, was how Mary Lou would look in twenty years, in 1931. Alice's husband,

Woodrow, a carpenter at the local wood mill, was a big, slow man, now going to fat. The pivot, the centre of gravity of the Barrow family was Lincoln, Mary Lou's grandfather; wiry, gnarled, he was in many ways an older version of Abner Pyle. The dining table, in common with the whole cabin, was spotlessly clean, covered in an impeccable blue-check calico tablecloth. Marty recognised the china and the cutlery. They had come from the Majestic.

"Ain't never seen these befo'," said Lincoln, holding up a knife. "This heah boy royalty or sump'n?"

"They'll be back in the Majestic tomorrow, Gramps," Mary Lou assured him.

The dinner began with corn on the cob. As he consumed it, Marty realised that he had never before truly tasted corn on the cob. It was succulent, almost a meal in itself. Then the chicken arrived, crisp on top and tender beneath, with fried potatoes and squash.

"Marty here works down at the track, Gramps," said Mary Lou, breaking the silence.

"The railroad track?"

"The running track," smiled Mary Lou. "At the school."

Woodrow started to serve the chicken in silence. Lincoln took his, surveyed it, shook his head and Woodrow added another slice of chicken.

"With Pop Warner and all them Injun boys?" he said.

"Yes, Mr Barrow," said Marty.

"Mary Lou says you ran against Jim Thorpe," said Woodrow, continuing to dissect and serve the chicken. He cut off a leg and put it on a plate which Alice served to Marty.

"Marty beat him, Poppa. He beat Jim Thorpe."

"I seen Thorpe run once," said Lincoln. "No man alive can beat that Injun."

"I shaded him last week, in a trial, sir," said Marty.

"Tain't possible. No nigra boy can run that fast," insisted Lincoln. "'Gainst nature."

"Marty wants to run for the United States in the Olympics next year," said Mary Lou.

"Olympics? What's them?"

"A big track meet, sir," responded Marty. "Every country in the world. In Sweden."

"And who zactly pays for a black boy like you to git out there?"

"The American Olympic Committee. It's all found, sir."

"And where's zactly is this heah Sweden?" asked Lincoln.

"Next to France, Pop," said Alice, with conviction.

Lincoln reached forward to spike another piece of chicken and placed it on his plate. "Now, Marty, I ain't never been no athlete, but one thing I do know," he said. He chewed slowly, swallowed and pointed his fork at Marty. "They ain't never gonna let no nigra boy run for no United States in no Olympics. You jest take my word for it."

Later that evening, Mary Lou and Marty walked down Lime Street in the gathering dusk towards his lodgings. She slipped her hand into his. It felt good. She stopped and looked at him. "They all like you," she said. She stood on tiptoe, reached up and kissed him on the cheek. He placed his index finger on the exact spot, trailed it round to his lips and licked them. She grinned.

"Not too fresh?" he asked.

Mary Lou shook her head. "Not too fresh," she said, smiling.

It had not taken long for news of Marty's activities to reach Pop Warner's ears on his return. First there was the coaching. The change in Jim's shot-putting technique was immediately obvious to Pop, and his hurdling was a revelation. Jim would now be able to take on the best timber-toppers on the Eastern Seaboard. But it was the technical changes made with the lesser mortals of his Carlisle team that had surprised Pop. For his quarter-mile hurdler, Little Rock, now took a smooth, fluent fifteen strides between hurdles; Half Moon was now launching the spear out to close on 150 feet; and his sprint relay squad had perfected a new baton pass that had sliced a full two seconds off their best time.

And it was not as if the track itself had been neglected. The infield was now like a bowling green, with clear distance arcs for the first time, the vault boxes and take off boards had been replaced and the track surface was sharp and crisp.

Pop knew in his heart that track and field were not really his game, but he had spent over a decade observing the work of the best track and field coaches in the East. He had talked into the night with Mike Sweeney, the Irish coach who had once held the world high jump record, and with Mike Murphy, the 1908 Olympic coach and inventor of the crouch start. These men were acknowledged masters of their craft, yet Marty Roother had introduced more innovations in a week than Sweeney and Murphy had done in twenty years. Pop watched Marty work out with Jim, and moved behind him as Jim easily cleared six feet. "You did a good job last week," said Pop.

"Thanks, coach," replied Marty, eyes still fixed on Jim.

"You given some more thought about to the Dean's offer?"

Marty turned to face Pop. "I'm grateful, Pop, I really am," he said.

"But you still want to run in this dam' fool decathlon in Stockholm."

"That's it."

"Think about it, boy. That decathlon, I looked it up-it's hell on earth. A fifty-six pound weight throw and a half mile walk."

Marty shook his head. "No, Pop," he said. "First day, 100 metres, long jump, shot put, high jump and 400 metres. Second day, 100 metres hurdles, discus, vault, javelin and 1500 metres," he recited.

Pop surveyed him, lips pursed. "How the Sam Hill do you know stuff like that?"

Marty paused. "Must have read it somewhere in the papers," he answered. "And there's a pentathlon too."

“Yes,” said Pop. “You got to be a real Hackenschmidt for that. Rassling’s the last event.”

“No,” replied Marty firmly. “Hurdles, long jump, discus, 200 metres and 1500 metres. Not sure about the order though.”

Pop nodded, bemused. “You seem to have it all tied up with a ribbon,” he said.

“I keep my ears open,” said Marty. He turned. “Mind if I try a high jump?”

“Be my guest,” said Pop. He pointed at Jim. “Put it down for Marty here. Five feet for starters.”

Marty shook his head. “Put it at six, Jim,” he said.

“Five six?” said Pop.

“No, six feet,” replied Marty. “It’s cool.”

“Cool,” repeated Pop. Shaking his head, he beckoned to Jim to place the wooden crossbar at six feet.

“What style do you use? The Western Roll? Eastern Cut-Off?”

Marty paused and shook his head. “I just kinda flop over,” he replied.

“How does that work, now?”

“On my back.”

Pop shook his head. “Then 1911 is sure as hell going to be a short season for you, Marty,” he growled.

Marty moved across to the landing area, smiling to himself, and slowly pigeon-stepped fifty-six paces at an angle to the right-hand upright. He looked at the landing area, a mound of builder’s sand. The Flop was out of the question. He would scissor-jump, a technique he had often used in warm-up. Jim approached him, pointing behind him to the high jump stands, with cross-bar now set at six feet. “You **sure** this is what you want, Marty?”

Marty nodded. He stood for a moment behind the scratch mark which he had made on the loose, dry cinders. Then he ran forward, at speed. He took off, cleared the bar in a sitting position by at least four inches, landing lightly on his feet. Jim whooped his approval. Pop stood transfixed.

“It’s cool,” said Marty. “Put it up to six four, Jim.”

Jim elevated the crossbar to six feet four inches, and stood at the right-hand upright. Again, Marty ran smoothly at the bar and cleared it by two inches.

"Shee-it," said Pop, open-mouthed.

Marty raised two fingers to Jim.

"Six five?" asked Jim.

Marty nodded. He stood at his mark, breathing lightly. The crossbar had suddenly begun to look high. This height would require a flatter layout, or his butt would hit the crossbar. He attacked it at speed and hit his take off spot perfectly. It was a well-balanced jump, his take-off foot directly beneath his body-weight. As he reached the peak of his flight, Marty dropped back, his body now parallel to the crossbar. His butt touched it lightly, but the bar stayed up and he landed flat on his back in the sandpit. Winded, he lay in the sand, groaning. Jim rushed to him and pulled him to his feet.

"You all right?" he asked.

Pop reached them and looked up at the still quivering crossbar, shaking his head. "Some jump," he said. "Who trained you, the Wright brothers?" He was relieved that only he and Jim had witnessed Marty's jump. It would be important to keep this quiet, for Scranton odds would go down if it got out that there was another goddam superman at Carlisle. "Nothin' broke?" he asked, anxiously.

Marty shook his head, shaking sand from his vest. "Just got to chill out," he said.

"Before you two get too cool," said Pop. "Jim, Dean Mackay wants to see you, pronto, after Marty."

Angus Mackay was surprised that Jim Thorpe had asked to see him in private. Despite the differences in age and status, the relationship between Mackay and Thorpe had always been one of equals, and Jim had never before asked for a private meeting. Mackay had often reflected that, had he confined his bets to the feats of Jim Thorpe, then he would always be ahead of Goldberg, for Jim always stripped big.

Mackay had known that it was Jim because the knock at the door was not a tentative one, rather a decisive thump. He smiled and stood as Jim entered, proffering him his hand. He beckoned Jim to sit in the brown leather chair in front of his desk.

"I'll get straight to the point," said Jim. "It's about Marty."

"Roother? I just saw him."

Jim nodded. "After track practice?"

"That I did, Jim."

"And you canned him."

"The boy was insubordinate, Jim. All college employees have to work to orders. That's the way of the world."

"I'll buy that," said Jim. "But Marty didn't come here to run pro for you. He left his job at the Majestic to be our groundsman."

"You have a point," replied Mackay. "But it's all for his own good, Jim. He'll be a made man. A thousand bucks, more than any Alabama boy could make in a lifetime."

Jim shook his head. "But that's not what Marty wants to do, Dean."

"No, he wants to run for diddly-squat in the Olympics."

"But, like I said, that's what he wants to do, Dean. You gotta respect that."

Mackay shook his head. "No, Jim. That's my final position. Roother runs or he goes."

Jim breathed in deeply. "Then I go too," he said.

"What do you mean?"

"I don't play football or run for Carlisle no more. I can go down to Texas with Marty and break some hosses. Or play pro ball with McGhee and the New York Giants."

"You wouldn't do that to us, Jim. You wouldn't," groaned Mackay.

"Try me," growled Jim.

Angus Mackay looked into Jim Thorpe's firm gaze and knew that his bluff had been called. "I'm between a rock and a hard place here, Jim," he said. "You know I'm a gambling man."

Jim grunted.

"Well, I'm in for over a thousand bucks. To some Chicago boys. Hard men."

"You mean they'll come and break your legs?"

"That'll be the best of it," groaned Mackay.

Jim was silent for a moment. "We got a track meet coming up in June, against Yale," he said.

"So what?"

"Marty comes in with me and we take them on. Together. You get big odds."

"Against who? I mean whom? "

"Yale," replied Jim.

"We've never beaten Yale. But we would only get 2-1 at best. Even if we win, that's not enough. Anyhow, Roother *can't* compete for us, Jim. He's not Indian."

Jim shook his head. "It won't be a straight college match," he said.

"Then what in God's name will it be then?"

"Just Marty and me," replied Jim. "The two of us, behind closed doors, somewhere quiet."

"Just the two of you? Against Yale? Against the whole Yale track team?"

Jim nodded.

"Why not?" he said.

Chapter 8
The Key to Yale

Jim was like some raw hunk of marble, demanding to be shaped. Marty had stood observing him through Pop's field glasses from the verandah of the pavilion for several minutes as Jim, unaware of his presence, worked out with the shot on the marshy grass at the beginning of the home straight, prior to formal daily team practice. For Jim was like a sponge for physical skills. Already Marty noted that he had absorbed and accurately replicated most of what he had told him a week before. In his throwing position, Jim was now staying well back over his right leg, allowing him to deliver a long, powerful impulse to the 16lb implement. Already, the ball was flying out close to 46 feet.

Marty laid down his field glasses and looked out over the crisp green infield and its clear white throwing arcs, at the now precisely-marked black cinder track. He had never thought that he would ever feel pride in manual labour. Now he did. He walked forward on to the track, knelt and picked up some of the track's cinder surface. He released it, but none stayed in his hand. The material was too hard, too dry and the track was consequently bony, lacking in spring. That afternoon, he had gone to Carlisle Carnegie Library, seeking a book on track maintenance. He had been politely but firmly refused entry.

But the assistant librarian had been a Jewish lady, Mrs Lowenstein, and she had shown the same kindness to him as another Carlisle librarian, Miss Mapstone, would do almost a century later. For Mrs Lowenstein had checked the index and had located a book on the subject by an Englishman, Charles

Perry, who had laid the track surfaces for the 1896 and 1908 Olympics. If he returned at six o'clock tomorrow, she would pass the volume to him at the back door. Mrs Lowenstein observed that it was, indeed, cheering to see a Negro boy like him wishing to better himself.

Racism in Carlisle was not quite what Marty had anticipated. True, it showed itself formally in trolleys and libraries and in the kind of work which blacks were allowed to pursue. It lay in Negro posture and language, in the deference with which they spoke, even in the way which a black man walked in the presence of whites. To live as a black, it was best to be silent and invisible.

But behind his mute acceptance lay his knowledge that this experience was temporary, finite. Here he lived in the cocoon of Carlisle. On September 13th, 1912, on his return from the Stockholm Olympics, he would return to his world. There, though the Negro had problems, they were not those of 1912. It was a pity that these men and women, daily walking, heads bowed, in the streets of Carlisle, knew nothing of men like Nelson Mandela, Martin Luther King and Muhammed Ali. He had the certain knowledge of the lives of these men, the dignity and the courage of their existence. They had not, but it would surely have given them strength and hope.

The Indians of Carlisle Industrial School came into a different social category. Closeted in the School from Monday to Friday, male and female students strictly segregated, they were normally only able to go into town on weekends. The Presbyterian formality of Mackay's educational regime and their natural dignity had long since removed all fear of Indians from the population of Carlisle, but they were still treated with some caution. The Indians were transients, destined to return to their barren, arid reservations, or to form the anonymous urban poor of Eastern cities.

Marty knew that he was now living in a privileged bubble, living his life outside the black working community in a sporting world detached from normal life. In some ways, it resembled the life from which he had come, closed, hermetic.

Pop's week away from Carlisle had given him space, swiftly transporting him from groundsman to coach, from things to people. He now saw that it had been inevitable. For the members of the Carlisle track team were raw, innocent, untutored, like children. It would have been a crime for him to have failed to come to their aid. And anyway, Pop was essentially a football coach, his knowledge of track and field limited to the most basic of generalities. Marty had loved every moment of it, and it had surprised him. For he had been cosseted, always on the receiving end of an endless flow of coaching and financial support. He had never in his life offered a word of advice to anyone, never felt the need. Now he was on first name terms with every man on the Carlisle team. He had now become family – and it felt good.

Marty laid down his glasses and walked up the home straight towards Jim who waved acknowledgement as he approached.

"It's going good," said Jim, flipping the shot into the air and catching it.

"Forty-five foot plus. And the circle's wet."

Marty nodded, looking at the pulpy mush of the grass circle from which Jim had thrown. For a moment, he thought of asking if there was yet such a thing as a concrete circle, but he refrained.

"Got something to ask you, after the vault," said Jim, dropping the shot to the wet grass and pointing over to the pole vault landing area. They walked together towards it, to where Jim had rested his bamboo vault pole on the track rail. Marty noted that, like modern poles, it was bound with sticky black electrical tape, though only at the top. The pole was thick and heavy, closed at the bottom with a crude wooden bung.

"Pop, he says he vaulted ten foot with an ash pole, way back in eighteen lickety split," said Jim, smiling and laying his hands on the pole's binding. "But they used to break and some vaulters, they got spiked. No box neither, least not the way Pop tells it. Just stuck the pole in some goddam hole in the ground. The good old days." He placed the pole on the ground in front of him, slipping his bottom hand to his top hand as he simulated the take-off action. "You ever vaulted, Marty?" he asked. "You seem to have done a peck of everything else."

Marty pretended he had not heard Jim's question. "What height you want?" he said, walking up the runway towards the landing area.

"Gimme ten feet, Marty, just for starters," Jim bellowed after him.

Marty lifted the heavy wooden lathe, placed on top of the cracked, weathered wooden stands and slowly creaked them up to ten feet. It looked surprisingly high. Thankfully, the sandpit was no longer of the mining variety and could now, with the extra sand and sawdust which he had added, be justifiably called a landing area. He raised his hand to indicate that all was ready, reflecting as he did so that Jim had given him no instructions on placement of the uprights relative to the take-off box. Jim stormed in, like a medieval knight in a tournament, the bamboo pole high in front of him. His approach-run was three quarters improvisation and one quarter Chaos Theory. Seeing too late that he was much too close to the take-off box, Jim threw in half a dozen stuttering strides, poked the pole into the box and was ripped from the ground. He sailed over on his back, like a sack of potatoes, clearing the crossbar by a foot, and landed on his butt with a thud in the soft sand and sawdust. Marty grimaced and pulled him to his feet. "Didn't see you measure your steps first," he said.

"Never seen the need. Just work it out on the way, natural-like." said Jim, brushing sand and sawdust from his vest. "So whaddya think?"

"It's shit," said Marty.

"That good?" said Jim, grinning all over his nut-brown face.

"So what do we do, coach?"

Marty noted that this was the first time Jim had ever called him 'coach'. He smiled. "Let's first get your steps right, Jim," he said, and for the next twenty minutes, Marty drilled Jim in a seventeen-stride approach run on the track parallel to the vault runway. Jim then vaulted six times, without the distraction of the crossbar. Marty nodded. It was now good, for Jim was now able to plant his pole in balance, hitting his take-off spot accurately. True, when he had left the ground he did not know if he'd land in Pennsylvania or Connecticut, but that was not surprising. He never had and he never would.

"That's it for today," said Marty, after the sixth vault. His coach Vince Harris had always said that it was important for a coach to know when to avoid perfection.

"But I got lots left," protested Jim.

Marty pointed up the hill, to the Carlisle athletes now slowly trickling on to the track. "The others," he said.

Jim nodded. "Got something to tell you," he said. "See you outside Macy's Drug Store at six."

It had taken some time for Marty to locate Macy's. The drugstore lay in a quiet, sequestered backstreet, just below the Industrial School, a small, sweet-smelling pharmacy, with only three wooden stools in front of its soda bar. Jim had not been there when he had arrived outside, so Marty had spent time examining the various nostrums on offer in Macy's. Hofstetter's Bitters, Moxie Nerve Food, Hinkley's Bone Liniment, Vital Sparks (God's Great Gift to Man) and the inevitable Peruna.

He looked up at the clock. Jim was now ten minutes late. Marty entered, moved to the bar and sat down. Leonard Macy, a little man, lean and lined, had observed Marty for some minutes. His face took on a stony look. "Anything I can do for you, boy?"

"A Doctor Pepper," said Marty, seating himself on a stool.

"A Doctor what?" replied Macy sourly.

Marty realised what he had said and paused.

"Do you have an ice cream soda?" he asked.

"Not for you, nigra."

The voice came from behind him, and Marty felt a hand gripping his left shoulder. He turned to see two young men, close behind him. They were steelworkers dressed in stained blue dungarees, kerchiefs round their necks, their faces streaked with grime. He could smell their sweat. Somehow, Marty immediately knew where he was and what was happening, and felt cold fear in the pit of his stomach.

Then he felt a slap on his right cheek. It was not hard, not hard enough, but he knew instinctively what it meant and it triggered his reflexes. His karate instructor had always told him that the first blow should be the last. He turned, his right fist shot out, piston-like, smashing his attacker on his right flush on the nose. He felt the crack of bone, and blood spurted out onto Marty's shirt. The man, groaning, dropped on to one knee, blood spattering to the floor. The other young man stood, frozen. Then he turned and scampered from the shop.

Marty felt sick. Sweating, he turned back to Macy. "It's cool," he said. He was shivering. "No problem."

"No problem at all."

The deep voice came from behind him. Then there was blackness.

Sergeant Block, bulbous and perspiring, walked down the silent row of prison cells, his ring of keys jingling in his plump hands, Pop Warner at his side. "There's not much I wouldn't do for you, Pop, you know that. You taught my boy Marnie to pitch."

"Come on, Cecil, let the nigra out," pleaded Pop.

Block stopped and looked at Pop. "You know, Pop, you're the only man on earth can call me Cecil?"

"That's your name, isn't it?"

"That ain't the point," replied Block. "This Negro boy of yours, Roother, he bust up two white boys."

"Only one," said Pop. "The other one ran. He was fast. Jim clocked him."

"Well, one white boy."

"It was self-defence," said Pop.

"He's white, Pop. And your nigra, he bust his nose," said Block.

"Three tickets for the West Point game if you let him out," said Pop.

"Make it four," said Block. "My mother-in-law, she loves Jim Thorpe."

"Four it is, then," said Pop.

"One other thing. Teach my boy Marnie to hurdle," said Block.

Pop shook his head. "I won't," he said. He pointed into the cell where Marty stood. "But **he** will, Cecil."

"Don't call me Cecil," said Block, smiling. He held up his keys and selected one.

They sat in the bare, Spartan pavilion, Pop, Marty and Jim round the football team table. Behind Pop, the blackboard still bore dim traces of last year's team formations.

"So it was all your idea, Jim?" said Marty.

"Jim said he wouldn't play for me if you were canned," said Pop.

Marty smiled his thanks to Jim. "And what did **you** say, Pop?"

Pop shifted uneasily in his chair. "It wouldn't never have come down to the line, Marty. The Dean's a fair man, he wouldn't never have gone through with it. Just he's got a few problems."

"A thousand of them," grunted Jim.

"OK, I'll buy that for a dollar," said Marty. "So what's the deal?"

"We run against Yale – just you and me," said Jim.

"Just the *two* of us?"

"That's how the Dean gets good odds," said Pop. "Six to one."

"How many events?" asked Marty.

"That's got to be negotiated," replied Pop. "We meet up with Yale next week."

"And have they bought the deal?"

Pop nodded. Just the general idea. Their coach, Mike Delaney, has given it the OK. He's a gambling man. But all of this has to be held behind closed doors. Nothing about this has to get out. Ever."

"Let's get back to the events," said Marty.

"Nine," interrupted Jim.

"And how many men would Yale field?"

"Nine," replied Pop. "One per event."

Marty shook his head. "So Jim and I, we'd be up against fresh men, specialists, in each event?"

Pop nodded. "Pretty much," he said. "Just one against one, in each event. Three points for a win, one for a loss."

"Why the one point?"

"If you have three fouls in, say, a long jump or no clearance in high jump or failed to finish a race you'd get zero. But as long as you record a mark, you get a point."

Marty looked at Jim. "What do you think, Jim? You've run against Yale before."

"They have a couple of fast men over the two dashes," he replied.

"Heffelfinger and a quarter-miler who runs around fifty seconds," said Pop.

"A skinny guy called Walsh who breaks two minutes for half mile and another who makes four and a half minutes for the mile," observed Jim.

"What about the jumps?" asked Marty.

"They have a six foot two man in high jump and a twenty three plus long jumper," replied Jim.

"And throws?"

"A big javelin thrower," said Jim. "Around one-seventy, and a forty-six-plus shot putter."

"So it all depends what events we decide on," said Marty. "But the most important thing will be us getting good rests in between events."

"We haven't sorted out the events yet," said Pop. "Maybe best we have to draw for 'em. Out of a hat."

"The problem is if we draw a half mile or a mile," said Marty. "That kills the legs."

"If we didn't draw, and it was left to a choice, then Yale would be bound to choose at least one endurance event, perhaps two," said Pop. "Sure as hell, they'd pick steeplechase."

"A draw gives us a better chance, Marty," agreed Jim.

"The big thing is to get it tied up tight with those Yale assholes," said Pop. "The rules. Those Ivy League boys would cut your throat and lick the knife."

"So what's the money?" said Marty.

"The money? What money?" responded Pop.

"What's in it for us?" said Jim, picking up Marty's cue.

Pop paused. "A coupla hundred bucks each – how does that sound to you?"

"Sounds great to me," said Jim.

"Four hundred sounds better, Pop," said Marty.

There was a pause while Pop cleared his throat.

"Twice as great," added Jim.

Every member of the Carlisle syndicate had put money on the Carlisle-Yale confrontation. Gilbert, a '*Chronicle*' director Harold Mathias, and a local Freemason Albert Silverstein had taken odds of 5-1 against Jim and Marty. Gilbert had put up $1000 for the impecunious Mackay, but his support had come with a price: should Thorpe and Roother lose, then there would be no expansion of numbers at the Indian Industrial School until after 1920. Mackay had been reluctantly forced to agree.

The event would be held behind closed doors, at a neutral venue. This had been at Yale's insistence. The Yale coach, Mike Delaney could see no public relations triumph in beating an Indian and an unknown Negro with a team of nine men, even if the Indian were Jim Thorpe. And the money that he and his Yale team would lay on themselves with Mackay would be in strictest confidence, to avoid any questions being asked by the Amateur Athletic Union's top suit, James E. Sullivan, based in New York. No matter that Sullivan and his amateur cronies had made small fortunes over the years laying bets on amateur events throughout the Eastern seaboard. No, the Shamrock Sullivan's word was law and he was a man to be treated with caution.

"Who knows about this match?"

That was Yale coach Michael Delaney's first question as they sat across the green baize table in the committee room of the Chattanooga's Adelphi Hotel.

"The Carlisle syndicate," replied Mackay. "Men of impeccable reputation."

"The other members of the Carlisle team?"

Pop shook his head. "None of them know," he said.

"And Thorpe and this nigra Roother are both sworn to strict silence?"

"Yes," said Pop. "You can trust them. You have my word on it."

Delaney raised both hands placatingly. "Sorry I have to ask all these questions, Pop," he said. "It's that horse's ass, Sullivan."

"The AAU bigwig?" said Mackay.

Delaney nodded. "The same," he said. "Sullivan gets a whiff of this and we've all had it."

"Down the tubes," said Pop, using Marty's phrase, ignoring Delaney's look of incomprehension.

"Before we draw," said Delaney, "Are there any issues?"

"Rest between each event," said Pop, abruptly. "How about fifteen minutes between each field event, thirty minutes between each track event?"

"Agreed," said Delaney.

"A referee," said Mackay.

"In case of any disputes?" said Delaney, nodding. He paused, lips pursed. "How about Cardinal Houlihan?" he said. "Ran for Notre Dame back in 1877."

"I remember Seamus Houlihan. Ran close on two minutes for the half mile," said Mackay. He looked at Pop, who nodded agreement. "Couldn't have chosen a better man myself."

Delaney reached down into a briefcase below the table and withdrew a black velvet bag and shook it. "I have eighteen balls here, one for every event." He held up a sheet on the table in front of him. "Each event relates to a numbered ball."

"That sounds fair," said Pop. "Can I have a look at your list first?" Pop scrutinised the sheet and handed it to Mackay. "You've got hammer and hop, step and jump here," he said.

"And three miles and steeplechase and mile walk," said Mackay.

"All standard track and field events," said Delaney. "But we're all sportsmen here. If you have any objection, take out three events. Any three."

"The walk, the three miles and the steeplechase," said Pop. "Take 'em out. Jim and Marty, they would need feeding stations."

"Sportsmanship," said Delaney, nodding "That's what it's all about, Pop. Fair play."

Pop did not reply. Delaney opened the bag, looked into it, and withdrew three balls. "Here we are," he said. "Numbers one, six and eight. Three miles, steeplechase and walk." He shook the bag again. Mackay stretched out his lean, bony hand.

"Could I just check out those balls first?" he asked.

Delaney handed him the bag, and Mackay carefully laid each ball on the table in front of him.

"Should be fifteen here," he growled. "You've got eighteen." He checked the list and looked back at the balls, then at the list. "You've put in half mile, hammer and mile twice." He returned the offending balls to Delaney.

"An oversight," apologised the Yale coach.

"Draw," said Pop, unsmiling.

All of the jumps, except hop, step and jump were drawn, which was good, and two throws, shot and hammer. But the 880-yards and mile had been drawn, the quarter mile hurdles, and only one dash, the 100 yards.

"It's tight as a crab's ass," growled Pop, as they drove back along dusty, rutted roads in his Stanley.

"It would've been a damn sight tighter if we hadn't pulled out those three extra balls," said Mackay. "Yale, too. Aye, it makes you think. Never get into a pissing contest with a skunk."

"We've got near a month to prepare," said Pop.

"Pull Jim out of some of our meets, Pop. Keep him fresh. Same with the Negro," said Mackay.

"You're right, but I got to get Jim and Marty up to speed with hammer," said Pop. "You must know something about it, Dean. You're Scotch."

"Scots," corrected Mackay. "But with us at the Highland Games, it's always been a shafted hammer and a standing throw. With those Irish guys at Yale, it's on a wire and they jump around in a sort of dance, with a couple of turns. That's a horse of an entirely different colour, Pop."

Pop looked straight ahead on the straight, empty road. "We'll ask Roother. He seems to know about everything else," he said. "For all I know, he can throw the dam' hammer into New Jersey."

"Your Booker T. Washington he's an Uncle Tom," observed Marty as they walked hand in hand through the crowds in the darkness, away from the church.

"How you mean?" asked Mary Lou. "Uncle Tom?"

"I mean he thinks that us blacks have to know our place. That all we're good for is manual labour."

"I think Booker T just wants us to be happy." Even as she spoke the words, Mary Lou knew that she did not believe them.

"So why do you read all those books, Mary Lou? What's the point? Books won't help you if all you're ever going to do is cooking and cleaning."

"I don't know," she answered. "I just got to."

"I'll tell you why, Mary Lou," he said. "Because you've got a mind, that's why. And that mind is saying – come on, work me."

She was silent. "Stimulate the phagocytes," she said.

"What did you say?"

"I read it in that there George Bernard Shaw. You gets them phagocytes going to get you healed up when you'se sick. The Doctor's Dilemma."

"Something like that," he said, smiling. "Now don't get me wrong. Your Booker T's a good man. But he's setting the black man's sights too low."

"Like Jim Thorpe was? With his?"

"That's right. But Jim had a good excuse – he didn't know enough and neither did Pop."

She looked at him. "I watched you one day, down at the track," she said. "Coupla days ago, with all them Carlisle boys." Mary Lou stopped and held both his hands, eyeing him. "They was all a-standing there, listening to you like you was some sort of god." She paused. "Marty, how d'you know so much about running and jumping and all them things?" she asked.

"How d'you mean?"

"I mean you know more'n Pop Warner, and he's coach."

He paused. "I'm like you, Mary Lou," he said. "I read a lot."

That night he lay in his bunk in the darkness, head cupped in his hands. He could take Jim forward, he could take Carlisle forward, but that was only technical. He could not advance the others, Mary Lou, Beth, John, Lincoln. For it could not be microwaved, his knowledge of the growth of his race, of its coming to the understanding of its strength and its abilities. Booker T. Washington was a man of dignity and integrity, anyone with half an eye could see that, but he was just plain wrong. Or, perhaps, it was simply that he was right for now, for the moment, that there was no point in trying to swim against the tide. Booker T. was the best product of his time; he was simply doing the best that he could, within the cramped, hostile world of 1911.

Anyhow, he reflected that he had not come back to 1911 to do anything other than to defeat Jim Thorpe, though he had not expected to coach his rival. No, he had not come back to change the world, only to tweak it a little.

"Grass, Pop," observed Marty, standing on a mound above the field. "This is a grass track."

They stood with Jim, Pop and Mackay in the grounds of the Hartford Cricket Club, Connecticut. They walked down on to the surface of the field.

"It was the best that we could do," said Pop. "None of the colleges could guarantee security. Neither could any of the high schools. And this Yale meet has to be kept quiet."

Pop knelt down and poked an index finger into the lush grass surface. "Whatever else they can do, these English cricket guys can keep their mouths shut," he said.

"For the money we're paying them, they can keep their eyes shut as well," said Mackay.

Jim looked out upon the field.

"It's flat," he said, "and firm."

Marty nodded. The grass of the Hartford Cricket Ground was crisp and cropped, as springy as any artificial surface. It already had six clearly marked lanes, its inner edge marked by pegs. The jumps landing pits were immaculate, flat and well dug. Marty bent and placed his hand on the dry turf. He flexed his right arm and put his left hand on it. He would have to push some weights, and soon.

It was like a dungeon. Kevin Flaherty's "gymnasium" was like a dungeon. Not much bigger than the shed in which Marty nightly slept, its darkness was not caused by dirt, rather because each of the great bulbous dumbbells and barbells racked upon its walls was made of black iron, as were those which lay, sullen, upon its concrete floor.

"Don't see many Negro boys down here," Kevin Flaherty's voice was light, almost crooning, and came strangely from a man of such size. For Flaherty was a giant and Marty could see that in his day he must have been impressive. Now, though still thick-muscled, Flaherty sported a paunch that was imperfectly contained by a broad black leather belt. Red-haired and freckled, he looked to be in his mid-forties, dressed incongruously in black vest and wrestling tights and wearing worn Roman sandals. On the wall, where there were no dumbbells or barbells, there were dim photographs and tattered vaudeville posters.

'Kevin Flaherty, the Irish Hercules, the Belasco Theatre, New York, 1888' said one poster showing a leaner, younger Flaherty holding aloft in one hand a barbell marked '300lbs' in white paint. Another poster from The Olympic, Philadelphia in 1895 showed him supporting on the soles of his feet a platform on which played a five piece orchestra. Yet another showed Flaherty, dressed in leopard skins and Roman sandals, juggling with 56lb weights.

"So who sent ya?"

"Saw your advertisement over in Mulligan's, Mr Flaherty," replied Marty.

"A quarter per session," said Flaherty, putting out a great paw-like hand. "Ten cents more for private tuition."

Marty fumbled in his trouser pocket and withdrew a quarter. He handed it to Flaherty. "Here's the quarter, Mr Flaherty," he said. "I've lifted weights before, so no tuition, thank you kindly." Marty started his limbering up routine by circling his arms.

"What's all that about?" asked Flaherty.

"Just loosening up," explained Marty. "For the session."

"Let's have no more of that dam' fool nonsense," growled Flaherty. "Get yourself under that weight." He pushed Marty back on to a bench. On a rack above it, lay a weight that looked to Marty to be around two hundred pounds. "I got me some of 'em new-fangled disc weights," said Flaherty, moving to withdraw some discs.

"No, Mr Flaherty," said Marty. "Leave 'em on."

"This is two hundred and twenty pounds," observed Flaherty.

Marty nodded and settled under the weight. He put both hands evenly on the bar and took it at full stretch off the stands. He lowered it to his chest, pressed it easily fifteen times and sat up. Flaherty looked at him, stupefied.

For the next hour, Flaherty took him round the tiny gymnasium, testing him in each exercise. In the end, it was more like circuit training than weight training, but for Marty it was exactly what he needed, an all-round toning of the muscles. By the end of the hour, he was drenched in sweat and Flaherty sat in the corner of the gymnasium, observing him approvingly.

"Never seen a nigra boy work out like you," he said. "Watch this." He rolled a massive, bulbous black barbell out on to the centre of the floor. To Marty it looked close to 250 pounds. Flaherty lifted the barbell on to its end, so that it now stood vertically, and leant it on his right shoulder. Then he put his right hand at the centre of the barbell's shaft and levered the weight on to his right shoulder. Slowly, painfully he lowered his bodyweight under the bar, his right arm straightening out as he did so. Finally, his right arm was straight and Flaherty stood erect, sweat dripping his freckled face, holding the barbell aloft. "There, bent press, me boyo, try that," he said, lowering the barbell to the ground with two hands.

Marty put the barbell on its end and placing it against his right shoulder took it in his right hand, as Flaherty had done. He leant down and tried to bend under it. It would not budge. He groaned. "God," he said.

"Don't ask God for help," said Flaherty. "God's no good. God's a rascal."

Marty lowered the barbell to the ground, shaking his head.

"Ye're a strong boy," said Flaherty. "But ye don't have the knack." He pointed Marty towards the tiny kitchen adjacent to the gymnasium, and Marty followed him into it. Flaherty reached up to a cupboard, took down a half-empty bottle of Blackbush Irish whiskey, uncorked it and took a long pull. He proffered it to Marty, who shook his head. "So what is it ye'll be after?" he asked. He pointed to a corner to his left, where there was a shower which consisted of what appeared to be a rusty, punctured can, from which issued intermittent drips. "A shower or a slunge?"

Marty looked uncertainly at the shower. "I think I'll try the slunge," he said.

Flaherty beckoned him to strip off and place both hands on the edge of the kitchen sink. He reached down into a bucket of cold water and withdrew a dripping sponge. First he thrust the sponge into Marty's face then, refreshing it in the bucket, applied it to his back. Finally he plunged the freezing sponge between Marty's legs. Marty yelped and Flaherty handed him a rough, tattered white towel.

"That's the slunge," he said.

Chapter 9
The Contest

"Jake, he tells me you was back home near midnight. Been up Connecticut way, he says."

They stood, hand in hand, at the edge of the Negro swimming hole, in the woods at the edge of town. It was close to dusk and mayflies skipped across its dark, limpid waters, dimpling its surface. Marty was silent for a moment. "Business," he said.

"So what kind of business you got, up Connecticut ways?"

"Way," he corrected her. "Track and field business."

Mary Lou pulled her hand away and walked from him. She stood silent, her back to him, at the grassy edge of the swimming hole. A stork flew across its still surface, dipped and, scooping a fish from its dark waters, flew high out over the forest. "You got yourself a lady up there, like the Dean got in town?"

"The Dean. What's Mr Mackay got to do with it?"

"Your Mr Mackay, he got a young black lady, by name of Missie Brown, down town. Light-coloured, same as you. I hears the Dean comes by once a week, just like clockwork."

"Perhaps he does – but Hartford, that's one helluva way to go for any woman," he said.

She turned to face him. "Hartford? You went all de way to Hartford?"

"Look," he said. "You're getting to be a very pushy young lady. Godammit, we haven't kissed but twice yet."

"Three times," she said, holding up three fingers.

"Come on, be fair. The first time was on the cheek. That doesn't count."

"OK," she said. "Twice."

"And nothing proper," he said. "Or rather improper."

She moved to him and put both hands on his shoulders, looking directly into his eyes. Now he could smell the strange sweetness of her breath, the light, musky odour of her skin. "Improper? What's dat?"

"What's that," he reproved her. "Not dat."

Her lips brushed his right cheek. "So what's improper?"

"Kissing more easy," he said. "More, more open like. The way I tried that night when you slapped me."

"And if I does it more easy like you say, will you tell me all about Hartford?"

"No," he said firmly, feeling his voice break. "I can't, Mary Lou. It's, it's all confidential."

Her lips continued to brush his cheek and lingered on the corner of his mouth.

"I'se confidential," she said, "I kin be as confidential as you likes." She took her hands from his shoulders and put her right hand on the nape of his neck and pulled him to her. Her mouth, slightly open, was soft and creamy. Marty's head now felt light and he pulled her to him, feeling again, the firmness, the tone of her slim body. She gently pushed him back, her breathing now deep. "So what zactly was you a-doing-up Hartford way?"

Marty gulped and shook his head. "A man's got to have some secrets, Mary Lou. I can't tell you."

"What if I gets more confidential?"

"That's blackmail. You know that."

"Ain't no federal law against it, not far as I knows. Not when it's a boy and his girl."

He smiled. "So now you're my girl."

"Sure looks that way to me," she said. "I ain't never kissed nobody like I just done you. Never ever felt the need. So stands to reason you must be my man."

Marty looked at her. He felt as if he were back at high school on his first date. For here he was at the swimming hole, trading kisses, like some fevered adolescent. Hell, he had gone further in his first fumbles at the back of the school gymnasium, twelve years back. Yet, strangely, he was enjoying it. "OK," he said. "So what do you want to know?"

"Same as before. What you was – were – doing up Hartford way?"

"You promise not to tell a living soul?"

"Cross my heart and hope to die." She reached up and kissed him again, her soft tongue travelling deep into his mouth.

Marty felt weak. Gasping, he pushed her away. "You certain you've never done this before?" he said.

She drew her right hand across her heart. "Like I says, hope to die," she said.

He shook his head to clear it, then pulled her down to sit beneath a tree.

"Jim and I," he said. "We're running in a track meet."

"Just the two of you, you and Jim?"

"Against Yale."

She placed her hand lightly on top of his. "Then that's all right then," she said.

"But, Mary Lou, it's going to be the *two* of us against the whole Yale team, in nine events."

"But you got Jim Thorpe," she said.

He looked at her and smiled, mock-wearily. "I know," he said, "And Jim, he can jump houses."

"I boobed," groaned Pop, staring gloomily at the sheet of events in front of him.

"*We* boobed," grunted Mackay. "We should have taken out hammer."

The two men sat with Marty and Jim around the table in the deserted pavilion as outside the Carlisle athletes ended their track workout and made their way uphill to college.

"No, Dean," said Marty firmly. "You did the right thing. You got them to take out the mile walk, the three miles and the steeplechase. Jim and I couldn't have won any of those anyway, and they would have killed our legs."

"Besides," said Jim, "the hammer's the second last event. We might have it all tied up by then."

"There speaks a confident man," observed Mackay wryly. "So, let's just look at this schedule they've given us. First event, hundred yards. Marty, that's your bag."

He looked down at the programme. "Pole vault. Any takers?"

Marty nodded. "I'll take that too," he said.

Jim looked querulously at him. "Thought you told me you'd never vaulted."

"No, Jim. I never ever said that," replied Marty.

"Yes, you did."

"When you girlies have finished your little spat, we'll move on," said Pop, tartly. "Half mile. Who's up for two laps?"

Marty looked across the table at Jim, who shook his head. "I'd need feeding stations," said Jim.

"Let's look at this, gentlemen," said Pop. "We have two endurance events, half mile and mile. Jim's outside range is a quarter mile, so he should tackle the shorter distance, the half mile. Might even take it in a sprint finish." He looked at Marty. "So, it looks like the mile for you, Marty."

"Okay, I'll take on the mile," said Marty.

"I've never seen any nig…I've never seen you as a distance man," said Mackay.

"You mean nigra, don't you, Dean?" said Marty.

Mackay was silent.

"The problem is that the rules don't allow us to just jog around," said Marty. "We get lapped, then we lose a point. So that's going to take a lot of starch out of my legs." He took a deep breath. "I reckon I can run close to four and a half minutes for a mile. I might take full points there."

"Four and a half minutes," said Pop. "That's good running for a…"

"For a black man?" said Marty, smiling.

"For anybody," said Mackay. "So you take the mile."

"High jump, Jim," said Pop.

"Long jump, Jim," said Mackay.

"Looks like that leaves me with shot put and Marty with the quarter mile hurdles," said Jim.

"No, not quite," replied Pop. "Marty takes the shot. Hammer, that's got to be yours, Jim.

"But I've never thrown a hammer in my life," protested Jim. "Horseshoes, yes, hammer no."

"No problem, Jim," said Pop. "Just got to cream some skinny young Yale boy. Swing the goddam thing a coupla of times round your head and let it go. Nothing to it, Jim. Piece of pie!"

Jim looked across at Marty and smiled wryly. Pop, unaware of the exchange of glances, exhaled slowly, and sucked his pencil for a moment. "So we got a coupla weeks," he said. "Let's get ourselves a game plan. First, drying out."

Jim groaned audibly.

"Drying what?" said Marty.

"Drying out," repeated Pop, as if talking to a child. "It's modern science. The McLaren method. No liquids, get the weight down. Like I do each fall with the football team."

"Hell on earth," groaned Jim. "Last year, I got so dry, I ended up sticking my head down the john."

"And I saw you, and lapped you until I got you dried out proper," said Pop.

"No," said Marty, firmly. "No drying out, this time out. It's going to be hard enough for us without that."

Pop said nothing, but glowered.

"And what about Black Jack?" asked Mackay.

"And what in the name of God is Black Jack?" asked Marty.

"A laxative," repeated Mackay. "The night before. Cleans out the bowels."

"That's right, Marty, gets the bodyweight down," said Pop, nodding.

"Takes all the toxics out of the guts," explained Mackay. "Every Scots ped takes his Black Jack, the night before a big race."

"I think we can safely leave our bowels to their own devices," said Marty.

"I go with Marty there," said Jim. "I spent a full two hours on the john last year before the Harvard game."

Pop shook his head wearily. "Okay, suit yourselves," he said. "But it all goes against sports science as I know it."

Mackay looked at Pop and then at Marty. "So what do you propose, Roother?"

"Getting Jim up to speed with hammer, just so that he doesn't foul out, and get no points. Me, I have to work out on vault and quarter hurdles. I've never run over quarter hurdles, and you have to get your steps right. And getting Jim's steps right in high jump and long jump."

"What about stamina?" asked Pop.

Marty shook his head. "Too late for that," he said. "Only tire ourselves out."

"Women," said Mackay suddenly. "What about women?"

Pop nodded. "Women weaken legs," he said. "It's a known fact."

"So no women, not till it's over," said Mackay. "We've all got a lot riding on this. Agreed?"

Marty looked at Jim. Both men nodded. "While we're on the subject of women…" said Marty.

"Yes?" said Pop.

"I want my girl to come."

"What girl?"

"Mary Lou Barrow," said Marty.

Pop, his face stern, looked at Mackay, then back at Marty.

"This Mary Lou girl…will she keep her trap shut?"

Marty nodded. "You have my word on it," he said.

"Then your Mary Lou can come along for the ride," said Pop. "We can squeeze her into the back of the Stanley."

"Probably the first time that lass has ever been in a car," observed Mackay.

"One other thing," said Pop. "What about food?"

"Plenty of pasta," said Marty.

"Wop food?" cried Pop in astonishment.

"Pasta?" said Mackay. "I would have thought that red meat was the thing. Build up muscle."

"Pasta," repeated Marty.

Pop shook his head in resignation. "That all right with you, Jim?" he asked.

Jim turned to face Pop and the Dean "I only got one rule on food, Pop," he said. "I never try to eat more than I can lift."

"Cricket," said Jim, shaking his head.

They sat at midday in the cool, silent shadows of the stand at Hartford cricket ground. Below them lay a sunlit grass field, crisp, manicured with its precisely pegged grass track and soft, immaculate sand pits.

"Saw some English boys playing cricket once, up at Harvard." Jim paused and chewed on a blade of grass. "Them English pitchers. Kept rubbing themselves. All day. Never stopped."

"Rubbing themselves? Where?" asked Pop.

Jim looked sideways at Mary Lou, paused, then looked at Pop. "You know where," he said.

"They're probably putting a polish on the ball. Though you can never be sure with those English," said Mackay. "Public schools."

Pop stood, stretched and pointed down to the track. "So what d'you think?"

Marty nodded in approval. "Looks cool," he said. "But then, I've never run on grass." He looked to his side, at Mary Lou. Even during the long journey to Hartford in the Stanley, she had acted as if she drove around in a car every day of her life. Now that she was here, she acted as if she was completely at home.

"Thought grass would be home away from home for a Southern boy like you, Marty," said Pop. "Not many cinder tracks down there in Alabama, not to my recollection."

Marty made no reply. Below, on the left, at the entry gate, the Yale team were slowly filing in under the stand, led by Delaney and a lean, stooped man about 6'4" in height. Mackay recognised him immediately. It was a senior Yale lecturer, Dr Halsey. Mackay looked at Pop and shook his head. Halsey was not renowned for an interest in sports.

Even at this distance, Marty noted that the Yale team, dressed in striped Yale blazers and grey flannels, looked much bigger than the students back at Carlisle. He picked out at least two who looked to be at least 220 pounds, and who looked much too old to be students. Delaney and Halsey watched their team make their way down into the dressing rooms below, and walk along the front of the stands, up the wooden steps towards them. Delaney shook Pop and Mackay by the hand, ignoring Jim, Marty and Mary Lou.

"Doctor Halsey, Senior lecturer at Yale. Pop Warner and Dean Mackay."

The men shook hands.

Pop intervened.

"And this is Jim Thorpe and Marty Roother," he said.

Halsey nodded curtly, but did not proffer his hand to either athlete. Delaney and Halsey sat in the row beside Pop and Mackay. Delaney checked his fob watch.

"Cardinal Houlihan," he said, "he'll be here in ten minutes. Coming up by rail from New York. Bringing some of the priests from St Aloysius with him to act as judges, so it's all right and proper. So it looks like we can get started prompt at two."

Pop nodded to Jim and Marty, who made their way down the steps to the dressing rooms.

"Never thought you had much interest in track, Dr Halsey," said Mackay.

Halsey slowly withdrew his pince nez from his bony, liver-spotted nose and withdrew a silk handkerchief from an inner pocket of his black jacket. He breathed on his glasses and polished them. “You are correct, Mr Mackay,” he said. ‘I have no interest of any sort in athletics. But this competition has a particular fascination for me, as a student of ethnic characteristics. You may remember my work on the comparison of the Anglo Saxon race with those of…other racial derivation.”

Mackay nodded. “The Darwinism of race,” he said. “Intelligence, criminal characteristics, physical capacity. I’ve read it. It’s the definitive work.”

“Thank you, Mr Mackay,” said Halsey. He replaced his pince nez. “The research was originally funded by the Englishman, Cecil Rhodes, and when he died, by his Anglo-Saxon League. Twelve years of study, measuring every factor from manual dexterity to bone length and cranial configuration. Everything that could be measured in an objective manner.”

“Including, as I remember it, athletic performance,” said Pop.

“Yes,” said Halsey. “Though I must confess that it was difficult to find other than those of Anglo-Saxon extraction in the official record books.”

“Well, Jim’s three quarter Crow and this boy Roother, he’s pure nigra,” said Pop. “But I got to tell you Doctor Halsey, we didn’t put our sawbucks on them and come up here to throw our money away.”

“Your Thorpe and Roother may of course be the exceptions who prove the rule,” said Halsey. “But my Mr Delaney here says this is the strongest team ever fielded by Yale.”

“They’ll have to be.” It was Mary Lou. She rose, moved down a couple of steps to face Halsey. “I never did get to read your book, Doctor Halsey,” she said. “But let me tell you one thing. This fine day, Jim and Marty are going to whup your Anglo Saxon boys and whup ’em real good. So just you go put *that* in your next book.” She turned and scampered away from them down the steps. Halsey made no response but stared after her, adjusting his pince nez.

"That big galoot down there, what the hell kind of degree is he taking?" asked Pop, pointing down to one of the Yale team now sitting on a bench below them at track side. The Yale athlete, beefy and thick-waisted, looked to be in his late twenties, and more than 230 pounds.

"He's not a person, he's a place," growled Mackay.

Delaney's face had now adopted a distant expression. "Name of Flanagan," he replied. "Taking a diploma with us in physical education."

Pop withdrew from his briefcase a pair of binoculars and peered through them. "I know him," he said. "I've got his number. Saw him last year at the AAU's at Travis Island. Come off it, Mike, your man Flanagan, he's no student. He's a 28-year-old, and he's a sergeant in the New York police."

"Change of career," said Delaney.

"Three hundred and sixty degree change if you ask me," said Pop, replacing his binoculars. "Last year he threw the hammer hundred and sixty odd feet."

"And what about that beauty over there?" said Mackay, pointing to a burly, freckle-faced young man circling his shoulders to loosen off as he came up from the dressing room to join his colleagues on the bench.

"That, that's Sean Casey," replied Delaney.

"I know," groaned Pop. "He put the shot near forty-nine feet last year. He's a fireman from Chicago. What's he majoring in? Thermodynamics?"

"No, but you're close," said Delaney. "Another member of our physical education faculty. The department is developing rapidly."

"Aye," said Mackay. "From zero to two since we first made our bet. And both of 'em throwing from here to Killarney."

Pop beckoned Mackay away and they walked down the steps of the stand, followed by Mary Lou. "Dean, we've been well and truly buncoed here," he said. He pointed down to a lean angular young man speaking to Casey and Flanagan. "That there's Con Keyhoe, the Irish high jump champion. Those bastards must have wired him and got him across the pond. Jumps around six five."

"This isn't Yale we've got here," said Mackay. "Jim and Roother are up against the whole world, Pop." He shook his head. "Specialists in each event, some of them the best in the business. God knows who else they're hiding down there. For all I know, they've got Hackenschmidt and Sandow."

Pop pointed down to the sunlit infield, where Cardinal Houlihan, dressed in full vestments, his priests on either side of him, sat at wooden tables, checking stopwatches and measuring tapes.

"Too late," said Mackay. "It's too damn late, and they're all signed up as students, you can bet on that. Anyhow, if we protested, all these Yale ringers seem to have shamrocks on their jockstraps and Cardinal Houlihan,' he's a Kerry man." He sighed. "Any point telling all this to Jim and Roother?"

"No," said Pop firmly. "Best they shouldn't know. Won't do their spirits any good." He pointed down to the track. "Look, they're setting up for the hundred yard dash."

Below them, to the left, Marty was stretching, just behind the starting line, for the hundred yards. Pop and Mackay could see the Yale runner, Charles van Heffelfinger, confidently prancing on the spot at his side. The runners were called to their marks by Father McGraw, a pimpled, bespectacled young priest.

"Look at those shorts," said Mackay, pointing to Marty. For Marty was wearing shorts at least six inches briefer than those worn by his adversary. "It's not decent."

"So what?" growled Pop. "This ain't no fashion show."

The two runners settled, then their hips rose into the 'set' position at the end of two stringed four foot wide lanes. The gun cracked, releasing them. It was not a race. At twenty yards, Marty had surged into a two yard lead and he ripped away from van Heffelfinger, left wallowing in his wake. At the tape, he was four yards up and easing.

Pop examined his watch. “Jesus God!” he said. “I’ve got Marty at 9.6!”

“Same on mine,” said Mackay. “Your nigra, he’s like shit off a shovel.” He looked behind him at Delaney and Dr Harley. “How do you like them apples?” he said to no one in particular.

Delaney, speechless, looked again, at his watch, then back at the immobile Halsey. His face, lined like a child’s sandpit after rain, was impassive.

“Let’s us get ourselves down to the vault, get Marty’s steps right,” said Pop, grinning.

Marty, sweat running down his face, reached the bench and sat with Jim at the end of the vault runway. He shook Jim’s hand, and reaching into his bag, gave him a brown leather measuring tape. They walked together towards the vaulting pit. The vaulting area was off-set, parallel to the track, in a rectangular, fenced off paddock. Marty re-examined the vaulting box. It was well set in the dry, springy grass but the landing area sand, though ample and well dug, was only level with the ground. Jim laid the end of the tape at the edge of the box, and Marty pulled it back down the runway, and drove a peg into the dry grass at one hundred and ten feet, a fifteen-stride approach. He ventured a glance down the runway at Mary Lou, standing with Pop and Mackay at the outer fence, almost in line with the landing area. She smiled and raised a right hand in recognition. Marty nodded. He looked at his opponent, Leo Paffenberger. A genuine Yale student, Paffenberger was a lean, bespectacled young man with freckles and a shock of spiky red hair. Marty had watched the Yale man swing easily over ten feet in a practice vault. Paffenberger was not fast, but he was neat on the pole and technically excellent in flight. He had looked to be close on two feet clear.

Marty picked up his pole and examined it. This was not going to be easy. Vaulting with a stiff, heavy bamboo pole into a sandpit was a far cry from swinging on a light, flexible glass fibre pole into a bed of springy foam. To begin with, the bamboo pole was close to twice the weight of the fibreglass implement. This inevitably meant aslower approach run. The bamboo pole's stiffness meant that his top hand was now at 11″6″, a full two feet plus down on his fibreglass handhold. And in training he had experienced difficulty in remembering to shift his left, lower hand up to his right at take-off, because with fibreglass his left hand had always remained fixed. And though the fundamental principles of bamboo and fibreglass vaulting were no different, bamboo vaulting was less forgiving and allowed for no errors at take-off. Too close at take-off and the vaulter was swept off the ground, too far away and his arms were almost ripped out of their sockets. It was going to be tough.

At the right hand side of the landing area, Cardinal Houlihan, an ascetic, white-haired man in his mid-fifties, took his place in a deck chair underneath a canvas awning, shielding him from the hard heat of the sun. His priests pushed the crossbar up to ten foot six inches, Marty's warm-up height, and the plain wooden crossbar wobbled for a moment. Marty stood, right foot in line with his take-off peg and lifted the bamboo pole in front of him to his right, till its point was at head height. He could see Jim at the left hand side of the take-off box, waiting to catch his pole after take-off. "1911, here we come," he said under his breath, and surged down the runway. He hit his take-off spot perfectly, stayed behind the pole, swung, turned and landed in the pit on two feet. It was an easy clearance.

Jim grinned all over his big open face as he caught the pole. "Miles to spare," he said. "What height you coming in at?"

"Eleven foot," replied Marty. "Just to make sure of a point." He looked to his right and saw that Mary Lou was beckoning to him.

She drew him close. "That Yale boy," she whispered, pointing at a young Yale athlete standing with Paffenberger, "He just moved your marker up a couple of yards."

Marty nodded, frowning. He secured his measuring tape and with Jim he re-measured his approach run, pegging it and marking it with a handful of sand for good measure. He looked around for the Yale athlete. He was now nowhere to be seen.

Marty walked back down the runway with Jim. “Keep your eyes peeled, Jim,” he said. “These Yale boys, they’re playing dirty pool.”

“Business as usual then,” said Jim, grinning.

Marty cleared the opening height of 11 foot easily, as did Paffenberger. The crossbar was raised to ’11′6″ which Marty declined, leaving it to his opponent. Frowning, Pop strolled up the outside of the fence which separated them. “Why’d you miss out?” he asked.

“Saving my legs, Pop,” said Marty. “It’s going to be one helluva long day.”

Pop was not convinced. He walked back to Mackay, shaking his head. Marty walked down the side of the fence and beckoned to Mary Lou. “Mary Lou,” he said, “when Pop’s cooled down, could you ask him for his umbrella from the back of the car? And water, a big jug of water.”

Paffenberger cleared 11′6″’ easily, and the bar was moved up six inches to 12″. Marty shook his head. “I’ll wait for the 12′6″’, father,” he said to the young priest standing alongside the landing area.

He looked at Paffenberger. The young vaulter was clearly troubled by Marty’s tactics. “I’ll take the same,” he said. “Twelve-six.”

Cardinal Houlihan, the sweat now dripping down his lean, lined face, looked over his shoulder at Delaney and Harley standing at the fence. “Looks like you’ve got a battle royal on your hands, me boys,” he said. Harley forced a thin smile in response.

Mary Lou approached Marty, carrying a jug of water and a rolled black umbrella. Marty nodded his thanks. He opened up the umbrella and placed it on the ground, then took the jug and gulped down some of its contents. “Take this to Jim,” he said. “He’s on next in the half mile. Make sure he has a couple of good slugs.” Mary Lou nodded and trotted back to Jim. Marty lay down on the dry grass, under the protective shadow of the umbrella.

Cardinal Houlihan picked up the tin megaphone at his left side. “The crossbar is now at twelve foot six inches,” he bellowed. “First jumper, Roother, Carlisle.”

Marty stood and went to his marker. The thick wooden crossbar now looked surprisingly high. He had regularly cleared over a metre higher, but not on grass in 1911 with a bamboo pole that weighed a ton. He lifted his pole in front of him and raised it to the vertical. Words ran through his head. “Drive into the box and high hands at take off.” The muscle images were fixed in his mind. Marty stormed down the springy grass runway and drove the pole in front of him into the box. At take-off, he was perfectly behind the pole, his hands high. The pole quivered as it took the force of his approach run and bent slightly. Marty soared. He could see the bar well below him as he pushed off. His clearance was over a foot over the crossbar as he pushed the pole back.

“Jesus Christ,” gasped Pop. “Jesus H Christ.”

If Houlihan had heard Pop’s blasphemy, he chose to ignore it. He had spent much of his Notre Dame student life on the running track, but never had he witnessed anything remotely like this. For the Negro Roother had just run nine point six and now he had vaulted just a few inches short of a world record, with plenty to spare. He withdrew a white silk handkerchief from an inner pocket and wiped his hot, sweating face, looking down the runway at Paffenberger. Cardinal Kevin Houlihan knew his track and field, and he saw that the Yale vaulter was now gone. Trembling, eyes glazed, he stood at the end of the runway. He had cleared 12’6” more than once in training, but the vaulting of the Negro boy had unnerved him. He strode up the runway, but he had no strength, no conviction at take-off and he failed to leave the ground.

“He’s done,” said Pop, both hands on Mackay’s shoulders. “We’ve got him, Dean, we’ve got him by the…”

“I get your drift,” interrupted Mackay dryly.

The two men watched as Paffenberger fouled out on his next two attempts.

He called across to Jim. “You ready for the half mile, Jim? Got your game plan, man?”

Jim took another gulp of water, and passed the jug to Mary Lou. He nodded. Behind him, the broken Paffenberger had declined his two final attempts. The Carlisle team were now two events to zero up. Jim walked across to Marty, smiling, both thumbs up and shook his hand.

“Focus in,” said Marty, sharply.

“How d’you mean?”

“I mean switch on,” said Marty. “We can put these Yale boys away for good if you can just take the half mile. Get inside their heads.” He paused. “So listen, Jim,” he said. “Listen up good.” Marty’s game plan was simple. Jim was to secure an immediate lead and slow the race down, keep the pace slow and kick late. Make it something closer to a dash. This would not only win the race but it would also save Jim’s legs for the power events to follow. A fast overall pace would destroy Jim and take all the speed out of his legs. It would therefore have to be avoided at all costs.

Cardinal Houlihan, sitting in the shade of a canvas cupola infield of the starting line, called Jim and the Yale man, Alan Tyndall, to their marks. From the stands, Pop scrutinised Tyndall, a lean, long-legged young man wearing brown, crocodile-skin running shoes.

“A pair of legs with a head on top,” he growled to Wildstein. At his side, Marty pulled on his slacks, buttoned up the fly and reached down for the jug of water. He gulped some down.

“All that water,” said Mackay. “It’s not healthy. I’ve given Jim the real thing.”

Alarm bells began to ring in Marty’s head. “*What* real thing?” he asked.

“Sherry and eggs,” replied Pop.

"Whipped up good," said Mackay. He looked down at Wildstein. "All strictly legal."

"Standard practice," agreed Pop.

"God in heaven," groaned Marty, cupping his head in his hands.

"Gentlemen, get to your marks."

Jim and Tyndall toed the starting line, with Jim on the inside.

"Get set."

The gun exploded and Jim took an immediate lead into the first bend, staying slightly wide as Marty had told him, blocking Tyndall. Then he slowed down, forcing Tyndall to check his speed. Marty grinned to himself. It was slow. It was good. Entering the back straight, Tyndall tried to pass. Jim, again, moved out, his broad shoulders blocking Tyndall, and then slowed down again. The two runners reached the furlong mark and Marty checked Pop's stopwatch. A slow thirty-three seconds. Jim was running perfectly to plan. Into the next curve, Tyndall, aware of the slowness of the pace, again attempted to pass, but Jim again accelerated and moved out.

"Foul," bellowed Delaney, but Cardinal Houlihan ignored him.

"Good, Jim," said Marty, under his breath.

But Tyndall was not to be denied. As they moved into the home straight, he moved out and kicked, suddenly putting six yards between himself and Jim as they completed the first lap. Tyndall heard the bell for the final lap and Marty again checked Pop's flickering stopwatch. Sixty-two seconds. Slow enough. It was still going to plan.

"Pull him in slow, Jim," he bellowed as Jim, still six yards back, moved into the penultimate curve. The sweat was now streaming down his nut-brown face and his breathing was now heavier. Marty looked across at Mackay. Sherry and eggs. What an asshole! Then he looked at Mary Lou. Her gaze was locked in to the race, as in a trance.

Coming into the back straight, Jim began to feel heavy, dropping back on to his heels in the soft grass. He had picked up speed, but Tyndall seemed to be no closer. This was not Jim's territory, the world of endurance and he could now feel the rasp of his own breathing. He fixed his eyes on Tyndall's freckled back, and again accelerated.

"Jim's getting to him," said Mary Lou excitedly, as the two men hit the final furlong at the end of the back straight. Marty checked Pop's stopwatch and nodded a little uneasily. Jim was on schedule, with a 28-second third furlong, but Tyndall was still running smoothly and with ominous strength. Halfway down the final curve, now four yards down, Jim kicked. His running was clumsy, but his sheer animal power took him on to Tyndall's right shoulder.

"Jim's *got* him," shouted Pop.

But as they came into the home straight level, Jim's lungs were raw, the air ripping them like sandpaper. He was hurting, bow-legged, as he passed Tyndall, who watched Jim pass and slipped easily behind him as they hit the home straight. Then, his leg cadence suddenly rising, he kicked again, moving into another gear. He took an immediate three yard lead, leaving Jim gasping, flat-footed, struggling behind him. This time there was no response from Jim. Tyndall raised his arms in triumph as he hit the tape, to be enveloped by Delaney and his Yale teammates. The time was two minutes two seconds, with Jim ten yards back. Jim stumbled across the line, down on to his knees. He vomited on to the grass. Marty was first to reach him. He levered Jim to his feet and pointed to the vomit on the grass. "Sherry and eggs," he hissed at Pop, as the Yale team chaired Tyndall from the field.

Cardinal Houlihan looked down at the Indian, who had dropped back on to the grass, the Negro above him. It was all over. He had seen many an athletic competition in his time, and he knew when a man was gone. It had been bad luck. Bad luck that an endurance event had been drawn early, but it had surely been God's will, for he had drawn the event-order himself.

Houlihan checked his watch. The Indian, Thorpe, was on next, in thirty minutes, in high jump against the spring-heeled Cork man, Keyhoe. He shook his head. Thorpe would not be able to clear his throat, never mind a high jump crossbar placed at an opening height of five foot six. The Carlisle people were now dragging him off into the stands, but there could be no second coming for the Indian. Thorpe was a busted flush.

Marty felt a great paw upon his shoulder. He looked round. It was Flaherty. The red-haired giant towered over the little group in the stand clustered around Jim, who was still breathing hard. Marty looked round. "Kevin," he said, "Could you rub Jim down? Just his legs. Leave the rest. Get the crap out."

Flaherty nodded. "Let's get him down into the dressing rooms." He lifted Jim like a baby and, followed by Marty, Mackay and Pop, made his way down into the darkness beneath the stand. There, Keyhoe placed Jim on a massage table in the Carlisle dressing room.

"Get his legs elevated," ordered Marty, "and, Kevin, get those magic hands of yours working."

Mackay checked his watch. "We've only got about thirty minutes before the high jump," he said. "And you've got 440 yards hurdles first." He looked down at Jim, and shook his head. Thorpe looked to be finished.

"Keep working those legs," said Marty. "And get some water into him. And for God's sake try to get Pop to slow things up, stretch that half an hour. Whatever it takes."

Marty stood at his mark in the baking heat. On his left, on his inside, was Daryl Baker, the Yale runner, the 1910 NCAAA Champion. Thick-set and powerful, Baker looked more like a thrower than a hurdler. Shaking his head, he declined Marty's offer of a handshake and went to his mark. Marty took a deep breath, and looked out on the curve at the first three-foot barrier. He had practiced over the first five barriers back at Carlisle, but never in his life had he raced over the one lap hurdles. Fifteen strides between hurdles, all the way, smooth and fluid.

"Get to your marks."

Marty put the dreams into his head. Positive images. He walked slowly forward to his mark.

Fluid to the first hurdle, no checking, no reaching. Stay loose. Pick up the hurdles early and stay loose. He got down on to one knee and placed his hands behind the line.

"'Get set."

The report of the gun released him, not into an explosive sprint-type start, but into a fluid, rangy movement, from his starting holes. Marty poured round the first bend and sighted the first hurdle early, making the fine, subtle movements which would take him in balance into the barrier. He took the first hurdle as if it had been placed there for his legs alone. Not with the driving, explosive action of a sprint hurdler, but with a simple, snappy up-down action of his lead leg.

"Got it," he said aloud.

The second to fifth hurdles came easy, but as he came to the sixth at the final curve he saw, too late, that he was too far away. Marty threw in a clumsy Seven League Boots stride and cleared the hurdle, but his rhythm, his fluency had now suddenly vanished. He was now where he had never before been, tiring, facing four hurdles with no idea of how to recover his stride pattern. Marty tried to keep his rhythm, but at the seventh hurdle he was much too far away, so he slipped in two extra strides and cleared the barrier too high. It was the same on the eighth and he could now hear Baker's breathing, as the two men came in to the ninth, at the beginning of the home straight. Marty looked to the penultimate hurdle. See it early. See it early. Feeling his legs begin to buckle in the lush grass, he pressed in on it, Baker a couple of yards back. Luckily, the hurdle came directly into his stride, as if in a sweet dream.

Marty took it well, sprinted off it, and poured on to the final barrier, took it, and creamed Baker by a full ten yards.

Pop rushed towards him, stopwatch in hand. "You ran 53.4 seconds," he spluttered. "World record."

"Forget about that," said Marty, gasping, hands on his knees. "How's Jim?"

Con Keyhoe could have been immediately recognised as a high jumper, even in 1995, thought Marty. Six foot four tall and split to the ears, the Cork man had dominated European high jumping for the past four years. Indeed, but for injury, he would have taken gold at the London Olympics in 1908. He stood at his mark, prancing on the spot like a nervous colt, his white, paper-thin face like a map of Ireland. He had not come all the way from The Emerald Isle for Delany's hundred dollars and the extra hundred dollar win-bonus. No, Keyhoe had crossed the Atlantic to meet Jim Thorpe. For Thorpe had established himself as one of the world's greatest jumpers and Keyhoe wished to return to Cork as the undisputed champion of the world. But now it looked likely to be a hollow victory. For Keyhoe had seen Thorpe spew up after the half mile, witnessed him being dragged off by his team like a sack of potatoes. Ireland had half a dozen men who could whip the Indian now. Thorpe was finished, so it had not been worth the trip, whatever the reward.

Jim lay on the dry grass under Pop's black umbrella, shielded from the sun. He reached to his right for the water jug, the water spilling over his face, and took a swig. He leant up on his elbows and smiled his cracked, toothy smile at Marty at his side. There was a raw core strength in him, which no fatigue could extinguish and it was slowly seeping back into his limbs. The Irishman Flaherty's massage had loosened him out and Cardinal Houlihan's problems on the adjustment of the wooden high jump stands had given him extra time to recover. Neither he nor Marty knew that Pop and Mackay had earlier removed two screws essential to the operation of the high jump stands, thus delaying the start by a further twenty minutes. Jim flicked his thick muscular thighs and rubbed them lightly, recoiling from the smell of the acrid Elliman's Horse Liniment which Flaherty had so liberally employed. So far, so bad. The half mile had taken him into an alien land of endurance, one in which his powerful muscles had no rightful place. But now he had almost returned to where he wanted to be, a world of power and strength. He was back.

"You want five foot six?" It was Marty, at his side.

Jim nodded. "Got to get a point. Get myself loosened out."

Marty watched as Keyhoe took his first attempt at that height. The Irishman, a left footed jumper, took a curved run like a flopper. But Keyhoe scissored in flight, dipping his trunk back and down towards take off, parallel to the crossbar, then whipped his left leg through to land on both feet, facing the bar. It was loose, fluid, graceful. Marty had never seen anything quite like it.

"Eastern Cut Off," observed Jim. "Fancy Dan." He rose and went to his mark. Without stopping, Jim ran at the crossbar from the left and hopped over, rolling clear with inches to spare.

"Great," said Marty. "How d'you feel?"

"Never felt better glued together," said Jim. He lay under the umbrella and closed his eyes. 'Tell 'em to wake me up when we get to six feet,' he said.

Keyhoe took five foot nine, then put in a massive clearance at six feet. Jim rose and brushed some dried grass from his sweating legs. He looked at the bar. "Six feet?"

Marty nodded. Jim took his mark and was clear in a flash, but the crossbar trembled. Delaney looked at Keyhoe and smiled. It was going well. The crossbar was raised to six foot two, but Jim shook his head. "I'll wait," he said.

"But, Jim, Keyhoe cleared six foot easy," protested Marty. He dared not tell Jim how narrow his own clearance had been. Jim stretched himself on the grass under the umbrella. "Them Cut Off jumpers," he said. "I told you, Fancy Dans. Look good,

Marty, but they go out real sudden." He shut his eyes. Marty looked down at Jim. The man was a marvel. Only forty odd minutes before, he had been dead meat, but here he now was, back in the moment. Marty watched carefully as Keyhoe took his first attempt at six foot two. He cleared it clean as a whistle.

Pop approached him, face like thunder. "What the hell is Jim up to, missing heights like that?"

"Jim's got it all under control," Marty lied. "Just you watch." He walked back, heart sinking, as the crossbar was raised to six foot four. Keyhoe was the first to jump, but Jim did not bother to watch. The Irish jumper's first attempt was perfect, his high point directly above the crossbar. But his left hip brushed the bar, which quivered and dropped to the sand, to groans from Delaney and the Yale team now clustered round the sand pit.

Jim rose slowly, yawned and hitched up his shorts. This time, he was more deliberate. He slowly placed his right foot on his take-off marker and wiped his lips with the back of his hand, his eyes focussed on the crossbar. Then he rushed, stormed in, on his take off mark. Seeing his speed had brought him too close, Jim chopped two strides, but over-compensated and took off too far from his marked take off point. He hurled himself into flight, seeming to Marty to hang, suspended in the air, lying on his left side, parallel to the bar. There was clear daylight at the peak of his flight and he landed in a heap in the sandpit, rolling over on his back.

"Well, I'll be dammed," said Pop.

"For certain," said Mackay.

Marty shook his head, speechless. Jim had been right. Keyhoe now fell apart, getting nowhere close on his next two attempts, his fine, fluid cut-off technique now in ruins. They were now 3-1 up on Yale.

To Mary Lou Barrow, the day had been like some strange and marvellous dream. Never before had she seen great track athletes in action, and it had stunned her, the fluid power of the dash, the gymnastic grace of the vault, the speed and fluency of the hurdles. And then there was the high jump. That Jim Thorpe could jump houses had simply been local folklore, like the Bogeyman, but now she had seen Jim in dynamic action and it had been glorious. After the high jump competition had concluded, she had stood under the crossbar which trembled a foot above her in the light breeze, and marvelled than any man born of woman could clear such a height. For Marty and Jim were like two Greek gods come to earth to compete against mortals, and she could not see how the Yale athletes could possibly match them. She watched from the stands as Delaney and his team went into a huddle on the infield, as back in the gloom Dr Halsey sat imperiously, face impassive.

"Look at their guy Casey," growled Pop, pointing down to the Yale shot putter, now warming up at the shot circle. "He's massive. He's got two chins."

"Last year he had three," replied Mackay. "He must be in strict training."

"He looks about 240 pounds," said Mary Lou.

"Me darlin', that's just his legs," smiled Flaherty.

The shot put took place directly in shadows, front of the main stand, so there was no need for spectators to venture into the blazing heat of the infield. Marty and Casey drew for putting order and Casey won, opting to put second. Marty scrutinised his opponent. The man was muscular, thick in thigh and chest, but he had a paunch to dismay Falstaff. But Marty knew that, for all his work on the weights with Flaherty, he had lost strength. Factor 2000 was fading fast and would soon be of little help to him now in 1911. Casey revealed little in his warm-up, putting a controlled and conservative 44 feet from a standing position. In contrast, Marty drew gasps by launching the 16 lb shot out to over 48 feet, using a full shift across the cropped grass circle.

Cardinal Houlihan called him up for his first put and Marty took an easy, cautious heave, putting the metal ball out to 47′8″' On his put, Casey took his position at the back of the circle, standing side on to the line of throw. His movement across the circle was a short hop, but his right leg drive was strong and the shot dented the dry grass at 47′2″'. Marty picked up the shot, moved to the circle and nestled it under his chin. This was the time to put on the pressure, so now it was eyeballs out. He drove across fast and snatched his right leg quickly underneath him, turning it in on landing. The shot felt light and flew from his hand. Marty turned away and walked out from the circle. It was good. He had no need to look. The distance board showed 49′11″' and in the stands Pop and Mackay whooped and embraced each other. Casey, his face now a fixed mask of determination, picked up the shot and took his stance. But his hop was rushed, badly balanced and his throwing position shallow and weak. The shot landed at around 45″ and Casey fouled, falling on both hands beyond the stop board.

Mackay stood. "*Got you, ringer*," he bellowed into the stand, to no one in particular. Delaney glowered. Pop dragged the Dean back to his seat.

Although he was now almost three feet in the lead, to Marty 49′11″' seemed strangely, unsatisfactorily short. He now had his man, so he cast all caution to the winds in his final put. It flew out to 50′2″', and he reflected, as he observed the scoreboard, that the extra three inches made a world of difference.

Casey, his plump, freckled face now red with sun, looked up into the gloom of the grandstand. Delaney, sitting with Hurley several rows behind the Carlisle contingent, stood, placed a hand into an inside pocket and withdrew a thick wad of dollar bills which he held aloft. Casey nodded and grimly circled his shoulders. This time, his hop took him further across the circle and he landed in a deep, strong throwing position. He shouted out as the shot left his hand, and Marty knew that this was a big one. The shot landed, denting the dry turf directly alongside Marty's previous throw. The Carlisle group stood as if to orders, but could see nothing as the Yale team rushed on to the field, engulfing Houlihan's priests. Father O'Malley placed a steel spike at the back of the dent made by Casey's put. The cloth tape was stretched back to the stop board, and Cardinal Houlihan stood above it, checking and re-checking. Finally he stood and picked up a battered steel megaphone.

"Fifty feet, two and three-quarter inches," he bellowed, but his voice was lost in the uproar around him. High in the stands, Delaney patted his wallet and smiled. It was moving their way, and the next event after the interval, the mile, would surely bring them level with Carlisle.

Mackay had taken Pop away from the stands, where the Carlisle group were enjoying lunch from a picnic hamper. The two men stood in the shadows at the rear of the grandstands, chewing on their sandwiches.

"What the hell's happened to you, Pop?" asked Mackay. "Never seen you like this before."

Pop chewed for a moment, his brows furrowed. "I don't get your drift, Angus," he said.

"This nigra boy, Roother, he's running the whole dam' show. Never in my life seen you so quiet."

Pop's lips pursed and he exhaled slowly before replying. "If'n it ain't bust, don't fix it," he said. "Me, I'm a football coach, Angus. That's why Pratt brought me to Carlisle in the first place. Track. That's another world."

"But this boy, Roother, he's just a raggedy-assed nigra from Alabama," said Mackay.

"No, Angus, you're wrong there," said Pop. "In a week, he put near twenty points on my track team. Roother's forgotten more about track than I'll ever know."

"But how?" asked Mackay.

"Beats me," said Pop. "Last week, I had a talk with him. Doesn't even know the rules of high jump. Wanted to *dive* over, like some goddam circus acrobat."

Mackay shook his head in disbelief.

"Then there was the bamboo vault poles – Marty didn't know that they had to be female poles."

"Neither did I," said Mackay.

"No, but you don't vault near thirteen feet," said Pop. He paused. "And what about the running corks?" he continued. "He got them from Sears Roebuck with his track shoes. Roother didn't even know what to do with them."

"Arm action," said Mackay. "For *gripping*. Everybody knows that."

"Well, Roother, he didn't have a clue," said Pop. "And yet he can run as fast as Duffey."

"Faster," said Mackay, shaking his head. "So what do you make of him?"

Pop shook his head and wiped the crumbs from his lips. "I've checked him out with some of the southern colleges down Alabama way," he said. "No one has heard hoot or holler any guy named Roother down there."

"And what about the pro circuit down Alabama way?"

"Same thing. There's a mulatto name of Sykes, he runs a yard outside evens, but no black down there runs anywhere near Sykes. Or the times he makes."

"Forget about the running," said Mackay. "Our man can hurdle like a Kranzlein and vault like an Olympic champion."

"And look at his shot – over fifty feet," said Pop.

"It's more than that, Pop," said Mackay. "It's the way the man speaks, like he's an equal. As if he's had a Scottish education."

"Like he's been to college," agreed Pop. "But come on, Angus, who cares, where's the beef? We're two up, with three events to go. I can near taste the money. You said it before – we'll eat it with a knife and fork. And Angus, don't forget – he works for you at three bucks a week."

"And vittles," said Mackay.

Marty's lungs were screaming as he hit the home straight for the final time behind Torrance. The Yale man had followed coach Delaney's advice to the letter, pushing them through the first half mile in 2 minutes 13 seconds, the Negro clinging to his shoulder. The third lap of the mile was where it usually started to hurt, so Torrance, feeling strong, had slipped in a fast 66 second lap. Still the Carlisle man had hung on and Torrance could hear the rasp of his breathing, coming in great painful gulps as he pinned himself to his right shoulder. Torrance tried to pick it up coming off the curve into the home straight, but Roother, responding, stayed with him. They ran, locked, their strides synchronised, to the screams and shouts of the tiny crowd at the finish Marty sought desperately to keep the shape of his running, his legs bowing as they struggled into the final fifty yards. From the side of the track, Pop could see that Torrance was now fading fast, but Marty could make no impression on the elusive half yard that still separated them. Five yards from the tape, he leant in and hurled himself at the finish line, staggering over it into Jim's arms.

"He took it," said Pop. "Marty took it."

Mackay looked questioningly at Pop as the Yale runners, uncertain, pulled Torrance to his feet. "I wouldn't like to live off the difference," he said.

Cardinal Houlihan stood at the top of the finishing steps, both hands raised for silence. "First Yale," he said, He was not allowed to complete the result because of the whooping of the Yale team.

"Fuck," said Mackay.

It was the first time that Pop had ever heard the Dean swear in public.

Marty's day in the sun was over. With a dead-heat in the mile, it was all up to Jim now with the score at four to three to Carlisle, and only hammer and long jump to go. His sweat dripping onto the cold stone floor, Marty lay gasping on the dressing room couch. He groaned as Flaherty tried to knead away the waste products of the mile. The Irishman had good hands. Marty could feel his thick, heavy quadriceps slowly, painfully, begin to loosen out under Flaherty's persistent pressure. His breathing eased from deep, rasping gulps, gradually becoming shallower, more tranquil, but the back of his throat still felt raw as if scoured with sandpaper. He pushed himself up on to his elbows, looked up at the slow second hand of the dressing room clock, and checked his pulse at the wrist. Jesus, it was still pumping away at around one hundred and forty beats a minute.

He looked up again at the clock. Jim's hammer competition would now be almost over. They had spent only two training sessions with Jim on hammer during the previous week. It had been the blind leading the blind, for Marty had never launched a 16lb hammer in anger. Between them, they had tried to work out the basic elements of hammer technique. Long, straight arms going into the first turn on the left heel, legs bent. Two turns rather than the conventional three, because beyond that, vertigo took control. Then it was simply a matter of giving the 16lb implement a good belt on delivery. Jim had yet again surprised him. For not only did he quickly pick up the rudiments of hammer technique, he also showed that he possessed the raw, agricultural power necessary for weight throwing. On their second session, he had launched the hammer out to a hundred and fifty-one feet, well within reach of his opponent, Flanagan.

The dressing room door opened and Pop entered, his face expressionless. "Well?"

"First throw, straight into the goddam cage. Second throw, a hundred and thirty feet. Third was a winner, a hundred and sixty feet."

"Great," whooped Marty, sitting up.

"No," said Pop. "It was a foul."

The score was now even up, with only the long jump remaining to complete the nine event programme. Marty, showered and dressed in slacks, shirt and baseball cap, stood beside Jim on the grass long jump runway. He lifted a few wisps of grass and let them fall from his hand. They drifted away from him, towards the long jump pit.

"Wind with you," he said. "Got your steps, right?"

Jim nodded. He looked across at the Yale jumper, Edward Pearce. The Yale man did not possess the physique of the classic long jumper. About five foot eight tall, thick and swarthy, he looked more like a middleweight wrestler.

"Delaney tells me he's cleared twenty-four feet in training," said Pop, standing behind them at the fence. "And the man's fresh as paint."

Marty looked at Jim. Pop's information had produced no visible response. Marty realised that Jim simply did not care. This was no arrogance. For him, the hammer was now history. This was long jump, and there was nothing and no one he could not beat.

Marty looked down the crisp, cropped long jump runway at the spectators clustered there behind the fence for the final event. Three jumps. Now he wished that he had let Jim run the mile, for he could jump twenty-four feet in his sleep, but hindsight was an exact science. Three jumps, but there was so much riding on them. For him, $400 would mean decent food, clothing, perhaps, even a new home. Mackay would be able to clear his debts. Pop would treat himself to a Model T. And there would no longer be any need for Jim to play baseball for money in the summer vacation, so he would stay an amateur.

In his first attempt, Pearce stormed in on the 8″ wide take-off board as if he were in a dash. It seemed impossible that he could gain any lift at take-up. Thus his jump was flattish, but it was long. The distance board slotted up '22′10″ a good first jump.

Jim stood at his mark, eyes focussed down the runway. Marty looked across the stand-flags, which were now fluttering. The wind had now picked up strongly behind Jim, and he would therefore have to make subtle adjustments on the runway. Jim strode off, in his strong, chunky style. He was too close to the board, but saw it much too late. His jump was long, but his right foot bit deep into the sand marking the edge of the board. Pop groaned audibly. It was a foul.

In his second attempt, Pearce tried too hard and failed to take-off, fouling and running into the pit. Marty looked across at Jim, feeling himself flush in anticipation. The wind had dropped back to a breeze, and he had therefore made no alteration to his approach run this time. He hit the board sweetly, but it was too safe and there was no guts, no real power in the jump. The board showed 22′10″, equal with Pearce's first attempt.

They were now in the final round, and Marty again looked up at the stand-flags. They were again fluttering unevenly. It was difficult to know what to advice. Jim looked up at the flags, and then across at him questioningly. "Stay with it, Jim," called Marty.

On his final attempt, Pearce hit the full eight inches of the board perfectly, at full speed. Somehow, he gained elevation, sailing through the hot summer air in a tucked position, like the bullet out of a gun. He landed at the end of the pit. Pop was directly in line with him. "Jesus God," he groaned.

Houlihan's priests set down the measuring tape, and Cardinal Houlihan stood above it. "Twenty-three feet, ten inches," he intoned.

Delaney and his Yale team erupted. Even Halsey forced a tight smile.

Marty felt the sweat trickle down his neck. He looked up at the stadium flags. They were now limp, inert. In his final jump, Jim would be running without the light following breeze that had accompanied his second attempt. For a moment, Marty considered warning Jim, but it was too late. He was on his way.

Jim hit the board at speed but he was too far back. He launched himself into space, using the running action that Marty had taught him. For a moment, he seemed to be suspended in flight, frozen, as if he were picking out his landing spot. Then both legs shot forward in front of him, his knees bent on landing, and he topped forward to the end of the pit.

There was silence. All eyes were focussed on the neat hole that Jim had left in the moist sand. Marty had reached the pit by the time the priests had laid out the measuring tape. Houlihan stood over it. “Twenty-three feet,” he said, pausing, “ten inches.” Jim had finished level, for both he and Pearce had scored the same distance in their second best jumps. Yale and Carlisle were now level on points.

Pop groaned. If only it had beens scored like a goddam pentathlon, then the College would be out of sight on any points – table. It would have to be decided on a final event, and he prayed that it might be a dash, or a hundred and twenty yards over the slats, and the College would be home and dry. He looked at the Dean.

“Say something, Dean,” he said.

“The Lord oppresseth those that he loveth,” said Mackay. “And who am I to deny the Lord?”

All of the remaining track and field events were placed in Houlihan’s black cardinal’s hat. Houlihan, eyes shut, placed his hand in the hat and withdrew a black numbered ball. He opened his eyes and scrutinised the ball. “Number five,” he announced.

Pop looked down the list of events, then stopped.

“It’s not the three miles?” said Jim.

“No,” said Pop.

“Not the walk?” said Marty. “Tell me it isn’t the walk?”

“No,” said Pop. “It’s not.”

“No, not the steeplechase?” whined Mackay. “I’m begging you, not the two mile steeplechase.”

“No,” said Pop. “It isn’t. It’s the 4 x 440 yards relay.”

No woman, let alone a Negro woman, had ever entered the august, austere sanctum of the Hartford Cricket Club dressing rooms. An officious steward had attempted to block Mary Lou's entry but Angus Mackay had brushed past him, observing that they had paid their money and that he did not give a docken. For they were now a strange, sudden family, bound together by the drama of the day. Thus, Mary Lou was with them when Pop locked the dressing room door from the inside, placing the key on the massage couch. He looked up at the small cell-like window which cast a single shaft of light into the dark, stone-floored dressing room.

"Check that window Kevin," he directed Flaherty. Suddenly, Pop was again in charge, but this time Marty did not mind. For Pop knew every man in the Yale team, which they would soon face, every facet of their running. "They know that Jim will run first and third and you second and last," he said. "Didn't take a Thomas Alva Edison to work that one out." He beckoned them to sit on the benches in the corner of the room as Flaherty, standing on tiptoe to look out of the window, signalled that all was clear. "They'll run someone fast on the first leg, try to take the starch out of Jim's legs."

"Who?" said Marty.

"Their quarter mile hurdler, Daryl Baker. He's quick, runs about 50.5." replied Pop.

Marty frowned. This meant that he was going to receive the baton for the second leg about twenty yards down, perhaps more.

Pop pointed at Marty. "On your first run, you'll be up against a steady man, their half-miler, Tyndall. He's strong, but he's got no real pace, around fifty-two seconds plus. You could eat him for breakfast off scratch. Then the third leg against Jim, they'll use their long jumper, Pearce. He won't have much gas, about fifty-two, maybe fifty-three seconds."

"And the final lap?"

"Sting in the tail. They'll use their fast man, Heffelfinger, their usual anchor man. He can run inside 50 seconds."

Marty frowned again. “That means that they might average close on fifty-one seconds,” he said.

Mackay looked at Marty. “We know that Jim here can run around fifty-one, but not twice in a row,” he said. “What can you run over a quarter?”

Marty’s lips framed “Forty-five.” Then he paused. “Back to back, I don’t know,” he said. “After all that I’ve done today, probably around fifty seconds.”

“Jim should average around 54 or 55, so it’s going to be as tight as a crab’s arse,” growled Mackay.

“It’s all about pacing yourself in the first run,” said Jim. “Only fifty seconds’ recovery until the next one.”

“We know that you can run fifty-one fresh,” began Pop.

“That takes it closer to fifty-four for Jim in the first leg,” said Marty. “Leaves me fifteen yards or more down. My aim will be to give Jim the baton level for the third lap.”

“And how much can you give their final runner?”

“Ten yards at most,” said Marty. “I’ll still have that first lap lying in my legs. And that mile.”

Pop stood and walked to the middle of the dressing room. He put out his hand, palm down and beckoned the others to join him. They formed a circle, placing their hands in layers on top of Pop’s hand.

At first, Marcus Wildstein and the other members of the Carlisle betting syndicate had been lost. For this was for them, an alien land. Baseball, football, prize-fighting, professional foot racing – these were sports in which they felt at ease, but not track and field, essentially a disparate series of separate sports. But, as the hot afternoon had slowly unwound, the contest had begun to exert a hold upon them. It was not the money, though like all men who had earned it the hard way, they had no wish to relinquish it. No, it went beyond that. It was something deeper, this battle between the high and mighty Yale and a Carlisle team represented by an Indian and a raggedy-assed Negro. That Yale had stiffened their squad with ringers had only increased their commitment to Thorpe and Roother, and now they were right in there with them, pitching with their men.

But, like all spectators, they were powerless and now all they could do to show their solidarity, to bind themselves to Thorpe and Roother was to descend from the remoteness of the grandstands and stand at the trackside as the two men prepared for the final event.

Cardinal Houlihan had faced an immediate problem. For Hartford Cricket Club did not possess a relay baton. His father, Eammon Houlihan, had always told him that necessity is the mother of invention, and he had therefore ordered Father O'Malley to locate a saw and cut up a broom handle. This had produced two crude but quite serviceable relay batons. He checked his fob watch. Five minutes to go.

Delaney tapped his inside pocket and sighed. He was now a hundred bucks lighter, but Casey's put had been worth every sawbuck. The Chicago fireman's ¾" in the shot-put had been the turning point, and now it was roses all the way. The fourteen pounds shot which he had slipped into Casey's big paw before his final put was now safely at the bottom of the Hartford duck pond. Hell, even Halsey was now smiling, if that wolfish grin could ever truly be described as a smile.

Jim Thorpe had not surprised Delaney. Nothing about Thorpe ever surprised him, for he had long ago decided that the Indian was something more than a man. But the black, Roother, he was something else. There was no knowing what he might do, and that was why Delaney had decided to play his ace in the hole. That ace was someone who was not a member of their team, Amos Pearce, the twin brother of their long jumper, Edward Pearce. Amos could run inside fifty seconds on a good day, and he would see off a tiring Thorpe by thirty yards in the third leg, leaving the nigra, Roother, somewhere back in Pennsylvania. It was money in the bank.

Cardinal Houlihan beckoned Father O'Malley to hand him the Colt 45 starting pistol. He took it, flipped it open and checked it. He would start this one himself.

"Gentlemen," he bellowed. "Get to your marks."

The two runners, Baker and Thorpe, took their marks, Jim on the inside.

"Get set."

On the report of the gun, Jim surged away, moving out to the right to block Baker's path. But the Yale man was having none of it. For a moment, he pinned himself on Jim's shoulder as they ran into the back straight. Then he moved out and, though Jim held him off for a further twenty yards, Baker continued on his path and passed him easily half way down the back straight. Baker then cut into the inside lane, keeping his pace high, hoping that Thorpe would follow him. He had seen the Indian in the half mile, and knew that he lacked endurance. Coach Delaney's orders had been to stretch Thorpe so that, still fatigued, he would be easy meat for their ringer, a fresh Pearce in the third leg, however, well the Negro ran on the second stage. But Jim ran to orders, keeping his pace below maximum as they hit the back straight, conserving his energy. Baker was now ten clear yards up and going away. At the furlong, he was twelve yards up, but Jim kept his head, his eyes fixed on the Yale runner's back. Baker pushed, coming into the home straight, seeing Tyndall, hand out in the distance, hearing the encouraging shouts of the Yale team. Behind him, Jim's hips began to drop, but he chugged along evenly as Baker moved further away. Baker made his pass to Tyndall.

"Fifty point two," said Pop, frowning.

Jim made his pass to Marty, sixteen yards down. Pop looked at Mackay.

"Jim was just over fifty-three," said Mackay. "Too fast."

He looked at Jim, who crouched on hands and knees on the grass, his breath coming in deep gulps. They pulled him to his feet. Jim, sweat rolling in rivers down his nut-brown face, smiled a sickly smile. He looked up as Marty, now only five yards down, tracked Tyndall down the back straight. Tyndall was no quarter miler, but his half-miling background meant that he could stay, holding on to a limited amount of basic speed. Already, coming to the furlong mark, he could hear Marty's breathing behind him behind him. Then, halfway round the final curve, Marty surged into the lead and took a further five yards out of Tyndall before he had reached the beginning of the home straight. At the finish, Jim stood, still breathing hard, shook his head as if to clear it, and wiped his face with the towel that Mary Lou had given him, still breathing hard. Marty was eating Tyndall alive and now looked to be in a ten-yard lead. Jim sucked air deep as Marty drove in towards him. When the pass was made, he took the wooden baton with a fourteen yards' lead, going into the third lap.

Mackay studied his watch. The Negro had run close to forty-eight seconds, yet did not appear to be tired. If Yale's long-jumper Pearce ran his expected fifty-two seconds, and Jim ran even fifty-four seconds, then he should come into Marty close on level for the final lap. Everything then depended on how much starch was left in the Negro's legs.

For Jim, it started to hurt early, in the middle of the back straight. He could feel his breath harsh in his throat, feel himself begin to sink into the turf. Suddenly, at the furlong mark, Pearce had passed him and moved away from him into the final curve.

"Jim's gone," groaned Mackay.

"Pearce is running like a shithouse rat," Pop said. "Better'n fifty seconds."

Marty took a gulp of water from the jug. He felt good, his breathing now coming smooth and easy. He looked across the track towards the final curve. Either Pearce was running out of his mind, or Jim was dying on his feet, for he was now over ten yards down as Pearce hit the home straight. Now well down on Pearce, Jim struggled to find the signals that would help him maintain some semblance of running form, as he came into the final straight. Far off, he could hear the dull, ragged shouts of the crowd. Marty stood at his mark, right arm out in anticipation. Even from this distance, he could see that Jim's legs had gone, that he was struggling to hold on to the shape of his running. Jim was dying on his feet. Somehow, the long jumper Pearce had taken him apart.

Mackay looked at Delaney, but the Yale coach's face betrayed nothing. The Dean knew running. He knew runners. Somehow, they had been buncoed, but he did not know how.

The Yale pass was made. Marty stood at his mark, quivering, his eyes staring, begging Jim to reach him. Jim, baton hand raised in front of him, wobbled towards him, almost falling as he made the pass. When Marty took the baton, he was a full sixteen yards down on Van Horn.

Mackay looked at his stopwatch. "Pearce ran fifty seconds," he said. "Impossible."

Pop nodded. "Their long jumper. Their 52 second man. "

"Jim ran fifty-four," said Mackay. "He ran his guts out."

He looked down at Jim who lay flat on his face, his eyes closed, on the infield grass. Flaherty dragged him to his feet and sat him on a bench. Jim's breath ripped in his throat and he sagged in Flaherty's arms. Then his eyes opened. "How's Marty doing?" he gasped.

Marty, running into the back straight, was now twelve yards down. He knew that he had to pull Van Horn in slowly, on a long rope. Too fast in the first furlong and he would sink deep into a sea of lactic acid in the final part of the race. But Marty felt fluid, he ran tall, and he could feel himself slowly pulling in Van Horn. By the time that he had hit the furlong mark, he had gained another three yards and was now only eight yards down.

Mary Lou looked over Pop's shoulder at his flickering stopwatch.

"Marty's inside twenty-four for the first furlong," said Pop, shaking his head.

"But our boy's too far back," growled Mackay. "Too much to find."

Coming into the home straight, Marty was still six yards down and his breath was now harsh, savage, coming into deep sobs. Now it was hurting. It was hurting real bad.

Then it happened. Van Horn suddenly looked back, over his right shoulder. It was not much, but it was enough, for it told Marty that his man was now in trouble. Marty desperately tried to lift his hips and drive hard with his arms. Slowly, he began to drag Van Horn in as, in front of him, the Yale runner began to visibly wilt.

Fifty yards to go. Only two yards now separated the two runners. But it was two long yards, and Marty desperately tried to hold form, as he felt Van Horn slowly come towards him on his left shoulder.

Ten yards to go, and it was all over, as a short yard still separated the two men wobbling towards the tape. Then, with five yards to go, Van Horn's legs collapsed under him and he fell. Marty fell too, but through the tape to win.

Cardinal Houlihan stepped down from the dais, dabbing his eyes. He shook Pop's hand, shaking his head. "Thank you, Mr Warner," he said. "It was a privilege." Houlihan looked across at the crestfallen Dr Harley. "And perhaps, for some it may have been an education."

Chapter 10
Mammy Boston

Marty and Mary Lou stood with Jim on the creaking wooden platform of Carlisle railway station, as the steam hissed gently from the engine of the mid-day train. Jim lifted his brown, floppy canvas bag and slung it up the steps and on the train.

"How long will it take you?" asked Marty.

"Back to the Oklahoma Territory? Most of today and a peck of tomorrow," answered Jim.

"And what are you going to do when you get there?"

Jim smiled his lopsided grin. "Rest up. Hunt, fish get me in shape for the football season."

"You thought about what I said, about next year?"

"Them Stockholm Olympic Games?"

Marty nodded. "We'll go together to Sweden, Jim, the two of us. Compete in decathlon and pentathlon. Have us a ball."

"A ball?" Jim did not understand.

"Yeah, it'll be cool."

Jim still did not understand. He mock-frowned and shook his head. "Cool," he said. "Cool."

"That's right, Jim, decathlon."

"Your decathlon sounds a lot like Yale again to me. All them different events. Only twice as bad." He paused, smiling to himself. "But I'll give it a try."

Marty grinned. "One thing, Jim," he said. "Just promise me one thing."

"Yes?"

"No baseball this summer. Promise me. No bucks for baseball. Promise me that."

Jim tapped his left breast pocket. "No need, Marty," he said. "Yale. Four hundred clams."

There was a shrill warning whistle. Jim shook Marty's hand, smiled to Mary Lou, climbed the steps and was gone from sight. Marty and Mary Lou watched the train trundle slowly, through the steam, out of the station. They turned and walked slowly down Main Street.

"What was all that stuff about baseball?" she said.

"Amateur status," he replied. "The Olympics. Jim's got to keep his amateur status for Stockholm."

She took his right hand in hers and gently swung it. "That's something I've wanted to talk to you about," she said.

"Baseball?"

"No," she replied, squeezing his hand.

"The Olympics?"

"I never heard tell of them till you told me," she said. "But no, not the Olympics."

"Then what?"

"My amateur status," she replied, smiling.

Angus Mackay had, on his return to Carlisle, found it difficult to process what he had just witnessed at Hartford, for it was not simply wondrous track and field, though it was undoubtedly that. After all, he had seen the great professional dashman, the English runner, Harry Hutchens; he had seen professionals honed to a fine edge, men running scared with money on their backs on Scranton's frozen cinders. Crivvens, he had even witnessed his countryman, the great Donald Dinnie, in his prime, launching hammers into the Tay, then go on to wrestle giants to the ground, toy with great athletes like naughty children. No, Mackay had seen all that, yet he had never come across anything to compare with the Negro Roother. For, in a single day, he had gone close to world record in vault and dash, taken one in quarter mile hurdles, and had failed by a whisker to beat an Irish giant in shot put. Then, to cap it all, he had run two quarter miles, both well inside fifty seconds, with less than a minute's rest between each effort. No man born of woman could achieve such things.

Thorpe, well, he had always been something else, something wild, a fierce force of nature, and Mackay had always distinguished Jim from mere mortals. He accepted that the raw, savage nature of Indian culture would occasionally throw up men of his calibre; that was only natural.

When he had first arrived at Carlisle, Mackay had found it difficult to accept the status of the American Indian, their lack of rights. It was not right. It offended his Presbyterian sense of fairness and justice. But he had found, in his educational work, a means of providing them with a democratic environment, an island on which they could be insulated, however temporarily, from the grim realities which they would ultimately face.

At first, Mackay had felt a similar sense of injustice about the status of the Negro, but it had not been long before he had been seduced, had unconsciously absorbed in his pores the American attitude towards the black man. Had the argument on their rights, their equality, ever been formally put to him, then the Dean liked to think that he would have defended them to the last. Fortunately, he had never been required to argue their case. As a result, he had subconsciously placed the Negro in a different category, as an inferior race, fit only for menial tasks. Until now, he had observed them in no other role.

What troubled Mackay was not simply Roother's performances, marvellous though they undoubtedly were. No, it was the way that the man comported himself, the manner in which he spoke, even the way he stood. Pop Warner had somehow taken it on board, accepted it, tolerated it and deployed it to his advantage. Advantage! Mackay was now clear of his gambling debts, with a few bawbees to spare, and firmly re-established as the darling of the Carlisle syndicate.

Throughout his life, Angus Mackay had possessed patience for little but his own thoughts. But Roother had disturbed him, forced him to dig deep and think again. So, indeed, had the Negro woman, Mary Lou Barrow, who had gone further than he had ever dared, to confront the great Dr Harley. She was what his mother would have called "a Nippy Sweetie".

They had both made him think, too, beyond the moment, to his work at Carlisle. For though Angus Mackay had not been, like Pratt, an Indian fighter, he had followed that soldier's chosen path, that of turning the Indian into a white man. And, though he had laced Pratt's programmes with a strong dash of the Scottish dominie, there had always been doubts, bats at the back of his mind.

And the girl, Mary Lou, she had made him think again of his Wednesdays afternoons with Missie Brown. He reflected that they spoke only on his arrival and departure. All the rest, the hot reason for his weekly visits, was silence.

He withdrew his hand from the soft wetness between her legs, and waited. A few minutes later, when she had finished with him, they lay, sweating, in his narrow bed, in the darkness, suddenly aware of its restrictions. Mary Lou broke the silence. "You recollect," she said, her sweet breath hot upon his cheek, "what I said to you, back at the railway station?"

"Recollect," he said. "Where'd you get that word – George Bernard Shaw?"

"Come on, you know what I'm talking about," she pressed.

"Your amateur status," he said. "No, I didn't think you were talking about the Olympic Games."

"I guess you seen it in my eyes," she said.

"I don't get your drift."

"They ain't…they're not clear," she said.

"So what?"

"Sometimes I wonder about you," she groaned, mock wearily. "Ladies who ain't, haven't done it, it's a known fact, their eyes ain't clear, they're a sort of…cloudy, milky."

"I didn't know that," he signed. "You got any more of that earthy folk wisdom?"

She sat up on her elbows and looked down on him. “Earthy folk wisdom? Who says things like that?”

“I do.”

“So what you gonna do about it?”

“Your milky eyes?”

She pressed her lips to his cheek. “Sure.”

He shifted uneasily. “I’m trying to take it steady. Don’t want to rush things,” he said.

“I ain’t noticed no rush so far. I ain’t complaining about no rush.”

There was again silence.

“It wouldn’t be fair to you, Mary Lou. I may not be here with you much longer.”

She withdrew her lips from his cheek. “What you mean – much longer?”

“I mean I don’t plan to stay here in Carlisle for ever. Got to be moving on.”

“And where zactly you planning to go?”

He gulped. “Back,” he said.

“Back to Alabama?”

Marty struggled for words. “No, not exactly.”

“So why can’t you take me along with you?”

“Where I’m going,” he said, “you wouldn’t want to come.”

“Surely that’s up to me.” She paused and took a deep breath. “Marty, you really think I want to stay in this here town and clean up for white folks all my life?”

“No, I guess not,” replied Marty.

“And you think that I let every buck do what you just done?”

“No, I don’t.”

“And do you think I don’t wake up nights, all hot, just a-dreamin’ of you?”

“I dream of you, too, Mary Lou, I swear. I think of you a lot.”

“That’s a mercy,” she said. “But if I hear you right, you’re telling me that’s it. You come here, you mess with me and, lickety spit, off you go. Like you never been.”

"But, Mary Lou, I can't take you where I'm going," he said.

Her reply was immediate. "You don't come from no Alabama, do you?" she said.

Marty paused for a moment. "No, Mary Lou. You're right. I don't."

"So where in God's name *do* you come from, speaking so strange. England?"

"No." He paused. "California. I come from Los Angeles."

"Then just you tell me why you said you come from Alabama?"

He felt a lump in the mattress and moved to avoid it, pressing himself closer to her as he did so. He felt the tension now in her body. "It's a long story, Mary Lou," he said.

"I got plenty of time," she said, her voice now hard.

Marty felt a thick lump in his throat. He knew that he had now crossed a failsafe point, that it would be pointless to continue to lie. Yet he found it impossible to frame the words. It had to be done. Yet he knew that it could not possibly be done. For weeks, he had imagined this moment, rehearsed it in his mind, but no plausible, acceptable scenario had ever come to him. He had lain in bed, night after night, thinking of what his own reaction would have been had someone claimed to have come back from the year 2080. Straight to the Funny Farm, neither foot touching the ground.

"Okay," he said. "First, I've got to tell you that what I'm going to say is going to sound…"

"Strange?" she volunteered, her voice softer.

"You got it in one," he said. "That's exactly what I mean. Strange, weird, impossible."

"So, strange, weird, impossible – I've got all that. So, zactly what are you trying to tell me?"

"I already told you I didn't come from Alabama."

"No, you jest said you came from California. Marty, we've been through all of that. So what are you trying to tell me now, that you don't come from California?"

"No," he mumbled. "I do. I do." He gulped. "It's when. It's *when* I came."

"But I *know* that, Marty. I was there. 'Bout three months back."

"No, no, I didn't. That's the problem."

"So you came up earlier, to Pennsylvania. Then you come on over here to Carlisle. So what?"

"No, no, no," he said, a note of impatience entering his voice. It was not impatience with her, rather with himself. Marty now had difficulty in finding the words and, when he did find them, they were not to his liking. Suddenly, it came to him. "Science fiction," he said. "H. G. Wells, H G Wells."

"I read everything that feller ever wrote," she said, nodding. "What's *he* got to do with it?"

"*The Time Machine*," he said. "H G Wells wrote that, didn't he?"

"Yes, I read it, a coupla years back. Crazy stuff."

"Yes, crazy. But not that crazy," he said. He felt the sweat chill on his skin. "Now, Mary Lou, a few days ago, you told me what Pop said, after Yale."

"Yes, when you finished in that there relay. Pop said to that Yale coach…"

"Delaney."

"Yes," she said. "Coach Delaney. I remember. Pop said he'd just seen the future."

"That's right. You got it."

"Okay, so what?" she said. "That was just one of them what you call figures of speech."

"I know. I know," he said, feeling his voice crack. "But Pop, he was right. Take my word for it, Mary Lou. Pop was right."

"So, Marty, what are you saying?" her voice now taut. "Just what you trying to tell me?"

"That…That's where I come from."

"Where?"

"The future."

Mary Lou felt her jaw go slack. She pulled herself abruptly over him onto the dirt floor and reached in the darkness for her clothes on the chair at the table. "You crazy," she hissed at him, into the darkness. "You plain crazy."

Marty lifted himself, cracking his head on the bunk above. He fumbled on the table on the right of the bed and his hand reached what he sought, the matches. He stood, struck a match, lit the kerosene lamp and lifted it so that its light spilt into the cold, dark, little room. He placed it on the table at the centre of the room, and stood in front of Mary Lou, her calico shift now on, as she struggled to lace her shoes. "Look at me, Mary Lou," he said quietly, standing naked in front of her, arms spread. "Just you take a good look at me. How do you think I can do all these things? Lift those railway wheels, whup all those Yale boys?"

Mary Lou stood, shivering in front of him, as the light flickered on his body.

"*Look* at me," he repeated. "You ever in all your life heard of any black boy can do what I do? You ever heard of any nigra who can vault dick?"

"Oh," she whispered. "It's them words." Her legs suddenly weak, Mary Lou sat at the table. "Dick. *Nobody* says them words."

He went to the bed, retrieved his trousers and pulled them on, buckling his belt. Then he sat beside her at the table, and placed his hands on hers. "It's true," he said, gently. "It's all true. And you're the only one here I could tell. The only one in the whole world." He paused. "Do you believe me?"

She did not reply, but looked at him. "Why you not just plain ole Marty Roother, like you was that first day? I liked him from the start."

"Well, I'm not plain ole Marty Roother. It might be better for me if I were, but I'm not."

"When?" she said abruptly.

"When what?" he said. "You mean what year have I come from?" He gulped. "Pretty far on," he said. "Nineteen ninety-five."

Mary Lou slowly withdrew her hands from his, pulled her right arm well back, and smashed her open palm hard across his left cheek.

After all, Jim reasoned, it was only a couple of young soldier boys playing for matchsticks. And it sure was going to be a long, slow trip back to Oklahoma Territory. Then a drummer, selling patent leather shoes, by name of Benson, from Philadelphia, joined the two soldiers and they commenced playing for dimes. Jim ran into a full house early, aces and queens, and picked up ten bucks. A few hands later, he had creamed them for twenty clams with four kings.

That was when the drummer was joined by his friend, Orwin, and they had all moved on to the observation car. Orwin was a plump, freckled, well-set young fellow and soon produced a silver hip flask. It was not long before the game had become something of a social occasion and, as dusk gathered and the train clickety-clacked its way across the Plains, Jim warmed to his task and placed his four hundred dollar clip before him on the table.

Next afternoon, as he made his way down from the train, blinking in the sunlight, on to the boardwalk in Prague, Oklahoma, Jim had only ten bucks and fifty cents left in his possession. That would have to see him through till September. But then there was still the baseball.

There was no one in whom she could now possibly confide. For what on earth could she tell them? What words could she use? Who could be told that the man she loved claimed to have been born in 1970?

For the next week, her mind afire, Mary Lou had absorbed herself quietly, doggedly, at her work at the Majestic. She could see that her colleagues could not understand the change in her, but it did not matter. Then, seeking solace in imagination, she sat until dark in the deserted NAACP Library, reading voraciously. She had deliberately avoided re-reading H. G. Wells' *Time Machine*. Anyhow, Marty had not claimed to have returned in any kind of machine. Indeed, he had not made it at all clear how he had managed to return to 1911, for in a long, rambling letter to her, he did not appear to be quite certain himself. This lack of clarity had, strangely, put him closer to her favour, for if Marty had come up with some detailed "Wellesian" scenario, she would have been immediately suspicious. No, his vagueness was oddly reassuring. In his account, he had simply gone to sleep in 1995 and woken up on a shelf in the Majestic laundry-room in 1911. That was surely too plumb crazy to be a lie.

And then there was Jim Thorpe. Marty had apparently come back to compete against Thorpe because Jim had asked him to. Marty's letter had not been clear on this point either. After all, Jim would be over a hundred years old in 1995, in no condition to ask a favour from anyone. Or had Thorpe come to him in a dream? She could not be sure. Marty's letter was unclear.

She had been troubled from the outset. For a couple of hours after she had discovered Marty in the laundry room, an Alabama boy, Alvin Roother, had arrived. She had pushed this boy Roother on to the Greville Hotel, where he had duly secured a position.

She had seen more of Marty than anyone else and it was obvious that he was no country boy from Alabama. She had over the years spoken with many Southern boys. Marty's accent resembled none of them and, more significantly, neither did his language which, if eccentric, was curiously grammatical. But it was not merely his language. No, it was the manner in which he addressed whites, important men like Pop Warner and Dean Mackay. There was no deference, no subservience in his voice. Marty acted like he was equal, indeed, in some ways superior to both men. Even Booker T

Washington and the most radical members of the NAACP did not comport themselves in such a manner.

But the situation was crazy, and it was driving her crazy. Mary Lou could think of only one person who might help her. Mammy Boston.

Mammy Boston would always remember the exact day when she first realised that she had the Eye. It had been thirty-five years back, when she had been sixteen years of age and employed as a maid at Armbruster's Farm, a few miles north of Carlisle. Ellie Boston had seen it in a dream, savages, a-whooping and shrieking, riding in circles around young soldier boys. It had come to her in brief, chaotic bursts, the gunfire, men falling, the thinning ranks of the blue coats. And the horses rearing and whinnying in the centre, hit by bullets or writhing on the blood-stained grass. By the time she had woken, bathed in sweat, every single blue coat was dead and the butchery had begun. Ellie had her letters, and that evening had scribbled down her recollections as best she could. It was a day later that the final words of her record of that dream had appeared, solemn headlines in an article in the Carlisle Echo. The words were 'Little Big Horn'.

It had not been long before Ellie Boston's remarkable powers had become the talk of the neighbourhood and news of them soon went far beyond the boundaries of Carlisle or, indeed, of Pennsylvania. At first, it had been parochial, local girls seeking advice on a swain, pregnant women eager to know the sex of their baby. Alas, for the most part, Ellie was helpless, for her powers were fitful, erratic and unfocussed. For her dreams and visions, her occasional glimpses of the future, were impossible to summon at will. Often, when they did arrive, she did not even know if they were past or future, dreams or distant realities.

But Ellie Boston, at five cents a time, would never lie. So, though the sex of a baby was a 50/50 chance, Ellie, if in doubt, always delayed a decision until taking an item of clothing from both parents. That done, her success rate was high, extending even to twins or triplets. For the rest, the rapidly maturing Ellie had found that the sheer volume of the problems brought to her began to give her an instinctive sensitivity in what became as much mentoring and counselling as prediction. Indeed, she found that the elements of soothsaying and advice began to fuse, until she had often difficulty distinguishing one from the other.

It had probably been a coincidence that she had bought the crystal ball only a few days before she met Chief Geronimo when he had visited the College in 1908. It had been a strange dream, not so much the Indian Chief's death from influenza as the images of men dropping through the air, shouting his name. No, the crystal ball gave class, a professional aura to her work, though it had never yet offered her a single glimpse into the past or the future. Not, at least, until the arrival of Mary Lou Barrow.

Marty sat high in the bleachers in the hot midday sun, surveying the infield, the lush summer grass which had now obliterated the throwing arcs which he had so meticulously drawn way back in April. The track, now devoid of the summer energy poured into it by Carlisle's now departed athletes, looked dry, lifeless. It was difficult to believe that only a few short weeks before, Thorpe, White Wolf, Louis Tewanima and a dozen other Carlisle athletes had re-written the record books on its now dry, barren surface.

Marty felt bad. He had four hundred bucks from Hartford burning a hole in his pocket; he could now afford to eat well, buy a house and approach with confidence the winter and the 1912 Olympic season. And with Jim clear of pro baseball, he now knew that he could change history. Yet he felt bad. For the week following the Hartford meeting had confirmed to him, what he had already begun to suspect. His body was beginning to fade. True, the Yale events had been compressed into half the time of a decathlon schedule. True, he had been forced to push himself to the limits of his endurance in the mile and the final relay. True, he had, as Flaherty had later observed, "gone beyond his potential."

All of that was unquestionably true. But the plain, unacceptable fact was that it had taken him the best part of a fortnight to recover from Hartford, twice as long as usual. In contrast, Jim seemed to be made of different stuff, for only a couple of days later, he had been back down at the track, badgering him for help with his hurdling. For Jim, there had been no Factor 1911 equivalent, merely the constitution of an ox, a little training and an iron will. But without Factor 2000 to aid his recovery, Marty had struggled and it was now clear to him that, without the legal pharmaceutical aids of the late 20th century, life was going to be hard for him. Like the Wicked Witch of the West, he was melting.

But his physical condition, that was the least of it. For he was in love with a woman who thought he was raving mad. He could not blame Mary Lou. Neither could he blame her for avoiding him all that week, for refusing to come out of her house when he had called on her. It had thus come as a surprise when she had sent him a letter asking him to meet her that Thursday evening, outside Mammy Boston's home.

To Mary Lou, Marty had not seemed to be entirely convinced when she had explained to him that Mammy Boston possessed the Eye. And it had appeared to make no discernible difference to him that her view was shared by most people in Carlisle and its environs. Mary Lou had splashed out, bringing with her fifty cents for the full hour. With Marty, she stood outside Mammy Boston's tiny, ramshackle cottage at dusk, saying nothing. Then she spoke. "Mammy Boston, she'll know if what you say is on the square," she said.

"And what if she doesn't find me somewhere on her ouija board? What if your Mammy Boston thinks the same as you?" Marty replied.

"We'll cross that bridge when we comes to it," answered Mary Lou, firmly. She turned to look directly at him. "Marty, look at it from my side. I can't tell no one, not my ma, not my brothers and sisters. You sure made me a lonely lady when you done told me what you did. Don't you see that?"

Marty nodded. "I see that," he said. "But if you don't believe me, and if your Mammy Boston gives me the thumbs down, then there's only two things I can be."

"What's that?"

"A liar or a lunatic. There's not much in between."

"Or a lying lunatic," she said, taking his hand.

He smiled, as a departing couple walked past them from Mammy Boston's cottage.

"It's us now," said Mary Lou. "Now you just behave yourself in there."

"I will be a model of propriety," he said, squeezing her soft, warm hand.

"Now, there you go again," she groaned. "*A model of propriety.* Who says that round these parts?" She squeezed his hand in return, and they entered the cottage.

The cottage floor was brown dirt, its interior frugal, containing only a central table with three chairs around it, a bed in the right corner, a wrought iron stove on the back wall and a sink on the left. Marty reflected that the spirit world did not appear to pay big. Mammy Boston was portly and placid, sixty-two years of age. She sat, her abundant bosom bulging over the black sash which bound at the waist her polka-dotted red cotton dress, peering into the crystal ball on the table in front of her.

"Jesus Christ," groaned Marty inwardly, as he caught first sight of the crystal ball.

Mary Lou heard his words and gave him the Iron Eye.

Mammy Boston beckoned to them to sit on each side of her, as she replaced the black velvet cover on the crystal ball. She closed her eyes and pulled their hands together under her own. Then her eyes opened. Mary Lou opened the tiny leather purse, and placed her fifty cents on the table. Ellie Boston shook her head. "Not yet, honey," she said. "Let's find out fust if the Good Lord, he wants to tell us sump'n." She looked to her right, to Mary Lou. "You fust, honey," she said, holding Mary Lou's hands in hers.

She closed her eyes and gave a long, low groan. "You gonna live a long, long time. Way, way longer than any folks hereabouts."

"Am I going to be with Marty?" pressed Mary Lou.

"Could be, honey, but not here. Somewheres else."

Mary Lou smiled across the table, to no response from a bemused Marty. She withdrew her hands.

"That's all I want for me," she said.

Mammy Boston's eyes opened. "But that's only 'bout five cents worth," she said.

"Nuff for me," said Mary Lou.

"Suit yourself," said Mammy. "There was plenty more a-comin' up, I'm a-telling you. A full twenty cents worth, or more."

"What about Marty here?" asked Mary Lou.

Mammy Boston nodded and placed her plump hands over those of Marty, closing her eyes as she did so. Her brows furrowed. "Nuthin's comin' through," she murmured, shaking her head as if to clear it. She got to her feet and waddled across to the sink, and took a thick, white, enamel mug from a wooden table beside it. She poured its contents into the sink and returned with it to the table. "Let's us look at them tea leaves," she said, settling herself at the table again. She peered into the mug, breathing heavily. "You don't come from hereabouts, that's for sure," she observed, shaking her head.

"Alabama?" volunteered Mary Lou.

"California," corrected Marty.

"No, not neither. No, not from nowheres."

"He must come from somewhere," pleaded Mary Lou.

"Yo's right, honey," said Mammy, shaking her head. "Stands to reason. Everybody comes from **some**where."

Ellie Boston suddenly started to sweat. She pushed the fifty cents back across the table to Mary Lou. "Heah, honey. You keep yo' money. I can't see nuthin, no how."

Mary Lou pushed the coins back across the table. "Couldn't you try your crystal ball?" she asked, pointing to the velvet-sheathed ball in the centre of the table.

Ellie Boston took a deep breath and withdrew a red cotton handkerchief from a dress pocket and mopped the sweat from her face. She placed her hands on the velvet cover, and reflected that it had cost more than the ball which it encased. She reflected too that never had a single image ever appeared to her from its opaque, milky depths. Suddenly, Mammy felt drained.

Marty stood. "Let's go, Mary Lou. Maybe we should have tried the ouija board."

Mary Lou again gave him the Iron Eye. Marty regained his chair, frowning. This was voodoo; this was chicken shit.

Mammy Boston re-pocketed her handkerchief, even though the sweat continued to stream down her plump face on to the table. Breathing more deeply, she withdrew the velvet cover from the ball, continuously shaking her head to clear it and showering Marty and Mary Lou with sweat as she did so. She peered intently into the crystal. Her eyes rolled. For suddenly, it was all there. Clear, distinct. She gasped audibly.

"What is it?" demanded Mary Lou.

"It's yo' man," said Ellie. "It's Marty heah."

"What's he doing?"

"He's a-runnin, he's runnin like the wind."

"Where?"

"Can't tell," said Mammy. "But he's a-runnin' on red rubber."

Marty sat up, goggling, eyes fixed on Mammy Boston.

"And there's a whole heap of people a-watchin."

"Thousands?" he said.

Mammy shook her head. "Millions," she said.

"There can't be millions," said Mary Lou. "They couldn't all get in."

She leant towards Mammy. “What else can you see in there?”

“Now he’s a-jumpin’ over a bar,” said Mammy. “Backwards on to a bed.”

“A bed?” said Mary Lou. “Who with?”

“No,” said Mammy. “Not that kinda bed. It’s higher, thicker. Can’t make it out no-how.” She again shut her eyes. “Can’t take no mo’,” she said. “I can’t take no mo’.”

“Try,” begged Mary Lou. “It’s important.”

Mammy opened her eyes and again peered into the depths of the crystal ball, pushing Marty away as he pressed in on her to look. “Lawdy!” she exclaimed. “Now he’s a-jumpin’ with a pole.”

“Pole vault,” said Marty.

“No,” said Mammy quickly. “It’s a pole like a spring.”

Marty was now absorbed. “Jeez,” he said. “Mammy, tell me if I go to Sweden, to the Olympics.”

Ellie Boston peered into the ball, then closed her eyes. “No,” she said, slumping back into her chair. “Maybe yo’ do and maybe yo’ don’t. I can’t see no mo’.”

Marty decided to make his move.

“Nike, Mammy, Nike,” he said.

Mammy shuddered, as if she had received an electric shock. Sweat rolling down her face, she peered again into her bowl.

“I see lotsa shoes,” she said. “Looks to me like rubber shoes, with marks on their sides and spikes in their soles.”

“Anything else?” asked Marty.

Mary Lou could see that Mammy Boston was completely exhausted. She stood, placed her hand on her right shoulder and beckoned Marty to rise, and he reluctantly did so. When they had left, Ellie Boston’s eyes opened and she replaced the velvet cover on the ball. She looked at the door, and then back at the crystal ball and shook her head. This was crazy stuff.

They walked slowly down the rutted dirt road from Mammy Boston's, in the thick, dense heat of the August evening. She pulled his hand into hers. To Marty, it felt better than good. "So what was all that 'bout running on rubber?" she asked.

"It's the track, it's not grass or cinder, it's a sort of rubber," he replied. "Faster."

She nodded. "I suppose so. And what about jumping on to a bed?"

"High jump," he replied. "It's a technique called the Fosbury Flop. We land on our backs."

"So you kinda jump backwards, like one of them acrobats in vaudeville?"

"Something like that."

"Crazy," she said. "How high they jump like that?"

"Some Cuban guy, he's jumped eight feet," he answered.

She looked above them, to the branches which stretched to the fringe of the road. "Eight feet. That's a foot higher than I can reach," she said. "How high **you** jump?"

"Not so high," he replied. "About seven feet."

"Jesus Lord," she said. "And what about that there bed?"

"To land on," he answered. "It's made of a sort of foam rubber. Five thousand bucks worth."

Mary Lou shook her head and said nothing. They continued to walk hand in hand down the deserted dirt road. "And what about vaulting with a pole, like a spring?" she asked, eventually.

"It's tough to explain," Marty said. "The pole, it's bendy, like real springy bamboo, so you can hold higher."

"So how high kin you vault?"

"Over seventeen feet," he said.

"Come on," she protested. "That's higher than a house."

"I'm not that good. A Russian guy has vaulted twenty feet. Hell, a woman has cleared close to fifteen."

She stopped suddenly and pulled him around to face her, looking him straight in the eyes. "Now, Marty," she said. "I bin good. I listened to all you said. But are you now telling me that gals run track and vault with a pole?"

He nodded.

"Since when?"

He shook his head. "I don't know when they started. Ever since I can remember, that's all I can say."

"And what kinda gals would they be?"

"Women just like you, cross my heart, hope to die."

Mary Lou sighed deeply. They sat down on the dry grass in the shadow on an oak tree. "All this ain't doing me no good, Marty," she said. "It hurts my head. You gotta help me here, honey."

He reached forward to hold her hands in his. "That's what I've been trying to do, Mary Lou," he said gently.

"But you see, Marty, when Granpappy tells me all 'bout them slave days, 'bout the war between the States, I can cotton on. It's a long way back, but I kin understand that. You know why?"

"No."

"Cos things ain't changed that much, that's why. We still slaves. So, they don't whup us no mo', but we still slaves. We got no say in nothing." She paused. "But what you a-telling me…" She sighed and started to whimper. Marty raised her hands to his lips and kissed them softly. "Yo's half white, ain't you?" Mary Lou said in a whisper.

He nodded. "My mother was black. My father was white."

"So now what you're telling me is that blacks and whites kin marry and have children?"

"Yes, that's right."

"Lord a-mighty," she said. "That's why your John Thomas is like it is."

He nodded. "I was wondering when you'd ask. My father is a Jew."

"Okay," she said. "So tell me. Why'd you come back here?"

"It's a long story," he said. "Can't quite put my finger on when it all started."

"Try," she insisted. "Use 'em all."

"Well, the long and short of it is, Jim asked me to come back."

"Jim Thorpe?"

"That's right."

"But, Marty, I got my numbers. Jim would be 'bout a hundred and thirteen years old."

"Well, it wasn't exactly Jim."

"Then who?"

"His ghost." he replied, waiting for her blow.

Chapter 11
The Fix

No one in the Carlisle syndicate was complaining now. Angus Mackay was now clear of the men with the hard faces; Wildstein was happy; Goldberg had been close to delirious. They had cleared ten times more at Hartford than they had in the previous five years combined, and the look on Halsey's face had been worth at least another grand per man. But Goldberg was convinced that they had merely scratched the surface, that there was plenty more in the pot from the Negro.

For Roother had not yet been exposed. Because for sure as Hell, no one at Yale was going to announce to the world that their famous track team had been whupped good by Jim Thorpe and some unknown black boy. They would be the laughing stock of the Eastern seaboard if they did. Thus, the syndicate would control a man who had run a full four yards inside even time over a hundred yards. In 1913, a year after they had cleaned up at the 1912 meet with their Canadian ringer Rae, they could run Roother at Scranton.

It would be like spearing fish in a barrel. For bets could be laid at long odds when the handicaps were announced in late 1912, all laid at exactly the same time across the East, before the bookmakers got wind that there was now a fast nigger in the Scranton woodpile. The syndicate were looking at eight to one, perhaps better, to clear a hundred thousand bucks or more. It was certain money. They would eat it with a knife and fork.

And the nigra Roother would surely not refuse. For they would cut him in for a big slice of the pie, to stay out of the

1912 Scranton, and out of the Olympic Games. Anything, enough to keep any nigra in grits till 1960 or beyond.

Jim had arrived at the Reservation on the Oklahoma Territory somewhat later than his friends and relations had expected – ten weeks later, to be exact. For on the train, after he had lost almost all his money, he had met up with two other Carlisle students, Jesse Young Deer and Joseph Libby. The two men were destined for North Carolina to play baseball for Rocky Mount for a princely fifteen bucks a week. Jim had tagged along, hit a few into the bleachers for manager Jim Argobast, and had made the team.

He had batted well in that first fortnight at Rocky Mount, hitting 0.253, and his base running was the best in the League. Then Argobast, short on strong-arm hurlers, had asked Jim to pitch. He had never pitched before, but an arm honed by Marty to launch a spear out to one hundred and fifty feet proved more than adequate to the task. Jim had done well, pitched 0.474, ahead of Rocky Mount's end of season average of 0.315.

The baseball season over, and a few baseball bucks jingling in his pocket, Jim had packed his bags and hitched the five hundred miles to the Oklahoma Reservation. There he had stayed with his sister, Martha, and her family, performing chores in return for room and board. Sometimes Jim thought back to the four hundred bucks he had lost on the train, but most times he didn't. On September 6th, 1911, he set out on the 1000-mile trek back to Carlisle and the football season.

To Mary Lou, until Saturday January ^{7th} 1911, football had simply been something for college thugs, more of a battle than a game. That day, standing in the driving rain at Indian Field, she had witnessed something that had changed her mind. For she had now seen Jim Thorpe play. Jim had caught the ball from the kick-off and had ripped the Syracuse defence to shreds, running a mazy seventy-five yards for a touchdown. Jim was like a grey ghost, and defenders could rarely lay a hand on him. When they did get close, Jim simply handed them off like naughty children.

On that grey January afternoon, Jim had been a one-man army. He had carried the pigskin for three hundred yards, had tackled like a man possessed, and his punts seemed to hang in the air for ever, waiting for him to get under them and snatch them from bewildered defenders. Mary Lou had even seen him drop kick a field goal from way behind the half-way line. The other members of the Carlisle team were good; indeed, some were excellent, but Jim Thorpe, he was a God. It was not necessary to understand the technical nuances of football to understand that.

Thus, Mary Lou was happy to sit with Marty high in the bleachers at Indian Field in the bright September sun, as Pop assembled his players around him below them on the infield. Marty pointed down to the group of players huddled around Pop. "Is that the whole squad?" he asked. "Only fifteen players?"

She nodded, munching an apple. "How many would Pop need? How many would you want?"

"Well, you've got your offence, your defence, your specialist teams. You know what I mean."

"Just you stop there," she said, looking around her. "We gotta talk later, but just you stop there, case anybody down there hears you talking like that. Pop's got eleven, and four subs, on the field. That's all he needs. That's all any coach needs."

"Christ," Marty said, "I've never seen anything like it in my born days. I saw Jim putting in rolled-up magazines for shin pads."

"So what? They *all* do," replied Mary Lou.

"But those boys, they've got no shoulder padding. No protection. No helmets, just those strange little leather caps."

She shrugged. “Me, I’ve only seen a few games, but that’s the way it allus seems to be,” she said.

On the infield with Jim, Pop, squinting in the sun, looked up into the bleachers and waved. Marty responded with a mock salute. “I see Marty’s brought his girl Mary Lou,” Pop observed.

Jim nodded and waved up at the couple. “Yeah, I remember she came to watch a few times end of last season,” he said.

“You think Marty knows anything about football?” asked Pop.

Jim shook his head. “Didn’t even seem to know the rules when I talked to him,” he said. “Thought we had squads of ’bout forty players.”

“Chance would be a fine thing,” said Pop.

“Didn’t even know ’bout the forward pass comin’ in a coupla years back.”

Pop shook his head in disbelief. “Strange,” he said, “makes you wonder where that boy’s bin all his life.”

“A man can’t know everything,” said Jim. “Football, that’s your territory, Pop.”

They walked, hand in hand, through the Negro quarter, in the growing dusk. “Don’t you go expecting the Ritz,” he said. “It’s nothing great. Just a couple of rooms.”

“Three bucks a week,” she said, “must be something fancy!”

The house was at the far end of the coloured quarter, fringing on Irish Town where Flaherty lived. Like most of the other houses, it was constructed of dull, grey, slatted wood, but looked to Mary Lou to be in good order. They climbed onto the verandah and Marty fumbled in his pocket for the keys. “Three bucks a week. Don’t expect much,” he said again, putting the key in the lock.

The door creaked open, set to reveal a sparse, wood-floored room with a wooden table and three chairs at its centre. In the middle of the back wall, was a cast-iron stove on which stood a coffee pot, and on each side, wooden shelving. On the left, was a cold water sink; on the right a door leading to the bedroom. Mary Lou noted that the room was warm and snug.

"I got the stove going before you came," said Marty. "Coffee?"

She nodded and sat at the table, looking around her. Marty picked up the coffee pot from the stove and brought it to the table with two enamel mugs. He poured out two cups of steaming black Arbuckle's. Mary Lou sipped hers, both hands around the mug. "Marty," she began, "I been to see Mammy Boston again. You left your handkerchief behind."

"And?"

"Mammy, she said she needs sump'n – like a handkerchief – to help her…"

"To help her see more things?"

She nodded.

"Mammy said, she said she could see you a-flyin' in the air."

"She said that before. Pole vaulting."

"No. This time, it was in a kinda rocket."

Marty nodded. "That'd be a plane."

"No, Mammy, she says she done seen a plane once, in a magic lantern show. So have I. That's made of wood and canvas and wires, and only holds a coupla men. No, she said this one was made of steel, and like a big house. Lotsa people in it."

"Where I come from, that's a plane, Mary Lou."

She shook her head. "And she said she saw you drivin' around in some kinda car. Real fast."

"That doesn't surprise me either. I've got two cars. Is that all?"

"No," she said, sipping her coffee. She laid down her mug. "She said, she said…" Mary Lou could not get the words out.

"Yes, come on, out with it, woman."

Mary Lou paused, as if afraid to release the words. "Mammy said she saw you takin' dollars…out of a hole in a wall."

"Everybody does that," he said, amused. "I always get my money out of a hole in a wall."

Instinctively, Mary Lou raised her right hand to him again, but stopped. "Marty, you gotta stop saying all them things. This is killin' me," she groaned. "I jest can't take no more. We'll both of us be in the crazy house."

Marty sipped his coffee. "I know, I know," he said, patiently.

She looked across the table at him, tears beginning to well in her eyes. "Help me, Marty," she pleaded. "You gotta help me out here."

"But how?"

She laid both hands out on his. "Let's us just keep this simple. Say that it's Sunday night." She paused. "Back where you come from, what would you be a doing?"

"Well, let's say I'd just competed in a decathlon, I'd rest up, have a couple of beers in my condo, that's my flat, and watch me a video."

"What's a video?"

"It's a sort of movie in a box," he said. "Like in a can of film."

"Like we saw at the movies last month, but all in a box?"

He nodded. "That's right," he said.

"Okay, I'll buy that. So what do you do with it? This box?"

"You put it into another box called a video recorder, and then the movie shows up on a big screen."

"And so this big screen, where does that come from?"

He paused. "Well, we have another box…with a screen, and the movie, it comes up on that screen."

"So you put a box in a box and the movie, that appears in another box. I gotta tell you, that sounds kinda weird to me, Marty."

Marty nodded. "I suppose it is when you say it like that, but that's the way it works. Cross my heart."

"And I suppose you gotta sit in a box to watch it?"

He smiled. "No," he said. "No need for any more boxes. You just sit in a chair with a coupla Buds."

"Buds?"

"Budweiser beers."

She shook her head. "Doesn't sound much fun to me," she said. "So why don't you tell me sump'n else? Sump'n I can understand."

He sighed and shook his head. "It's hopeless. I don't know where to start, Mary Lou."

"Let us start with how you make a living?"

"That's easy," he answered, "Decathlon. I run, I jump, I throw."

"And people *pay* you money for that? Just for watchin' you runnin' and jumping?

"No, not many people watch decathlon. But I got a shoe company called Nike that pays me half a million bucks a year."

"For doing what?"

"Wearing their shoes."

"Half a million bucks, just for wearing somebody's shoes," she said, her voice growing higher in disbelief. "They gotta be some kinda shoes."

"No, not just for that. For wearing their sweat suits as well."

"So you're paid half a million bucks just for wearin' suits and shoes. What else?"

"Well, I appear in advertisements."

"Like Houdini? In all the papers?"

"Something like that."

"And they pay you good money for that?"

"Yes, and I push Pepsi."

"What's Pepsi?"

"Pepsi Cola."

"Like Coca Cola? But that's for old people. For their health."

"Not where I come from, it isn't," he said.

Football, Angus Mackay reflected, was the only thing that really worked. He looked down from his office, as in the distance on the grit road below, Pop and his muddied players trudged slowly up the hill into the college grounds. He had taken over in 1906 on Brigadier Pratt's summary dismissal, full of great hopes and dreams. Pratt had been, for his time, a liberal, a radical, taking Carlisle away from being a post Little Big Horn repository for child hostages to the status of an educational institution. Alas, over the years, he had become hard, imperious, impervious to Government criticism. That was why he had to go in 1906. Pratt had done some great work, but his time was over. But Government policy had not changed. The American Indian was to become a white man, albeit one denied either citizenship or a vote. Thus, Mackay had, on his appointment, been forced to preserve Pratt's rigid policy in banning from Carlisle all Indian custom and language.

Angus Mackay had always been a pragmatist. If, therefore, he had seen that Indians could be seamlessly integrated, painlessly transformed into white men by educational process, then he would have done so. But he had seen from the start that it simply did not work. The Jesuits had claimed that it was the first seven years of life that put the stamp on a man. And though the Presbyterian Mackay had little time for Papists, he had been forced to admit that the Jesuits were probably right. For you could not take the Indian out of the man, no matter how much plumbing, carpentry or engineering you drilled into him. For inside each one of his students, there was a something that could not be touched.

Mackay had therefore decided to turn a blind eye to the use of Indian language and no one in Government had given a hoot or a holler. Washington had, in any case, no objective measure of the success or failure of Indian schools. For they had long known for certain that there would be no more Little Big Horns, and that Indians would simply vanish into their barren reservations or melt into the stews of industrial towns. For the moment, that was enough.

There was now only one area in which the native Indian could still hit the white man where it hurt, and that was football. There, Pop Warner's scrawny Indians had for years rocked the beefy, pampered offspring of Eastern industrialists by regularly whupping their asses good on the gridiron. Outweighed by up to twenty pounds or more a man, Pop's Indians had reduced the cream of Eastern colleges to rubble.

From the start, Carlisle's players had stuck rigidly to Pratt's sporting ethics, expressing in practice what the deans and physical educationalists of the East merely parroted in rhetoric from their lecterns. The white man had broken every treaty which he had signed with the Indian, but paradoxically Pop's Indians had always stuck by the rules of the white man's game. Thus, win or lose, they had shamed them every time they had taken the field. That would be Pratt's lasting legacy, one in which Mackay and Pop were happy to share.

Still looking down from his window, Mackay waved down to the players, though expecting no reply. He observed that the Negro boy Roother was there, talking with Jim Thorpe. It was a pity that he was black and not an Indian. If he had an eye for a ball and could take a hit, then he was surely a running back or a wide receiver. Mackay liked Roother. Indeed, he could almost accept him as an equal. But not quite.

Running Deer struggled slowly to his feet, reached deep into his mouth and withdrew a back tooth. He looked coldly into the eyes of Mulgrew, the Penn state player who had just slugged him, raised his right arm, making a fist, and then dropped it limply to his side. "Well done," he said.

Fifty yards upfield, Jim Thorpe crossed the Penn line for the first touchdown of the game. High up in the bleachers, Mary Lou by his side, Marty applauded. Jim had just taken the Penn team apart. He was, Marty decided, half dancer, half sprinter, gliding and then exploding, leaving tacklers grasping for air. Jim jogged back upfield, a broad grin all over his tanned face.

Marty looked at Mary Lou, shaking his head. "Penn are just sluggers," he said. "And no one seems to give a damn." He pointed down to the infield. "Hell, Mary Lou, they've put two of our boys out of the game already, and we're only into the first quarter."

"That's the way it's played by those East coast boys," said Mary Lou.

"But we've got umpires down there," Marty protested.

"White men," replied Mary Lou.

It had not been easy for Marty to follow the play, for this was not the game of football to which he was accustomed. For one thing, there was so much passing, most of it lateral. Indeed, this 1911 game looked to him more like rugby union than American football. The twenty-yard forward-passing limit, though now gone, had clearly been a major restriction, though neither quarterback could, in any case, have guaranteed accuracy much beyond twenty yards and most balls wobbled like jelly in flight. And the wide receivers did not seem to have planned lines of running. But the major difference lay in the fact that there were no specialists, with the same eleven men playing attack and defence. Thus, the whole brutal eighty minutes was played by eleven men and four substitutes. The game ended at 24 – 6 to Carlisle but, had the umpires observed the laws, then Carlisle would have creamed Penn by at least fifty points.

Jim walked across the track towards them, grinning, blood seeping from cut lips on to his grey Carlisle uniform. "So what d'you think?" he asked.

Marty paused. "Never seen anything like it in my life, Jim," he said. "Cross my heart."

"You got any pointers, coach?" Jim grinned.

"Football's not really my game, Jim," replied Marty. "But I got a few ideas which might work. If you can clear it with Pop, we'll talk about it on Monday."

Jim wiped his mouth with the back of his hand and looked at the blood. "That reminds me," he said, pointing up the hill. "The Dean. He wants to see you. Right away."

Dean Mackay beckoned Marty to sit in the chair in front of his oak desk. "So what do you think of Pop's boys?" he asked.

"Great, Dean," said Marty. "They were just great."

"Pop, he's done as much for Carlisle as I've ever done, or I'm ever likely to do," growled Mackay. He took off his glasses, removed a handkerchief from his inside pocket, breathed on their surfaces and began to polish them. "No one ever remembers your college for basket-weaving or carpentry. But football, that's a horse of an entirely different colour." Mackay replaced his spectacles on his thin, bony nose. He reached out and placed both hands in a triangle on the table in front of him. "I've got a wee proposition for you, Marty," he said slowly.

"You remember I talked to you a few months back about the Scranton New Year Handicap?"

"The Pro race? Yes?"

"Well, let me tell you a wee bit about Scranton, Marty. It's a hard town, full of hard men. Foot-racing, it's like a religion with those miners. They know running. They know runners."

"You told me all about it last summer, Dean."

"Aye, Marty. But that was before Yale. That was before you took the smile off Hurley's face. You did us proud that day, Marty, both of you. You did us proud." He paused. "But the Winter Handicap, that's the big one. New Year's Day. Just like Powderhall, back in Scotland. A hundred and thirty yards. A thousand dollars in prizes."

"That's not much," said Marty.

"No, Marty," said Mackay. "Like I said before, the big money's always in the betting. That's where you can clean up." He rose. "As I speak, Marty, as I stand here, there are twenty men on the East Coast hiding away, prepping for Scranton."

"Prepping?"

"Preparing," said Mackay patiently. "All in some hideaway, eating good, getting their rubs every day, finding yards, all just for twelve short seconds in Scranton, on New Year's Day, just like Powderhall." He stood and walked backwards and forwards behind his desk as he spoke, eyes glazed, as if speaking to himself. "And it's not just the East Coast, Marty," he continued. "No, runners come there from all over. St Louis, San Francisco, even England. The Colonies."

"But, Dean, I told you last summer," said Marty. "I don't want to turn professional."

Mackay stopped and turned to face Marty. "Aye," he said, nodding. "I know what you said then. Decathlon. The Olympics. Sweden. But just hear me out, Marty, just hear me out. You run at Stockholm and you're out in the open. Oh, you may have your Olympic medal round your neck, but that's all you'll have. You're exposed."

"So, I'm exposed. So what?" Despite his response, Marty could see where this was leading.

"That would mean that if you went for the 1913 Scranton Handicap, then the handicapper would put you so far back, my old mother could beat you. You won't be worth a cent to anyone."

"But, Dean, I don't care," said Marty. "I won't be around here in 1913 anyway."

Mackay stood, placed both hands flat on the table and looked Marty in the eye. "Be straight with me, Marty. How much do you have in the bank? Two, three hundred bucks from Yale?"

Marty nodded.

"The odds at Scranton will be juicy, Marty. And this time we'll cut you in for a big piece of the action. Five grand, maybe more."

Marty shook his head.

Mackay's voice took on a more plaintive note. "It's not just for me, Marty," he said. "No, if'n you win we'll be able to put twenty thousand bucks or more into Carlisle, get ourselves a proper gymnasium, perhaps even an indoor track. That money could change everything here."

"Dean, this is blackmail," protested Marty.

"Aye, Marty, you're right," agreed Mackay. "But what d'you say, man? For the college. For Carlisle?"

Marty raised both his arms to the side and shrugged. "I can't," he said. "It's just not in my plans. Sure I'd like to help the college, Dean, but it's not in my plans. If I run at Scranton this year, then it's goodbye to Stockholm. You must know that."

Mackay sighed, turned his back walked to the window and looked out without speaking. Then he turned to face Marty. "What does it get you, running at Stockholm for Sullivan and his AAU cronies? Nothing." He paused. "You've seen some of our college facilities, Marty. They're like something out of the Dark Ages. The Scranton Dash, it's once in a lifetime, money in the bank. We'll never get another chance like it."

Marty rose, shaking his head. "I'm sorry, Dean, really I am," he said. "I'd really like to help you out, but it's no." He turned and left the room.

Mackay watched the door close behind him. He knew that Marty was right. The syndicate would have to rely on their Canadian Rae, a runner they had been preparing for a year, a good bet. They might be able to use Marty at Scranton in 1913, after Stockholm, but he would by then be exposed, and the odds on him would be low. Aloysius Gilbert would not be a happy man.

Marty now understood that his release of random fragments of the future was proving to be of little help to Mary Lou. For the plain fact was that, only a few years after the Wright brothers, she could hardly be expected to conceive of a Boeing 747. She had never travelled by train and only once by car, when they had visited Hartford. Indeed, though she had made nothing of it at the time, Hartford represented the greatest distance she had ever ventured from Carlisle. On the other hand, her prolific and promiscuous reading had given her a much broader view of the world than most of Carlisle's citizenry. Understandably, that knowledge was patchy, chaotic. Thus, she possessed only the vaguest idea of the location, even the existence, of many European nations, and little knowledge at all of the rest of the world. Similarly, she knew more about Shaw and Wilde than she did about the recent history of the United States and, because of the NAACP, more about distant Negro history than she understood of the government of Pennsylvania.

But Mary Lou could not conceive of the ownership by a Negro of a house with running water and an inside toilet, of possessing a car or a bank account, or attending college. Perhaps that was not surprising. For she possessed only three dresses, two pairs of shoes, ten dollars and fifty cents in a tin box under the bed. That, and an agile, intelligent mind and a pair of slim, muscular legs that went on forever. That was it. He did not, therefore, know where to start when Mary Lou again visited his new home. But when he started by telling her of Mackay's offer and of his immediate refusal, her reaction was immediate. "All that money," she said. "Why didn't you take it?"

"Because I'd lose my amateur status, that's why," he protested.

"You should be so lucky," she said. "I'm still waiting to lose mine."

Marty struggled to keep his face straight. Mary Lou was incorrigible.

"Give me time," he said. "Give me time."

"OK, so you would lose your precious amateur status. So what?"

"So I can't go to Stockholm, to the Olympics, to beat Jim, that's so what."

She beckoned him to refill her mug with coffee. He went back to the stove.

"Now just let me get this clear in my head," she said, as he returned. "You've got history books – where you come from?"

Marty noted that she had avoided the words 'nineteen ninety-five'. "Of course, he replied, refilling her mug.

"And what did they, your books, say about Stockholm? About Jim?"

"That Jim won in the decathlon and the pentathlon."

"So that's done. That's history and you're not there. Just you tell me how you aim to change that?"

"I go to Stockholm, that's how!"

"If'n you win, all the history books will change?"

"I suppose so." He felt the words go limp from his mouth."

"But you've already read them history books."

"Let's say I go up to Washington and put a bullet in President Taft's head," Marty said. "History would change, wouldn't it?"

"But you won't," she said.

"But that's not the point," Marty said. "I *could*, and that would change everything."

She paused. "But Taft, he dies normal, don't he?"

He shook his head. "I don't know. History isn't my strong point."

"Perhaps it shoulda bin," she said. "But do you hear what I'm trying to tell you? You do something big like that and everything changes."

"But you do something small and everything changes too," he responded.

"You're right, but it's ornery people and nobody ever notices. It never gets in the books, does it?" She paused and sipped her coffee. "Let me ask you sump'n else," she said. "You told me once you knew for certain you had been back here."

He nodded. "Yes. I saw myself in an old photograph, in a museum."

"Or someone who looked like you," she said.

"No, it was me for sure."

"But nothing else? Nothing about them Olympics?"

"No."

"So let's say that ole photograph, it *was* you. That's on the record for sure. But not them Olympics. Don't that tell you sump'n, that you never made it? That you don't change nothing?"

"You're forgetting one thing that I have changed already," he said.

"What?"

"Jim losing his medals in 1913."

"How come?"

"I told you before, in all the history books, Jim played pro baseball last summer. So he lost his medals. Sullivan and his AAU assholes banned him."

"And?"

"The money he won at Hartford. Jim didn't have to play pro ball. So that means he'll keep his medals now. Just I aim that they won't be gold. Don't you see that?"

Mary Lou sighed again and slowly sipped her coffee. "That's the first thing you've said that lines up," she said. "I got no answer to that."

"All this is killing my brain," said Marty. He rose and withdrew a crumpled envelope from a back pocket.

"I got a letter here from Mr Sullivan of the Amateur Athletic Union."

"So what does he say?"

"I got to go to New York next week to register as an amateur."

"Can I come with you?" She smiled and put her hand over his. "We go to New York. You can get your amateur status, and I can lose mine."

Only a month had kept James E. Sullivan out of the history books. Those four weeks in 1894 had prevented him from getting ahead of Baron Pierre de Coubertin, to create the first modern Olympics in New York. Only the clogged arteries of the AAU committee structure had stopped him from heading off the Frenchman and linking with the AAA of England to create an Anglo Saxon Olympic games. Instead, de Coubertin, using his fancy European Freemasonry of counts and princes, had got his nose in front and had held the first Games in Athens in 1896. At first, Sullivan had considered ignoring de Coubertin's Athens achievement and going ahead with an Olympics in New York in 1900. After all, Athens had been a tatterdemalion affair, a thing of shreds and patches, consisting mainly of untrained Greeks. Hell, they had been forced to scour the ships in Piraeus harbour for sailors to fill the lanes and the athletic standards had been dismal, in most cases poorer than your average East Coast club meet. But those thirty days in 1894 had been critical, and when Sullivan had been told of de Coubertin's 1900 Paris Games, he had lost heart. Again, he had miscalculated. For de Coubertin had been cut out of the 1900 Olympics by jealous countrymen, in a Games which had stretched for three long months and had not even been called an Olympics.

Sullivan's big chance had come in 1904, when he had secured the Games for St Louis, linked with the St Louis Exhibition. But the Olympics had not attracted international competitors and had become little more than an American inter-club competition. De Coubertin had not even deigned to attend. Surprisingly, the failure of the St Louis Games had played into Sullivan's hands, for the Greeks suddenly re-appeared, demanding that there should be Intercalated Olympics in Athens, between four-year Olympic cycles. Sullivan had immediately jumped onto the Greek bandwagon and had delivered a powerful American team to Athens in 1906. He had made strong contacts in Greece and had sensed that de Coubertin's grip was beginning to weaken. The American team's success in Athens had done his political prospects at home no harm either. On his office wall, he boasted the framed telegram from Teddy Roosevelt to the American Olympic team. 'Uncle Sam is all right' it said.

In 1907, things looked as if they might be going his way. The Olympics had been scheduled for Rome, but Italian Government funds, depleted by the costs of the Vesuvius eruption, were diverted from the Rome Olympics and the Italians had pulled out. The English, with whom Sullivan had always had strong links, stepped in and produced an outstanding Olympics at London's White City. Alas, the relationship in London 'twixt the Americans and the English had turned out to be little short of poisonous, and there was now little prospect of a USA/Great Britain axis against de Coubertin.

The Frenchman had, since 1896, been acutely aware of the fragility of his Olympic movement, for only the London Olympics, for all their problems, could really be called on international sports festival. Sullivan was still a real threat, so de Coubertin had taken the only possible course. He had invited his arch-enemy into the Olympic family. Sullivan, feeling that it would only be a matter of time before his Tammany Hall skills would see off an effete Frenchman, had agreed and had come into the body of the kirk. By the Berlin Olympics of 1916, he reasoned, James E Sullivan would surely head the Olympic movement, or create a professional Games, like those goddam Ancient Greeks.

Sullivan sat at his desk, awaiting Roother's arrival and scrutinised the letter from Aloysius Gilbert. He could not see what Gilbert could possibly gain from what he had written. There had to be a buck in it somewhere, though for the life of him Sullivan could not yet identify its exact location, except possibly Scranton. For James E Sullivan, for all his devotion to the amateur ideal, had always possessed a good eye for a dollar. Thus, every brown paper envelope passed between athlete and meet-promoter had been skimmed and every meet-organiser seeking athletes had been forced to pay tribute to Sullivan. And no bookie, looking for advice on odds on amateur meets, ever looked further than the AAU Secretary. Sullivan had a finger in every track and field pie, and no one could go into the pie-making business without his express approval.

James E Sullivan was not used to a Negro looking him straight in the eye. But this fellow Roother did, sitting in front of his desk at the AAU office. Sullivan lifted Mackay's letter in front of him. "Mr Roother," he began. "The letter I have here makes some very grave claims against you. Relative to your amateur status."

"Letter?" said Marty in surprise. "Whose letter?"

Sullivan shook his head. "That is confidential, Roother," he said. He opened his desk drawer, placed the letter in it and closed it again.

"And exactly what does it say?" asked Marty.

"Amateur rules are quite clear, Mr Roother. Nobody can profit from amateur sport."

For a moment, Marty thought that Sullivan had found out about the Yale meet. His heart dropped and he flushed. "So what exactly are these charges?"

"That you coach track professionally at Carlisle College."

Marty smiled in relief. "That's all there is? That's it?"

"This is a serious matter, Roother," said Sullivan. "No professional coach is allowed to compete in amateur track. Those are strict AAU rules."

"Then we have no problem, Mr Sullivan," said Marty. "I'm employed at Carlisle to take care of the grounds, not to coach."

"But you **are** coaching?" Sullivan went back to his drawer and withdrew a sheet of paper. He scrutinised it. "Louis Tewanima, Running Deer, Jim Thorpe. You have coached all of these Carlisle athletes?"

Marty raised both hands. "Of course I've given the boys some help. But that's not what I'm paid for, Mr Sullivan."

"Can you *prove* that? Do you have any contract to that effect?"

Marty exploded. "At three bucks a week! A contract! Get real, man."

Sullivan scowled. "I would advise you, Roother, to keep a civil tongue in your head."

"Then let's treat this seriously, Mr Sullivan," replied Marty. "Can *you* produce a coaching contract? A man's innocent until proven guilty. That's the Constitution, even in 1911."

"The AAU doesn't have to prove anything," answered Sullivan. "We have evidence from an impeccable source that you have been paid to coach at Carlisle."

"This is crazy," protested Marty. "You don't have a shred of evidence that I coach for money, except some goddam letter that you won't even let me see. This wouldn't stand up for ten seconds in any court of law."

Sullivan stood, walked around the desk and sat on its edge looking over Marty. He smiled. "There may be another way," he said. "To the advantage of both of us."

"And I can compete in Stockholm?"

Sullivan shook his head.

"Stockholm would put nothing in your pocket," he said. "But running for me at Scranton in 1913 would."

"Why not this year's race?"

"I already have a man running there, at long odds," he said. "You have no form, and I would get big odds on you at Scranton in 1913. Two bites of the cherry. And you would come out of it with enough money for a lifetime."

"I'll give it some thought, Mr Sullivan," he replied.

Marty left Sullivan's office knowing that all hope of Stockholm had now gone. Sullivan was the A.A.U. He had all the cards.

Jim's thick, bulbous buttocks looked as if they had been traversed by a lawn mower. Marty shook his head as he looked at him, standing singing in the wet mist of the showers with the other Carlisle players after the 39-0 defeat of Pittsburgh. As Jim turned, Marty could see on his back five clearly defined diagonal weals. His puffy right eye was half-closed, his thick lips cracked and bleeding, his legs blue with bruises. Jim smiled as the warm water gushed over him. He turned off the shower, pulled a dark blue Carlisle bath towel from a hook in the drying area and began to dry himself, wincing as he drew it across his back. He pulled his towel around his waist and walked towards Marty into the noisy, crowded dressing room. Jim reached into his locker, pulled out another towel and began to dry his hair. "So you're all registered now," he said. "I can whup your ass in Finland."

"Sweden," corrected Marty.

"Same thing," said Jim, continuing to rub his hair dry.

"But I'm not registered," said Marty.

Jim stopped drying his hair and looked at him. "Why not?"

"Because I'm a professional, that's what. Sullivan says I'm a pro because I coached you and Louis and the other guys."

"But that's crap," said Jim, laying down his towel. "Pop didn't pay you for that."

Marty nodded. "I know that, and you know that…"

"And *I* know that." The voice came from Pop, standing just behind them. He put his hand on Marty's shoulder. "Come into my office, Marty," he said, nodding to Jim. Pop walked across the dressing room and closed his office door behind him. He beckoned Marty to sit on the single chair in his cramped, cluttered, little office and sat on his desk above him. "Now just what's all this about, Marty? What did Sullivan say?"

"It's like I said to Jim, Pop," replied Marty. "Sullivan said I was paid to coach."

"James E Sullivan is a horse's ass," growled Pop. "And he hates nigras."

"He's a motherfucker," said Marty dismissively.

Pop's eyebrows rose. "I'm not concerned with his domestic arrangements. He doesn't have a leg to stand on in this. I'll write and tell him the true story and what's more, I'll get the Dean to do the same. We'll clear this up in no time, Marty, just you mark my words."

The next morning, Pop was in Dean Mackay's office. There was no problem, indeed, Mackay could not have been more sympathetic, more helpful. This, he told Pop, was a disgrace, an affront to natural justice. He would therefore support Pop's letter with one of his own.

A day later, two letters were therefore dispatched by hand to James E Sullivan, both strongly supporting Marty Roother.

Chapter 12
Preparation

Numbed, Marty had read and re-read the letter from the AAU, signed by its secretary, James E. Sullivan. "The Appeals Committee has duly considered your case, but has found no good reason to alter the Secretary's decision of 9th October 1911. You are therefore under suspension from amateur athletics as from this date. Any appeal against this decision should be made to this office by 31st April 1912, and will then be considered by the Committee at its next meeting of July 6th 1912."

July 6th 1912. By that time, the United States Olympic team would be halfway across the Atlantic to Stockholm. There was, in any case, no reason to believe that the AAU would reverse its decision, for no stronger evidence in his favour was likely to be presented. History would not change. He would not be competing against Jim in Stockholm.

Mary Lou slowly scrutinised Sullivan's letter, sitting with him at the dining table at his home. She gloomily shook her head. "Looks like they fixed you good here," she said.

"I suppose I could try taking them to court," he replied.

"No," she said. "Not unless you get Clarence Darrow hisself to take your case. You black, honey. You black."

"You're right, Mary Lou. The courts won't go against people like the AAU. Anyhow, this is 1911. They'll say it's nothing to do with the law. It's a private club."

"That feller Sullivan, he knows that. Those AAU guys, they got all the cards."

"They printed the deck," he said.

"What do I do?"

She took both his hands in hers. "You do zactly what you came back here to do," she said firmly. "You help Jim, then you take him on, after Stockholm."

"And whup his ass."

"Just maybe," she said. "Then what?"

"Then I go back."

She frowned. "Going back. We'll talk 'bout dat later. What 'bout this Scranton race? It's big bucks. You could set up Carlisle college good. And my folks."

Marty nodded. "I owe Jim and the boys and your folks that," he said. "Yes, I win big in Scranton, coach Jim for Stockholm, then take him on when he gets back. You're right, honey. It all still fits. Just not the way that I expected."

She frowned.

"Cep'n I don't see no place in all this for little ole me," she said. "Is it because of what happened back in New York?"

"There was nothing wrong with New York," he said.

"I warn't much good to you. Didn't know what to do when we got together."

"You didn't hear me complaining, did you?"

"No, but I knows you been with all those other girls. They all could do it, couldn't they?"

"Yes, I suppose they could, but I didn't feel the same about them. It's not just about doing it. It's not a track meet, Mary Lou, Not a competition."

She laid her hands warm on his. "I'm glad you said that," she said. "Just wanna please you."

"Please me? Mary Lou, you please me all the time, just by being around. Maybe it wasn't Jim – maybe you're the real reason I came back."

She shook her head. "No," she said.

"Okay," he said. "So I came back to beat Jim."

"No," she said, placing her palm on his cheek. "Jim, he asked you back, but you wouldn't've come if'n you had known zactly who you was."

"Were," he said, smiling.

"Were, was, you didn't know, did you?"

"You mean Factor 2000?"

"Whatever. All that junk. Up till you found out, you thought YOU was the man. Then you stops and thinks, *am* I? Come on, Marty, you can level up with me."

He nodded. "You think of nothing else, since high school, only about being the best that you can be. You train your butt off, year in year out and then you let these crooks fill you full of shit. And you close your eyes to it. Then one day you think – where does the shit end, and I begin?"

He paused.

"Where is the ME?"

"You must've been talking to my friend Alvin, for that's exactly what he said. And I can feel it even now. My arms are down by an inch, my chest by over two inches. I can only train once a day now."

"Cos you're working."

"All I used to do was train, eat and rest up."

"And take whatever them people gave you."

"That's right. Oh, I can win this Scranton Dash cos I've still got a lot left and because it's a handicap race, but Jim, he's a great athlete. By next year, all this Factor 2000 is going to be down the pan. So, it looks like it's going to be pretty much even up for me against Jim by then."

"But that's right, ain't it? That's the way you wanted it to be all the time. Fair?"

"It's the way it always has to be," he said. "Fair, or it's all pointless. And that's why I'm here and that's why I coach Jim."

Later they lay together, in the darkness, their sweat drying on them.

"That was it, wasn't it?" she said burrowing her head into his shoulder.

"Yes," he said. "That was surely it."

She lifted her head. "And?"

He placed an index finger on her soft warm lips. "Don't ask me for a score," he said. "Just you take my word for it."

"I only aims to please," she smiled.

"You please," he said. "You sure as hell do please," He was silent. "You know," he said, "I said it before, but maybe I didn't come back for Jim. Maybe I just came back for you."

"So how you reckon you gonna get me back with you?"

He pulled her to him. "We get as close as we got tonight," he said, "they won't be able to get us apart."

They now had Roother, but Angus Mackay was surprised to find that he did not feel good about it. Since Marty had suddenly agreed to run at Scranton he had felt queasy in the stomach, a strange, acid taste in his throat. He felt that something had rotted at his core. For someone in the syndicate, someone that he trusted, had surely ratted on Marty to the A.A.U. And for days, since showing Sullivan's letter to Pop, he had not been able to look his coach in the eye. He wondered if Pop had noticed.

Pop, well, he had been Pop. He had cussed and raged, he had paced impotently up and down Mackay's office, then he had raged again. It was odd. A strange, unspoken bond had grown between Pop Warner and Roother. It was not the same as his relationship with Jim. Thorpe, he had always had to be pushed, squeezed, even occasionally bullied. With Roother, it was different. He appeared to be self-driven, to have a clear view of his objectives. Unlike Jim, he had a strong, focussed desire. That was rare. Pop had always known that it was not difficult to find talent. It was the talent for having a talent, that was rare as hen's teeth. Jim had it, but it needed coaxing. Marty Roother required no such external stimulus. Pop realised that with Roother, roles had somehow been reversed but had, surprisingly, shown little resentment. For Marty somehow gave him fresh energy. And, though he would be able to take little credit from their athletic achievements, he had wanted to be there in Stockholm when the two greatest athletes in his lifetime finally met in combat. That would now never happen.

But Pop could not understand it. Roother had no history with the AAU. Indeed, he had no record anywhere. Only a few years back, Sullivan had wiped out A. F. Duffey, the world's best dash man, because of a series of articles on shamateurism that the runner had penned for the eccentric Bernard McFadden's magazine. But, Pop reasoned, Roother had never crossed Sullivan; he had not been around long enough to make enemies in the AAU.

If Teddy Roosevelt had still been in the White House, then Pop would have gone direct to him with an appeal. And Teddy, always a stickler for fair play, would surely have gone out to bat for Marty. But not that tub of lard, William Taft. Hell, they had been forced to take down a White House bathroom wall in order to bring in a bath big enough for the 300lb. President. No, he had seen this all before. When the *blazerati* had it in for you, then you were dead meat. They made the rules. They were both judge and jury. They were the l rules.

Mackay had immediately submitted Marty's entry to Scranton and, two weeks before the handicaps were announced, they had heard on the grapevine that Marty would run off a novice handicap of five yards, a good mark, but not generous

In his negotiations with Pop, Marty had been no easy touch. He had insisted on Flaherty as his trainer at twenty bucks a week, and a six-week preparation period, all expenses paid. That and a grand up-front, win or lose, plus ten percent of winnings. Marty had wanted to train at Carlisle, and Mackay's only success had been in getting him to train away from the College, where there would be no prying eyes. He had therefore arranged that the training camp would be based at Coalburn, a derelict, worked-out Scotch mining town fifty miles to the west. Even there, Marty had gained a minor triumph, for he had insisted that the girl, Mary Lou Barrow, come with him. They had thought long and hard on this issue, for this was contrary to all pedestrian practice. It was well-known, even to the layman, that a man in training had to retain his vital bodily fluids. But Roother had been adamant, and they had reluctantly agreed. Roother and his companions had made their way to Coalburn in Pop's Stanley Steamer.

Angus Mackay slowly poured out for Pop Warner a steaming mugful of Arbuckles. The coach always took it black, no sugar and capable of floating a discus. He poured cream into his own and stirred it. "So what's the news from Coalburn?"

"It's early days," said Pop. "Can't say I know what our boy's all about, lifting these heavy weights with Flaherty."

"Preparation, it's not my line of business," said Mackay. "But it's common knowledge, Pop. Weights make you slow. Even my granny knows that."

"Forget about the weights, Angus," said Pop. "We've got another problem. Someone's out there clocking them."

"But we're the only ones who know where they are."

"Barring James E. Sullivan," said Pop. "We think that his man's been down at Coalburn."

"Sullivan's man?"

"Fellow name of Hanagan," replied Pop.

"Trying to clock Marty?"

"What else? But Marty has done them in a weighted belt, so Hanagan's come up empty so far." Pop frowned. "But that's not the point. How the Sam Hill did Sullivan know where Marty's prepping? And what's his angle?"

"Perhaps he's got money on Scranton," said Mackay.

"You mean on Marty?"

"We don't know that."

Pop laid down his mug and looked Mackay straight in the eye. "Angus, I *know* you. You're holding something back. Level with me. Sullivan could be in on Scranton, couldn't he?"

"In on what?" Mackay felt himself flush.

"Scranton. Marty. He's just checking out his investment. Sullivan's in for a slice of the syndicate pie."

Mackay gulped. “OK, so Sullivan might be in for a piece, but who knows? Nothing wrong in that.”

“Nothing wrong?” exploded Pop. “That horse’s ass put paid to Marty’s Olympic chances, now he’s planning to make a fortune out of him in 1913, if he can get him to pull out or take a dive at Scranton. That stinks, Angus, and you know it.”

Mackay stood, went to a cupboard on his left, withdrew a bottle of Scotch and proffered it to Pop, who shook his head. He poured himself a shot and put it down in one, then returned to his desk. “No,” he said. “Sullivan isn’t putting any money on Marty. Yes, he’s checking him out, but I’m not sure where his money will go at Scranton, probably with the syndicate’s man Rae. So he’ll want Marty to take a dive.”

“Now how the Sam Hill could you know that? Are you psychic? You been going to Mammie Boston? Level with me, Angus. Level with me.”

Mackay stood, returned to the cupboard and poured himself another shot. This time he sipped it and took it to his desk. “Okay, okay, Pop. I was going to tell you anyway.” He took a sip of his scotch. “Pop, I’ve been out of line here, way out of line. I did it for the right reasons, for the college. A new gymnasium…”

“A gymnasium, the college, what’s that got to do with Scranton?”

“I thought that we could make big bucks at Scranton on Roother, and put most of it straight into the college. And I told Gilbert.”

“You’ve got me there, Angus,” said Pop. “I’m lost.”

The Dean paused.

“I think that it might have been Gilbert who told Sullivan that Marty coached here for money,” said Mackay. “I should have kept my mouth shut to him about Scranton.”

Mackay gulped down the remainder of his drink and nodded. “The syndicate slipped Sullivan two grand to take Marty out of amateur track and told him they would have Marty in contract for Scranton, 2013, so that they could both make another killing then.”

Pop shook his head. "Which was a lie. Anyhow, they couldn't know that Marty would play ball, just took it for granted. He's running for us. Anyhow, Marty says he won't be around in 1913.All this is burning my brain, Angus. I think I'll have a shot of that Scotch now," he said.

"You don't drink in the morning."

"I do now," said Pop. He took his Scotch, gulped it down in one and put his glass forward for a refill. "I hope you're proud of your goddam syndicate, Angus," he said.

"I'm not," said Mackay, filling Pop's glass. "

I'm not surprised – but we can still get the money for the College Marty's a shoo-in for Scranton."

"No he's not," said the Dean. "As I told you, the syndicate have all their money on someone else this year, this chiel Rae. A ringer to end all ringers."

Mackay sighed. "This is where it gets a wee bit complicated," he said. He sipped his drink. "Before Marty ran at Yale, before they had seen Marty, the syndicate had been prepping another man up in Canada, a Scot name of Rae, the one I told you about. And they put early money on him, at big odds."

"But this Scot, Rae, surely his form would be known by now."

"No," said Mackay. "Rae came to them at eighteen, straight from rugby, running a few yards off ten seconds for a hundred yards, raw, no training. He had never competed, not even as an amateur. So they entered him in half miles and mile, and he ran on those boondock Canadian circuits."

"Always losing," said Pop.

"But always trying," said Mackay. "Those handicappers are fly, they can always spot a non-trier. Rae could run a fair half mile, around two minutes four, but he needed feeding stations in the mile."

"Typical dash man," said Pop.

"He didn't run many, 'cos they didn't want to take the edge off his sprinting," said Mackay.

"But all the time they were training him as a sprinter," said Pop.

"This boy's like shit off a shovel," said Mackay. "They say he ran just inside thirteen seconds in a trial in Canada, over the full Scranton distance."

"But that's still well over three yards slower than Marty," said Pop.

"Yes, but a little bird says he might be getting nine yards start to Marty's five," said Mackay. "Nine! So Marty, four yards back, is no certainty, Pop. So that's where the syndicate has put its money, on this guy Rae. So the syndicate plan is, Marty, he pulls out or goes out early at Scranton, and they keep him warm for next year's race."

Pop nodded. "At big odds. I suppose you've told Marty all this?"

Mackay shook his head. Pop groaned. "Angus, you've been in with the bad guys here," he said.

"I know. But look at it this way, Pop, Marty will get the same money for losing, or staying out. He'll come out with some cream – and there'll be more to come. He'll be a rich man."

"That's not the point, Angus. Marty, he's an athlete, he's a warrior, and he's decided to run for us. He won't want to take the fall. I'm telling you that now. And he says that he's leaving after Stockholm."

"Then if he doesn't make the right noises, they might send someone up to Scranton to try to convince him."

Pop exploded. "What *is* this, Angus? Tammany Hall? You're using this boy like a piece of meat."

Mackay flushed. "Come on, Pop, don't come the saint with me. Your college footballers aren't exactly Caspar Milquetoasts. You've been using Jim Thorpe for years. By the time he leaves here, his body will be a junkyard."

Mackay could see that he had hit his target. Pop gulped and reddened. "Yes," he said. "I've thought a lot about that, about what's going to happen to Jim when he leaves Carlisle. Hell, Jim's an ancient student, he's twenty-one. But he knows the score, we've talked it over many a time. Jim loves sport. He wants to play forever."

"Nobody gets to play forever," growled Mackay.

"No, and somewhere at the back of his brain, Jim knows that, said Pop. "I've told him that when his football days are over, he'll always have a place with me, coaching. Jim won't be dumped. I can promise you that."

Mackay smiled. "I'm glad I got this off my chest, Pop," he said. "So what do we do?"

"First, we tell Marty the full story," said Pop. "Let him make his mind up, 'bout how he wants to play it. After all, he's doing it for the College."

"Who'll tell him?"

"I will," said Pop. "I'll drive with you across to Coalburn on Sunday."

"And what if Marty decides to be a trier?"

"Then that's his decision. We've already put all our money on him, so to hell with the syndicate, even if they try to pay us off," said Pop. "But don't you on any account tell them that. They've got to think he'll withdraw, or go out in his heat, finishing way back. If'n Marty even wins his heat, we still get some money back for the College. If he goes on and takes it in the final, then it's great for us but goodbye to your syndicate buddies, Angus.

Mackay nodded. Already he felt better.

The town of Coalburn was like a black, suppurating wound. It consisted of a single street of industrial cinder, of shacks, deserted shops and broken boardwalks, on whose surface endlessly ran jagged rivulets of dark, brackish water. At its peak in 1885, Coalburn had housed one hundred and twenty-four Scottish miners and their families. But by 1902, the deep coal was exhausted, the Coalburn Mining Company had departed, and the Scots miners who had worked the pit had left for Scranton, Cleveland and Pittsburgh. Now, only the rusted mining wheel creaked in bleak memory over a town dominated by pyramids of coal slurry. Only a handful of families remained, scratching a sparse living from opencast mining or from work in neighbouring farms. Coalburn was a sad, stricken landscape, its shop windows like gouged eyes, its broken houses patched and peeled. On the outskirts, it was just possible to see the dim markings of a long-lost soccer field, its goalposts now peeled, blackened stumps. Like the town, like the pit, all energy had long departed.

Mrs Susan McCarthy was more than a woman; she was an event. From the moment she opened her door, she had engulfed her visitors from Carlisle, ushering them into a dining room heavy with heat from a glowing stove, placing before them steaming bowls of Scotch broth. Susan had been, in her springier days, ample, even voluptuous, though her late husband, Donald, would never have thought to employ such a word. Now, at forty-five, Susan was ample, capacious. Donald McCarthy had been crushed in a fall of coal in 1898 and with the insurance money she had set up a boarding house for the bachelors of the town, two of whom had stayed on in 1902 to work an opencast mine. It was from them and the products of a vegetable garden that Susan pursued a frugal existence. That and the yearly visits of the Carlisle syndicate's contingent to prepare their men.

Susan evinced neither surprise nor dismay that Marty Roother was black, or that he had brought with him a female companion, and the lumbering, Irish giant, Flaherty. She had always enjoyed the capacity to absorb everything that came her way. Anyhow, the young Negro was surely a fine figure of a man, and the girl, she was a peach. As for the trainer, Flaherty, Susan had never seen anything quite like him, not since they had visited the Majestic Theatre in Benton back in 1896. There, the German Sandow had lifted a fully-grown elephant, and had later proceeded to dance around the stage, carrying upon his shoulders a five-piece band. This fellow Flaherty looked to her to be able to bear the weight of the Pittsburgh Philharmonic, were the mood to take him.

Susan had seen more than a few automobiles in her time, though none recently, but she had never seen anything to approach Pop's Stanley Steamer. When she had served the main course, she and her lodgers, Hamish and Colin, had stood on the porch, gazing at it, listening to the quiet hissing of its slowly cooling engine. In the past, Angus Mackay had always delivered the athletes himself. In doing so, he had invariably left behind a bottle of malt whisky. This time, the Bowmore Malt had been delivered by the Irishman, Flaherty. It was the same rich, peaty dram that she had first tasted as a young woman back in Lochgelly.

Lochgelly. Susan had seen a power of running in her youth, runners training on Sundays or after a day at the pit face, runners without a backer to cosset and nurse them, to take them to some remote location for preparation, men with no more chance in the big money handicaps than she had herself. She had watched them leave for the big races in Edinburgh and Newcastle, and return, heads down, having failed to survive even their cross-ties.

Similarly, for all their careful preparations, none of the syndicate's previous runners had ever survived beyond the cross-ties at Scranton. They had usually been cut down by men honed to a fine edge, men who trained to run with money heavy on their backs. For that was always the test. They had brought to Scranton men who would run well in their final trials, some good enough on paper to take the big handicap. But none of them had ever stripped big; they had withered in the cold winter cauldron that was Scranton.

Pop and Jim had never thought to see Angus Mackay so penitent. They sat with Marty, Mary Lou and Flaherty in the dim brown light of Susan McCarthy's living room, as the Dean poured out the whole sorry tale.

"Let me get this straight in my head, Mr Mackay," said Marty. "The syndicate sold me out to Sullivan, so that my amateur status went down the tubes. But now you're telling me that all their money's on this Scotchman, McCrae..."

"Rae," corrected Mackay.

"Rae, McCrae, who cares?" Marty exploded. "So it's all bets off. I won't be here for next year's race, their bucks are on Rae, so there's nothing in it now for Sullivan or your syndicate. So why can't they get Sullivan to give me back my amateur status?"

"It's not as easy as that," Mackay replied. "You're entered at Scranton. Your entry's been paid."

"But I haven't earned a cent," said Marty.

Mackay shook his head. "That makes no difference to the AAU," he said. "You've signed pro forms."

"Now just wait a minute." It was Mary Lou who spoke. "Marty only entered because your syndicate lied to Sullivan, and paid him to take Marty out."

"I know." Mackay's words came through clenched teeth.

"What you mean is that Marty runs at Scranton and goes out early so that the syndicate and Sullivan can still get good odds on him come next winter," said Mary Lou. "That's the long and short of it."

"Is that it, Mr Mackay?" Jim said. "The syndicate gets a double bite at the cherry. I know Sullivan. He runs the AAU. He could give Marty back his amateur status tomorrow if he had half a mind to."

"Yeah, he thinks that he can pay off Marty to take the dive and run next year," replied Mackay. "But if Marty shows fast next month and even makes the Scranton final, then he'll be cut down to a low handicap. Low odds, no big bucks there next year for Sullivan, or anybody."

"Except the College, if'n he wins, with your money on his back," said Mary Lou

"This is a sad, sad business, Angus," said Pop.

"But if he takes a dive, Marty will probably get the same money, then more next year," said Mackay. "He'll never have to work again."

"That's not the point," said Marty, struggling to control his rising anger. "And I'm not going to be here next year. And I wanted to compete against Jim in Stockholm."

"And whup my Indian ass," said Jim.

"You got it," smiled Marty.

"You can still do that, try to whup my ass," said Jim.

"How?"

"After them Olympics," Jim said. "I'll take you on here, back at Hartford."

"Promise?"

"You got my word on that, Marty," said Jim.

"Well, that's surely something," said Mackay, brightening. "So where does that leave us?" He looked at Marty. "What are you going to do? Are you going to run to orders, take the dive?"

Marty looked at Mary Lou. "Keep putting your money on me, heat to final," he said. "I run to win. I don't know any other way."

The reports back from Coalburn to the syndicate from their spy Brodie were both unequivocal and encouraging. The Negro had now moved on to weekly time trials, over one hundred and twenty-five yards, having brought across Jim Thorpe, giving Jim a three yard start. The first trial, held on a still, dry, December day, Brodie had clocked at 12.5 seconds, with the Indian winning by two yards. Brodie had tracked Roother throughout the trial, and there was no question that he was a trier. But twelve and a half seconds was as fast as he could run. A week later, the two men had raced again, with the same result, and a slower time of 12.6 seconds, albeit into a slight headwind.

When the runners had departed, the syndicate's spy Brodie had checked out the track surface. It was hard, fast, industrial cinder, identical to Scranton. The Negro was fast, but he was at least three yards off the pace, with Rae off nine yards, and there was no way by which that distance could be found in a fortnight. When Brodie had reported back to the syndicate, he had been well satisfied. Clearly this had been why the syndicate had been content to have Flaherty and the girl with Roother. Heavy weights slowed a man down, that was common knowledge. As for women, they were poison to any athlete in hard training. Roother was clearly out of condition and in contrast, reports from Rae's camp were of trial times that would make the Scranton race a formality. Indeed, reasoned Gilbert, the problem might be in slowing down their man Rae in order that he would win without concealing his true form. This might leave him with a handicap still good enough to pick up money in subsequent summer events. Still, it might be best to avoid being too greedy. If Rae eased off perceptibly in the Scranton Final, then there would be dozens of aficionados who would pick it up and the handicappers were not fools. They could usually pick out non-triers.

Marty had never run at such speeds in his life, certainly, not at a bodyweight of over two hundred pounds. For the lead-filled canvas belt which Flaherty had created for him, meticulously stitched by Susan McCarthy, had added over ten pounds to his weight. That, and ponderous lead-plated running shoes, had ballooned his running weight to over two hundred pounds in his trials. Under such conditions, he was delighted with his trial times. Whenever he took the belt off, Marty felt sharp, he felt good. He had almost come to like the crisp, black cinder path by the railroad that was now his training track. In them, there was suddenly a life, an energy not possessed by the synthetic rubber tracks to which he was accustomed. There was in them a strange, hard reality.

Mary Lou had been pure gold. For though they had not pursued an entirely celibate course, she had held in check her newly-discovered sexual drive. They had therefore spent their spare time in the Stanley Steamer, driving far from the darkness of Coalburn, deep into green Pennsylvania countryside.

For Kevin Flaherty, celibacy possessed neither merit nor meaning. Thus, within a week, Susan McCarthy seemed to shed at least ten years. And on rest afternoons, when Marty and Mary Lou had driven off, her home rocked to the vigour of their endeavours. On one such occasion, when it was over, they had lain together in silence. “Kevin,” said Susan. “Did I ever tell you about that German, Sandow, at the Majestic. A braw chiel.”

“Aye,” said Flaherty. “That Sandow was a strong feller, and no mistake.”

“I once saw him lift a big barbell, with one hand. Then he put it down on the stage and opened it at each end. Each of the globes was hollow.”

“Bejasus,” said Flaherty.

“But, Kevin, a man stepped out of each globe. He had lifted those two men. Did **you** ever do that?”

Flaherty paused. “I don’t know,” he said. “What were their names?”

Scranton, 28th December 1911

The coal dust crusted their lips, lay bitter in their mouths and throats. Its dark grains hung in the still, frozen Scranton air, blackening every tree and plant which dared to survive the town’s sulphurous atmosphere.

Their party had arrived late at night, trundling through silent, corrugated streets gripped by frost, on the Stanley’s stiff, unyielding tyres. Scranton was a dark nightmare, lit as much by the skyward flames of the Carnegie Steelworks as the guttering gas lamps which lined its streets like sentinels. Their lodgings were situated in the shadow of steaming slag heaps on the outskirts of the town, the property of a retired miner, the Chippewa, Joshua Two Wings, an ex-Carlisle student. Joshua kept a spotless house, on three storeys, occupied by black miners and steelworkers, and had allocated four rooms to the party. Joshua had not missed a Scranton Dash since his arrival in 1887, but never had he seen a Negro worth a bucket of warm spit. The smart money seemed to be on a Scotchman, name of Rae, who had now dropped to 3-1 having been as high as fives, back in November.

Joshua had never before housed whites, and Dean Mackay's insistence that Flaherty and Mrs McCarthy stay with him had come as a surprise. On her arrival, Susan McCarthy, sensing the embarrassment of some of the Negro lodgers, had drawn a coal-stained finger down her white face. She had scrutinised it. "Seems to me like we're all black here," had been her words. That had broken the tension, had brought a smile to Joshua's brown, leathery face, and had made his Negro lodgers feel at ease.

And Flaherty's presence, that was an honour. For Joshua had been a member of the audience back at the Grand Theatre, Scranton in 1896 when Flaherty, the Irish Giant, had lifted a full-grown elephant overhead and had bent solid iron bars as if they were liquorice. Indeed, he still possessed a tattered, well-thumbed copy of Flaherty's manual "Muscular Manhood". Mary Five Fingers aside, he had followed its tenets for sixteen years. Mary had been a constant and reliable companion since the death of his wife in 1902. Joshua had not re-married, for the women of the Reservations had no desire to exchange their soft, sweet air for the fug of Scranton. Anyhow, Joshua reckoned that whatever damage that Mary had done had been more than redressed by his daily workouts with his McFadden Patent Chest Expanders.

Joshua found the Negro Roother to be a rum kind of fellow. To start with, he ate with a knife and fork and talked real funny, like no black whom he had ever encountered. And the presence of the girl, Mary Lou, had come as a real surprise, for it was a well-known fact that women were death to an athlete. And he had also been surprised at the lack of meat in Roother's diet, for it was common knowledge, too, that rump steak was central to pedestrian's preparations; that, and sherry and eggs just before a big race. But Roother, he seemed to favour Scotch and wop food, pasta and porridge and the like. And though porridge was no problem, Joshua had been hard put to locate any source of pasta in Scranton's shops.

Pop and Jim had now deliberately distanced themselves from the syndicate, and had lodged with Joshua in a cramped single room. Mackay had remained with his colleagues, aware that any detachment might arouse doubt about Marty's intentions. As far as Gilbert and his partners were concerned, the hired hand Roother would withdraw, depart early, in the first round, way back, running tight, and Mackay did not intend to put any doubts in their minds at this moment.

The pumps and furnaces of Scranton's mines and steelworks never for a brief moment stopped for breath. Many workers had, however, altered shifts to attend the Dash, as had their colleagues throughout Pennsylvania and the Eastern Seaboard. The Handicap had first been brought to Scranton by immigrant Scots, who had created a direct replica of their revered New Year Powderhall event. Somehow, the Scots had infected Poles, Germans, Irish and Czechs with their love of professional footracing, men running with the weight of money on their backs. Scranton's still, cold air throbbed with running and rumours of runners.

The California School was said to be bringing over a Mexican who was rumoured to be as fast as a shithouse rat. The Mex, name of Alvarez, was virtually unknown but rumoured to be good for close to even time, and running off a generous handicap of six yards. The Limeys had shipped across a Lancashire miner, name of Crench, reputed to be a yard faster and running off seven yards. The Welshman, Thomas, was said to be the great grandson of the legendary runner, Guto Nyth Bran, who had run twelve miles inside the hour over a century before, although, no mention was made of the fact that Guto had died on completion of his great feat. Then there were stories of Scotsmen running off long marks, men who had run like stags in obscure Canadian Highland Games. The town seethed with running rumour.

Mary Lou had, for the past two months, lived in the strange, rarefied atmosphere of track and field. She had liked the taste of it. During their stay at Coalburn, she had been asked by Marty to act, if not as a coach, then as a second pair of eyes. Marty took her through his running drills and practices, in which single aspects of sprinting were isolated, focussed on and then moulded into the full sprint action. Thus, there was the angle of the arms, a rough right angle, and the "clip-to-hip" drill which focussed on the range through which the arms should travel. There was the "running tall" drill, in which the hips had to be high, the shoulders low. There was even a drill called "jelly jaw", to relax the face and mouth.

Marty seemed to have a drill for everything, for knee pick-up, for leg-cadence, even for eye-focus. Mary Lou had daily taken him through the ritual of the drills at sum maximal speeds, and had slowly developed an eye, a feel for sprinting. Thus it had not long before she could detect tension in his neck and shoulders, over-striding, low hips, high shoulders. She took him through his drills, as a music teacher would put a pupil through the scales, to secure that strange paradox of power without tension.

Marty closed the door of the living room behind him, and locked it. He beckoned Mackay, Pop, Jim and Mary Lou to sit with him at the fire. He sensed trouble.

"Houston, do we have a problem?" he said.

"Houston who?" asked Mary Lou.

"Just an Alabammy figure of speech," Is there anything that I should know?"

"No," said Mackay. "We laid on you early, before Gilbert, one of them a roll-up bet, and we got good odds. Roll-up means if'n you win in your heat, the winnings go forward to the next round, then on into the final. So that could be big bucks."

"But you're clear that they have their money on Rae and they still want me to withdraw or throw the race in the first round?"

Mackay nodded.

"Aye, but it's got more…more complicated," he said.

"The syndicate have now sweetened it. They've now told me that they will give you two thousand bucks to pull out, or a thousand to take a dive in the first heat. You will be kept out of the way in the summer, and win big for them here next year. And they will cover our losses and give us a slice of their winnings. That's the whole story, so far."

"Two big hits, if their man Rae wins and Marty takes it next year," said Jim.

"And there's more," said Pop.

"Sullivan has told them that he will give you exactly the same deal."

"So how has Sullivan suddenly come into the picture?" asked Marty.

Pop shook his head.

"I don't rightly know," he said. "Rumour has it that he tried to take over the Olympic set-up back in 1906, but he didn't cut the mustard with the Olympic aristocracy. The buzz is that he needs big bucks to set up his own pro running circuit before the 1916 Olympics. Two big hits at Scranton might give him the bucks to do it."

"But Marty could've picked up a passle of medals for us at Stockholm," said Jim.

"Sullivan doesn't give a docken," said Mackay. "Marty's black, and Sullivan hates blacks."

"Specially sassy blacks," said Marty.

Mary Lou spoke.

"You're all treating Marty here like you owns him," she said.

There was silence.

"What do you want, Marty?" said Jim.

"If I win the first heat, Dean, will that give you enough from the syndicate to keep the College in funds?"

"No, though the syndicate did offer to give me a piece of the action if they win on Rae, and you take the dive. That would cover our losses on you, with an extra slice for the College. "

"But surely they must have it somewhere in the back of their minds that I'm not going to take the fall, and that means that you will be persona non grata with the syndicate from now on? You're happy with that?"

Mackay nodded.

"Aye," he said." My old granny, she had a saying, Marty. "You have buttered your parsnips, so now you must lie upon them."

Chapter 13
Scranton

Marty stood at the centre of the frozen infield and looked around him, out in the misty winter gloom at a sea of cloth caps. Scranton Stadium was full, gorged. Ten thousand, one hundred and thirty-six spectators had paid a dime to brave the winter cold on its rough, broken, terracings, and five thousand others had put up a dime more to set their asses on wooden benches in the leaking, corrugated-iron-roofed stands on the straights. Hundreds of others had paid nothing, squeezing or battering their way through and over rotten wooden fences, risking emasculation as they scrambled over the jagged glass that studded the stadium's high concrete walls. In all, 17,196 miners and steelworkers had come to lay money on the fastest men on earth.

But it would not merely be fast men. For there was also a 300 yards' handicap, and another over a mile on the Scranton Stadium's cramped, black, four-lane cinder track. Marty scraped up a handful of black cinders and held them in his hand, and allowed them to slip slowly through his fingers. A residue of the cinders stayed in his hand. That was good, for Jim had told him that it meant clay and a quick, firm surface. But he had been hard put to it to scoop up any cinders, for the surface was now freezing fast. Fortunately, it was well-rolled, but soon it would set like concrete.

Earlier, the members of the syndicate had come down to see him in his dressing room, all smiles and synthetic bonhomie. Aloysius Gilbert had said little, but had hinted to Marty that it would be best that he go out early, preferably in his heat, and way back. Marty had smiled and had said that they could trust him to carry out his side of the bargain, they could be certain of that. Gilbert had smiled back, secure in the knowledge that the emetic that Joshua Two Wings had been paid $50 to insert in Marty's evening meal would surely do the trick, whatever the Negro's competitive intentions.

It was nothing remotely like a sweat suit, but it would have to serve. Mary Lou had elasticated the waist of a pair of grey flannel trousers and had then done the same at the bottom of both trouser-legs. The resultant track-bottoms were clumsy and had little of the warmth or flexibility of modern sweat-pants, but they would surely serve their purpose. Topped by a warm woollen jersey, they were, certainly, superior to the dressing gowns and blankets being deployed by most of the other competitors in the Scranton Dash.

Marty lay on the massage table in the cold, shadowy stillness of his dressing room as Flaherty gently kneaded reeking horse-liniment into his legs. Flaherty paused, smelt his fingers and shook his head and grinned. "Bejesus, Marty," he said, "at least ye'll *smell* fit."

Marty smiled distantly and lay back as the Irishman flicked the soft belly of his right calf. Earlier, he had watched the first event of the meet. It had not been a footrace No, it had been a contest between a pigeon and a greyhound, for a wager of three hundred dollars. The bookies threading the vast, dark, steaming crowd had taken $10,000 in bets, with the greyhound at evens and the pigeon at 3-1 against. Jim had placed $50 on the bird and had advised Pop and Marty to do the same. "Trust Jim," he had said, and they had.

It had been no contest, for the pigeon had taken the race by a clear five yards. To be certain, Jim had stayed tight on the bookie's shoulder and had picked up their winnings. He returned to them with a wad of crumpled greenbacks, his face wreathed in smiles. "We raced 'em lotsa times, back in the

Territory," he said. "The pigeon wins, so long as its mate is at the finish. It's got something to go for."

Something to go for. Marty lay back, eyes half-closed, as Flaherty gently teased his thick, soft quadriceps. He had come all this way, ninety years back, to run for real, to **be** real. That was what he was running for in this cold, dark place, to be real. It was not, therefore, enough simply to win. He wanted to win big, to be the fastest of the Fast Men of this Year of Our Lord, 1912.

Mary Lou sat high in the stand parallel to the home straight, jammed in between Mackay, Jim, Pop and Flaherty, relishing every moment, her cheeks hot with a mix of fear and anticipation. She loved it. Scranton had a charge, an energy, a danger. It was that danger, the dollar-weight that would in moments be applied to its frozen surfaces that gave the Scranton Dash a force, a power beyond conventional track competition. It was the certainty that in seconds lives could be transformed, that the training of years could take a man from the mine or the foundry, to a better life. But the Dash was a handicap race. There was no knowing who would vanish in the cross-ties or who would suddenly find that vital yard in the final. It was that terrible uncertainty that produced the cold spot at the pit of Mary Lou's stomach that she so loved and hated.

Jim sat beside her in the freezing stand above the home straight, his hands numb, sipping Scotch from a hip flask. The pristine, one hundred and thirty yard dash straight below them was divided into six lanes, all separated by foot-high strings. The Scranton track was now flint-hard, and Jim had counselled Marty to wear short, stubby training spikes, rather than his new racing-shoes. Otherwise, it would be like running on stilts.

Pop scrutinised his programme. There would be thirty-six heats, with only heat-winners moving forward into the next day's six semi-finals, or cross-ties, as these goddam Scotch officials chose to call them. The cross-ties would produce six runners for the final on New Year's Day. Pop had been at Scranton twice before with Jim, who had acted as trial horse in training for two other syndicate runners. Alas, both had tightened up and been blown away in the cross-ties. Scranton was unlike amateur track, where form was common knowledge. For no one knew where there might lurk an unknown hick on a long handicap, who had suddenly 'found' yards somewhere up in the Adirondacks. Neither did anyone know how a fresh, fancied amateur, however swift, might perform with bucks heavy on his back. No one knew who would choke up under pressure or who would suddenly strip big and make Scranton his and his alone.

Pop looked around him at the dark, lowering skies. Black rain. For Pop, Scranton had always meant black rain lashing down, reducing the track to a pulp. Now it was hoar frost, though even the frost now gripping the infield grass was flecked with soot. Scranton was as far from the sunny swards of inter-collegiate track as it was possible to be, but Pop was not unacquainted with the runners of the area. Jim had met some of them on the football field, men scarred by factory and mine, ringers brought in by Ivy League colleges to stiffen up their teams. The toughest tackles of college football were gnat bites to men who had burrowed like rats in a three-foot coal seam or daily faced the blast of foundry furnaces. Jim had taken big hits from men like these, often when the pigskin was miles away, but after the game he had been happy to share a jug with them. These and men like them would be the runners whom Marty would face. Hard men, men with little to lose. It was as well, reflected Pop, that this was a straight dash, in lanes. In a longer race, without lanes and on a curve, pro running was a full-contact sport and Marty would have been cut to shreds. But he knew that the money was down and that he Jim and the Dean were now in deep, with no long boot to get out of it.

Pop leafed through his programme. Thirty-six heats, with only the winner of each heat moving on into the six "cross-ties". The winner of each "cross-tie" would compete in the final. Marty was off five yards, with forty others level or behind him, from scratch onwards. The longest handicap was sixteen yards, light years for a dash man, but occupied by a 45-year-old veteran, Hamish McLeod, whose lean, white legs were little more than a series of varicose veins held together by ligaments. Marty was in heat 17, and Jim and Mary Lou made careful notes on the heats preceding him. The early handicapping was good, with every heat going to two yards or less. With a following breeze and an unscarred track, times were fast, in the 12.5 sec to 12.7 sec range. The fastest was the little Mexican, Alvarez, off six yards, at 12.6 seconds, but the Welshman, Thomas, had also won well, winning, hands high, at 12.4 seconds, with a couple of yards to spare. The Maine runner, a rangy ex-amateur, Van Houten, running off a generous eight yards, had been a tad slower at 12.6 seconds, while the English runner, Crench, running from the same start, had narrowly qualified, in the same time.

"They're up," observed Pop, pointing down to the track, for the runners in Heat 17 were now discarding blankets and dressing gowns behind the starting line.

Mary Lou noted that Marty was slow in removing his clothing, discarding first his grey woollen jersey, removing his flannels to expose his legs only at the last moment. All of the runners wore black, numbered bibs, with white numbers Powderhall-style, giving them a strange anonymity. Pop passed his field glasses to Mary Lou, and she peered down onto the track. She could see Marty vainly trying to scratch with a trowel an indentation for his front foot on the track's rock-hard surface.

The runners took to their marks and on the terracings the flat caps were now still and silent. Mary Lou checked her programme. Marty, in lane three, was giving away between three and nine yards in starts. Mary Lou felt the hot throb of her pulse in her temple as she watched her man screw his front foot into the icebound track, and settle into his marks. The surface was rock-hard and there would be no angled front wall from which to drive out. She returned the field glasses to Pop, and placed her right hand on Jim's shoulder for comfort. Jim grinned his toothy grin. "Gun up," he said, pointing to the start.

The gun exploded in the still air. Marty powered out, eating cinders. He had taken his first man, on his left, in twenty yards and gobbled up the two runners on his right at fifty. He was deep into the front – markers at eighty yards and now easing up at a hundred yards, was two yards clear. The crowd erupted. It was always great to see a fast man rip through the field in such a manner.

"Twelve and a fifth," observed Pop. "I got Marty at twelve point two, playing Dixie." He looked behind him, at the syndicate, sitting gloomily three rows behind them. "How d'you like them apples?" he said, to no one in particular

December 31st 1911

The vomit splattered from Marty's mouth, on to his jersey and down on to the track. He dropped, coughing, on to his knees at the entrance to the arena, both hands to his face. Still it continued to pour out, through his fingers, lumpy, viscous, soiling the frozen black cinders. Flaherty quickly lifted him to his feet as the buzz of the crowd at the track entrance grew and together they walked back down the tunnel, out of sight. Marty's odds rose from evens to 3-1 against. It was fully five minutes before he reappeared, his face ashen white, wearing an unsoiled jersey and flannels, to answer the starter's call for the fifth cross-tie. Snow had begun to drift down, flaky, forming a thin white skin on the flinty, black cinder surface.

The first and second heat winners were two local miners, Headley and Walecinski, both off long starts of ten and twelve yards but only scraping inside thirteen seconds by the thickness of a vest. The English miner, Crench, had made it through, taking the third narrowly in 12.9 seconds. The revelation had been the Welshman, Thomas, who had wiped out Alvarez, running 12.8 seconds, into a blizzard. Rae had won by a short yard, in the same time.

It was clear, even to spectators high in the stands, that the Negro Roother, was still in deep trouble, as the starter called the six runners to their marks for the final cross-tie. Shaking his head as if to clear it, he struggled to pull his woollen jersey over his head, then snagged his spikes on his flannel trousers as he tried to withdraw his feet. The snow, swirling into the runners' faces, continued to come down in thick, soft flakes, giving the athletes a ghostly quality. Marty looked down the track into a silent whiteness and ritually adjusted shorts which required no adjustment. This time, he made no attempt to dig a hole for his front foot. There was no point. The snow-skinned track was now like iron. He had again drawn a middle lane, lane four, with all of his men in front of him, on starts from four to nine yards. Marty was not concerned about the starts, for it was always lethal to look. As a decathlete, he had long ago learned that it was essential to drill through four feet of space, oblivious of the competition. Sprinters ran in a tunnel. If he could see anyone, if for a moment he was aware of him, then he had lost focus and was in deep shit. Somehow, the snow made everything easier, for it blocked out the periphery. It cocooned him. Now, as the starter's voice boomed above him to his left, he could see only a white void. Marty could not even feel the snow on his left knee as he got on to his marks. That was good. On the "set," he lifted his hips.

The gun barked and unleashed him. Marty flowed out and ran as in a dream, his movements silky, feeling only muscle-flow, hearing nothing, seeing nothing. He was running loose; he was running tall; he was running easy. The product of a thousand drills was now being effortlessly expressed through Scranton's frozen cinders. This was the way it should be. When he snapped tape, he was a clear yard up.

"Twelve point five, maybe better," observed Pop. "Into a wind, and on snow."

"Fancy running," shouted Jim, as Mary Lou continued to shriek beside him.

"And him sick as a dog," added Mackay.

"Fifty bucks worth of syndicate sick," said Pop, smiling.

The Carlisle syndicate were still aggrieved, but optimistic. For their man, Rae, had been slick as greased ice at 12.8 seconds with surely at least two yards left in his legs, perhaps more. And, though Roother had somehow survived the immediate effects of Joshua Two Wings' potion, the Indian had assured them that it lingered in a man's guts for days. Roother, he assured them, would be soft as your pocket in the final. That was the Navajo's opinion, and it was good enough for the syndicate.

Still, Marty's lack of professional ethics rankled with Gilbert and his colleagues. For this had nothing to do with sport. He was their man, even if he had not actually taken their money. A pro, a black, a hired man like Roother, ran to orders. After all, they had put good money into his pocket at Hartford.

The syndicate had so far seen nothing of Sullivan. Perhaps, thought, Gilbert, that was not surprising, for it might have been unwise for the cardinal of amateur track and field to be seen at the Scranton pedestrian carnival.

1st January, Scranton

FINAL

Lane 1 Crench (England) 7 yards 4-1

Lane 2 Rae (Canada) 9 yards evens

Lane 3 Headley (Scranton) 10yards 2-1

Lane 4 Roother (Carlisle) 5yards 3-1

Lane 5 Walecinsky (Scranton) 12 yards 4-1

Lane 6 Thomas (Wales) 7yards 2-1

There had been slight movement in the betting in the day before the final, with bets from the Carlisle Syndicate taking the odds on Rae down to evens. A mountain of nickels and dimes had poured in on the two local miners, Headley and Walecinski. This was based on sentiment, for neither man looked to have an extra yard in him, both having won their cross-ties in modest times. Late money had come in on the Englishman, Crench, who had struggled in his heats, and whose odds had consequently risen, but the odds had stayed high on Walecinsky, who had taken a tumble in the cross-tie, taking enough skin off his knees to furnish parchment for a diploma. No, it looked to the cognoscenti to be between Roother and Rae.

Joshua Two Wings had no reason to believe that he did not continue to enjoy the confidence of Gilbert and the Carlisle Syndicate. Nevertheless, he had paid a sawbuck to each of his lodgers to act as guards on the evening prior to the race, had double-locked his larders and had even brought in fresh water from a neighbour. It was wise to take no chances when big bucks were at stake, though Gilbert and his friends were not to know that Joshua himself had studiously prepared Marty's pre-race "vomit". He had picked up a few bucks on his man, and so had Jim and Pop.

At six o'clock on the night before the race, came the rain. It poured relentlessly from sullen skies, black and heavy, running in dark, jagged rivers through Scranton's slimy cobbled streets. It took less than three hours for the track's flinty cinders to melt. Pop, Flaherty, Mackay and Jim looked grimly out of streaked windows and reflected that the Scranton Dash would now be a lottery.

Marty swiftly realigned himself, all hopes of a fast time now gone, but that was of no importance. All that now mattered to him was that he took the Scranton Dash, took it big, and put bucks into the College and the pockets of Pop and Jim. He sat in the dim lamplight of the living room, listening to the rain rattle on the roof above, and looked across the chess table at Mary Lou. He reflected that she had grown into another woman, a companion as well as a lover. She had entered this closed world of foot racing as if she had been born to it. Though she was always around, she had kept away from his bed, allowing him to focus his energies on the Dash, a pliant part of the cocoon placed around him by the College group.

Mary Lou, head down, made her move. "Check," she said.

Marty reviewed the board and shook his head, flicking over his king. "If you could run, I'd never beat you," he said.

She smiled her flashing, open smile. "You're darn right," she said, surveying the chessboard. "And when this Dash is over, I'll turn this dam' game into a contact sport!"

The streets of Scranton were now dark with men. They streamed towards the stadium, their hobnailed boots and clogs rattling on the slimy streets. The rain had gone, the stadium was gorged and the assault upon its walls and fences began. An hour later, 21,000 sodden spectators jostled, steam rising from them, on its cinder terraces.

High in the stands, Mackay pulled on his hip flask and handed it to Jim. “Look at that track,” he said. “No day for a scratch man, giving away up to seven yards on mud.”

Jim grunted. He pointed down to the entrance to the track, where Healey, the white-coated starter, was in deep conversation with a stocky, moustachioed man in a black homburg. “Look, Pop,” he said. “Something’s up.”

The four men sat, huddled high in the dark, frozen stands, two on each side of a shivering Mary Lou. Below them, in the icy mists, the rain had now stopped, but the Scranton track was now little more than a black pulp. But the massed crowds, the steam of their bodies, rising above them, mixing with the mist, were composed of men inured to the rigours of the town’s harsh anthracite mines. They wound their way down to the Ring to place their hard-won bucks with bookmakers who stood, swigging brandy from hip-flasks, bellowing their odds up into the frozen terracings.

Suddenly, Flaherty rose to his feet.

“Two hours to go,” he said. “Time for Marty’s rub-down. “

“This early?” said Pop, looking at his watch.

“Yep. He reckons that he needs a full hour for his warm up.”

Pop sighed.

“Never in my born days heard of such a thing. Mark my words, that boy will wear himself out. And I don’t for the life of me know why he drinks all that water.”

“Hydration, he calls it,” said Jim.

“Sherry and eggs, that’s what he needs,” said Mackay. “that’s what all the top men take back in Scotland.”

Then, below them in the Ring, there was sudden movement on the boards. They were wiped, as big money arrived on the Scranton man, Headley, a front-marker, off twelve yards. He was suddenly taken down to evens, with Rae steady at 5-4 and Marty still at 3-1.

Pop shook his head.

"Can't for the life of me work this out, Headley at evens," he said.

News of Marty's spewings had now reached the crowd, and his odds rose to 4-1. In the depths of the dressing room, he did nothing to alter that opinion, coughing and spluttering as he stripped off for the final. Thus it was that he now stood in the john, spitting out the fake vomit which Joshua had provided him.

"This guy Headley, Marty should see him off easy," said Jim.

Mackay peered at his programme.

"What about this boy Rae. Pop, the syndicate man?"

Pop shook his head.

"Rae? He's no problem," he said.

"You could've fooled me," replied Mackay. "That chiel ran close tae twelve and a half seconds in his cross-tie."

Pop grinned. The Dean always seemed to return to Scots dialect when he was worried.

"Yes," said Pop. "But I've been watching Rae. He hit it flat out in his last run, but he was as tight as a crab's arse at the finish. Rae doesn't have a yard left in his legs. Marty will eat him up at the start and spit him out at the finish."

Jim nodded.

"The money for the college is safe, Dean. The syndicate have blown it again."

"Thalassotherapy," said Mary Lou suddenly. "Marty told me you could buy that instead of showers for your football team."

"And what the Sam Hill would that be?" asked Pop.

"Jets of cold water shooting out at you from all angles," she replied.

"Figures," said Pop. "Lines up with all that stuff that Marty says about being cool, and chilling out."

"And that chiel Houston, with all his problems," said Mackay. "All that cold water might help clear his head."

Pop nodded, and peered down at the track through his binoculars.

"Forget about Houston, Dean, we might be the ones with the problems," he said.

Mackay took the binoculars from him.

"Hold on," he said. "Hold on a wee. Take a keek at those boards. The odds on Headley have dropped to two to one on. There's been big money suddenly landing on his back. Someone down there knows something, Jim, get ye down to the track and see what's happening."

Mary Lou sat silent as Jim made his way down. Scranton had been a revelation to her. For she had imagined that track, unlike college football with its ringers and sluggers, would be pure, pristine. But she reflected that the Yale experience had been pretty much the same. When prestige or money was at stake, then ethics went out the window, even in the Ivy League. But not with her man. Not with her Marty.

Jim returned to them, twenty minutes later, his face sombre.

"Headley, he's Sullivan's man," he said. "Word is that he got ten to one on him, way back in September in a private bet. His trainers have had him in prep somewhere in the boondocks for six months."

The Dean scowled.

"That's why he wanted tae keep Marty out-he'll win a fortune. And do ye know who it was we saw speaking to the starter an hour ago?"

"It was a little guy, one of Sullivan's buddies," said Jim.

"Hanagan," growled Pop.

Jim was again dispatched down to the track to investigate further.

Mary Lou sat quiet, attempting to process the Byzantine world in which she was now immersed. For last night, Marty had told her that he had been approached by someone of the same name. He had offered Marty amateur re-instatement if he pulled out of the final, or took a dive. Marty had asked him for a signed letter from Sullivan to that effect, but she had not heard if he had yet received it.

Ten minutes later, Jim returned to them.

"You come up with anything, Jim?" asked Pop.

"Nothing that you would want to hear, Pop," he replied.

"Get it out, Jim," growled Mackay.

"I slipped ten bucks to a miner, a ringer for Cornell, the guy who near bit off my ear a coupla months ago," said Jim. "Nice guy."

"Forget about yer lug, Jim," said Mackay. "Tell us the worst."

Jim took a deep breath.

"Headley, so far he's been running in his heavy shoes," he said.

The Dean groaned and shook his head. "He already has seven yards start on Marty," he said." These heavy shoes-how much does it mean in yards, Pop?"

Pop bit his lip.

"One yard, mibbe two," he said. "Marty is in trouble. Real trouble."

It was a closed skill. A sprinter ran in a tunnel, with peripheral vision a distraction, an enemy. All that he could now see was four foot of space through which his force would be applied, loosely and fluidly, oblivious to all around him. He was in the moment.

Marty could see only the tunnel before him, bounded by track-strings. Somewhere in the distance, he heard the starter call them to their marks. There was a silence, broken only by a drunken shout, high in the stands.

"Gentlemen, get to your marks." The command was given in a strong Scottish brogue.

Marty settled into starting-holes, which oozed mud, oblivious to the black water seeping into his shoes, or to his right knee settling deep into the cinder pulp. He looked up the straight, blocking out the space on either side.

"Get set."

Marty's hips rose; his eyes focussed a yard ahead, in perfect balance. The gun exploded and he drove out. It was a good start. The gun exploded again, bringing the finalists down to a canter. From above him on his left came the starter's gruff voice.

"Roother, false start. One yard penalty."

Marty shook his head as a white-coated steward directed him to his new starting position. He looked up at the starter. "That was a fair start," he said.

The starter's dour expression did not change. "A yard back," he said again. "The starter's decision is final."

Marty shook his head and tried to scratch a starting hole at his new mark, a yard back.

In the stand, Mackay peered down through his field glasses at the track. "Like you said, Jim, looks like the money's moved."

"What do you mean, the money's moved?" demanded Mary Lou, angrily, the colour rising in her cheeks. "Moved where?"

Jim made to reply, but Mackay's stern look stopped him. He pointed down to the track.

"Get to your marks."

The six finalists again settled.

"Get set."

The moment hung. Then the gun again released the runners. Again, there was the report of the recall gun.

"Roother, one yard back," rasped the starter.

There was sustained booing all around the ground as the red flag went up, for as before there had been no sign of a false start. The Negro had clearly held fast. Marty said nothing, but walked back and slowly dug fresh starting-holes.

Mackay handed the field glasses to Pop, gloomily shaking his head. "They've got him," he said.

Mary Lou peered through her binoculars.

"No," she said. "Marty's there, he's still in his tunnel.

A hush again settled on the crowd as the finalists again took to their marks. The gun exploded. The third start was a fair one, but Marty had deliberately "hung", and was a further yard back on his first stride. But he kept his focus. Acceleration was difficult on Scranton's slimy cinders, but Marty surged across them, throwing up mud and water behind him as he did so. He was flowing, eating up the cinders, sucking in the field. At fifty yards, Mary Lou could see that Marty had passed the Welsh runner Thomas, and was closing fast on Headley and Walecinski in the lanes on either side of him. At sixty yards, Rae was suddenly gone, clutching the back of his left thigh.

Mary Lou stood, gripping her programme, her screams lost in the roar of the crowd. Everyone in the stands rose, for the Negro boy was gobbling up the yards between himself and the front markers, Headley and Walecinski. At eighty yards, he had taken the Pole, whose legs bowed in the thick mud. At a hundred yards, Headley had tied up, his arms threshing wildly as Marty passed him.

But out in lane one, Crench was still a short yard up and with only ten yards to go, he looked to be holding well. Marty was now running out of yards.

"Marty's got him," roared Pop, crunching his programme. "He's *got* him."

Marty powered through the final ten yards and took the tape in his teeth, tasting the blood as it cut his lips, and landed face first in the mud beyond the finish. He rose, wiping the cinders from his face and walked away from the finish, hands high, engulfed in the roars of the crowd, his legs and body now black with mud.

There was a hush as Marty jogged back to collect his clothing at the start. In the stands, the finish-judges conferred. Finally, a message was transmitted down to a group of six officials below, who slowly began to chalk on blackboards. The officials walked off, boards held close to their chests, and posted themselves at the ends of the straights and in the middle of the home and back straights. Then, the shrill sound of a whistle, and 'Roother' appeared on their boards.

The Carlisle group found Marty in the darkness of the dressing room, lying silent, face down, on the massage table. Flaherty stood, grinning, above him. Jim placed his right hand on Marty's left shoulder. Marty turned on to his back, looking up at Jim. "What time did I run?" he asked.

"The Dean got you at twelve and three eighths seconds," Jim replied.

"Eighths? Come on, Jim, that's Confederate money," said Marty, propping himself up on the table as Flaherty adjusted it behind to support his back.

"Well, twelve point four then," said Jim. "Fancy running on mud."

Marty exhaled slowly, shaking his head." Add my start and that's at least three yards inside even time, Jim, running on shit. I never ran so fast."

"It was all a fix. From the start," said Jim.

"The start!" said Flaherty. "You can say that again!"

"The starter was paid off," said Marty.

"By Sullivan?" asked Mary Lou.

"Yes, lass," said Mackay. "Sullivan's money was on Headley."

Jim nodded. "And to be sure, to take you out for certain, Hanagan paid off the starter."

"Dean," said Marty, sitting up. "I've got a confession to make to you."

"You mean you took my sherry and eggs before the final?"

"No. I ran in my heavy belt in the heats, "said Marty.

"Like I said to Halsey at Yale. Never get into a pissing contest with a skunk," said the Dean.

Flaherty handed Marty his shirt. "My old grandfather put it different-he used to say, never bet on anything on two legs," he growled.

Jim nodded, then looked over his shoulder to the door. "We gotta get back to Carlisle. And we sure need your brains, Marty."

"What for?"

"Football now. To whup West Point," said Jim.

Behind Jim, the dressing-room door creaked slowly open to reveal a small, bowler-hatted, moustachioed man, engulfed in a loud, grey, check suit. Squeezing behind him into the cramped little room, two burly, flat-nosed men whose faces looked to have been thatched.

"And who might you'se be?" asked Flaherty, still seated.

"I answer to the name of Hanagan," replied the little man. "I represent the best interests of Mr Headley's backers."

"Sullivan?"

"I didn't say that," said Hanagan.

"Then to what do we owe the pleasure of this visit?" asked Flaherty.

"We come here to deliver justice," said Hanagan. "Your boy Roother, he didn't run to orders. Go out early. A pro runs to orders."

Marty sat up on the bed. "You took your chances," he said. "I didn't get any letter."

"That's not the point," said Hanagan, pointing his index finger at Marty. "A pro runs to orders."

The thug on Hanagan's left suddenly moved forward towards Marty. Flaherty rose quickly to his feet, towering above him. Brodie's man made to lift his right fist but Flaherty trapped it in his Gotham-ham of a hand and squeezed. Marty heard the bones crack. The man screamed, holding his crushed fingers in his other hand and slumped back against the wall, sobbing.

The other heavy moved in on Jim, whose right fist came out like a whip, taking him on the side of the nose with a crunch. The man dropped to his knees and Jim grabbed him by the hair and tossed him to the side wall like a sack.

Hanagan stood quivering at the door, his beady little eyes goggling.

“Any trouble here, boys?” It was Pop at the door, with the other members of the Carlisle team crowded behind him.

“No, Pop,” replied Jim. “No trouble at all.”

Chapter 14
West Point

Marty sat high in the bleachers in the thin, sleety January wind, shaking his head as below him, on a black, sodden field, Carlisle prepared for the West Point game, now only four weeks away. Gus Welch, Pop's quarter back was, despite Marty's coaching, still shaky on his spiral pass and the ball wobbled like a top, even on short throws. There was still no pace, no power on the ball and it was both easy to intercept and difficult for receivers to catch.

The sleet eased. He stood and walked down on to the field, behind Pop, who, unaware of his presence, continued to bawl expletives through a battered tin megaphone. As he approached, Pop noted him and dropped his megaphone to his hip. "That sprint start position of yours, for defence," he said. "Marty, that's a real lalapaloosa. These West Point boys are animals, but they won't get to Gus Welch less'n they use a Gatling."

Marty nodded. "Looks real good, coach," he said. "But the pass…" He picked up a ball. "D'you mind if I show Gus again?"

"Be my guest," said Pop, blowing his whistle. The players stopped and gathered round him. Pop beckoned Gus Welch towards him, and pointed to Marty.

"Jim," shouted Marty. "You catch for me?"

Jim replied with his open grin and nodded. He trotted off and stopped about thirty yards from Marty and the group.

"Further," roared Marty.

Jim re-started his jog, stopping at forty yards.

"Further," bellowed Marty again.

"You want Jim to stay in the county, Marty?" growled Pop.

Jim stopped fifty yards away, and Marty picked up the pigskin. He pointed to Gus Welch. "You hold it here, Gus. Like this," he demonstrated, taking the ball with his right hand.

"Plenty of skin on it, fingers across the laces," he said. "Just like you hold a javelin, Gus." He removed his hand from the ball and pointed to his wrist. He made a flicking, rotational movement with it. Marty took the ball in his right hand, withdrew it and rifled it off. It spun like a bullet through the still, winter air and landed over Jim's head, ten yards beyond him. The Carlisle players broke into spontaneous applause and gathered round Marty.

Pop flipped Marty another ball. "Let me see you do that again," he said.

Again, Marty launched the ball towards Jim who had now moved even further back. He caught it cleanly on his chest.

"We sure could do with you against those Army boys, Marty," said Pop. "You sure you ain't got some Indian blood in you?"

"'Bout as much as you have, Pop," replied Marty.

Pop and Angus Mackay sat in the Dean's office, sipping malt whisky. It was early evening and only the tick of the grandfather clock broke the silence.

"Thought I had you all figured out, Pop," growled Mackay.

Pop sipped his malt slowly. He loved the dark, peaty taste of Laphroaig. "I don't zactly get your drift, Angus," he answered.

"I mean this nigra boy, Roother. Okay, so I know you've never set out your stall as a track coach and Roother, he seems to know track…"

"From soup to nuts," said Pop.

Mackay nodded. "But football, that's your dish. You know, I reckon only one man on earth knows more than you do. That's Walter Camp and he near as dammit invented the game."

Pop reached forward to the desk to re-charge his glass. He grinned. "You're right, Angus. If I do say so myself."

"And yet, now this boy, Roother, he's your right hand man on the football field."

"Only in offence," said Pop. "Marty, he doesn't know jack shit about defence."

"Jack shit?"

Pop grinned again. "It's a phrase he sometimes uses." He shook his head. "It's odd, Angus. Marty, he knows nothing about defence. Nothing but offence…did you see those quarter back drills, last time out?"

Mackay nodded.

"It was like George M. Cohan, and Yankee Doodle Sandy," he said. "Like some kind of dance."

"Well," Pop continued. "He's got a three-step drill, a five-step drill and a seven-step drill."

"Sounds to me like Roother's got a drill for just about everything," said Mackay. "He got himself a drill for wiping his ass?"

"Probably got that too," growled Pop. "And he's got step drills for wide receivers, to get 'em clear of defence. Angles like Pythagoras." Pop paused and took a sip of his whiskey. "You're right, Angus. It's like a dance. I never saw plays like it, not in all my born days." He paused again. "But then, suddenly, Marty goes dark on me. Starts talking about something called specialist teams. Seems to think we should have a defensive team and an offensive team."

"Chance'd be a fine thing," growled Mackay.

"And that's not all," Pop went on. "There was maybe another team, just for punt receiving. But I'm not sure."

"Just how many players does your boy Roother think we have out there?"

"No idea," said Pop. And I almost forgot," he said. "A specialist kicker."

"And what did he mean by that?"

"Well, I didn't ask, but I reckon he meant someone who comes on just to punt and kick goals."

"And that's *all*? The man doesn't earn his corn by making hits and running and blocking?"

Pop shook his head. "Don't reckon so," he said.

"Well, don't that beat all?" said Mackay, shaking his head. "Next thing, he'll be wanting coaches for every position."

"That's not all," Pop was warming to his theme. "You ever seen Marty throw a football?"

Mackay shook his head. "Missed that," he said.

"Marty spins that ball fifty yards or more, Angus. Like a bullet. And he can place it on a dime."

"Nigras don't play football," growled Mackay. "That's a known fact."

"This one does," said Pop.

"Tell me something," said Mary Lou.

"Tell you what?"

They sat opposite each other in Marty's sparsely furnished living room, as her chicken stew bubbled on the fire that crackled in the hearth. Outside, the wind whistled, cold and sharp, down Bleeker Street.

"Like something that's gonna happen soon, so I know it's gonna happen. So I might maybe make a few bucks."

Marty's brow furrowed. Then he nodded. "Okay, what about something on Roosevelt?" he said.

She smiled. "Yeah. Something about Teddy."

"Teddy? Teddy who?"

"Teddy Roosevelt, that's who," she replied. "What other Roosevelt is there?"

"Some guy called Franklin," he said.

"Roosevelt Franklin?"

"No. No. Franklin D. Roosevelt. I think they called him FDR."

"So what does the D stand for?"

Marty shrugged his shoulders.

"Seems to me," she said, "you don't know much 'bout this here country of ours. So just how did you pass your time at college?"

"I picked up my classes," he said, defensively.

"Don't seem much like it to me," she said. "Seems to me that all you ever done was running and jumping." She pointed a finger at him. "So your ole FDR, what zactly did he do?"

"Something called the New Deal. What did your Teddy Roosevelt do?"

"The Rough Riders," she replied. "San Juan Hill. The National Parks. Don't they teach you **nothing** at school?" She looked at him across the fire and shook her head. "Think, honey," she said. "This here is 1912. What happened in 1912?"

Marty breathed deeply. "Got it," he said. "I think there was some kinda war."

Mary Lou leant forward to stir the stew, then licked the ladle. "A war? Now we're getting somewhere," she said. "Where? Mexico?"

"No, in Europe."

She shook her head in disbelief. "So what would folks like us be a-doin', a-fightin' in Europe?"

"No idea," Marty admitted.

She returned to the stew, gave it another stir. "So who we fighting against? Betcha two bits it was them English."

"No," he said. "It wasn't the English. It was the Germans."

She shook her head. "Come on, Marty," she said. "Why the Sam Hill would we be a-fightin' them Germans? We got lotsa Germans round here. Some of them're right nice people too. No way we would fight them Germans. You musta got it all wrong."

"No," said Marty firmly. "It was the Germans, for sure."

"So just you tell me how them Germans would want to come all the way across here to take over these United States of America? It's too far. And stands to reason they got better things to do."

"I don't know, Mary Lou," he said. "They just did."

"Marty," she said. "I said it before, and I'll say it again. You can run and jump real good, but you sure don't know much about the history of these here United States of America."

"Never saw the need," he said. "Why don't you ask me again 'bout **my** time?"

"You sure you know enough?" she said, grinning. "Sure don't want to push your memory-box too hard." Mary Lou picked up the mug of coffee on the table and sipped it slowly. "Well, let me see," she said. "You told me 'bout them men in the moon. I took that on board – just some guys in a plane going a weeny bit higher."

"More than a weeny bit, honey."

"And I can take them motion pictures with sound – just means a gramophone."

"So what *can't* you take?"

She paused, and shook her head "You ain't told me that much yet," she said.

"That's because I'm trying to *spare* you," he said. "If I told you some things I know, it could drive you crazy. You ever thought of that?"

She stood, took his empty mug from him, walked to the stove, removed the coffee pot and re-charged both their mugs before returning to her chair. "Us blacks a-getting the vote and a-going off to college, and all that stuff," she said. "That's real tough to take."

He nodded.

"So when does all that happen?"

"Soon, I think," he replied, "'bout twenty years from now. Don't know for sure."

"College, twenty years," she said. "Too late for me."

He nodded.

"And Blacks hitching up with Whites. You *sure* of that?"

"Yes," he said. "But not everywhere."

"And them telephones you talked about, the kind you carry about in your pocket?"

"Mobiles."

"I just can't get that into my head. Folks standing in Main Street a-beating their gums to folks in China. That sure beats all."

"Yes, putting it that way, I suppose it does."

"So where does the sound come from? Cos there ain't no wires in there?"

"It comes from satellites," he said.

"Satta what?"

"Sort of stations up in the sky, spinning round the earth."

"Railway stations in the sky? Come on."

"No, no, Mary Lou," he shook his head, "Not railway stations. More like telegraph stations."

"So tell me, who put them up there, these telegraph stations?"

"We did, with rockets."

She shook her head. "You're joshing me, Marty."

"No," he said. "I swear to God. We put them up there."

"So how does it all work?"

"Well the sound goes up to the satellite and bounces back to earth."

"So you're telling me that what I say goes thousands of miles up there and then bounces down to China?"

"Got it in one."

"No I don't," she said, shaking her head.

"Anything else you want me to try and explain?"

"Don't rightly think I want to try. You ain't zactly covered yourself in glory so far, Marty." She paused. "So let's us try something else. What do you find back here, that's so all-fired different?"

Marty sipped his Arbuckles and did not answer for a moment. "Most of all, I think the smell."

"What kinda smells?"

"Horses, mainly. Didn't really expect so many horses. Leather. I never really smelt leather before. Then there's the smell of the stores. I never smelt stores before either." He sighed. "Everything smells more. Including me."

"You trying to tell me you never smelt yourself before?"

"Yes, I suppose I did, but I wasn't aware of it. But then, I could shower every day, sometimes twice a day."

"Twice a day," she said, shaking her head. "Honey, you coulda cleaned yourself to death."

He nodded.

"So now you're smelling yourself?"

"Yes and it's weird. It's a sort of sweaty, musty smell."

"That's the way most folks smells, leastways as long as I've been around."

"I suppose so." He paused. "And then there's the dentist."

"Don't talk to me 'bout no dentist," she said.

"I see these grown men shaking before they go in. Even the footballers."

"Why shouldn't they? There's real hurt in there."

"Back where I come from, you go to the dentist and it's like getting a haircut."

"Some haircut," she said. "You ain't been to no dentist here. Them rich folks, they give 'em a slug of cocaine, but poor nigras, they just rip your teeth outa your gums, with you a whoopin' and a-hollering. Anything else?"

"And all your patent medicines," he said. "Peruna, Ka Tar No, Simmons Liver Regulator. A bunch of shit."

"So you gets ill, what do you take where you come from?"

"We have penicillin, vaccines, antibiotics."

"Don't know nuthin' 'bout them," she said, shaking her head. "What about TB? What about diphtheria?"

"No one dies of things like that anymore."

"What about catarrh? My grandpappy had that in his hips. Peruna done save him."

"Mary Lou," he said, patiently. "That's what they call a cure for which there is no known disease. I'm no medical man, but I'm damn sure you can't have catarrh in your hips."

"Well, let that pass," she said. "What else bothers you?"

"The clothes, for sure. It's got to be the clothes. Even the shirts. They're so heavy, so rough."

"Ain't you the Caspar Milquetoast." She said, pursing her soft, thick lips in mock-disgust. "I suppose you sashays around in silks and satins."

"No," he said. "I don't, but it's just that my clothes, they were easier on the skin."

"Your poor skin," she said, mocking. "You got your shaving to your lordship's liking?"

Marty exhaled slowly. "Those first days, at your brother's pad. Cold water. A cut-throat razor. You know some days I had to break the ice in the bucket in the yard? But I think I got the shaving sorted now."

"Courtesy of your Mr Gillette?"

"Man's greatest benefactor," he said. "Well ahead of your Simmons and his Liver Regulator."

"Marty," she said. "You must be the only nigra boy in these parts who shaves with them there Gillette safety razors. You know that?"

"Take it from me, it's worth every cent," he said.

Her expression changed, her features softening. "You finds it hard here, don't you?"

"Not so much now, at the track. Jim and the boys help me out. But back at the hotel, where I first met you…I never thought a man could work so hard for fifty cents."

"But you're rich now."

He nodded. "I got my own pad and two thousand bucks in the bank."

"That's real rich hereabouts," she said. "You pick up some more bucks running pro at Scranton again and you don't have no need to go back to work."

He did not answer her. He could not. She looked at him, knowing that she had touched a nerve. "Stew's near ready," she said, laying a warm hand on his. "You want it now, or you got something else in mind?"

Walter Camp sat high in the stand as, below him, the Carlisle Team filed slowly out on to the field. It was two hours before the start, and all the players were dressed in team blazers. Camp had never claimed to have invented the Gridiron game. He had been content to let others do that for him. But Walter had never really taken to the English sport of rugby football, the game which the East coast colleges had embraced in the early 1870s'. True, it was a manly contest, but with its lineouts, its scrums and its mauls, the English game, was too chaotic, too messy, too lacking in clarity. Your East coast college boy, Camp had reasoned, he needed a contest that was simpler, more direct. That was why he had cut teams down to a neat eleven players, from two unruly mobs of twenty. That was why the scrimmage had been boiled down to a single snap, the mauls and lineouts consigned to history.

By the first years of the 20th century, college ball had become a simpler game and had begun to attract big crowds. Clearer, but not cleaner, with eighteen deaths per year. But it was only after the bloody photograph of Swarthmore's quarterback, Bob Maxwell, had made the national press that President Teddy Roosevelt had summoned Camp and the other leaders of college football to the White House. And they came, at a brisk trot, for they knew that the Colonel Roosevelt who had led the charge at San Juan Hill was no Caspar Milquetoast.

Roosevelt had made it clear to the nation's coaches that college football would have to clean up its act, or else it would be consigned to the dustbin of history. As a result, rules were changed, injuries dropped dramatically and in 1906 the forward pass had been introduced, opening up the game. Of course, there was still plenty of slugging, much of it from Ivy League colleges like Harvard and Yale, but the serious injuries and the death-rate had dropped and the threat of a ban had receded. His game was safe.

New York Times

West Point. Feb 1st, 2012. Jim Thorpe and his redoubtable band of Carlisle Indian gridiron stars invaded the plains this afternoon to match their prowess against the moleskin gladiators of Uncle Sam's Military Academy, and when the two teams crossed the parade ground in the semi-darkness of late afternoon, the Cadets had been shown up as no other West Point team has been in many years. They were buried under the overwhelming score of 27 to 6. Standing out resplendent in a galaxy of Indian stars was Jim Thorpe, recently crowned the athlete marvel of the age. The big Indian Captain added more lustre to his already brilliant record, and at times the game itself was almost forgotten while the spectators gazed on Thorpe, the individual, to wonder at his prowess. To recount his notable performances in the complete overthrow of the Cadets would leave little space for other notable points of the conflict. He simply ran wild, while the Cadets tried in vain to stop his progress. It was like trying to clutch a shadow. Thorpe went through the West Point line as if it was an open door; his defensive play was on a par with his attack, and his every move was that of a past master.

Thorpe tore off runs of ten yards or more so often that they became common, and an advance of less than that figure seemed a wasted effort. His zigzag running and ability to hurl himself free of tacklers made his running highly spectacular. In the third period, he made a run which, while it failed to bring anything in points [a team-mate was declared offside], will go down in the Army gridiron annals as one of the greatest ever seen on the plains. The Indians had been held for downs on West Point's 3-yard line, and Keyes dropped back behind his own goal line and punted out. The ball went directly to Thorpe, who stood on the Army's 45-yard line, about halfway between the two sidelines. It was a high kick, and the Cadets were already gathering around the big Indian when he clutched the falling pigskin in his arms. His catch and his start were but one motion. In and out, zigzagging first to one side and then to the other, while a flying Cadet went hurling through space, Thorpe wormed his way through the entire Army team. Every Cadet in the game had his chance, and every one of them failed. It was not the usual spectacle of the man with the ball out-distancing his opponents by circling them.

It was a dodging game in which Thorpe matched himself against an entire team and proved the master. Lines drawn parallel and fifteen feet apart would include all the ground that Thorpe covered on his triumphant dash through an entire team.

West Point's much-talked-of defence, which had helped Yale to four first downs in a full hour of play, was like tissue paper before the Indians. To a corresponding degree, the Indian defence, which had been considered so much inferior to their attack, was a wonder.

Marty later reflected that what transpired could never have happened eighty years later, for early in the second half, Jim had been flattened by a heavy tackle and lay motionless on the sodden turf. Marty had been close enough to overhear the exchange between the West Point captain, Leland S Devore, and the referee, John Evans. Evans had been pressing to observe the two-minute time limit, only to be interrupted by Devore.

"Hell's bells, referee," he said. "We don't stand on technicalities here at West Point. Give Jim all the time he wants."

Suddenly Jim was back on his feet as if nothing had occurred. Moments later, he carried the pigskin sixty-five yards only to have the score disallowed for offside. In that second half, with Gus Welch spinning inch-perfect passes, Jim punting kicks that stayed in the clouds forever, and running slick as greased ice, Carlisle's Indians took West Point apart. At one point, two of the cadets' halfbacks decided to put paid to Thorpe. Heads down, they charged Jim who had suddenly stopped. The two West Point men missed him, collided and went down like logs, then groggily got to their feet. The coach, Captain Graves, allowed them to stay on, on one condition, that they put paid to Thorpe. "Benedict," he said to the smaller of the two men, "take that as an order. You too, Eisenhower."

Marty and Mary Lou stood outside the doors to the main stand in the gathering dusk, awaiting the arrival of Pop and the Carlisle players.

"Five step drill," said Gus Welch pointing his index finger and winking as he emerged with Jim, Pop and the other members of the team. They made their way up the winding, grit-surfaced road to Student Hall, where the after-match reception would be held. It is quite literally Ivy League, army-style, thought Marty, looking above him as he approached the ivy-covered, grey-brick building, the light dim behind its stained glass, mock-Tudor windows. Behind Pop, Jim and Gus, he walked up the steps towards the entrance, with the rest of the Carlisle team behind them. At the top of the steps, framed in the entrance, stood a plump, uniformed steward, every straining button of his dress-coat doing its job. His eyes drifted behind Pop and Jim to Marty and Mary Lou, and he raised a soft, manicured hand. "May I ask who is in charge of this group?" His voice was low.

"Reckon that must be me," replied Pop.

The steward's face took on a stony aspect, and he looked pointedly beyond Pop to Marty and Mary Lou. "They can't come in," he said.

Pop was nonplussed.

"Cadet House rules," said the steward.

“If they don’t come in, then neither do we.” It was Jim, now standing beside Pop. There were rumblings of agreement from Gus Welch and the other team members.

“What’s the problem?” Cadet Eisenhower, now impeccably attired in dress uniform, appeared, limping, behind the steward, now unrecognisable from the muddy, sweating, gridiron star of a few hours before.

The young steward pointed to Marty and Mary Lou. “Cadet House rules,” he repeated.

“Mr Roother here is an officer, part of my staff,” said Pop. “And this is his…fiancée.”

“No rules against team staff,” said Eisenhower, reaching forward to take Mary Lou’s arm.

Captain Graves suddenly loomed behind Eisenhower. “None that I heard of, Cadet Eisenhower,” he confirmed, reaching to take Marty’s right hand and pull him forward.

The steward realised that all resistance was now futile, lowered his head, and raised both hands to usher Marty and Mary Lou into the lobby. The team followed and stood, engulfed in the high-ceilinged, oak-beamed anteroom, its walls covered in brown, fading photographs and paintings of long-past teams.

Marty scrutinised Eisenhower. Crew cut, his bronzed face marred only by the still bleeding scratches of the day’s encounter, he looked taller than Marty had expected. He accepted the firm grip of Eisenhower’s right hand. “Nice to meet you, Mr President,” he said.

Chapter 15
Physical Culture City

It had started off as no more than a dull ache, low on the right side of his jaw. At first, Marty had thought that it was simply a food-trap which had inflamed his gums, and he poked around at the back of his mouth, but found no identifiable point of pain. It was only when he had finished his day's work with a fast three hundred metres with Jim that the throb began to intensify. Jim had advised oil of cloves and Mary Lou had agreed. Marty had duly purchased a bottle of the oil at Mulligan's and on his return home had rubbed it deep into his gums. He had spent the rest of the evening with the bitter taste of cloves in his mouth.

But the throbbing continued undiminished, and soon became almost unbearable. Thus, late that evening, Mary Lou had taken him to Mammy Boston, who supplemented her work on the astral plane with primitive forms of alternative medicine. Mammy was unequivocal. Marty was not suffering from some minor gum inflammation. No, he almost certainly had an infected wisdom tooth, and he would surely have to visit the dentist, Mr Weiss, in the morning. To tide him over, Mammy provided Marty with two bottles of Kilmer's Painkiller and observed him carefully as he consumed almost an entire bottle. As he left, on unsteady legs, Mammy had handed him a box of Thayer's Slippery Elm Lozenges, known to be particularly effective with gum infections.

It was fortunate for Marty that Mary Lou was with him, for under the influence of Dr Kilmer's alcohol-laden potion, he might have found it difficult to make it back home. The pain in his tooth had not completely gone but it was now dull, distant, blurred by the impact of Kilmer's elixir. Marty was not in good shape. Mary Lou helped him to undress, pulled the blankets over him and tucked him in. He lay in the lamp-lit gloom, her face close to his.

"I'll jest make myself up a bed on the floor," she said, lightly patting his right cheek, now swollen to twice its normal size. Marty did not respond, for he did not hear her. He was now far gone, in a deep haze.

Early in the morning, the pain jolted him from his sleep. His anguished groans awoke Mary Lou, who poured some Painkiller into a cup and handed it to him. She tried not to register alarm at the sight of Marty's now grotesquely-swollen face. "We got to get you to Mr Weiss," she said, "and quick."

Solomon Weiss peered into Marty's mouth and nodded. "Wisdom tooth," he pronounced. "Infected. Got to be yanked, right away."

Solomon had always thought it fortunate that he had been unbeaten in arm-wrestling during his period at Boston College of Dentistry. Thus, he had become renowned in Carlisle for fast, if not entirely pain-free, extractions. True, he had sat at the feet of Hardcastle, that master of molar extraction and had revelled in his mentor's scientific analysis of leverage and rotation, but Weiss' sheer animal strength had proved to be his ace in the hole. For the august, academic Hardcastle, for all his biomechanics, had rarely relieved struggling young bucks of their molars without benefit of anaesthetic, rarely had to address their desperate writhings.

That was where Weiss' assistant Muldoon had proved invaluable. Seamus Muldoon, a horny-handed son of Erin, had once traded bare-knuckle blows with the great John L. Sullivan and Jim Fitzsimmons and still had the bumps to show for it. His job was to keep Weiss' patients still, while his employer pursued his arduous and painful task.

Weiss turned to open his instrument-box on the table beside him. “A buck,” he said, palm extended to Marty.

Marty now almost delirious with pain, sat up slowly in Weiss’ shiny padded leather chair. “For what?” he mumbled.

“Extraction,” replied Weiss. “Straight extraction.”

“No painkillers? Nothing?”

Weiss sighed, picked up a pair of chrome-plated pliers and held them in front of him. He opened and closed them. “Cocaine, that’s five bucks more,” he said. “You won’t feel a thing, young man, I promise you.”

“Cocaine,” mumbled Marty, nodding.

“Money in advance,” said Weiss.

Marty fumbled clumsily in his pocket, located six dollars and handed them to the dentist who turned, walked back to a table by the door and carefully placed them in a black metal box. At the door, hung a white medical tunic, its front caked with blood. Weiss slipped on the tunic and opened the surgery door. “Muldoon!” he roared. “Muldoon!”

Seamus Muldoon lumbered in, craggy, unshaven. Weiss’ assistant had a face that looked as if it had been poured in concrete. Muldoon buttoned up the back of his employer’s blood-stained tunic and quietly slipped behind Marty. Like many big men, he was surprisingly light on his feet. Weiss turned, opened a glass-fronted cabinet on the wall beside the door and withdrew a large hypodermic syringe and a bottle of clear fluid. He opened the bottle, held it at an angle, inserted the syringe through the cork and watched as it slowly filled. Standing directly in Marty’s line of vision, he pointed it towards the ceiling, pressed on the syringe and smiled as the clear fluid squirted forth.

For all his pain, for all his delirium, Marty felt his stomach squirm with fear. This was surely not the way it was.

“Just a couple of little pricks,” said Weiss, pressing Marty firmly back into the chair. He nodded to Muldoon, who positioned himself behind Marty. Weiss leant forward, placed the syringe within Marty’s mouth, and inserted its needle into his gum. Marty felt it cut deep into his flesh. It was agony. He felt the tears stream down his face in reflex as Weiss squeezed the cocaine into his gum and moved the needle around. He withdrew the syringe and examined it. "Just one more," he said, nodding to Muldoon. Marty now felt hard pressure on both of his shoulders. Weiss again inserted the needle, this time into the side of the gum, and Marty, now helpless, felt it penetrate, slicing flesh. He moaned, feeling his jaw freeze and swell to what felt like ten times its normal size.

"That's it," said Weiss, laying the syringe on a table beside Marty. He inserted a thick, salty index finger into Marty's mouth and massaged the gum, then picked up his pliers and again examined them. "Here we go." He inserted the pliers, gripped Marty's wisdom tooth firmly, pressed down hard and twisted. Nothing happened. Marty, wriggling, felt as if a nail driven by a hammer had pierced his jaw. He bellowed, squirming, but was now helpless in Muldoon's firm grip. Weiss shook his head, withdrew a handkerchief from his tunic pocket and wiped his sweating brow. No question of it, this was going to be a Lalapaloosa. He re-inserted the pliers, took a firm grip, pressed down and rotated hard.

The molar broke. Blood spurted from Marty's mouth, spilling on to Weiss' soiled tunic. The dentist withdrew a chunk of the tooth and dropped it behind him into a spittoon on the floor. He placed his pliers on the table and handed Marty a glass of water. "Gargle," he said.

Groggy, Marty took the glass, sat up, gargled and spat blood and fragments of tooth into a tin basin which Weiss held before him. Weiss looked over Marty to Muldoon, frowned and shook his head. From the Negro's reaction, he had missed and had not fully numbed the nerve of the wisdom tooth. Either that, or he was dealing with something more than an infected molar. For the moment, that was of no matter. The remains of the shattered tooth would have to be withdrawn, and quickly. Weiss checked his wristwatch; his next appointment was in ten minutes. He pressed Marty back into the chair, to be again firmly pinioned by Muldoon. "Just a little bit of cleaning up to do," he said, inserting his pliers again. Marty howled.

Jim, Pop and MacKay were the first to visit Marty at his home.

"Goddam butcher," growled Pop, looking down at Marty, now sleeping, his face obscenely swollen. He saw that Jim was close to tears.

"Only one thing for it," said MacKay.

"Bernarr."

Bernarr McFadden scribbled industriously. He wrote in a garbled shorthand, decipherable to no one but himself. This he later transcribed to block capitals, before dispatching the final product to his mistress, Marguerite, for transfer to typed manuscript for his monthly *Bernarr McFadden's Magazine*.

He paused to check his fob watch. Pop Warner's Negro boy would be in Physical Culture City with Jim Thorpe in a couple of hours, driven over by Pop in his new Model T. He returned to his work.

"For ages past, the medical men (poor useless fools) have tried to manufacture health, yet in the meantime, mankind has steadily grown weaker. They begin at the wrong end and go backward; they study disease, instead of health, with the inevitable result that they fail to conquer disease."

Bernarr warmed to his task. It was going well. His editorial, like most of his magazine, contained not a shred of scientific evidence, and was merely a construct of McFadden's vibrant, fertile imagination, but that was of no matter. The Journal now sold well throughout the English-speaking world, tapping into a mixture of naïve Utopianism, a dislike of conventional medicine and a reaction to the pollution of industrial life.

McFadden's "Physical Culture City" consisted of little more than a couple of streets forty miles north of New York, by the shores of the River Manalapan. Its first bricks had been laid back in 1905. At that time, Bernarr had built himself a palatial mansion of wood and brick and a printing factory. Alas, in the subsequent six years, for all his blandishments, few of his readers had shown any great desire to share Bernarr's earthly paradise. His parishioners still numbered less than one hundred, a motley band of naturists, vegetarians, and anarchists.

Bernarr's main enemies were alcohol and smoking. These, and big cities, prudishness, muscular inactivity, corsets, gluttony and drugs. The list was comprehensive and gave him great freedom to manoeuvre in his editorials. Prudishness presented him with most of his problems and he had always been required to tread carefully. The letter from 'C.R.', to which he was now responding in the second half of his editorial, was typical of some of his correspondents' concerns. It first warmly commended him for his denunciation of religious magazines which published advertisements for quack medicines. 'C.R.' agreed with him that he was cleansing bodies to make them fit temples for the Holy Ghost, but then proceeded to take issue with his editor. McFadden should stop publishing 'pictures of naked men and women,' for 'C.R.' had a boy who was not yet twenty-one years of age. "Several years ago I found that he was practising a vile secret habit. If there is anything in the world which would make a boy continue the evil habit I refer to, it is that caused by the nude pictures that you choose to publish."

Johnny Five Fingers, thought Bernarr, sucking on his pencil. Father to all ills that flesh was heir to. If it had resulted in even a fraction of the dire consequences that 'C.R.' and his ilk claimed, then Bernarr would not have retained the strength to grip a pen. 'C.R.' was in any case on weak ground. Hell, most of the semi-nude photographs in the magazine were of Bernarr himself, demonstrating an infinity of exercises. They showed him half-naked, suspended from trees, or performing unlikely callisthenics on door-lintels, chairs and bed-rails, poses hardly likely to stir either male or female pulses. True,

Bernarr had found, back in 1905, with his Madison Square Garden competitions for 'The World's Most Perfectly Developed Man and Woman', that subsequent photographs of scantily-dressed athletes had immediately tripled magazine sales. But even then, the male competitors had been obliged to wear tights and the women had not dared to bare even an inch of flesh. This discretion had not, however, prevented five thousand desperate souls from failing to secure admission on the first sell-out night of competition or sell-outs for every single night of the contests. There were always big bucks in the body beautiful, and there always would be.

Bernarr reflected that during the six years of their existence, no Negros had ever featured in any of his Madison Square Garden competitions. There was no stated ban, it was simply that none had ever cared to enter. His reflections were prompted by the physique of young Roother as he lay on the examination-table of his 'surgery'. For Roother was a fine figure of a man, at least 46" round the chest and a lean 32" in the waist, with the abdominal definition of a young Eugene Sandow. None of his New York medallists could have lived with this fellow, had he entered the competition.

Bernarr peered into Marty's mouth. "You eat much in the way of red meat, Mr Roother?" he asked.

Marty nodded. "Meat," groaned Bernarr, shaking his head. "A poison, it corrupts the whole system. Heats the blood. Inflames the passions." He turned to Jim and Pop, who sat in armchairs behind him, struggling to consume glasses of warm carrot-juice. "I reckon that horses' ass of a dentist has messed up your boy, Pop," he said. He lifted a glass of carrot juice from a table and gulped it down in one, and beckoned Marty to dress. "There was an abscess behind that tooth. Impurity in the blood. Meat, Pop. You take my word for it." The words, driven by the power of positive ignorance, poured from his mouth.

Pop laid down his carrot juice with some relief. "Is there anything you can do for our man, Bernarr?"

"You bet your sweet ass there is, Pop," said Bernarr, confidently. "Two, maybe three weeks here. Sweating, colonic irrigation, fasting, roots and berries. Cleanse his system, flush out all them pesky toxins. Your boy will soon be right as rain."

Pop reached down into his briefcase and withdrew a bottle of Dr Kilmer's Painkiller. "What about this?" he asked. "Any good?"

Bernarr took the bottle and scrutinised the label. He went to the sink, opened it and emptied it of its contents. Jim groaned inwardly. What a waste. Kilmer's was good strong stuff.

"Poison, Pop," declared McFadden. "Poison."

Marty buttoned up his shirt. "So what will all this cost me?" he asked.

"I got a bunk for you down in the barn," replied Bernarr. "Fifty bucks a week, but all found."

Whatever it was that Bernarr McFadden 'found', it was certainly not food. In that first week of virtual isolation, Marty lost about two pounds of solid muscle, as he struggled to survive on McFadden's diet of water and vegetables. By the weekend, he was reduced to wandering in the nearby woods, in search of berries.

The barn's facilities were Spartan. A bunk, a chair, a table, but no fire. The only commodities in ample supply were the profuse literary works of Bernarr McFadden. Marty read them all, with growing fascination. Impotence, constipation, cancer, catarrh, tuberculosis, depression, all of man's physical and mental ills could, in McFadden's view, be avoided or cured by natural living. This meant no meat, alcohol or tobacco but instead the inhalation of vast quantities of clean country air, cold showers, and the consumption of gallons of pure water. That, and the ingestion of fields of vegetables and endless exercise. McFadden's exercise-programmes involved an infinity of free-standing activities, using everything from axes to stones, tree-branches, bed-rails and door-lintels. His programmes had travelled far across the face of the earth and

Marty's cabin was lined with framed letters of thanks from Fijian aboriginals to aristocrats of the court of the Czar.

The natural, puritanical nature of Bernarr's belief meant that his magazine contained little in the way of advertising. Accepted products such as tea, coffee and cocoa were just as poisonous to McFadden as Peruna and Ka We To. What McFadden's Magazine had in spades was a plethora of Bernarr McFadden.

The pain in his healing wisdom tooth was still there, but with every day it became less intense. Bernarr McFadden expressed contempt for all conventional drugs and to cope with the pain provided Marty with an ample supply of Cola leaves from the jungles of Columbia, apparently unaware that their primary constituent was cocaine. As far as McFadden was concerned, if it was natural, it was good and Marty found that chewing on the leaves dulled the pain and even produced pleasant feelings of euphoria.

After breakfast, McFadden invariably retired to his study to edit his magazine and to deal with his vast correspondence. His 'editing' was a fiction, since most of the articles in the magazine, whatever the name of the author, were written by McFadden himself.

McFadden's purification programme was inflexible. Thus, every day of that first week in Physical Culture City began with a cold shower at the bath house, a log hut by the shores of Lake Manalapan. Bernarr placed great store by the efficacy of cold showers, a euphemism for high-speed jets of freezing water projected at an infinity of angles within a glass cubicle. The shower was followed, once every 48 hours, by colonic irrigation, another McFadden euphemism for an enema of warm, soapy water, conducted by a female nurse with arms like Gotham hams. This proved to be less unpleasant than Marty had feared. He left the bath house that first morning for McFadden's sauna, adjacent to it feeling surprisingly good, having expelled a brown, X-Files sludge which McFadden assured him was toxic waste, but which Marty felt no inclination either to discuss or inspect. The sauna which Bernarr had constructed was a direct copy of a Najavo sweat house, replete with an arboretum of branches of eucalyptus. Every morning, after forty minutes of sustained sweating and self-flagellation with birch-boughs, Marty made his way to his cabin for breakfast. He was surprised to find at the end of his first week that breakfast was now to be shared at McFadden's mansion with Bernarr and his friend Marguerite, a radiant, attractive brunette in her late twenties. The meals were unvarying, consisting of raw vegetables, rolled oats, nuts, raisins, bran, honey and milk. Conversation did not take high priority in the McFadden household. Instead, Marty and Marguerite were treated by Bernarr to a relentless monologue on the evils of prudishness, corsets, meat and cities.

During his first days, Marty was still weak, the poisons from the abscess still in his system. His walks were therefore at a slow pace, on pine-needle paths in the green, spring woods. As he had passed through McFadden's 'Physical Culture City', on his way to the woods, he had observed no sign of life in the fifty-odd cabin-type houses in its single main street. There were no shops, no telephones, no newspapers. It was like a ghost town.

By the beginning of the second week, he was beginning to feel much better. A letter from Mary Lou lay snug in his back pocket to be read and re-read. The wood echoed with the gurgle of birds and the rhythmic cooing of doves, the sun shafting through the virgin leaves. Scranton seemed another land, as did even Pop, Jim and the boys of the Carlisle Team. Less easy to forget were the agonies of Weiss' dental ministrations.

For the moment, the purpose of his return to 1912 had receded, but as he became stronger, the date of September 13th 1912 returned to him. That was the day after he planned to compete against Jim, the day on which he would return to the future. He reflected that, in a way, his illness would cleanse him, clean the drugs of Factor 2000 out of his system, leave him clean to take on Jim after the Stockholm Olympics.

But there were bats at the back of his soul. For he would return to riches, to fame, and it would only take a few months for his medical advisors to pump him full of enough chemicals to ensure Olympic gold in Sydney. But he would do it as a fake. For that was what the whole shebang was, a pharmaceutical freak show, fakes against fakes, Glaxo-Wellcome versus Roche. And he was a star of the freak show, a fully signed-up member of the club. The true athletes had long departed the scene, but no one had the guts to admit it. And soon there would be the gene-warriors, genetically-programmed for success, no more substantial than holograms. OK, so 1912 was no athletic paradise. There was the chicanery of Scranton, the slugging of Ivy League teams, the ringers, but it all had a rugged reality, far from the fantasies of pharmacists.

But the real shadow was of greater substance and had nothing to do with track and field. It was Mary Lou. Until he had met her, women had been sexual wallpaper, an anonymous part of the seamless tapestry of success. But Mary Lou had no care for who he was; she did care about what he was. She was now part of the fibre of his life and lay at his core. Mary Lou had nothing but a couple of pairs of shoes, a Sunday go-to-the-meeting dress and fourteen bucks in a tin box beneath her bed. But she had a vigorous, enquiring mind, a lust for knowledge and a generosity of spirit. Marty knew that he could not, indeed would not, leave her behind.

Every day since his arrival he had explored with his tongue the pulsing volcano at the back of his mouth. At first, it had been a great, soft hollow of pus and pain. Surprisingly, Bernarr McFadden at no point made any further attempt to examine it. Bernarr's belief in the cleansing forces of nature was absolute, unswerving. Fruit and fibre, colonic irrigation, evacuation and perspiration, sun and fresh air, these were to be Marty's physicians.

Marty had, by the end of the second week begun to encounter some of the other residents of McFadden's Physical Culture City. They were a motley bunch, identical only their eccentricity. There was Abel Clark, a retired New York fireman whom McFadden had cured of a stomach cancer by placing him on a diet of carrots and water; Herb Wasserstein, the Boston shipping magnate who had abandoned wife and family and now devoted himself to the study of the works of the theosophist Madame Blavatsky; Sadie Brome, a 35-year-old dancer who had been a lover of Isadora Duncan, and who now dedicated herself to a form of exercise based on the figures depicted on Greek vases. Then there was the actor Junius Brutus Tasker, who had stolen his first two names from the father of the great Edwin Booth. Junius Brutus had dedicated his life to the hypothesis that the works of Shakespeare had been written by Queen Elizabeth I, who was not the Virgin Queen, but rather the illegitimate son of the Duke of Norfolk.

These and ninety-odd others constituted the population of McFadden's Physical Culture City. Together, they had dug a well and had gone into the production of 'Malapan Spa Water' at 10 cents a bottle, a cent going into Bernarr McFadden's pocket for every bottle sold. Clark had helped them build a power unit, using the energy of the river Manalapan to provide electricity, and Sadie Broome ran a community bakery. There appeared to be little in the way of cash in Physical Culture City. The community, apart from those who had come to take cures, seemed to live entirely on barter.

Day by day, the hollow in his gum became smaller, less painful, but each day he lost weight, almost all of it solid muscle. Marty could almost see his deltoids shrink. But by the middle of the third week he began to feel sharp, began to feel good. He, therefore, decided that before dinner on Friday he would inform McFadden that he was now ready to return to Carlisle.

When he arrived for dinner that evening. He found Bernarr McFadden in the living room in deep conversation with a stocky, dapper, middle-aged man of medium height. On seeing Marty, McFadden drew his guest forward. "Marty," he said. "Meet Houdini."

The entire dinner was a blur to him. Marty ate as in a dream, and did not taste the food. Houdini. It was as if he were dining with Jesse Owens or Wyatt Earp. McFadden, a long-time friend of the Houdinis, had asked the magician to write a series of articles for his magazine, and Houdini, ever eager for publicity, had agreed. He would even give an extempore concert for the citizens of Physical Culture City on Saturday night, when his wife and his assistant would join him.

Marty was surprised to find that Houdini spoke with a slightly foreign accent, and that he always referred to himself as 'Houdini'. Thus, it was "Houdini will appear next month at the Belasco", or "Houdini will appear before the Kaiser in November." Marty did not dare to address him directly, but listened intently to the conversation between Houdini and Bernarr McFadden. It was the first time that Marty had heard McFadden in true conversation with anyone, but in Harry Houdini he had met his match. For the words flowed in torrents from the great escapologist and the argument grew progressively more heated as the subject of spiritualism was broached. For McFadden was an ardent believer, while Houdini was at best agnostic.

It was approaching midnight when McFadden, clearly getting the worse of the debate, suggested that Houdini might entertain them with a 'trick'. Marty noted that Houdini's expression hardened slightly. He had clearly no liking for the word 'trick', but natural courtesy held him back. Houdini asked for a pack of cards but McFadden informed him that he had no truck with gambling of any kind. A pack could not, therefore, be found. Houdini paused and looked round the table. "Mrs

McFadden," he said. "How many churches are there round here, say within a radius of five miles?"

"Too dam' many," growled Bernarr McFadden.

Marguerite paused. "Three," she said.

"Four," corrected Bernarr.

Marguerite nodded. "That's right, darling. Bethlehem, St Luke's, Maryport and Stanton."

"Do all of these have church bells?" asked Houdini.

"Yes," replied Marguerite, nodding.

"And could you hear them here, on a clear night like this?" pursued Houdini.

"Yes," replied Marguerite. "But they only ring on Sundays and at weddings and funerals."

Houdini nodded. "Mrs McFadden, please could you provide me with four slips of plain white paper?"

Marguerite was despatched and returned with four slips of paper.

"Mr Roother," said Houdini. "If you would be so kind, as to print the names of the four churches on these slips of paper?"

Marty duly printed the names. Houdini took from Marty the four slips of paper, inspected them and folded them. Then he placed them carefully in a glass bowl on the table. "Mrs McFadden, please make your choice," he said.

Marguerite placed her hand in the bowl, withdrew a slip and handed it to Houdini. He unfolded the slip and held it in front of him.

"St Luke's," he said, replacing it in the bowl. He took his watch from an inner fob pocket and examined it. "Three minutes to midnight," he said. "In exactly three minutes, the bells of St Luke's will ring thirteen times." He looked at Bernarr. "St Luke's, would you recognise them?"

McFadden nodded. "Rusty as hell, Harry," he said, "couldn't mistake 'em."

They sat in silence for several minutes. Then, on the stroke of midnight, there was the sound of bells, rough and sharp in the still night air. They rang thirteen times.

Bernarr McFadden sagged. "St Luke's," he whispered.

Houdini had seen no good purpose in presenting an escapology act to the citizens of Physical Culture City. True, the act had enraptured audiences from Maine to Moscow, but it was best suited to theatres, to large audiences. There, orchestras had played endless drear ditties whilst audiences imagined Houdini behind the velvet curtains of his cabinet, going through agonies as he writhed to free himself from a wilderness of locks and chains. But Houdini rarely took more than a few moments to divest himself of his restraints. Early experience of sand-clogged locks and others which were impossible to open because they had never been devised to do so had taught him to insist that every lock was first opened in front of him. Houdini took few chances. Once clear of restraints, he would sit, still and silent, in his cabinet for anything up to half an hour, whilst his audience were entertained by the orchestra. Occasionally, he would poke a sweating face and carefully bloodied wrists through the curtains to a now almost hysterical audience. Sometimes, Houdini would beg for water, on others he would complain that his legs had gone numb and plead that his leg-chains be loosened. Whatever his reasons for complaint, Houdini's requests were invariably refused by his challenger, usually a local locksmith or a chief of police. Equally invariably, boos and hisses swelled from the audience, but the challengers (now identified by the audience as enemies) were obdurate. After at least two more such appeals, and with almost an hour gone, many of the audience began to become restive. Had Houdini lost consciousness? Had the Great Houdini suffered a heart attack? As the clock ticked towards the hour, there were shouts for the management to intervene. Then, suddenly, the curtains parted and Houdini was there, before them, sweating, bloodied, his clothes now in shreds, carrying in his hands the symbols of his bondage, a tangled spaghetti of chains, locks and wires.

Their hero, their Samson, their God, was now free and the audience exploded with joy and relief.

But here Houdini reasoned that a small audience required, not the grand gesture, but an intimate entertainment. Thus, he and his wife Bess regaled the audience with a blizzard of card-tricks, sleight of hand which he had first performed twenty years before when they had travelled in vaudeville. Then, he and Bess had performed his mind-reading act, before finishing with his pièce de resistance, automatic writing.

Houdini signalled to the back of the room to a colleague and the lights of McFadden's crowded living room dimmed. Houdini's colleague, a lean, bearded middle-aged man in a black suit, wheeled through the centre of the audience what looked like a wooden coat-stand. He placed it in front of the audience and retreated to the shadows at the back of the room. Houdini now held in front of him a rectangular slate, about 18″ by 15″. Holes had been bored in two corners of the slate and Houdini passed through them wires on to which hooks were attached. Bernarr McFadden was brought forward and he took the slate and suspended it on the frame, allowing it to hang freely. Houdini beckoned members of the audience forward to inspect the slate. "Mr Roother," said Houdini. Marty, at the back of the room, saw all eyes turn towards him. He reddened. "Mr Roother," Houdini continued, "I would kindly ask that you procure a paper and pencil."

Marty did so.

"I would like you to go out of the house, walk anywhere you like, then write a phrase or symbol on a piece of paper. Anything you like. Put it back in your pocket and return to the house. Will you do that for me?" asked Houdini.

Marty nodded. He went to the front door and walked out into the dusk. It was clear to him that this was some kind of mind-reading trick, and he resolved to put it beyond even the Great Houdini. He withdrew the paper and pencil from his pocket and printed on it 'September 13th, 1995', the planned date of his return, and placed it in his inside jacket pocket.

"Have you done as I requested you, Mr Roother?" asked Houdini, taking the paper from him and holding it aloft, before returning it to him.

Houdini presented Bernarr McFadden with a cork ball and asked him to examine it. He then asked him to roll the ball in a plate containing a white, paint-like fluid. Houdini then took the ball and threw it at the slate. It stuck, as if glued to the surface. Then slowly, it began to roll across the surface of the slate, to sighs from the audience. In a few moments, the words 'September 13th, 1995' appeared in white on the surface of the slate. Marty felt his jaw go slack, his cheeks flush.

"And Mr Roother, may I ask you what you have printed on the sheet of paper?"

Marty's reply stumbled from dry lips.

The applause was immediate, rapturous, and the lights went on. Houdini immediately beckoned Bess and his assistant to take their bows before the audience.

Marty was transfixed, stunned. Then he looked more carefully at Houdini's bearded, black-coated assistant and his heart stopped.

It was his father.

Chapter 16
Getting Back

"Row Five, Seat Six, St Patrick's Church, 104 East 25th Street, New York City," growled Marcus Jones, slowly beating a path for them through the woods with his walking stick. Father and son walked together in the watery sun, which struggled through spring leaves in the dense, green forest which encircled Lake Malapan.

"Bob and I, and our Aetherians we won't take any chances. St Patrick's was there in March 1995, and not a brick had changed in a century. Anyhow, it was the same way that Miss Boggis had made it back, before me, from Paris. Psychokinetics."

"Psychokinetics, you just made that word up," said Marty.

"You're right, but however, did you know that? "

"Instinct," said Marty.

"Well, that's what it is, the power of the mind. Collective power."

"So why didn't you tell me that you were going?" said Marty.

His father stopped, turned and took him by both shoulders. "Come on, Marty," he said. "You would have gone straight to the men in the white suits. Anyhow, you were too busy doing your own thing – MLJ. Armani. Nike. 9000 points. All that shit. No need to bother you."

Marty observed his father. Despite the beard and the loose, unflattering trousers and shirt, Marcus Jones looked leaner, younger. "You're looking good, Pop," he said.

Marcus tapped his stomach. “That’s Houdini for you. The man’s a fitness freak. You know he once ran a 2.05 half – mile? We work out together most days.”

“But Bob Goldstein told me you went back to work with Edison.”

His father grunted his agreement. “Bob was right,” he said. “I did. In 1898. Been there, done that. Yes, I got myself into Edison’s team for a couple of years.” He shook his head. “What an asshole. Edison worked eighteen hours a day, expected all his people to do likewise, paid us peanuts, stole all our best ideas and kept the profits for himself. Not a nice man.”

The two men stopped and sat on an upturned log. Marcus withdrew a Scout knife from a trouser pocket, picked up a short, thick branch and slowly began to whittle it. “Then it was off to Paris, France,” he said. He paused and observed the product of his whittling. “You know, Marty, I always thought I could paint.”

“You’re pretty good,” said Marty. “So how long did you spend there?”

“Just over a year,” replied his father. “About a week in our time. But even there, amongst all these great artists, it didn’t make a blind bit of difference. You would have thought something, just a little, would have rubbed off, but no, it didn’t. Sure, I could draw, I could paint, but I had no real talent.” He paused and resumed his whittling. “But I sure had me a real good time.”

“And where did you go from there?”

“I had a year and a half as a gofer for Teddy Roosevelt, when he was Vice-President. That was when I found out you couldn’t change anything.”

Marty felt himself flush. “You mean the past. You can’t change the past.”

Marcus lifted his now fully whittled branch in front of him and inspected it. “When Teddy became Vice-President to McKinley, I tried to get the President to take on more security but no, he wouldn’t listen. So they got to him.”

“How do you mean?”

"History never was your strong suit, Marty," observed his father. "McKinley, he was assassinated in 1901, just like they say in all the history books and there wasn't a damn thing I could do about it." He spun the whittled branch out into the spring undergrowth. "Nothing in the world," he said. "Same as the Titanic." He picked up another stumpy branch and again began to whittle, shearing off thick shards of wood. "I phoned up the Steamship Company, but they just wouldn't listen. Hell, you can hardly blame them." He shook his head. "No, there's not a blind thing you can do, Marty, least not with things like that, not with the big things." He chuckled. "Else I could've got little Annie Oakley to kill the Kaiser, 'stead of just shooting a cigar out of his mouth, when Buffalo Bill was over in Germany." Marcus suddenly stopped his whittling and looked at his son. "Did Houdini do the bell trick?" he asked

"Yes, how do you know that?" said Marty.

"Let me try to tell you how it all works," said his father smiling. "His wife Bess asked Houdini for a trick, or he got lucky and someone else asked. They always do, and always close to midnight."

"Right," replied Marty. "McFadden, he was the one who asked."

"OK," said his father. "So Houdini asked for the names of three or four local churches and got someone to write them down for him."

Marty nodded.

"Houdini, he put them in a bowl and asked someone to take out one of the slips of paper."

"Right on," said Marty.

"So let me tell you the name of the Church," said his father. "St Luke's."

"Jesus Christ!" gasped Marty. "How come you knew that?"

"Because I bust my buns opening the lock at St Luke's twelve hours before, that's why," growled his father. "By midnight, I had been in the bell-tower for most of the day. Houdini, he had palmed these slips and replaced them with four of his own."

"With St Luke's written on every one of them," said Marty.

"You got it," said his father. "So at midnight I pulled that bell rope thirteen times."

"OK," said Marty. "But what about that stunt with the cork ball?"

His father shook his head. "I don't know how he pulls that one," he said. "Houdini, he doesn't tell me everything." He paused and looked at his son. "Marty," he said. "I am an A1 asshole. Hell, I haven't stopped talking since we started. I haven't asked you why you came back."

Marty did not reply for a moment. He reflected that it had always been the same. His father had never had much patience for anything but his own thoughts. Marty sat beside his father on the log. "It was Jim," he said.

"Jim? Jim who?"

"Jim Thorpe," replied Marty.

"Jim Thorpe? So how did that come about?"

"I heard voices," said Marty. "Saw him everywhere I went."

"So what did Jim say to you?"

"Are you ready?" replied Marty.

"Ready for what, for Christ's sake?"

"To come back and take him on."

"So that was when you first went to see Bob Goldstein?"

Marty nodded. "Dunk told me you were back here and about Lucy Boggis. So I got back and I ended up as a groundsman at Carlisle. I go back home on September 13th after I've whipped Jim."

Marcus Jones ran his tongue beneath his lower lip. "I saw Thorpe play last year 'gainst Harvard," he said. "I never in my life saw such plays, not even from Payton or O.J. So you've picked up with ole Jim."

Marty told him of his experiences at Carlisle, of the match against Yale, the Scranton Handicap, of Mary Lou. "You hit pay-dirt there, Marty," said his father. "Jim Thorpe. Pop Warner. Pity I wasn't around when you met up with that asshole Sullivan. Might have got you to Stockholm. Might have got you an Olympic medal."

"Not from what you've just told me, Pop."

His father nodded. "So what's your game plan now?"

"To go to the Stockholm Olympics to help Jim, then whip his ass when we get back. After that, it's September 13th 1912, the laundry room at the Majestic and back home with Mary Lou."

His father's expression hardened. "That may not be quite as easy as you think, son," he said. "OK, so far all of our people have got back, but they sure as hell haven't arrived home with any company."

"Perhaps none of them ever tried."

"Yes and no," replied his father, his expression still sombre. Miss Boggis she tried to bring back a painting by Picasso. She made it back on time but God knows what happened to that painting."

"So you're telling me that Mary Lou can't come back with me?"

"No, I'm not saying anything of the sort," said his father. "But this time travel, it's not like algebra, it's not an exact science. They parked themselves in the right place at the appointed time and allah kazam, they vanished. That's all we really know."

Marty looked at his father and pointed a finger at him. "Wait a minute," he said. "You shouldn't be here now. Bob, he said you were in 1910."

His father sighed. "Like I said Marty, it isn't an exact science. Still maybe it's fate, maybe that's why our paths have crossed."

"I don't get your drift," said Marty.

"I don't know if I can get back," replied his father.

"What about St Patrick's?"

"You were right. I was due to go back there three years ago," said his father.

"But it went wrong," said Marty

His father growled assent. "I went to sleep one night in the appointed place, and went through my psychokinetic routines. When I woke up, it was May 1910."

Marty's heart sank. "Didn't you get a message back?"

"I did," replied Marcus. "I scheduled to get back for a year later, May 20th 1911."

"Same date, same time, same place."

Marcus nodded. "When I got there, the church was closed, locked and bolted. No way in, less I used dynamite. So I sent more messages, got the OK, and went to St Patrick's, week in week out." He shook his head. "Nothing happened. Day after day, but nix. Hell, I gave ten confessions, just to pass away the time."

Marty stood and spoke as if he was talking to himself. "So you think this whole thing is locked into a specific year or day and date. Once a year or no deal."

"How do I know?" said his father. "Maybe it's some black hole that only opens up for business once a year. Hell, maybe it's only once a lifetime. May 20th is my next shot."

"I'll put it in my next message, with Mammy Boston," said Marty. "So they're all clear about it back home." He paused. "So what happens…if nothing happens?"

Marcus Jones could sense the change in the atmosphere. "Look at it this way, Marty," he said. "I've had me a good deal. I've met some people I never could've met, done things I never could've done, and you've noticed – I've hardly aged. So I've had fifteen years of bonus life. I'll come out of it good."

"If you get back."

"If I don't, I'll put all my money on 1, 2, 3 in the Kentucky Derby – I'll stay on here and live like a king. Either way it's win, win, win."

The two men sat, facing each other across the rough wooden breakfast table in Marty's Spartan, sparsely furnished cabin. Marcus looked across at his son, spooned a mouthful of oats and bran, wiped his mouth with the back of his hand and smiled. "He's a fraud, that bastard McFadden," he said. "But this is one thing of his that works. Since I've been taking McFadden's bran, I can set my watch by the movements of my bowels." He continued to eat, observing his son. "You know," he said, "It looks like we've had to come back a century just so we can talk. Hell, we haven't sat and talked like this for years."

"I've been around, Pa," said Marty, defensively.

"No," replied his father, abruptly laying down his spoon. "No, Marty, you haven't. Let me put it another way, you've been around, but you haven't been in the neighbourhood."

"The neighbourhood? What the hell's the neighbourhood?" responded Marty.

"You know what I mean," said his father. "You went from being Marty to being MLJ. That's what I mean. OK, so you were there, but you weren't in the neighbourhood."

Marty did not reply. He stood, went to the stove and poured himself a mug of steaming Arbuckles. He sat down and surveyed the mug, both hands around it. "OK, Pa," he said. "You're right, but now I've come back to the neighbourhood."

"To 1912"

Marty nodded.

"You know Marty I think we might both have come back for something. To find something good, something honest," said his father.

"And did you find it?"

His father shook his head. "Somebody once said that a Golden Age was only evidence of bad memory. Whoever it was, he was right." He sipped his coffee.

"So it's all been a complete waste of time?"

"No," said his father. "I found Houdini, the ultimate pro. He's as close as I'm ever likely to get." He smiled to himself. "One of the greatest men of all time and he's as pure as Sir Galahad."

"But why Houdini, why is he so good?"

"I've thought a lot about it," his father replied. "First, sex. I don't think Harry Houdini has much of a sex drive. Or maybe he has, but it's all focussed on his wife, Beth. Hell, I don't think he's laid a hand on any other woman in his life. That clears him to be the best at what he does."

"Which is fooling the public."

"Sex, it often fucks us up," said his father. "So we can't see straight. So does power. Okay, so maybe it's not power that does it; maybe it's the way we get it that fucks us up. Either way, it's the same thing." He paused. "And Houdini has the power, too. He never takes any new illusion on unless he has total control. No variables." Marcus looks across at his son. "All this way back to talk like a dime store Socrates. I'm boring the pants off you."

Marty shook his head. "No, Pa, you're not. Jim's the same. He's pure athlete, pure, unadulterated athlete."

"He doesn't have a girl?"

"Yes, Jim's got a girl. But it's sport that drives him. Jim's completely honest. Not like me!"

"So that's why you came back. To fight clean."

Marty nodded. "I won't compete again in Olympic track when I get back," he said. "I've finished with that freak show for good. It's whupping Jim, then back to 1995 with Mary Lou. Then it's college for her, coaching for me."

His father smiled, reached across and placed his hand over that of his son. "What…what I said about sex and power, all those things. Don't take it too much to heart. Take those out and you take the grit out of the oyster. The secret is in how you balance them all out." He paused. "You love this girl, this Mary Lou?"

"Yes, I do," said Marty.

"A good woman and a coupla friends in town," said his father. "That's all any man needs." He lifted his mug to his lips and drained it. "But let me ask you one question, Marty. If you know you can't both get back, are you willing to stay here?"

As Marty made to answer, he heard the door creak behind him. He turned to see Mary Lou and smiled. "Mary Lou," he said, standing. "Meet my father."

Marcus Jones had immediately taken to the girl. He had asked Marty if he could have a few moments alone with her, while his son packed for his departure from Physical Culture City. They had walked together along the rocky shores of Lake Malapan.

Mary Lou glowed. The girl had asked nothing about the future, only about himself, about his experiences since he had returned. *Perhaps,* he thought, *Marty had told her all she wanted to know about the future.* Perhaps, what his son had told her about it had confused and frightened her. But, no question about it, Mary Lou shone. It had not taken Marcus long to discover that she was one hell of a lady, a heavyweight. Voraciously curious, she had never let her education interfere with her studies. Mary Lou bled him of his experiences with Edison and Roosevelt and the French painters. Though uneducated, she was not far being from an intellectual equal and she would soon test Marty to his limits. And it was clear to Marcus that she loved his son. That made it all the more difficult for him to tell her that there was no guarantee that she would make it back to 1995.

"I go back next month," he said. "And I'm taking a couple of paintings with me."

"Them Frenchmen?"

He smiled. "Them Frenchmen. Gauguin. I got one cheap, for a hundred bucks," he said. "Back where I come from they'll fetch well over a hundred million. I'll put all the money to psychic research and a prostate cancer charity."

Mary Lou wrinkled her nose. "So what's that gotta do with me?"

"Well if I can get back with these paintings, then there's a chance that you can make it back, too. And I'm also going to get my Scottie dog back too.

"It's gonna be tough," she said. "The Majestic Hotel where Marty come in, it burnt to the ground last week. I ain't told Marty yet."

"Jeez," said Marcus. He hesitated. "Then maybe these will help." He reached into his right jacket pocket and withdrew a pair of handcuffs. "Take these," he said, handing them to her. "They belong to Houdini and he's about as psychic as any man I've ever met. Perhaps they'll manage to keep you together."

She looked at him, sensing the doubt in his voice. Marcus shrugged and raised both hands. "Hell, Mary Lou," he said. "I've told you I don't know how it works. At least, I'll be back ahead of you. When I get back home, we'll all give it our best shot. I'll be with Lucy Boggis and the others, putting some bang into the telepathic buck."

"And what happens if the paintings and the dog don't make it back?"

"I've told you," he said. "We'll all give it our best shot. Psychokinetics. After all, you're pretty much family. It's only another one to get back."

"No," she said, tapping her stomach. "Two."

It was only when they returned to the cabin that Mary Lou told them of Jim's injury. It was a Charley horse, a rupture in the thick belly of his left hamstring, sustained during a dash session with Pop Warner on Carlisle's now untended track.

The news of the injury had set Marcus to thinking. In his youth, he had read everything on Jim Thorpe that he could lay his hands on. Nothing in the literature had ever made any mention of a June injury in 1912. It was the type of injury that in that time would have kept Thorpe out of the Olympic Games, for in those days athletes possessed no effective means of treatment, and Jim would have been unable to make the American team. Even if he had made it, he would have been in no shape to take on a pentathlon, a decathlon and two individual events in Stockholm. Unless something had happened. Unless there had been some intervening factor. And that factor might well have been his son. For Marty certainly knew enough about athletic injury to help Jim through to Stockholm. Without him, without Marty's aid, Jim would struggle. So perhaps, some things in the past could be changed; perhaps, anything could be changed.

Certainly, he reflected, the bank balances of certain American bookmakers had changed since his arrival in 1897. For he had brought back with him the results of the Kentucky Derby from 1897 to 1912. He had been generous and had spread his bets through a range of bookmakers and his advance knowledge had kept him like a poor man with money since his arrival. So something could be changed.

Chapter 17
Danville, Alabama

Jim lay on his bunk, head cupped in his hands, legs flexed, staring at the ceiling. He reached down for the hundredth time and rubbed the back of his left leg, frowned, then stretched to the side with his right hand, fumbling for the earthenware jug on the stone floor beside him. He lifted it to his mouth and tilted it, but only a thin trickle of the corn mash whiskey dripped to his lips. The jug was empty. He groaned and cursed under his breath. Jim replaced the jug on the floor, lay back and gently probed the centre of the back of his left leg with his fingers, digging deep. He sensed that he could detect a hole in the thick bulbous muscle of his hamstring. Of course, he could not. For the tear, though substantial, was deep, well beyond his reach, in the dense cluster of short fibres at the centre of the muscle.

Jim reflected that there was no worse condition than that of the crippled athlete. Of course, he had been hurt many times before. That had always, however, been an impact injury, the product of his insistence that 'Jim run', no matter how many Ivy League thugs blocked his path. Jim would dodge some, run over others and hand off most of the rest, but there was often one player who could not be passed. That was when a leather-capped bullet head would smash into hip or thigh, or a swinging fist would cause gouts of blood to spurt from his nose or loosen his teeth. Jim could, quite literally, take all such injuries in his stride. A hot bath, a few grogs and a few days later he was a new, if slightly stiffer, man. His body had always seemed to have an almost infinite capacity to repair itself. It had never once let him down. Up till now.

This was different. A cluster of treacherous fibres deep in the depths of his hamstrings had betrayed him. Jim's knowledge of anatomy did not extend to the understanding that it took only a few millimetres of recalcitrant tissue to rupture to produce the knife-pain that had brought him to such a summary halt. That was now unimportant, irrelevant. For the moment, Jim knew that he could not beat a child to the mailbox.

He rose awkwardly, lowered himself to his feet and limped to the cabinet above his washbasin. He rummaged through its contents, till he had located Dr Kilmer's Kiowa Cure. The fluid was contained in a sticky brown bottle and was half-empty. The Kiowa Cure was for bronchial problems, but that was of no matter. Jim uncorked it with his teeth, tasting a stale sweetness as he did so, and poured the sticky brown mixture down his throat. He had no great liking for its sickly taste, but that was of no concern to him. Kilmer's was at least sixty percent proof and a more than adequate substitute for his empty jug of corn mash. Jim drank the Kilmer's to the dregs, then licked the rim of the bottle and replaced it in the cabinet. Then, he cautiously bent down and tried to touch the floor with his hands, legs straight. But no, the knife-pain was still there. He had tried this exercise every day since the injury, which had occurred during an early-season dash-session with Pop Warner. Alas, since then there had been little obvious change. When the injury had first occurred, Pop had simply grunted 'Charley Horse', had handed him a bottle of evil-smelling horse-ointment, then had set out in his Model T to check out some Navajo boys for the 1912 football season.

Jim was alone. His new girl, Alice, had returned to the Reservation to care for a sick mother and most of the rest of the Carlisle team had departed to their tribes for Easter. He sat for a moment on the side of his bed, then returned to his back, his head again cupped in his hands, his eyes on the cracked, flaking cream paint on the ceiling above him. *Perhaps,* he thought, *this was what it would be like when he got old, when his tissues had inevitably lost the elasticity of youth, when the words 'let Jim run' would finally meet with no response.* Jim found it difficult to conceive of a future when he could no longer run like a stag, jump like a deer, put up punts that hung in flight for an eternity. For this was the way it had been for him, what he wanted it to be forever. There could surely be no better life. Yet he knew that deep in the back of his left thigh lay the future, that sad time when it would all come to an end, when another reality, one without sport, would have to be addressed. That future time when his legs had lost their power, when hands ceased to applaud. Jim felt a weight at the pit of his stomach.

The door of his room opened. It was Marty, carrying a discus. He was smiling. Marty flipped the discus across the little room to Jim, who quickly sat up and caught it with two hands. "OK, Jim," said Marty. "Let's us get your ass in gear for Stockholm."

Mary Lou had been surprised when she had been called up to Dean Mackay's office. True, her experiences with him at Hartford and in Scranton had been agreeable, but Mackay, with his severe manner and his deep, rasping Scotch voice, had always made her feel uneasy.

The Dean, lean and ascetic, framed in his leather-covered chair behind his desk, came straight to the point. "Something just arrived here for you, woman," he said, reaching down to open a drawer on his left. "A parcel – New York postmark." He withdrew a long, cylindrical package encased in brown paper and laid it on his desk in front of him. Mackay stood, picked up the parcel and handed it to her across the desk. Mary Lou returned to her chair in front of his desk and sat down. She felt beneath the brown packaging the hard shape of a cylinder.

She looked down at it. "First parcel I ever got in my born days," she said.

"From someone who didn't seem to know your address, but probably knew you were spoken for by young Marty," observed Mackay. "I suppose that's why they sent it here, to the college."

Mary Lou made to rise. Mackay rose and beckoned here to remain seated. “Hold on, lass,” he said. “Bide a wee, there’s something that’s bothered me for months.” He put both elbows on his desk and leant towards her. “Be honest with me, girl. Your boy, Marty, he doesn’t come from Alabama, does he?”

Mary Lou did not answer, but lowered her eyes to the parcel.

“No. “I thought not,” said Mackay. “The long and the short of it is that he doesn’t come from America either,” he said. He paused. “Stands to reason. Me, I’ve pushed it back and forwards in my head for months. Just couldna get it out of my mind.” He sat further back and placed both hands under his chin, both elbows still on the desk. “Then it all came to me, sudden-like.” He took his elbows from the desk and he leant back in his chair. “Your boy Marty, he’s come from the wrong side of the blanket,” he said. “And I hope you won’t take offence.” Mackay now spoke as if he were speaking to himself. “It’s the way the boy talks, the words he uses, it’s like he’s been educated like, like…”

“Like a Scot?” volunteered Mary Lou, struggling to keep her face straight.

“Could well be. He do say some strange things sometimes.”

The Dean did not pick up the note of sarcasm in her voice.

“Marty has what might well be described as an extensive vocabulary,” said the Dean. “He says some things that people haven’t thought of yet. There’s no way that he could have learnt that picking cotton, unless he had gone to Harvard. You saw the way he spoke to Halsey and those Yale people.”

Mary Lou shook her head.

“He’s a weird one, that’s for sure,” she said, standing.

“Before you go, lass, I just had a call. There’s something else has just arrived for you, down at the post office.”

“What is it?”

“It’s a dog, lass. It’s a wee dog.”

Marty stood with Jim at the wooden fence at the side of the running track. It was all Pop's fault. For Pop had run Jim through a dozen sixty yard short-recovery dashes, without rest on Carlisle's now lumpy, untended surface. Jim's hamstrings, soon suffering from the bumpy surface and poorly-conditioned from the football season, had hit fatigue and ripped. Injury had been almost inevitable. Marty had given Jim a spare pair of track bottoms which Mary Lou had made him for Scranton and had Jim walk for a vigorous mile, to warm up his muscles. He was now sweating hard.

"Stand side-on to the fence, Jim," he said. "Right side to it, hold on with the right hand, like in ballet."

"Ballet?" grunted Jim, his broad brown face creased into a grin. "You ain't getting me into no ballet, Marty, I can tell you that for sure."

Marty smiled. "No one's gonna have you dancing in Swan Lake, Jim. It's just for support." He stood facing Jim three yards away, supporting himself on the fence with his left hand. Then he slowly began to swing his right leg, pendulum style, till his foot was beyond head-height. "Swing your left leg like this, Jim. Feel the stretch."

Jim gingerly began to swing his left leg.

"Higher."

Jim's left foot reached chest height.

"You feel anything yet?"

"Not much."

"Higher," ordered Marty.

Jim nodded and swung the leg to shoulder height. "Reckon I can feel it a touch now," he said.

"No problem, keep it at that height, and keep swinging," said Marty.

"How many?" said Jim.

"A set of twenty, then rest," responded Marty.

Jim continued to swing. "It's getting easier," he said.

"A hundred more and it'll be easier yet," said Marty.

Jim continued to swing his left leg religiously and completed his second set. Half an hour later, he was able to jog for the first time, without a limp.

Mary Lou dared not take the package home. Instead, she took it to the laundry room at the Excelsior, where she had first discovered Marty. Locking the door behind her, she carefully stripped away the brown paper, to reveal a stiff cardboard cylinder, the type used for posters and prints. As she did so, two brown paper envelopes dropped from the interior of the cylinder. Mary Lou picked them up, flattened them, and laid them on a shelf beside the towels, then fumbled in the interior of the cylinder. Something was curled up inside it. It felt like rough fabric. Mary Lou slowly, carefully, teased the fabric out of the cylinder and opened it out, placing heavy slabs of carbolic soap at each edge to keep it flat. It was an oil painting. She surveyed it. For sure, it was damned rude. The painting was of a flat-nosed nude coloured woman of ample proportions, seen from above. She lay on her back, weight on her elbows, legs spread wide apart. Mary Lou had never ever seen a woman's parts exposed in such an outrageous manner. Come to that, she had never seen naked breasts, either. Yet here it was. And even a cursory knowledge of the human condition told her that the stiff nipples, the sheer raw, abandoned nature of the woman's posture could indicate only one thing. This woman was ready for it. She felt her breathing deepen, her face flush. Mary Lou sat on her knees and studied the painting for a few moments. She knew now who had sent it and she felt cold. Mary Lou stood and went to the shelf to retrieve the two brown envelopes. She opened the first, which was bulky. In it, was five hundred dollars, in new fifty-dollar notes. She folded the money into a purse on her belt and ripped open the second envelope. It contained a single sheet, and was a letter from Marty's father.

Dear Mary Lou,
As you read this, you will know that I have made it back, but, alas, the painting and my dog did not. A hundred bucks to the Poor Fund at St Bartholemew's has ensured that the painting gets to you. It's by a Frenchman called Gauguin, and will be worth a few million bucks, forty years or so from now.
The five hundred bucks is for you and the baby, just in case you don't make it, or decide to stay. On the other side of this sheet, you will find the first three horses in the Preakness each year until 1916. Invest your $500 in that, and you and your folks will live off the fatheads of the land till well into the century.
It's not for me to say what you or Marty should do. My advice is to both stay or both go. If you decide to try on September 13th, then we'll bust our buns and turn on all the lights for you back here. I suggest that you get your Mammy Boston and her buddies to push from your end. But say nothing to Marty.
See you in 1995.

Yours
Marcus Jones

She now knew that it had occurred just as she had feared. Marcus, the human material of the year 2000, had made it back. The painting, the stuff of 1912, had not, and neither had the dog.

She replaced the painting in the cylinder and opened the laundry room door. She would say Marty nothing of this to his father She would simply have to take her chances on September 13th.

"You a getting close to where you want to be," she said.

Mary Lou sat opposite him on the hard wooden seat of the coloured section of the South East Railway, on its way to Danville, Alabama. She munched on a sandwich.

Marty peered out through soot-stained windows as the train trundled slowly through Lynchburg. "Don't get your point," he said. "We've got more than 500 miles to Danville and my great grandparents, Mary Lou."

"Don't mean that," she said. "You knows what I mean."

"I *know* what you mean," he said, gently correcting her. He paused. "But yes. I think I do know what you mean. Near the real Marty. I must have lost ten pounds of solid muscle these last three months."

"All that stuff," she said, wiping the crumbs from her mouth.

He nodded. "All that stuff," he said. "I think I'm just about clear of it now, so I just got to get myself ready for September 12th. It'll be even up between Jim and me by then."

"Yet you're training Jim up. You're *helping* Jim," she said. "Most folks would think that real strange."

"You mean helping him, just so's I can whup him?"

She nodded.

"Look at it this way," she said. "Coming back near ninety years to do it, then getting him in shape when he might beat you…" She shook her head.

"That's not what it's all about," Marty said. "It's about sport, it's about being fair. Jim's hurt bad. If'n I had left it all to Pop, Jim wouldn't even be on the boat to Stockholm, let alone able to meet me afterwards."

"So you builds Jim up just so you can knock him down."

"That's one way of putting it," he said. "Coming back to beat Jim Thorpe when he was half-fit, I didn't come all this way to do that. I want Jim to be at his very best."

"You like him a lot, don't you?" she said.

"I love Jim," he answered. "You see, Jim is what he does. He's the pure athlete. You get exactly what you see. Nothing hidden, nothing held back."

"That the same with me?"

He nodded. “Four people in the world I trust,” he said. “My father, Pop Warner, Jim and you.”

“That in any particular order?”

“Don’t you to start getting uppity with me,” he said, smiling.

“But you had plenty of women where you come from.”

“Yes,” he said. “I’ve had plenty, but I’ve only been with one, “

“So how would you feel if I keeps something from you?”

“Disappointed,” he replied.

For a moment, Mary Lou thought of telling him about the baby and about what had happened with his father. The words trembled on her lips. She placed her hands on his. “No need,” she said. “No need.”

Marty had been in Danville once before, in April 1990, when he had been only 15 years of age. When he and his mother had arrived, there had been virtually nothing. Just Main St, USA. The cotton fields and the mills had long since vanished, leaving no record of the Grovers of Danville, Alabama. It was as if his family had never been. It was as if the generations of men and women who had poured their sweat into that sour soil had never existed. After his mother had checked the records at the library, they had travelled out to the town graveyard. There, she had found not even a stone or a cross to mark their passing. Simply mounds of moss-covered boulders, bumps on weed-infested fields, the only record of the passing of countless generations of their kind. And when they had attempted to locate the family home on Lincoln St they had found nothing but shacks lost in the long grass, like the ribs of long-dead animals. His mother had held his hand and wept. Marty had not shared her tears. To him, Danville had simply been a strange, boring place. He had longed to get back to his friends, to L.A., to his Nintendo.

Marty had knocked on the weathered wooden door of the Jones' shack for several minutes, to no response. Then he had gone out back, to find only a postage-sized stamp fenced garden, clucking with half a dozen scrawny chickens. He returned to the porch and sat on its steps surveying the silent, backed-dirt street, still in the hot spring sun. For a moment, he wished that Mary Lou had not stayed back at the railway depot.

"They'se all down at the fields." An old man stood at the base of the steps, directly in front of him. He was like an older Abner, but bowed, bent with the weight of the years. He was dressed in tattered denim dungarees, spittle oozing out of a corner of his mouth. "Them Jones. You some kin of them?"

Marty nodded. "Close," he replied. He looked down at the old man's bare feet. Both big toes had gone, as if amputated.

The old man noted his gaze and spat on the dry road. "Ah kept a-running away back in the old days," he said. "They soon stopped that. Sure fixed me good."

Marty felt his gorge rise. "How far is them cotton fields, sir?"

The old man turned and pointed down the silent dirt road to his left. "Bout a coupla miles thataways," he said. "You know when you gets there."

Marty checked the impulse to slip the man a sawbuck, but resisted it. It would have been an insult. The old man had such dignity, such strength. Marty nodded, stepped down from the porch and walked down the street, feeling the hot sun heavy on his back. He reflected that it now must be close on 90°. The Negro quarters were like a ghost town. Not a soul was to be seen.

He came to the first field after walking for about a mile. Row upon row of serried, unpicked white cotton, stretching as far as the eye could see, deep into the heat haze. A mile or so later, he came upon the first cotton pickers, men, women and children bearing baskets and canvas bags, hundreds of them working in the broiling sun. Some of the children could not have been much more than five years of age and many of the men were not much younger than the old cripple whom he had just left.

Marty stopped by a young woman, picking at the edge of the road, which bisected the fields. “The Jones,” he said. “You know where they’re working?”

She stopped and pointed up the path. “They’se up there aways,” she said. “By the pump.”

He walked up fifty yards to the water-pump, which stood above a stone water-trough. Negroes carrying cups and pails stood in a queue, filling their vessels before returning to their families in the fields. He stood at the pump and looked out to his right. Marty could immediately recognise Mammy, from an old lithograph. His great-grandmother was in her mid-thirties, a fine, upright, big-bosomed woman, dressed in a long, bright floral cotton dress tied at the middle. Beside her worked what Marty assumed was her husband George Jones, a heavily-muscled young man around 6′2″ and 200 pounds, the sweat rolling in streams down his face. Around them worked six children, aged from around six to fifteen, though Marty could not be certain that they were all Jones. He stood for some time watching them, unsure of what to do.

The family toiled remorselessly, plucking chunks of fluffy cotton from the bushes and placing them in buckram bags. He could see that there was a spare tin cup on a stone shelf by the water-trough. Marty picked up the cup and stood in the queue, his eyes still fixed on the family. Having reached the top of the queue, he placed his cup below the spout and pulled on the pump. His cup filled, he turned to drink. The cup had not reached his lips when it was dashed to the ground, from behind.

“No water for you, boy.” The voice behind him was gruff and harsh.

Marty bent to pick up his cup, to be pushed on the shoulder blades, falling on his face into the dust. He rose, stood and cleaned himself off, to see before him a big-bellied white man, about 220 pounds, dressed in jeans, waistcoat and brown ten-gallon hat. The man was unshaven, the sweat trickling unevenly down his plump, ruddy face.

"Like I said, no water for you boy, not less'n you works heah."

"Didn't mean to cause no offence, sir," said Marty, replacing his cup on the stone plinth.

"Didn't mean no offence, boss," said the man, fingers on each side of his belt.

Marty looked to each side. He saw that the Jones and the other workers had now stopped working.

"Like you said," said Marty "I don't come from hereabouts."

"Boss," said the man, poking him in the chest with a podgy finger.

"Please don't do that," repeated Marty.

"Boss," said the man, pushing him again.

"I'm asking you nicely, sir," said Marty. "Please don't do that."

"Boss," said the man, again pushing him in the diaphragm.

Marty moved in reflex. His right fist sank deep into the man's soft gut. The fat man gasped and buckled, but somehow stayed erect. Marty followed with a left into a marshmallow belly. This time the overseer went down on to both knees, his eyes glassy, then fell flat on his face. Marty stood, frozen. Then he turned and ran.

Marty arrived at the Jones' shack gasping, the sweat clamping his jeans to his thighs, and sat on the porch, his lungs heaving.

"You in some kinda trouble, son?" It was the old man in the street below.

Marty's breath came in deep gulps. "You could say that," he gasped.

"Next train out of town's a quarter of five," said the old man. "You got the time."

Marty, still breathing heavily, nodded. He reached into his back pocket and pulled out a clip of bills. Then he peeled off three hundred and stuffed them into an envelope and into the old man's right hand, closing his left hand on it. "This, this is for the Jones family," he said. "And there's a letter with it. Will you make real sure that they get it?"

The old man opened his hands and surveyed the money. "Them Jones, they sure won't have to work no more cotton," he said.

Marty reached back into his clip. "Don't tell anyone where it come from. Just tell 'em some guy up North, a friend of the family."

"That there friend of the family, he got a name?"

"Tell 'em it's Marty," he said. He pulled out a ten spot and handed it to the old man. "This is for you, sir," he said. "I didn't get your name?"

"Pappy Jones," said the old man. "That's my name."

When the Company men had arrived in swarms in Lincoln Street, Pappy Jones had proved more than willing to assist them. He told them, yes, there had been a strapping young buck up from Kentucky somewheres about, who had asked him the way to the cotton fields. He had set the young fellow on his proper path, but had seen neither hoot nor holler of him since. The Company men and their dogs had raged around the Negro quarter for an hour or more, then made their way back to the fields, or into Danville.

When the working day had ended and the family had returned, Pappy Jones had first locked the doors. Then he gave George and Martha the envelope which the young stranger had deposited with him. Shaking their heads, the couple had counted and re-counted the money, all in old notes, so clearly not counterfeit. And with the money had been a slip of paper.

Next day, Martha had checked the advance entries for the Preakness and three other events on the same day, to find that they had not yet been announced. However, a fortnight later, they were published and to her surprise all three horses were listed. Heartened, Mammy felt that this was worth at least fifty bucks of anybody's money and found that something called an accumulation would release two thousand dollars on such a bet. It was worth taking a chance, for the family already had more than enough to buy a place of their own and could now do some sharecropping on their own account. And if by some chance the Preakness came up good, then for the family it was surely goodbye Danville and hello Harlem.

Marty had been uncharacteristically silent in their first few moments on the train back. Before it had moved from the station at Danville, Mary Lou had noted the depth of his breathing, that his shirt, wet with sweat, was sticking to his chest, that he kept looking back, out on to the station platform. She made no comment, neither had she resisted when Marty had shepherded her to the john and locked the door just before the train had left the station. When the train had trundled off, they had returned to their seats.

She looked across at him. "You got any intention of telling me what happened back there?" she asked.

Marty withdrew a handkerchief and mopped his wet brow. "Ran into a little trouble," he said.

"White trouble?"

He nodded. "Got it in one. Wasn't any of my doing. Just worked out that way."

"Did you get to see your folks?"

"Yes and no," he replied. "They were all working out in the fields. Before I had a chance of talking to them, this horse's ass, this boss guy, he started pushing me around."

"So you took him out? You hurt him?"

"Not much," Marty replied, shaking his head.

"Yo's in Alabama now, Marty," she frowned. "Here they strings black boys up for beating up white folks."

He nodded. "That's why we go to the john every station, till we're clean across the state border and close the door. These people, they got telephones, they could phone ahead."

"If'n they knows you took the train north," she said.

"We can't take that chance, Mary Lou."

She nodded. "You're right, but what about your folks?"

"I left them three hundred bucks. And the Preakness result."

"How does you know they'll make a bet?"

"I don't," he replied, shaking his head.

Mary Lou sat back and surveyed him. "So was it all worthwhile? You a-comin' back?"

"Oh yes," he answered. "I fixed my folks up good. OK, so I didn't get to speak to them, but maybe that's just as well. After all, what could I have said to them? Who could I say I was?"

"Only what you done told me," she replied.

"And just look where that's got me. No. It worked out all right. And it told me something I should have seen from the start." He paused. "I can't do anything for my people back there, Mary Lou. The only reason I can take this *'yes boss, no boss'* stuff and a cold ass in the outside privy is because I know exactly who I am and because I don't have to take it for ever."

She lowered her eyes. "Because you're going back."

He shook his head. "Because **we're** going back," he said. "You can count on it."

"I spoke to your Pa," she said. "He told me that President Wilson…"

"Wilson, who's he?"

"The next President," she replied. "Me, I never heard tell of him. But your Pa, he says he's next in line." She paused. "Well, this President Wilson, he won't even see the NAACP. Says their head man gotta be changed, fore'n he even talks to them."

"It all figures," said Marty. "The time's not right. Doesn't matter how much justice you have on your side, if the time's not right." Marty looked out of the window through the smoke on to the farmland below. “Reckon we’re fifty miles short of the state border,” he said. “Then we’re home and dry.”

Marty now knew how Michelangelo must have felt. For Jim was like a great, glorious lump of marble on which he had found that he could chisel endlessly, fashioning whatever shape he pleased. All through the hot Carlisle May of 1912, the two men worked out together on the track’s now crisp, flat surface. It was an unending joy.

Jim’s hamstring injury, though deep, had healed rapidly under Marty’s patient ministrations. After their first session of stretch-therapy, it had only taken Jim a fortnight before he was able to stride evenly, at close to full speed. Two weeks later, Jim was able to sprint flat out, running a yard inside even time in a trial. The injury had not, in any case, prevented him from working on field event techniques, in such events as the shot, discus and javelin. Like all decathletes, Jim was a skill-hungry animal, more, Marty reflected, like some physical computer with a capacity of a hundred million megabytes, capable of assimilating in his muscular memory any movement, pattern, however complex, that Marty entered on its keyboard. For there appeared to be nothing that Jim could not do. Pop had let it slip to Marty that while he had been with McFadden, that Jim and his partner Alice had taken gold at the National Collegiate Ballroom Dancing Championships, and Marty had not been surprised.

Marty’s main problem had been to find enough hours in the day to deal with all the decathlon techniques which Jim was required to absorb. For Jim had insisted that he would compete not only in decathlon and pentathlon in Stockholm, but in high jump and long jump as well, against specialists. Thus, five days a week, the two men had toiled on the Carlisle track as, beside them, Pop had worked out the college track team.

Pop had been surprised that he had not felt even a twinge of jealousy for the Negro to whom Jim now looked entirely for coaching support. But, he reflected, the rapport, the comradeship between the two men was something almost palpable, something pure and marvellous. Yet Pop knew that, on Jim's return from Stockholm, Marty would take him on in competition. The date, September 12th, had already been agreed, as had the events of the pentathlon: 200 metres, hurdles, javelin, long jump and 1500 metres – the best of five events to be adjudged the winner. So, for all the rapport between the two men, there was always an edge in every session, albeit one laced with friendship. Jim could feel it, so could Pop and the entire track squad. The two men exuded it from every pore in every jump, every lung-bursting run, every grunting throw. And Marty made no attempt to hide his objective, to whup Jim's butt good on his return from the Stockholm Olympics.

That baking summer of 1912, Jim went through Eastern Seaboard track like Grant through Georgia. By early June, he had taken the scalp of America's best high jumper, Alma Richards, and beaten one of its top broad jumpers, Calvin Bricker. Even the Irish whales from the New York Police Department, behemoths like Pat McDonald and Ralph Rose, with shamrocks in their jockstraps, had to be at their best to beat Jim in shot put. And everyone remarked on Jim's turn of speed over the slats for he recorded 15.6 seconds on a slow track into a headwind. Jim was number one choice for Uncle Sam in pentathlon and decathlon, and also made the team in broad jump and high jump. Thus ended that hot, joyous summer of 1912.

Chapter 18
Stockholm

Marty and Mary Lou stood, pressed close together in the bubbling, excited crowd which thronged New York's Dock Three. A few yards away, a sweating brass band pumped out a jangled Sousa march in front of a vast, drooping canvas Stars and Stripes flag ten yards wide and ten yards high. Looming above them, like the Woolworth building, soared the SS *Finland*, bound for Stockholm, Sweden, packed with America's finest. Marty reflected that he had seen only one black face in the national team, their dash man, Howard Drew. This American squad, the most powerful on the face of the earth, was a white man's team.

"It's only a month," he said, pressing his lips to her cheek.

She frowned.

"Five weeks," she replied.

"And then I come back and take on Jim." He kissed her neck. "After that, we're on our way back home."

"Back home," she said, limply.

He felt the darkness, the uncertainty in her voice and gulped. "And for starters, I'm gonna beat the odds."

"And how zactly d'you plan to do that?" she asked.

The hooting of the ship's sirens caused him to pause. "Howard Drew," he said. "My Pa told me that Howard went out in his heat with a pulled muscle."

"And you think you gonna change all that? Change what was written in them history books?"

"Yes," said Marty. "The big problem on the boat will be de-conditioning. If I keep Howard in shape, then he can take gold. I saw him at the Trials. He's greased ice."

"And if'n you can change that..."

"Then I can change anything," he completed her sentence. Mary Lou knew what he meant.

"I spoke last night to Mammy Boston," she said. "She tells me she bin getting some real strange dreams."

"Messages from my father and his people?"

"Seems like they could be," said Mary Lou.

"What kind of dreams?"

"All about people a-looking in screens and typing."

Marty was silent for a moment. "E-mail," he said. "I think that's what she's seeing."

"E what?"

"It's like television. I should have told you about it before. People send messages round the world to each other on things like typewriters."

"Typewriters," she said. "Across the world. Well now, don't that beat all."

"I should have told you before," he said. "There's so much to explain. The good thing is that dad and his people are trying to get something back to Mammy. We're going to need all the help we can get on September 13th."

Above them, at the top of the ship's gangway, a steward holding a tin megaphone bellowed a first call for passengers to take their places on board. Over the top of the crowd, Marty could see Jim, in an ill-fitting blue blazer, chatting with Pop Warner and Louis Tewanima at the ship's rail. Pop gestured to him over the crowd to make his way up to the ship. The band began to play a slightly tinny, off-key 'Star Spangled Banner', mingling with the ship's siren as it sounded three times. James E Sullivan, glowering with self-importance, followed by porters carrying his trunks, bumped into Marty as he rushed past. He did not stop to apologise.

As Marty kissed Mary Lou goodbye, he had felt a pang, almost like a pain above his heart. It was a shiver of doubt. Not for the first time, he considered that it might be better to stay here as a nigger, rather than try to return to 1995 as a man of colour. He could still feel the hurt, now deep in his chest as he stood waving down at Mary Lou from the SS *Finland*'s rail. The gangways were removed, the ropes slipped and they were off. He waved long after she was a distant dot and there was no real purpose in waving any more.

Pop Warner had felt insulted when Sullivan had offered him a berth in first class with Gustavus T Kirby and the other poo-bahs of the American track and field establishment. It meant that Sullivan thought that he, Pop, was one of them, one of the ass-lickers, and that did not go down well with him. He had been civil in his reply to Sullivan, but had refused and asked to travel below decks with the rest of the Olympic team.

Pop had watched with heavy heart as they had embarked, followed by servants laden with trunks, the East Coast establishment who ruled American track and field. Sullivan, he reflected, was not by birth one of them, one of the Ivy League brigade characterised by Gustavus P Kirby and John F Rockefeller. Sullivan was from another world, a Tammany Hall Neanderthal, delighted to swim amongst the scions of Wall Street. For them, Sullivan was simply a convenience. He would do all of their dirty washing for them. Sullivan knew where all the bodies were buried, who had paid off whom, the precise destiny of every brown paper envelope. He was the one who did all the dirty work with which the Ivy League blazerati would not deign to sully their hands, leaving them free to lecture on the moral virtues of the amateur. Sullivan would make sure that there was an endless flow of Dom Perignon, a ready supply of nubile young women for Kirby and his friends during the voyage to Stockholm. His Swedish satrap, Per Lindblom, had already made similar arrangements for their stay in Stockholm.

Pop had often wondered what these immensely rich men derived from their contact with amateur sport. Because, for all their pompous pronouncements about athletics and its values, they had no real dedication to the welfare of youth; none of them had ever delivered a single programme for the development of their sport. All were fully paid-up members of Status Quo AC. Pop had observed them closely at the Olympic trials. Most of the time, they had sat in the stands in conversation with each other, oblivious to the intense competitions on the track below them. The rest of the time, they were ensconced in a private bar deep in the bowels of the stands, sinking double Jack Daniels. If these men had any real passion for sport, then they concealed it well.

Feeling the ship begin to throb, Pop made his way down the narrow gangways in the depths of the ship, behind Jim, Marty, Louis and the little mulatto sprinter, Howard Drew. The mulatto was as slick as shit off a shovel. If he could survive the trip, then he would surely win at Stockholm.

Pop had been just about to turn in that first night on the SS *Finland* when there had been a knock on his cabin door. It was Mike Murphy, the team coach.

"Come in, Mike," growled Pop. "Sit down if'n you can find the space to park your ass." He bent down underneath his bunk and withdrew a bottle of Jim Beam. "Have yourself a snort, a long one."

"Better make it a short one, Pop," replied Murphy, sitting on the edge of Pop's bunk. He looked around the cramped cabin. "Nice place you got here."

"Hot and cold running dust," grunted Pop, handing him a glass.

Murphy was clearly nervous. "You crossed James J Sullivan again, Pop?" he asked.

Pop shook his head. "Nope, not that I know of."

"Sullivan, he took Scranton hard when Marty wouldn't play ball, and then Jim roughed up his lunkheads," said Murphy, sipping his whisky. "I hear he lost a packet in Scranton."

"That's not my problem," said Pop. "Just what are you trying to tell me, Mike?"

"Sullivan's got it in for Jim," said Murphy. "He's told me to push him hard, to bust his kazoos every day. Kill him off."

Pop poured himself a glass and sipped it. "A man can lose condition in a coupla weeks on a boat, Mike. Maybe that's what Sullivan meant."

"I know him as well as you do, Pop," said Murphy. "But no, that's not what Sullivan's talking about. He hates Indians, Jim crossed him, so he wants him to be busted up good. The nigra Drew too."

"Why Drew?"

"Sullivan wanted to run pro for him at Scranton next year, now that Marty is exposed. Bigger odds if Drew goes out early in Stockholm."

Pop nodded. "That's it. It's Scranton all over again, the same deal. Marty crossed Sullivan back in Scranton and Jim flattened one of his heavies. And now Sullivan's paying him off."

"Just like I said," said Murphy, proffering his glass. "Another short one, if'n you can see your way to it."

Pop grinned and poured Murphy a long one instead. Murphy surveyed the glass, mock-frowned but gulped it down just the same. "So what's the deal with Sullivan?" asked Pop.

"A grand to do the business, if I can train Jim and Drew out of gold. Another grand if they don't medal."

"Sounds like Sullivan's real serious," said Pop.

"Thorpe and Drew are both pretty sharp now," said Murphy. "They don't have to do much till Stockholm, just to keep that edge. You know the score, Pop. You can't make a man much fitter in a coupla weeks, but…

"You can sure as hell slow him down," Pop finished the sentence.

Murphy nodded. "You got it, Pop. Heavy workouts, too little rest, Black Jack."

"Black Jack?" exploded Pop. "That goes through a man's guts and ends up in his boots."

"A coupla weeks of that would slow up Teddy Roosevelt," said Murphy, nodding.

"So what are you going to do?" asked Pop.

"Nothin'," Murphy paused. "Pop, I'll level with you. My pump, it's shot. I've got maybe a year. Perhaps less."

"Jesus Christ, Mike," said Pop. "I'd no idea."

"I've got me some life insurance," said Murphy. "Enough for Mabel and my boy George. They'll come out good."

For once, Pop was almost lost for words.

"But you're telling me that a couple of grand would come in handy," he said lamely.

"Tell me about it," replied Murphy. "But you know me, Pop. I ran pro for nine years. Never ran to the book. Never took a dive. Not once." He shook his head. "And I'm not taking one now. Not for a horse's ass like Sullivan."

"But he can make it hard for you," said Pop.

"Maybe," replied Murphy. "But not if Jim and Drew do zactly as I tell them."

Later, Jim Thorpe had visited Sullivan's suite in first-class. Coach Murphy, he complained, had insisted on daily three mile runs round the SS *Finland*'s heaving deck and that he lose five pounds in weight by the time the ship docked in Copenhagen. The high mileage, groaned Thorpe, was killing his legs, draining them of the power essential for decathlon and pentathlon. Sullivan had been obdurate. Coach Murphy probably had good reason for endurance runs. Did Thorpe not require to run 1500 metres in both events? Thorpe would simply have to buckle down to it, or be taken off the team. Sullivan had smiled when a crestfallen Thorpe had slowly closed the cabin door behind him.

Only a couple of hours later, it had been the turn of the mulatto, Howard Drew, to arrive at Sullivan's suite. Drew's complaints were not much different from those of Thorpe. Coach Murphy was insisting on two training sessions a day, one of them in the bowels of the ship, lifting weights with those Irish whales, the throwers, McDonald and McGrath. Everyone in track knew that heavy weights could only slow down a dash man; it was common knowledge. Then there was the Black Jack, a laxative which had all but ruined his guts. Coach Murphy had insisted that he take in nightly as part of what he called "the cleansing process". Drew felt that he was now surely clean enough, had begged that he be allowed to pursue his normal training programme and to be excused Murphy's medication. Again, Sullivan was obdurate, unrelenting. Drew would follow Coach Murphy's dictums, or he would be off the Olympic team.

That night, Sullivan slipped Murphy an advance of two hundred dollars. The coach was working to orders. Murphy was busting their buns and Thorpe and Drew would be good for nothing by the time they reached Stockholm. What James J Sullivan did not know was that both men were working to Marty's schedules, which involved light sessions of speed work, light weights at high speeds and technical activity, if the sea was calm. Thus, Sullivan was off Murphy's back, their ailing coach would pick up a few bucks, and Drew and Thorpe could focus on success in Stockholm.

King Gustav had been regaled with stories of the great Jim Thorpe by the Swedish-American coach, Ernst Hjertberg, whom he had employed to train his athletes for the Stockholm Olympics. At first, it had seemed to him impossible that any man could do what Hjertberg had described to him, to beat America's best jumpers, to compete on even terms with its finest hurdlers and throwers, then in winter to rip to shreds the defences of Ivy League football teams and kick goals from vast distances – Thorpe's feats simply beggared belief.

Hjertberg had gone further, telling him that the Indian could also play both basketball and baseball to national standard and with a student partner had recently won the National Collegiate Ballroom Dancing Championship. When Thorpe had won first the pentathlon and then the decathlon, King Gustav began to think that his coach had understated the American's talents. For Thorpe had slaughtered with ease the best all-round athletes that Europe could put to the field. And he had gone close to medals in high jump and long jump, and Gustav had wondered if there was any athletic skill beyond the compass of the burly American.

The Americans were surely gods. They had demolished the world's best sprinters, jumpers and hurdlers, and had taken almost every field event. Only in the distance runs, where their student-based system was at a disadvantage, did they fail to make any impact.

But there had been one negative, and that had been their manager, Sullivan. He had informed his Swedish colleague Hjertberg that the Finns were planning to tell the IOC that Sweden had parked their team at the Olympic stadium for three months or more before the Games. This was clearly in breach of amateur rules, and would take Sweden from the top of the table, into oblivion and disgrace.

But Sullivan had offered Sweden a convenient solution. Ten thousand bucks would be enough to square the Finns, and he would be willing to discreetly conduct the negotiations on behalf of Sweden. Accordingly, that sum was withdrawn from the royal coffers, delivered to Sullivan, and no more was heard of the matter.

Sweden would therefore achieve its highest-ever Olympic ranking, second, one medal ahead of the USA, and the distinction of conducting the greatest Olympic Games of modern times. True, they had stretched the rules a little, but their coach Hjertberg had regaled him with accounts of the shamateurism and corruption of Sullivan's AAU, of the brown envelopes of its Eastern indoor circuit. And the English, they were little better, with their Boat-Race crews spending months in training camps. The world of the amateur athlete was a fantasy, even de Coubertin had confessed that to him. It would surely only be a few years before the amateur passed into the mists of history.

But for Gustav there would always be that precious moment to remember, that moment, always for the rest of his life. The King of Sweden had found it difficult to keep his face straight when, he had handed his decathlon medal to Jim Thorpe with the words "Sir, you are the greatest athlete in the world," Thorpe had looked him straight in the eye and replied "Thanks, King."

Chapter 19
Battle of Friends

On the completion of the Stockholm Games, Marty had high-tailed it on the first boat back, leaving Jim to compete in money meets (for the benefit of James Sullivan and the AAU) in Scandinavia. He had worked out hard every day on the SS *Sparta*, just as he had on the SS *Finland* on the way out. Marty reckoned that he had lost about 16 lbs of solid muscle in those eighteen months since Mary Lou had first discovered him on the shelf of the laundry room at the Majestic Hotel. He was now down to a spare 180 lbs, no longer the god who could bench-press 300 lbs and squat with 200 lbs more. No, those drug-enhanced days were now long past.

Marty could not wait to get back to Mary Lou. Martin Luther Jones had not realised it was possible for a woman to be both lover and friend. Marty Roother had. This meant that September 13th, the day after his match with Jim, lay heavy in his thoughts. For Marty had no idea if either or both of them could make it back to 1995. Come to that, he could not say with any certainty that his father had now returned, if he had disappeared into some Black Hole, or had perished in the 1944 Normandy Landings. There was, for the moment, with no recent communication with Goldstein, no means of knowing.

For the first time in his life, Marty was afraid. He now realised that he would rather live with Mary Lou in 1912 as a coach at Carlisle than return without her to 1995 as MLJ. He could stay on as a twenty-bucks-a-week assistant to Pop, run as a pro before they sliced his handicap to scratch, perhaps, even go match-racing for money in England or Australia. And his father had left him the Preakness results for 1913 and 1914. They would never be poor, not by a long chalk. And yet he longed to take Mary Lou back; to take her back, not to all the cheating and the crap and the cokeheads, but to a life where she could have a career, go to college, be a woman. Each night, for the first time since his childhood, he prayed. Marty promised God that if they both made it, then he would give up track and return to college; take a teaching degree and teach sports to kids.

When the SS *Sparta* finally berthed at New York, Mary Lou was there, standing at the quay, in the same dress, as if she had never left the spot. They had booked in at a black hotel in Harlem and for a week, they had not left their room, except to eat. Mary Lou was like some deep, warm pool in which he loved to lounge and linger. Even that torrid week in Harlem did little to sate their passions, but they returned to Carlisle on August 23rd with Jim due to return from Europe a day later. The events had been agreed with Pop before the departure to Stockholm. It was to be the classic pentathlon, consisting of long jump, javelin, 200 metres, discus and 1500 metres. It was to be as in Stockholm, but on a simple win-lose basis, no smart-ass points tables. The competition would be held in secret, away from Carlisle, at Hartford on the same crisp, bouncy grass track where they had beaten Yale a year before. Pop, Mackay and Flaherty would act as judges.

Pop had never seen Jim in such a serious mood. Neither for that matter had Dean Mackay. "Meaner than a junkyard dog." had been Flaherty's view, as he had observed Jim work out with Pop at the college track in the week before the competition.

And yet Pop knew that Jim near as dammit loved Roother. David and Jonathan, Mackay had once called them, though Pop knew for sure that no David or Jonathan could run inside even time for a hundred yards or clear six foot six in high jump. He knew that Jim placed most of his Olympic success at the door of his friend Marty Roother. The black boy had transformed Jim, taking him from a raw, undisciplined animal to become a professional athlete. He remembered something that Marty had once said to him. “An amateur does it till he gets it right. A pro practices till he can’t get it wrong.” Those words would be repeated by Pop to his teams for the rest of his life.

Somehow Pop knew that this was it, that Jim and Marty would compete and that they would then see no more of the Negro boy. True, Marty had not said so, but Pop knew it. So did Jim.

The trip to Hartford had been quiet, the atmosphere in the group subdued. When the Carlisle group arrived, the smooth university lawns were just as they had been back in 1911, when Marty and Jim had teamed up to whup Yale’s ass. The sandpits were flat, moist and well dug; the track precisely pegged out, its pennants twitching in an autumn breeze which was bringing leaves fluttering down on to the grass track’s pristine surface.

Marty had never in his athletic life broad-jumped from a grass runway, but his short warm-up jumps for the first pentathlon event felt good. The Hartford grass had life and energy; flat and dry, its resilience had been enhanced by a brief shower only a day before. As he measured his approach run, Marty reflected that he had not broad-jumped in 1912, for in the match against Yale, Jim had taken the event.

He watched Jim closely in his warm-up jumps, and it passed through his mind that he had coached him only too well. For gone was the chaotic, unstructured approach which he had witnessed in his first meeting, the hope that the 8-inch wooden board would somehow magically land beneath his take-off foot. Jim’s approach was now disciplined and accurate, and all of his warm-up jumps were beyond twenty-three feet. That was a distance that Marty could normally jump in his sleep from a half-distance approach run, but these were different times. And

Jim was now well-focussed. Marty watched him after they had finished their warm-up jumps. He now moved as if to barbaric music.

It took Marty four practice jumps before he finally managed to secure an accurate take-off. For, though the Hartford grass was relatively flat, a tiny bump screened the take-off board from sight until a couple of strides from take-off. Marty's "steering", that point where he picked up clear information on his position relative to the board was normally five to six strides out, and the bump meant that he now "saw" the board a little too late.

"Roother up," bawled Pop, standing with a clipboard with Flaherty, Mackay and Mary Lou at the take-off board.

Marty slowly withdrew his sweat-top and track bottoms, laid them on a bench and stood, coiled, on his mark. High-hipped, fluent, he drove in on the board and took a clean six inches of wood, in perfect balance, landing easy in the soft sand. It felt sweet from take-off. It was good.

"Twenty-four feet two inches," called Pop, as Jim started to peel off his jersey and trousers at the far end of the runway. "Thorpe up."

Jim took his time. He stood, knees bent, eyes focussed on the runway. He roared down the narrow strip of turf, his stride long and rangy; but Jim was trying too hard; he was too tight. True, he took a full eight inches of board, but he had no control, no lift, and he skidded into the pit.

Pop observed the tape. "Twenty-two feet ten inches," he shouted, as if informing a stadium crowd. "Roother up."

Marty looked at Mary Lou as she raked out Jim's landing prints. He could see the sweat bead on her forehead, feel her tension. She looked up at him and forced a half-grin.

Marty's second jump was almost a carbon copy of his first, and he landed at twenty-four feet three inches. Jim responded well, but his second jump was well short, at only twenty-three feet six inches. Marty sensed that Jim was now at his limit, for he simply did not possess the technical stability to maintain form, to respond at this level of intensity. He knew that he had him.

"Roother up."

Marty walked slowly to his mark. This was surely the moment to put it away for certain, but he knew that in such situations the danger always lay in trying too hard. The aim had to be to stay loose, in a technical cocoon, otherwise energy simply melted away. He picked up some loose grass and let it drop. It floated fast away from him. A backwind had picked up. Marty paused for a moment, considering what adjustments he would have to make to his approach run in order to accommodate the wind. He decided to gamble big, and put it back by a foot; he stood, coiled, behind his mark.

Marty ripped down the runway, the breeze giving him extra speed. He could feel the board big under his foot and he flew. When he landed, he knew beyond doubt that it was twenty-five feet or more.

Then Flaherty's voice boomed out, "Foul."

Marty's heart dropped. He trotted back to inspect the board. It was only a tiny indentation in the sand beyond the pristine white take-off board, not much more than half an inch. But it was enough.

"Thorpe up."

Marty pulled on his bottoms at a bench beside the pit and looked up the runway at Jim as he stood at his mark. Somehow, he now looked bigger, looser. He stood behind his mark, idly flicking his dark brown thighs. The wind had now dropped, so Jim had made no adjustment to his approach run marker. He stood, focussed, at his mark.

Jim's approach run was somehow quite different from his previous jumps. True, it had exactly the same number of strides, but it was of a quite different quality. Now, Jim was loose and supple, sucked into the board, making subtle adjustments in his final strides. He hit seven inches of board and soared.

When Jim landed, Marty realised that the measuring tape was an irrelevance. This was the winning jump.

Twenty-four feet six and a half inches," boomed Pop.

Somehow, Marty was not disappointed. He had given it his best shot, but he had just witnessed something marvellous. He shook Jim's hand.

"Thanks, coach," Jim grinned.

Marty had thrown the whippy wooden 1912 javelin many times in training with Jim at Carlisle, but had always found the implement difficult to master. He had also found it difficult, without specialist javelin boots, to secure a firm plant of his left foot in his throwing base. But the main problem lay in controlling the javelin's angle of attack. Marty still held the implement flat, in line with the shoulders, as he always had with a modern javelin. Habit died hard. But he was unable to control its point and as a consequence his first two throws stalled badly, landing tail first at around 160 feet. Jim, well accustomed to the vagaries of the primitive spear, had slung it out to 148 feet in his third throw. A modest one hundred and fifty feet would do it, a distance he could probably throw with his weaker arm. That would level him with Jim. In his third and final throw, Marty decided to slow down his approach run and focus on lining the javelin up with point higher, close to his face. If he hit it right, it would fly to two hundred feet, no question of it.

It did. The javelin flew a full fifty feet beyond Jim's mark, over the heads of Flaherty and Mackay. Mary Lou shrieked with joy. But the point had been too high, and the javelin died and landed ominously flat. Marty jogged out towards it, feeling the sweat bead hot on his forehead. It would be a close call. Flaherty looked at Pop, who shook his head.

"Foul," he said.

"Flat."

"Fuck," said Marty, under his breath. He was now 2-0 down, with the 200 metres to come.

The rivals loosened out together, jogging easily on the firm, springy turf without exchanging a word. Pop viewed them through his binoculars. Jim had never been in better shape, one hundred and eighty pounds of lean, mean muscle and bone. Marty looked to Pop a tad lighter than he had been at Stockholm, but still in good shape.

"If Jim as much as blinks, he's gone," observed Flaherty, loading his starting pistol.

"If is the worst word in the world," growled Pop, checking and re-checking his stopwatch before handing it to Mackay. He blew his whistle to summon both men, and nodded to Flaherty to set up the finishing tape. Mary Lou, her heart thudding in her forehead, walked with Pop and Mackay and sat at the top of the judge's steps at the finish as Flaherty walked across the grass with Jim and Marty to the start of the two hundred metres.

The two athletes stopped at the starting line and Flaherty checked his gun. Jim smiled his broad, toothy grin and put out his right hand to Marty.

"May the best man win," said Marty.

"I sure hope not," grinned Jim.

Marty smiled. He was going to miss the big man. But now he was going to whup his ass, and whup it good. He had to, or it was all over. He took up his position on the inside lane with Jim directly outside him.

"Gentlemen, get to your marks," called Flaherty.

Marty dropped on to his right knee and screwed both feet into the turf. He had never been happy without starting blocks, but now there could be no room for negative thoughts. Jim dug in. Marty settled. Then all was still.

"Get set."

Both men lifted their hips. Then the gun cracked, splitting the silence.

Marty drove out hard but his front foot slipped and he lost an immediate yard. On his outside, Jim blasted out as if it were an indoor sixty-yard dash.

Mary Lou could see that Jim had opened up an immediate lead, picking up more than a yard over the first fifty and he looked to be moving away. Her heart dropped. Never had she seen Jim move with such speed. Mackay glanced down at his watch. The Indian must have covered the first hundred yards on the curve in close to even time. Jim was running like a man possessed. He was running smooth.

Marty could feel that Jim had the edge, that he would be down on him coming off the bend, but he stayed cool, flowing round the curve. The grass felt light under his feet and he was running loose, with rhythm. He was slick.

Jim hit the straight a long two yards up and running tall, just as Marty had taught him. He focussed on the tunnel ahead, knowing that it was good.

Behind him, Marty hit the straight and began his “lift” into the final half of the dash. Then, though he was not looking, he saw it. Jim’s hips sagged slightly and with them his rhythm dropped. He had hit the bend too hard. Marty smiled; he was now syrup; he was hot chocolate. He would suck Jim in.

Mary Lou could see, even from the front, that Marty was now pulling Jim in on a long rope. Jim was running like a god, but Marty was now taking yards out of him. With fifty yards to go, he was level. For a moment, they were locked together, and then Marty pulled away, to win by a clear two yards.

“Twenty-one point seven,” observed Flaherty, looking at his watch.

“Two-tenths slower for Jim,” growled Mackay. “Fastest he ever ran. A second faster than Stockholm.” Mackay shook his head. He would never fathom Marty Roother.

Flaherty re-set his stopwatch. “It looks so easy,” he said. “That boy, he’s loose as water.”

The Hartford discus was a Quasimodo of an implement, a distant relative of the smooth "Obol" to which Marty had been accustomed. Its edge was thick, its wood rough but Marty had no beefs. He had practiced for a fortnight with a similarly Brobdinagian implement at Carlisle. It had no feel, no flight-quality, but it had the convex shape of a discus, and that was all that mattered.

They threw from a grass circle and the competition was over in the first round. Marty launched the clumsy instrument out to 149 feet, and Jim had no answer, finishing a full fifteen feet back. It was now two events all, with only the 1500 metres to complete the competition.

The skies suddenly cracked and the rain lashed down, grey and warm. In a matter of moments, the Hartford track was awash, and there were pools of standing water. The Carlisle group retreated to the concrete stand and sat in its shadows on wooden benches as outside the rain poured down relentlessly, thudding on the corrugated iron roof above them.

"Two events all. Even up," said Pop, surveying his now sodden clipboard. "Just like I thought. This is going to go down to the wire, gentlemen."

"You know, Pop, I reckon this is the best track and field my ageing eyeballs are ever likely to witness," said Mackay. "And, God help me, I'll never be able to tell a soul."

"You mention that Jim ran against a pro and he's history," said Pop.

"Jim will always be history," said Marty under his breath. Mary Lou heard him and frowned a warning.

Pop looked out onto the torrent. "So are we going to try to finish this?" he asked. "Are we going to settle it all for good?"

"Suits me, I'm all wet through anyway," said Flaherty.

Mackay nodded.

"Let's just make it a straight four laps," suggested Pop. "A mile. No one's got a cat in hell's chance of finding the 1500 metre start-line now, not in this mud."

Marty looked across at Jim, who nodded agreement. "Four laps," he said. "Then it's all over."

The Carlisle party splashed out to the start through the driving rain, across the deep, slimy pools which now spanned the Hartford field. Marty sloshed across, the rain streaming down his face and body. This would no longer be a track race, where speed and power would be decisive. No, this would now be a cross-country race. No matter. At 190 pounds, he was a full fourteen pounds lighter than when he had run the equivalent of a four and a half minute mile. He was now in even better shape and far fresher than he had been in Los Angeles after two days and nine decathlon events. Jim had run the equivalent of around five minutes for the mile in Stockholm, a full one hundred and fifty yards slower.

As they approached the start, the rain stopped and the sun shafted strong through the sullen clouds. It hit both men, causing steam to rise from their wet vests. Marty and Mary Lou stood at the starting line on the sodden turf as Pop re-charged his starting gun and Mackay and Flaherty set their stopwatches.

Marty looked across at Jim. "I'll let Jim take it out," he whispered to Mary Lou. "Jim won't push it. I'll just tuck in behind and go away from him in the final lap."

"Use your speed?"

Marty nodded. "Jim's never front-run at pace. It's not in his nature. He'll play it cool, and try to keep it slow. I'll have plenty left."

The words felt strange coming from his lips. Distance running had never been his forte, and, like most decathletes, had always been relatively timid over any distance much beyond 400 metres. But today, lighter than he had ever been, running against Jim, more than half a minute slower, he felt confident.

"Okay, boys, this is it. The big Bazonka." It was Pop. He held out his hands to them both and gripped them firmly, saying nothing. There was no need. Then he picked up his Colt and walked to the starting line. “Gentlemen, get to your marks.”

The two men moved up to the line, which was now barely visible beneath the lying water. Marty looked to his side at Jim. In the end, after all that had happened, it would now be decided in four laps. He set himself on the line, Jim on his inside, and snapped back into the moment.

“Get set.” Pop’s words came to him as from afar. The gun exploded.

It was not quite as Marty had imagined, for Jim launched himself into an immediate lead, splashing purposefully through the standing water, throwing it up into Marty’s face. The two men rushed into the first bend, with Marty closing the two-yard gap that Jim had set up, settling on his right shoulder at the entry to the back straight. The two men splashed hard through the first furlong.

“Thirty-four,” observed Flaherty. “That’s flying – on mud.”

Jim and Marty, still locked, finished the first lap in well inside seventy seconds. Marty had been surprised by Jim’s aggressive pace, but he felt good. Glued together, they strode up the back straight into the third furlong.

Pop checked his watch. “That’s our Jim,” he said. “Lightning in a jug. You never know what he’s a-gonna do next.”

“That’s because he doesn’t know himself,” grunted Mackay.

“Two minutes twenty, two minutes twenty-one,” bellowed Flaherty as the runners splashed through the half mile, still locked together.

“Jim’s running liked a canned dog,” said Pop. “Trying to take the starch out of Marty.”

But Marty felt good on Jim’s shoulder, even with the mud splattering into his face and chest. He pinned himself on Jim’s brown, sweating back, his breathing still coming clean and easy.

Then, as they came into the home straight to end the third lap, Marty heard Jim suddenly grunt, and knew that he was now weakening. Jim had made his play. He had shot his bolt. Marty hung loose and easy behind him as Flaherty clanged the bell for the last lap. He winked at Mary Lou as he passed. Ahead of him, Jim's hips were gradually sinking, and he could hear his breathing, now coming in deep, harsh gasps. It was time to show who was the man, to achieve what he had returned to the past to achieve, in the Year of our Lord 2012.

At the start of the back straight, Marty made his hit. He moved up another gear, immediately putting ten clear yards between himself and Jim. Suddenly, he was away and gone.

Jim did not respond, but chugged steadily on, now a full twelve yards back, his breath rasping like sandpaper in his throat.

"Marty's got him," gasped Mackay. "He's caught Jim cold."

Jim held firm, but he knew that his plan had failed, for Marty was now moving steadily away from him. He could now hear his own splashing strides, feel the rasp of his breath, like sandpaper in his throat. He fixed his eyes on Marty's broad, rippling back, desperately trying to maintain some link with him. Jim could feel himself fading, sinking into the marsh that was now the Hartford track.

Then, in the middle of the final curve, Marty felt his legs go. It was sudden, as if someone somewhere had flicked off a switch. Now, fifteen yards up, his rhythm suddenly vanished. He splashed into the home straight, legs bowed.

Drive with the arms, that was what he had always done. Stay loose, keep form and drive with the arms. Somewhere, deep in his muscular memory, he remembered and he worked the elbows hard. But it was no longer running, merely a remote, distant parody as he squelched into the final straight.

Behind him, even through the depths of his fatigue, Jim could see that Marty had gone. He remembered their practices together. Keep your shape and drive hard. He started to dig in and sensed that the gap between them was slowly shrinking.

With fifty yards to go, Jim was now less than six yards down and gaining, clawing back the yards, but there was surely too little time. Marty, his breathing audible to the spectators at the finish line, felt as if the tape was receding from him. He could now barely support his weight.

With ten yards to go, Marty was still a yard clear, legs buckling, mouth open, eyes rolling. Behind him, Jim made his final desperate hit. Calling upon all that he had, all that he would ever have, Jim launched himself at the tape.

The two men fell through it, locked together, and skidded, face down, aquaplaning, legs and arms tangled. For a moment, they lay draped together in the watery slime, their breathing in strange synchronicity. Then Marty wobbled on to one knee and stood, pulling Jim to his feet. Arms draped around each other, lungs heaving, the two muddied men staggered back to the finish.

"I think Marty got it," said Pop.

Mackay shook his head. "Jim for me," he said.

"Can't split 'em," said Flaherty.

The three men looked across expectantly at Mary Lou. "Jim and Marty, split 'em?" she said. "Who would ever try? Dead heat."

The three men sat in the Dean's office, around his desk, at its centre a half-empty bottle of Talisker malt whiskey.

"Gentlemen," said Pop, raising his glass," today we have been privileged to witness the greatest competition in the history of track and field athletics."

Flaherty raised his glass and nodded.

"And none of us will ever be able to tell a soul," he said.

Pop sipped his malt.

"Or Sullivan and his AAU will be down on Jim like a ton of bricks," he growled.

The Dean surveyed the Talisker.

"Last orders, gentlemen," he said.

"He filled three tumblers with an ample portion of Talisker, emptying the bottle. There was silence.

"My reckoning is that tomorrow will be the last that any of us will ever see of Marty Roother," said Pop. "We don't know where he came from and we don't know where he's going."

"Hold on," said Flaherty. "He came here from Alabama and he's going on to California."

The Dean shook his head. "Pop's right," he said. "He may well be off to California, but he sure as hell didn't come from Alabama. "

"I'm with you on the Alabama, Dean," said Pop. "My best guess is that Marty came here from Texas. All that stuff about Houston."

The Dean pouted his lower lip.

"No, Pop," he said. "It's my belief that our boy Marty Roother is a Scot."

He sipped his whiskey.

"I should have seen it right from the start, from his vocabulary, from the way that he stood, the way that he spoke."

Pop frowned.

"But Marty, he didn't speak anything like you, Dean," he said.

The Dean sat silent for a moment.

"No," he said. "He didn't. But take my word for it our boy Roother is a Scot-and a gentleman of noble blood. "

"Jesus wept," said Flaherty. "How did you ever manage to work that out, Dean?"

"Let me tell you a wee story," he said. "The Duke of Ruthven, back in 1880, he hired a black lady from Jamaica, by name of Flora Rioch, to act as a governess to his three wee boys. Rumour has it that she bore him a son in 1885, and she took him with her, back here to the USA ten years later. And that was the last that was heard of Flora Rioch, or her son."

Pop shook his head, and took a sip of his whiskey.

"So let me get this clear-what you are really trying to tell us, Dean, is that our boy Marty was in receipt of ten years of your precious Scotch education," said Pop.

"There is no other possible explanation," said the Dean. "And there's something else-I could sometimes pick up some of the rhythms of the Fife dialect when he spoke to me. "

"All that doesn't get anywhere near explaining how your black Scotchman could arrive here from nowhere and run world record times in all the dashes and hurdles, and do pretty much the same in vault and broad jump," said Pop.

"And Marty, he would have taken even Eugene Sandow apart with the barbells," said Flaherty.

The Dean nodded.

"No, gentlemen, I must freely admit that even the possession of Scots blood and the receipt of a Scottish education cannot fully explain any of what you have just described. The source of Marty's athletic talents, that will be a question which all three of us will take with us to our graves. All that we can be absolutely certain of is that what this man Marty Roother has showed us was the future. "

Mammy Boston had been relieved that Marty and Mary Lou had returned to her. For she had been getting more of them crazy dreams again, about Marty swinging on poles and a-running like the wind on red rubber. But now other, darker things had come through to her, a strange, curved devil-sign that meant diddlysquat to her and a recurring phrase which meant even less.

Marty and Mary Lou sat facing her at Mammy's round black wooden table with the cloudy crystal ball at its centre. Mammy somehow knew for certain sure that this was the last time the couple would come to her.

"I bin getting this devil sign real often," she began. She slowly traced out with a pencil a shape on a sheet of paper in front of her, and then pushed it across the table towards them. It was a single curved line. To Mammy it appeared to be a hill, or a mountain peak, but it could equally have been a witch's hat, albeit one without a brim.

"This gotta mean somethin'," said Mary Lou. "And you certain sure it came with these dreams 'bout Marty?"

Mammy Boston nodded. "All jumbled up," she said. "Can't make nuthin' of it."

Mary Lou picked up the paper and held it close, shaking her head. Then she laid it back on the table and turned it through a half circle. "Could be we're looking at this thing the wrong way around," she said.

Marty looked over her shoulder at the shape which now resembled a tick, as on an examination paper.

"Looks like sump'n from school," ventured Mary Lou. "Them times in spelling when you gets it right."

"A tick," said Marty. He paused. "Got it," he roared, standing. "It's the Nike sign."

"Nike?" Mary Lou looked in stupefaction at Mammy Boston who was now leaning back, trance-like, eyes blank, but scribbling letters frantically on a sheet of paper on the table in front of her. She scrawled in broad loose letters, sweating as she did so. Then she stopped and dropped her head, exhausted, on to the surface of the table, her sweat soiling the paper upon which she had written.

Marty bent over Mammy Boston and gingerly slid the paper from underneath her. He surveyed its sweat-stained surface, shaking his head. "Can't make head or tail of any of this," he said. "It's not even English. T-D-T-I-O-J-S-U. Where'd this come from? Vietnam?

"It's not a word, honey," said Mary Lou, taking the paper and looking at it again. "Maybe, maybe it's some sort of code."

"T-D-T-I-O-J-S-U," he read it again. "English letters. Perhaps it's some kind of…anagram."

"A what?" asked Mary Lou, looking at him.

"You know, a sort of play with words, like in a crossword. Look, there are some words here – or maybe just one word, I don't know."

She shook her head. “It ain’t just one word, not in English anyways.”

“OK, so maybe it’s more than one word.”

“O sit jut,” she said. “Nope, missed off the D.”

“Dot is jut,” she offered. “You know anyone called Dot?”

“Yes,” he smiled. “But she doesn’t jut.”

“Just,” she said, suddenly. “Take out the J-U-S-T and what we got left?”

“O-I-T-D.”

“Toid,” she said, frowning. “It. Do. Do it!”

“Just do it,” bellowed Marty. “**Just do it**!”

If’n it doesn’t work out for you two over in California, you could always come back and coach for me,” offered Pop. “Twenty bucks a week.”

“And vittles,” added Mackay, smiling.

“And I could make it up with a buck or two a week in the gym,” offered Flaherty.

They stood with Marty at Carlisle station awaiting the arrival of the midday train. A few yards away, Mary Lou stood, surrounded by her brothers and sisters, making final farewells to her family. Jim pulled Marty to one side. “And we could always play football, or go try out for the New York Giants,” he said. “I seen you bat. Or we could go round us up some horses down Texas way.”

“Cool,” said Marty. “But I’ll take a rain-check on that one, Jim,”

He looked up the track to watch the arrival of the train, slowly hissing towards them, steam spuming, its bell jangling. Then his eyes wandered across to Mary Lou who stood, tears streaming down her face, hugging her parents. She detached herself at last from them and walked towards him, the younger children clinging to her dress.

“I promise,” she said, over her shoulder to her parents.

“What did you promise, honey?” he asked.

"That you gonna make an honest woman outa me," she whispered under her breath.

Marty walked across to Lincoln and shook his hand.

"You take good care of my li'l girl," said the old man.

"You can count on it, sir," Marty answered.

Mary Lou walked up the steps and vanished into the train, to the shouts of her family who crowded below the train window. Marty re-joined the Carlisle group and placed their cases up on the train just as the stationmaster called for passengers to embark.

"Looks like now we'll never know who was the better man," said Pop, shaking his head.

Marty shook Jim's hand. "Pop," he said. "Jim was always the better man."

He looked down at Jim, knowing that it would be for the last time.

"Just one thing, Jim," he said.

"Something I want you to do for me. One last thing, one last time. "

Jim nodded.

"Say – are you ready?"

Jim smiled and responded, and his voice rose, strong and firm over the hiss of steam and the grind of the train's wheels, as they left the station.

The Majestic Hotel had not been rebuilt. The hotel had never, even at its zenith, made anywhere close to top dollar for its owners, the Weinbergs. They had therefore simply pocketted the insurance money and had high-tailed it to San Francisco, leaving behind them a charred heap of beams and rubble, to the care of the City Fathers – and more than a few unanswered questions for the police.

It was suitably dark when Marty and Mary Lou gingerly picked their way across the wreckage, carrying in their suitcases blankets, pillows and tarpaulins. Above them, sullen

September skies threatened rain and Marty felt a first ominous spit on his cheek as Mary Lou looked up and pointed out to him the exact spot where the laundry room had been located.

"We about three storeys below it," she gloomily observed.

"That's about as close as we're ever gonna get," said Marty, laying down his case and hugging her reassuringly.

"You sure your pop knows what he's a-doing?"

Marty was tempted to reply that psychokinetics was not exactly rocket science, but he resisted the temptation. "Don't you worry, honey," he said instead. "Pop's got it down to a fine art, just you wait and see." He felt the words wither in his throat and hoped Mary Lou did not notice.

Together, they carefully flattened out the area, clearing it of bricks and charred, splintered wood, and placed a waterproof tarpaulin on the ground. The rain now began to fall slowly, rhythmically. Mary Lou quickly opened her case and withdrew two thick blankets and pillows. She laid them on the tarpaulin. Marty pulled out a second tarpaulin and placed it above the blankets, sealing them off. The two of them lay down and pulled the blankets over them, snuggling together, feeling the rain thud remorselessly on the tarpaulin which sheltered them. It soon became like a sauna and the sweat started to stream down their faces.

"I want you to know…" she began, her breath hot on his face.

"You want me to know what?"

"That all that's happened, it's all bin worth it," she answered. "Whatever."

"Don't you speak like that," said Marty, uncertainly. He fumbled in his trouser pocket and withdrew the Houdini handcuffs. He put his left wrist in a cuff and pulled it together, hearing its welcome click as the rain continued to pound on the tarpaulin above them. He reached down for Mary Lou's right wrist, placed the cuff around it and locked it. They were now together. "You ain't seen nothing yet," he smiled in the darkness.

"One thing," she said, her voice thick and drowsy.

"Yes?"

"Howard Drew, the guy you coached in the Olympic dash. How'd he do in them Olympic Games?"

"He did just great," said Marty. "Howard did just great."

He felt her sag into sleep and felt a hot flush that had nothing to do with the sweaty cocoon within which they now lodged. Howard Drew had gone down with a hamstring pull, just as they had said in all the books. Nothing had changed, and he felt his heart sink. Then, suddenly, far off in the distance, a church clock struck thirteen.

It was a fly walking slowly across a yellow ceiling. Marty watched the fly, gradually becoming aware of the softness of the mattress beneath him. He fumbled to his right to feel the mattress, then slowly above him to touch a pillow. A red sweat engulfed his face and neck. He was back.

He reached slowly across with his left hand, feeling for the handcuff on his wrist. Marty lifted his hand above him. His cuff was still closed, as was its dangling partner. The bed was empty. Mary Lou had not made it back.

Marty felt the tears start to well in his eyes and run salty down onto his lips. He sat up, sobbing, his body limp. Then he stood, unlocked the cuffs, reached for a handkerchief and dried his eyes, and moved to the window. There, below him was Carlisle 1995, dank and grey. His eyes ranged round the empty room, the tears still streaming down his face. He sank to his knees, sobbing as, before him, the grey rain lashed the verandah windows.

Suddenly, the telephone rang. Slowly, Marty rose to his feet and sat on the edge of the bed, putting the phone to his ear.

"Yes?"

"You come right on in," It was a woman's voice.

Marty was disoriented. "Who's that? Who's speaking?" he shouted.

"Well who do you think it is?" The voice was unmistakable. "It's ME!"

"Mary Lou?" he shouted. "Mary Lou! Where are you, woman?"

"In here, in the john."

Marty scrambled across the room to the door of the john. He could now hear dim sounds behind it. Wiping his eyes with the back of his hand, he timidly opened the door. There in the foaming jacuzzi sat Mary Lou, as above her on the television set flickered a Richard Pryor show.

"This ole guy, he's real funny," she said.

"Yes," he replied, lamely, wiping his eyes with a towel.

"Real cool, just like you tole me, Marty. Nigras in the movies."

Marty slowly pulled her out of the jacuzzi and kissed her warm wet lips. Then he carefully towelled her down and helped her don a fluffy white bathrobe.

"Just how long you been watching this?"

"Not long, 'bout four hours," she replied. "It's great."

"Then I think it's about high time that you see the world that you're gonna live in."

He drew her by the hand across to the bedroom window and they looked down on the town below. It was not now the Carlisle that he had surveyed a few moments before. For *the* rain had now stopped, and an autumn sun beamed down upon the bustling town.

"Are you ready?" he asked.

She nodded and kissed him. "Of course I'se ready," she said. "*I was born ready.*"